THE WICKED + THE DIVINE

VOL. 2, FANDEMONIUM

GILLEN

McKELVIE

WILSON

COWLES

KIERON GILLEN
WRITER

JAMIE McKELVIE
ARTIST

MATTHEW WILSON
COLOURIST

CLAYTON COWLES
LETTERER

HANNAH DONOVAN
DESIGNER

CHRISSY WILLIAMS
EDITOR

DEE CUNNIFFE
FLATTER

ALISON SAMPSON
#7 MAP DESIGN, PP 6-7

TOM MULLER
#7 FLYER DESIGN, PP 25

THE WICKED + THE DIVINE, VOL. 2, FANDEMONIUM
First printing. July 2015
ISBN: 978-1-63215-327-2
Published by Image Comics Inc.
Office of publication: 2001 Center St, Sixth Fl, Berkeley, CA 94704.

For information regarding the CPSIA on this printed material call: 203-595-3636
and provide reference # RICH – 507826. Representation: Law Offices of Harris
M. Miller II, P.C. (rights.inquiries@gmail.com).

This book was designed by Sergio Serrano, based on a design by Hannah
Donovan and Jamie McKelvie, and set into type by Sergio Serrano in Edmonton,
Canada. The text face is Gotham, designed and issued by Hoefler & Co. in 2000.
The paper is Escanaba 60 matte.

GILLEN McKELVIE WILSON COWLES

THE WICKED + THE DIVINE

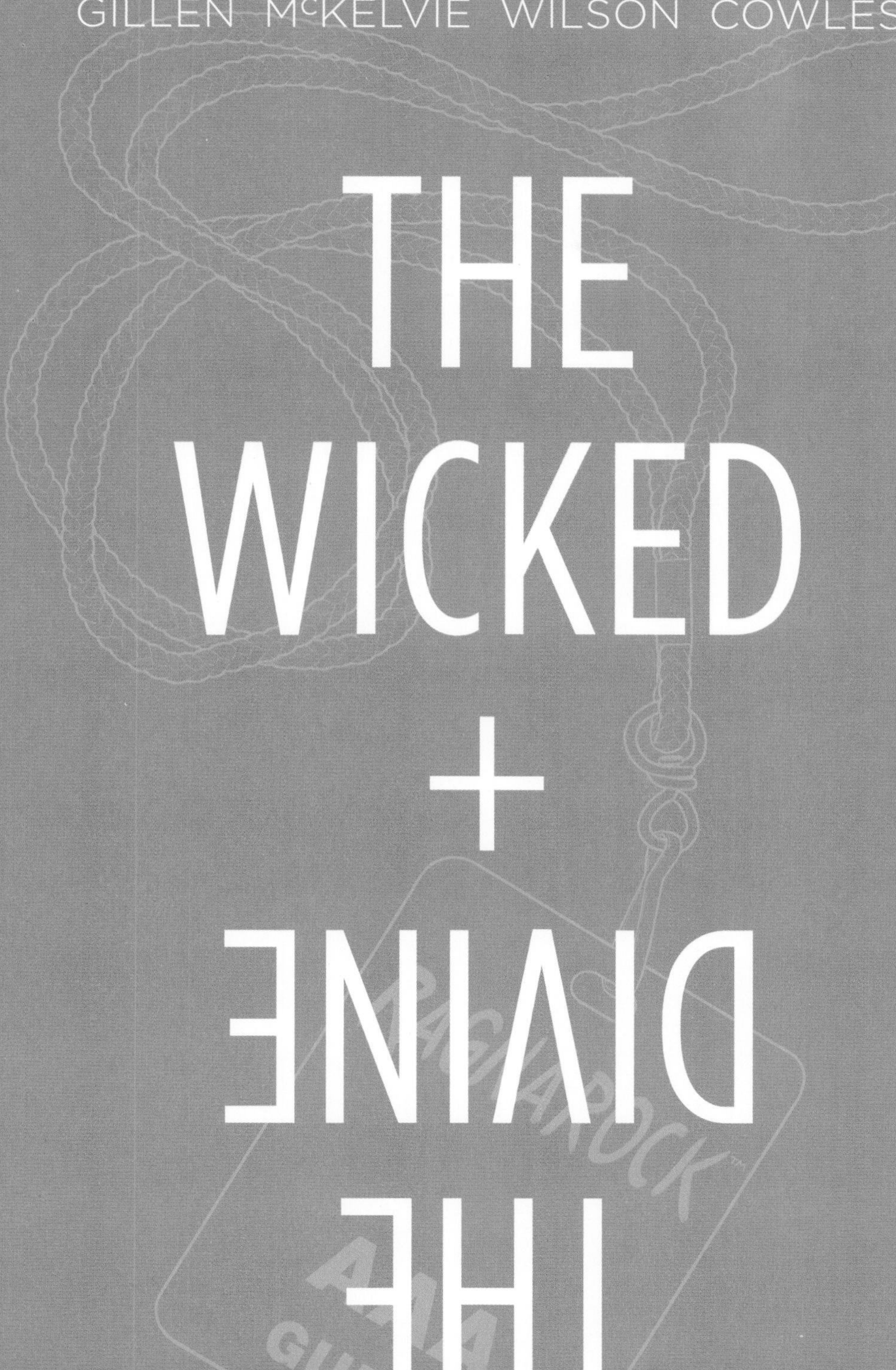
RAGNAROCK
AAA
GUEST

VOL. 2, FANDEMONIUM

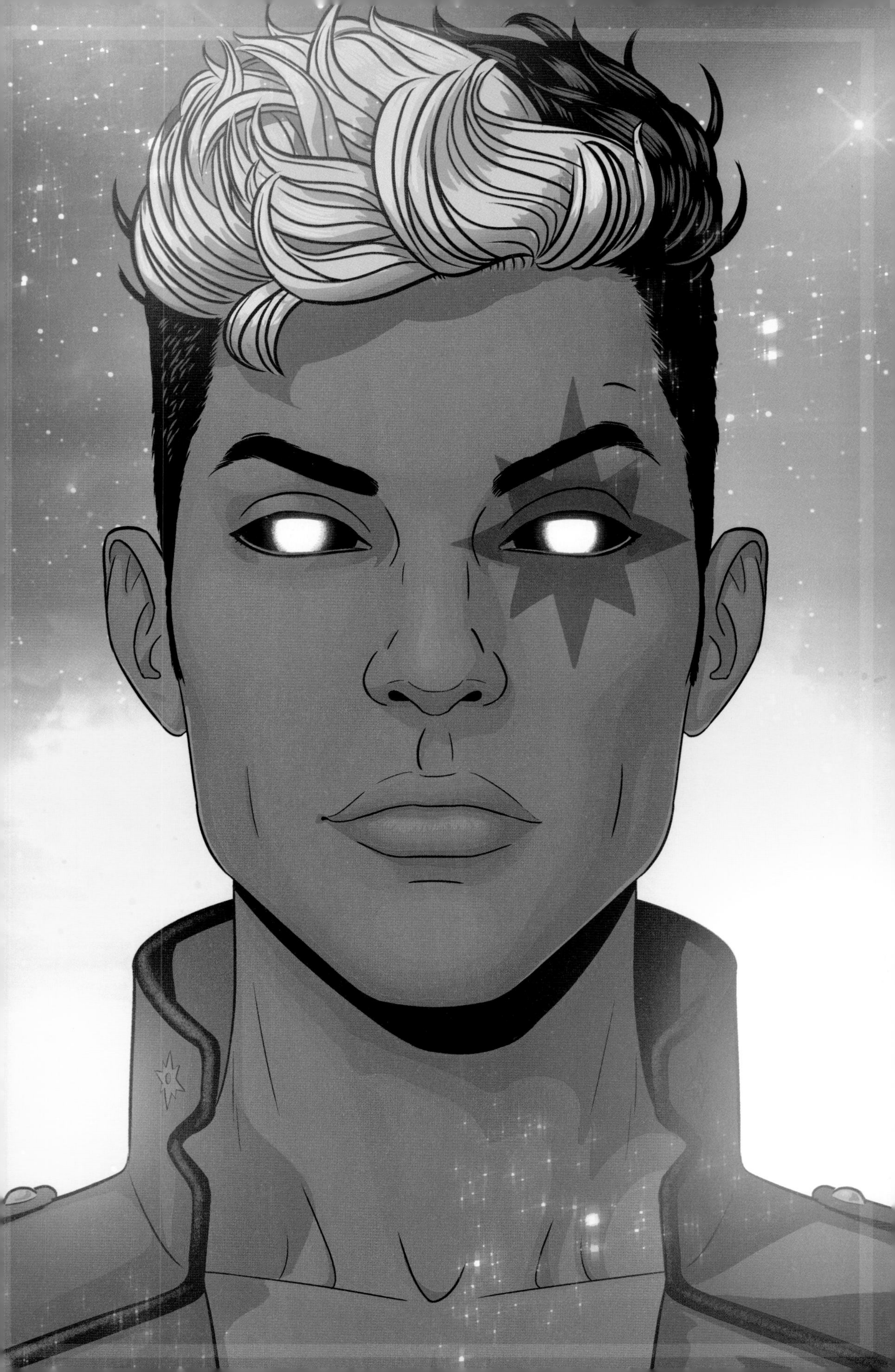

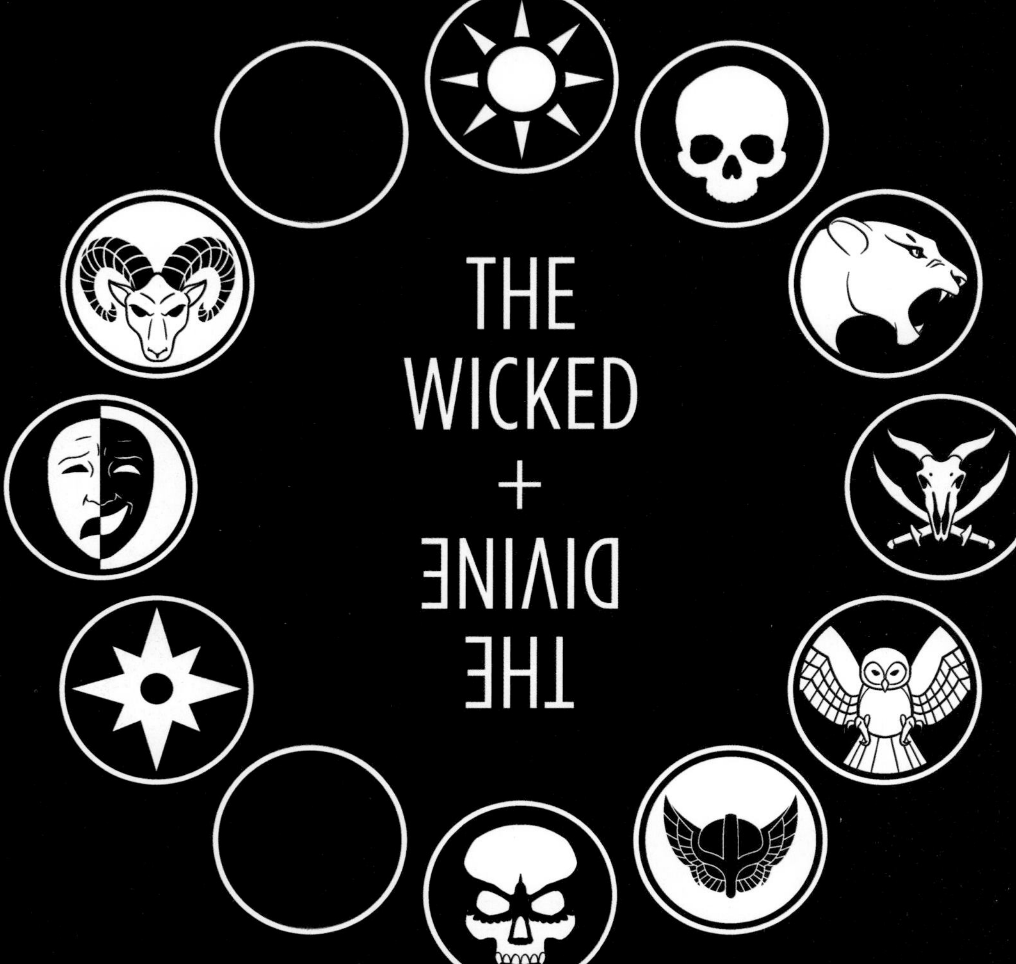
THE
WICKED
+
THE
DIVINE

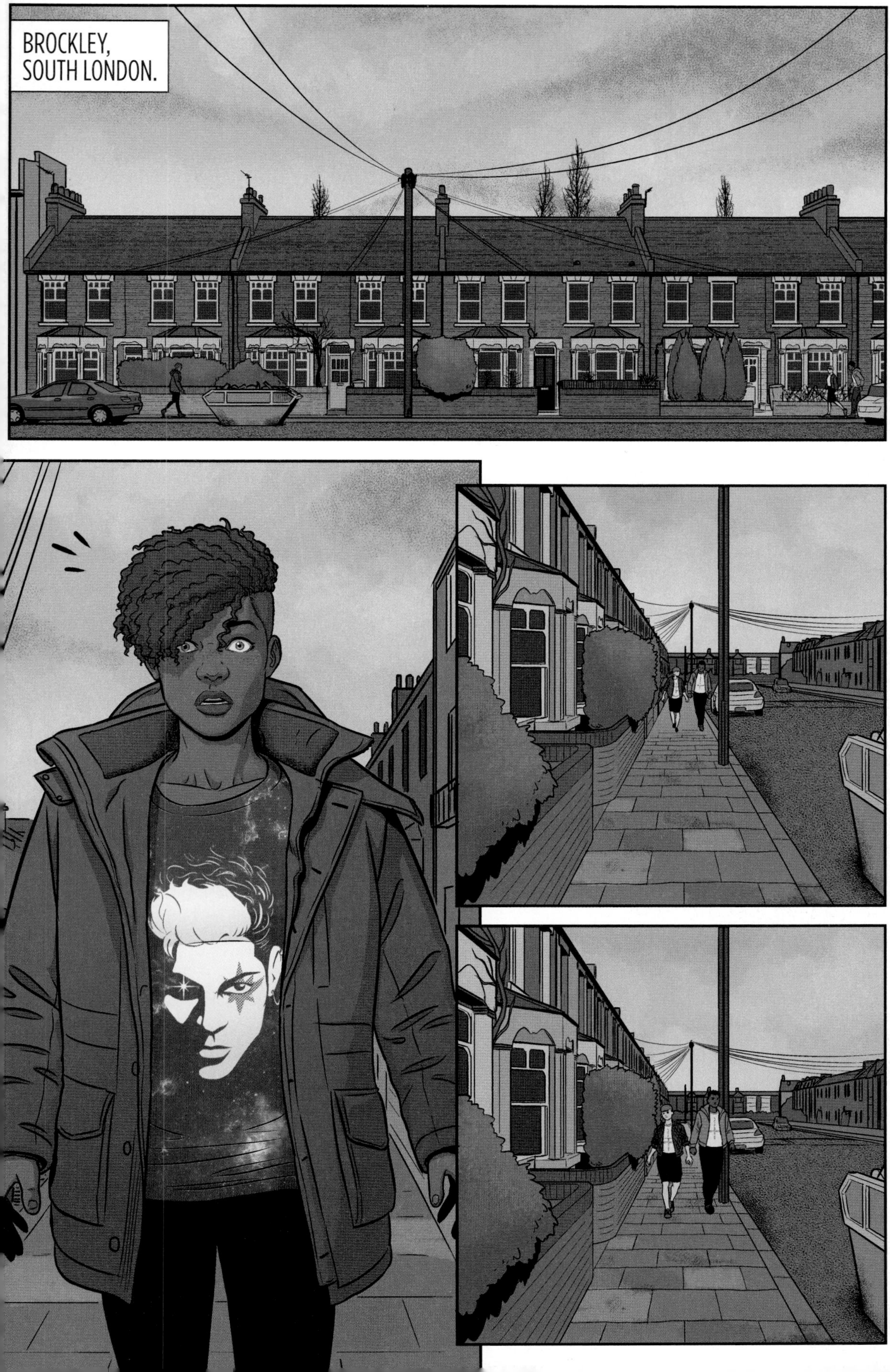
BROCKLEY,
SOUTH LONDON.

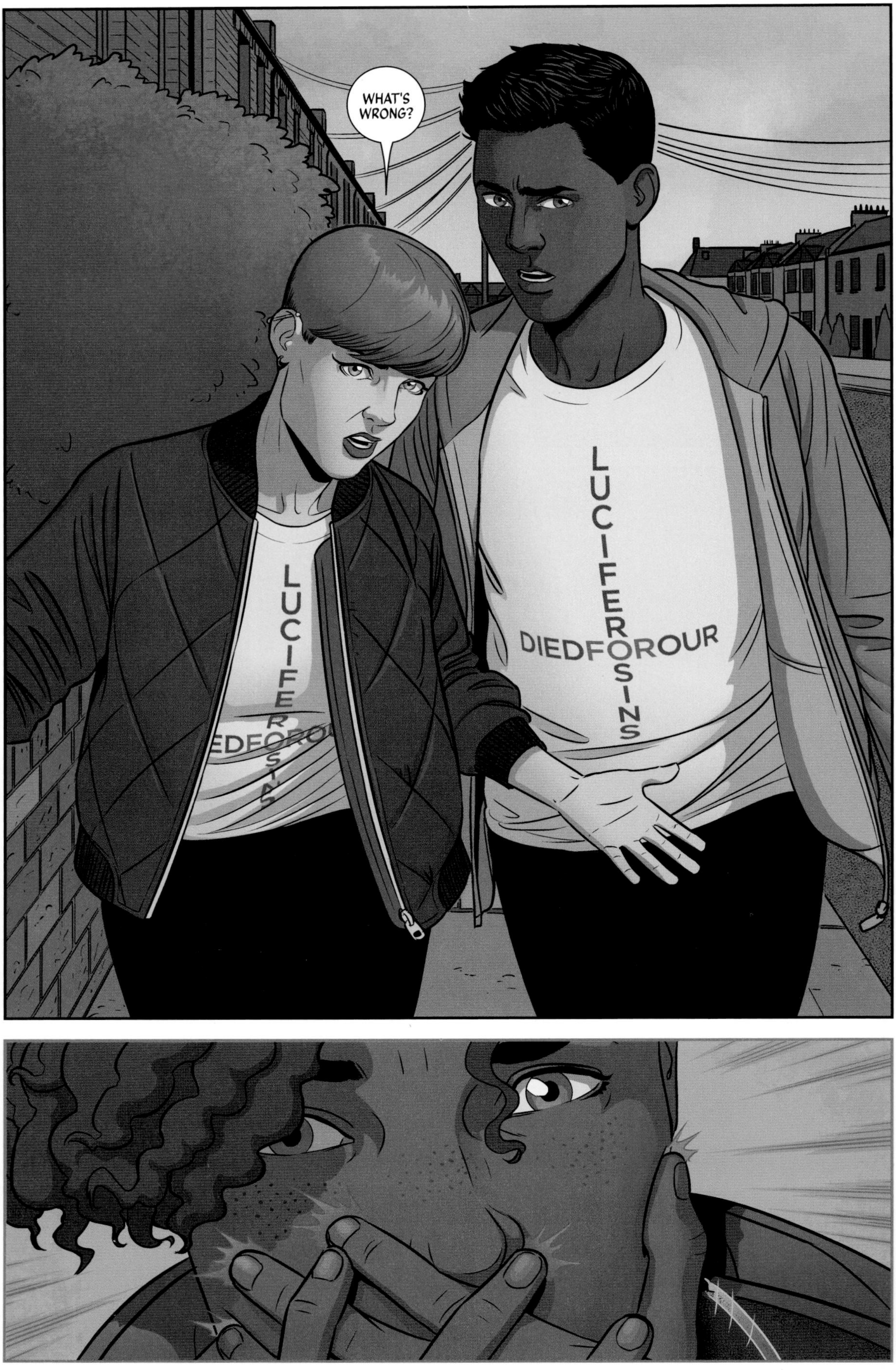
WHAT'S WRONG?
LUCIFER DIED FOR OUR SINS
LUCIFER DIED FOR OUR SINS

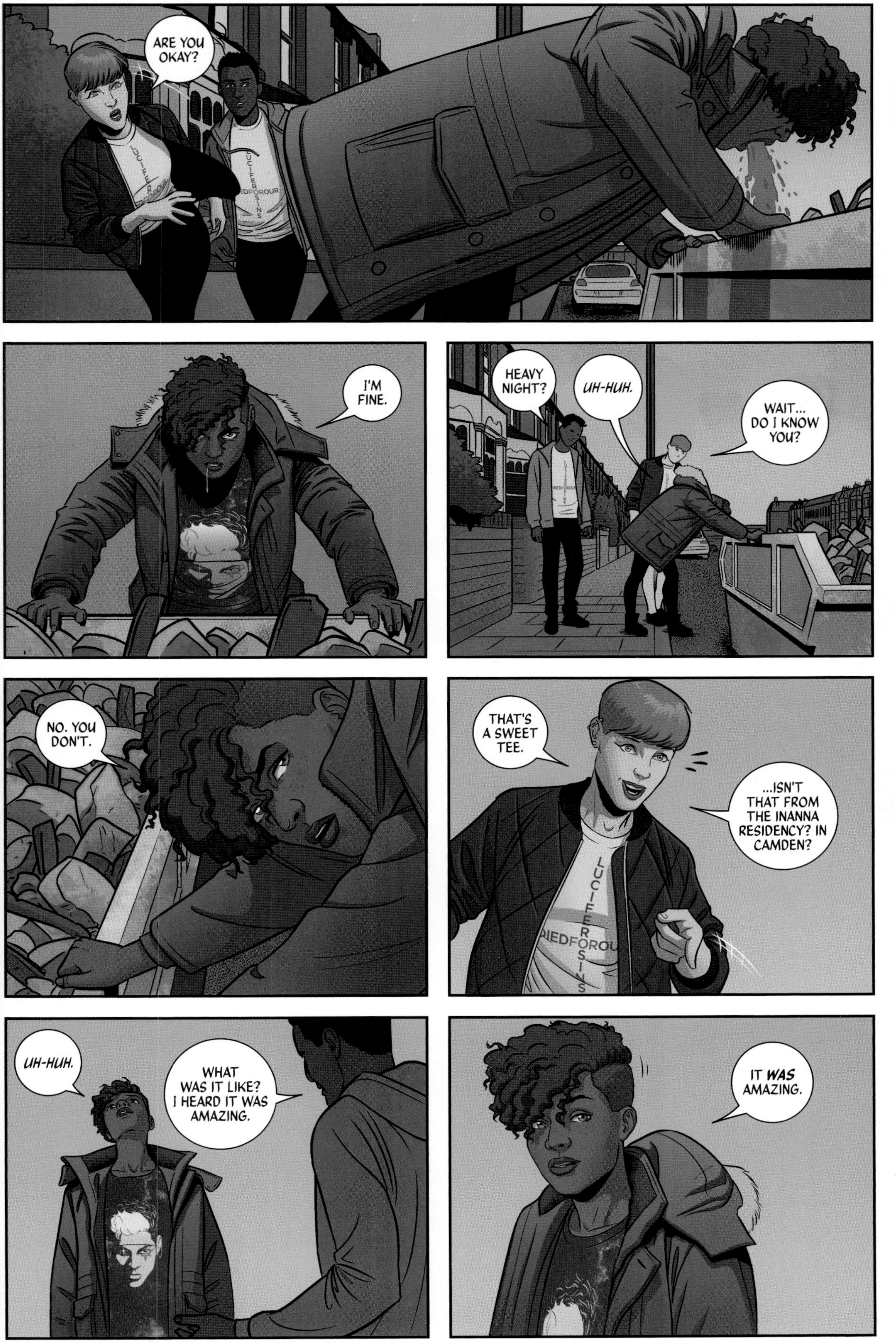
ARE YOU OKAY?
I'M FINE.
HEAVY NIGHT?
UH-HUH.
WAIT... DO I KNOW YOU?
NO. YOU DON'T.
THAT'S A SWEET TEE.
...ISN'T THAT FROM THE INANNA RESIDENCY? IN CAMDEN?
UH-HUH.
WHAT WAS IT LIKE? I HEARD IT WAS AMAZING.
IT WAS AMAZING.

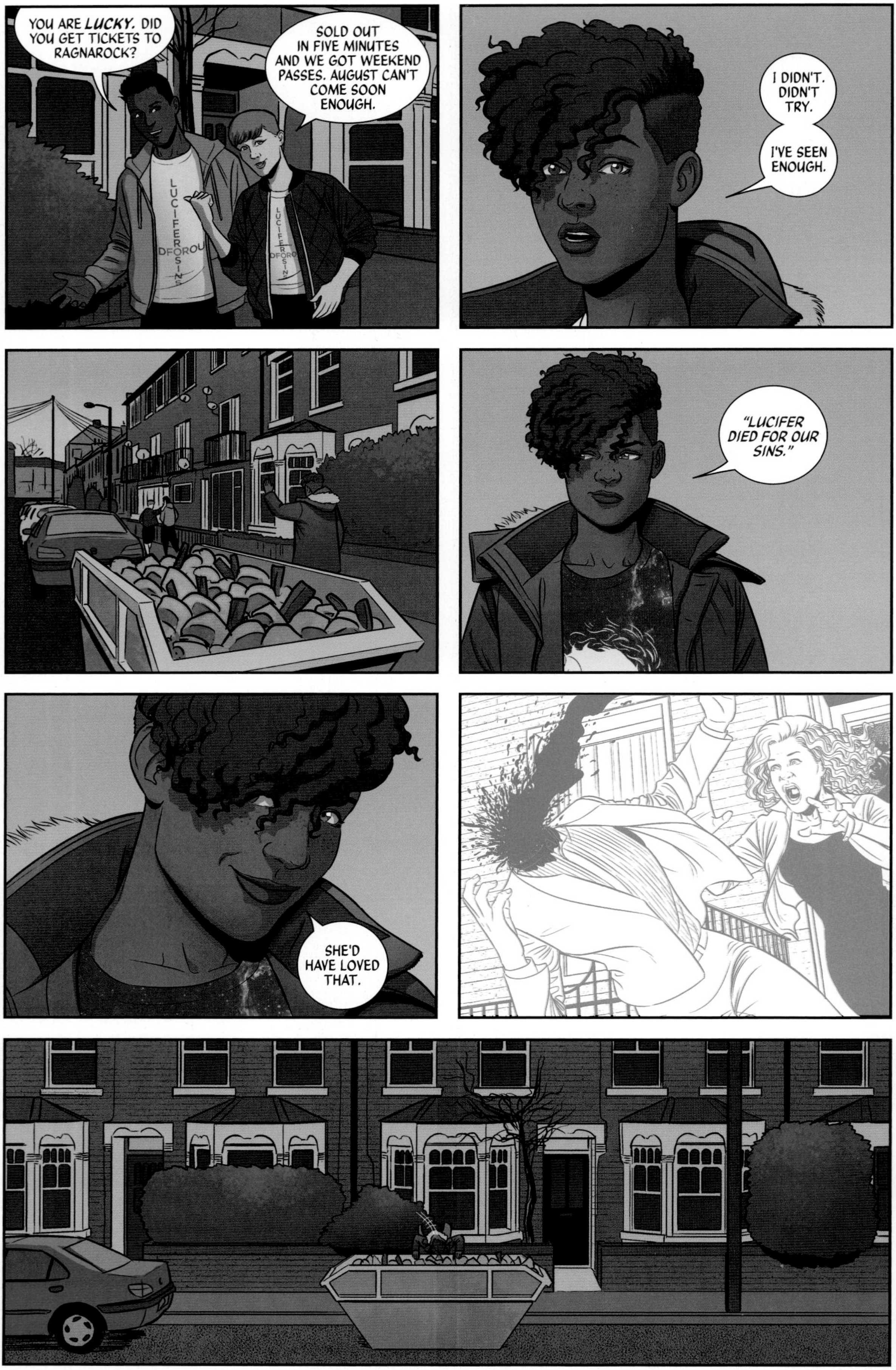
YOU ARE LUCKY. DID YOU GET TICKETS TO RAGNAROCK?
SOLD OUT IN FIVE MINUTES AND WE GOT WEEKEND PASSES. AUGUST CAN'T COME SOON ENOUGH.
I DIDN'T. DIDN'T TRY.
I'VE SEEN ENOUGH.
"LUCIFER DIED FOR OUR SINS."
SHE'D HAVE LOVED THAT.

HUMAN TRASH

28 FEBRUARY 2014

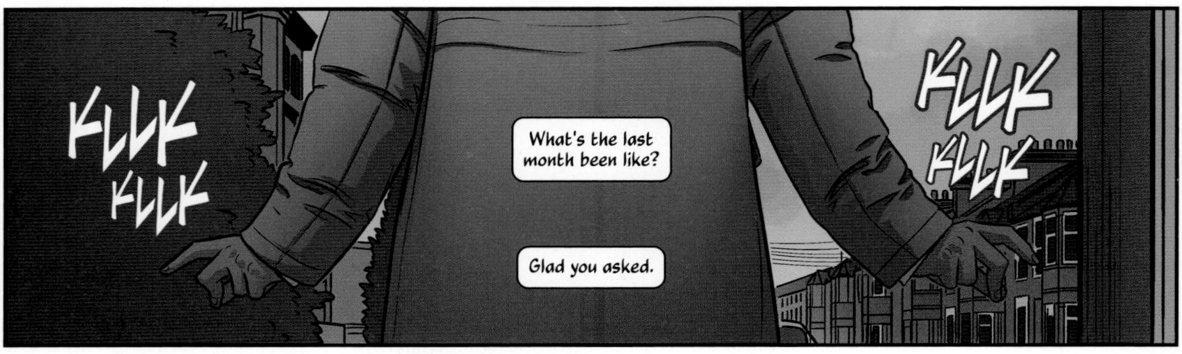
KLLK
KLLK
What's the last month been like?
Glad you asked.
KLLK
KLLK

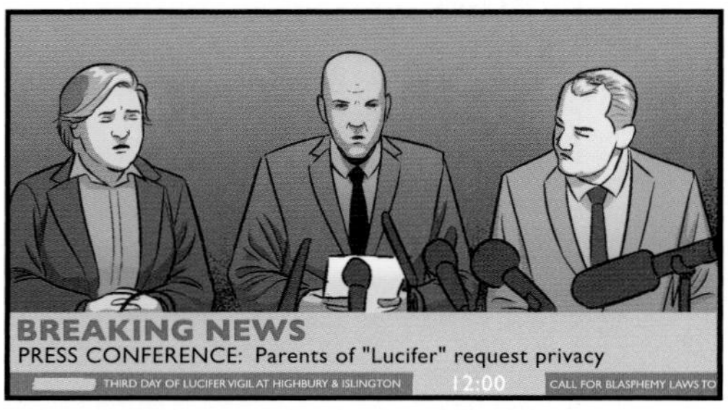
BREAKING NEWS
PRESS CONFERENCE: Parents of "Lucifer" request privacy
THIRD DAY OF LUCIFER VIGIL AT HIGHBURY & ISLINGTON
12:00
CALL FOR BLASPHEMY LAWS TO

"THE FUNERAL WILL BE HELD AT AN UNDISCLOSED LOCATION. WE REQUEST PRIVACY AT THIS DIFFICULT TIME.

"FOR ALL THE CLAIMS THAT SHE WAS A GOD, SHE WAS ALSO OUR LITTLE GIRL."

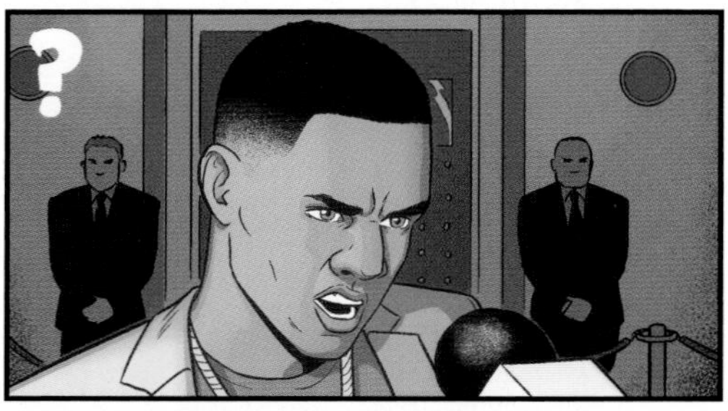
?

"NO, I DIDN'T GO TO THE *[BLEEP]* FUNERAL. THE LAST THING HER FAMILY NEEDS IS SEEING ANYONE WHO WAS BEATING ON THEIR NOW-DEAD-DAUGHTER STANDING THERE IN HIS BEST ALEXANDER McQUEEN.

"WHAT THE *[BLEEP]* IS ***WRONG*** WITH YOU?"

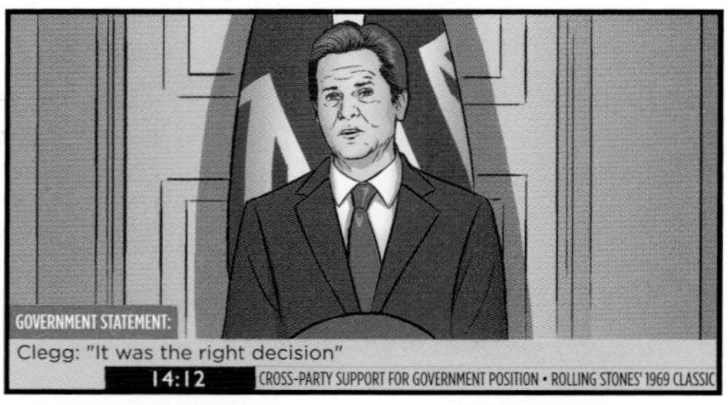
GOVERNMENT STATEMENT:
Clegg: "It was the right decision"
14:12
CROSS-PARTY SUPPORT FOR GOVERNMENT POSITION • ROLLING STONES' 1969 CLASSIC

"WHILE THIS GOVERNMENT CANNOT OFFER THANKS TO THE PANTHEON FOR ITS ACTIONS, THE INFORMATION 'ANANKE' SHARED HAS CONVINCED US THAT THE SAD DEATH OF THIS YOUNG GIRL WAS THE ONLY SOLUTION TO THE SITUATION.

"IN ACTING SO SWIFTLY, MANY LIVES WERE SAVED. IT WAS THE RIGHT DECISION."

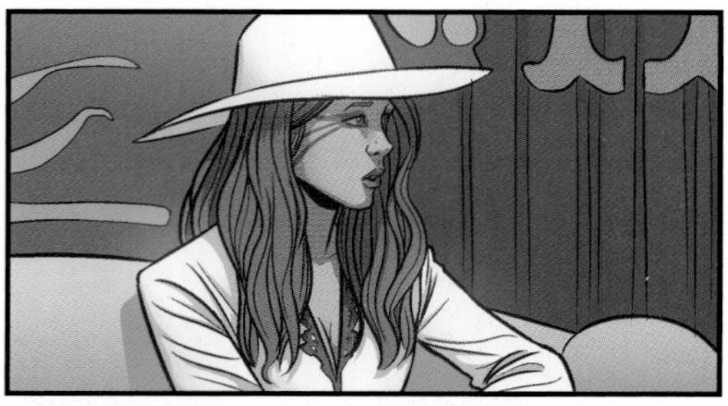

"I CRY FOR HER EVERY NIGHT. I CRY EVERY MORNING.

"THE ONLY COMFORT IS THAT I KNOW I'LL BE SEEING HER AGAIN SOON. IT MAY BE NINETY YEARS FOR YOU, BUT FOR US, IT'S LESS THAN TWO."

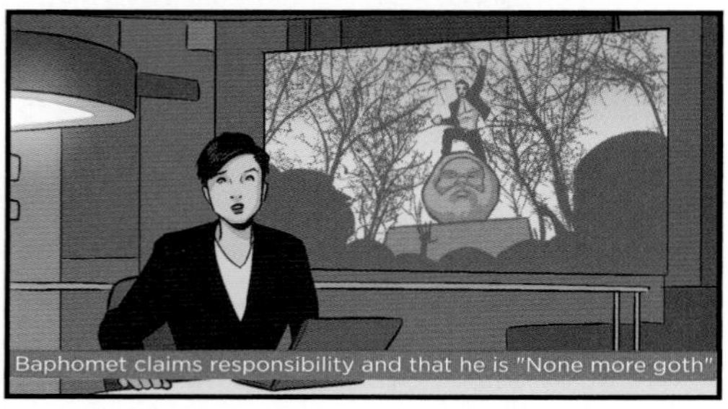
Baphomet claims responsibility and that he is "None more goth"

"LAST NIGHT, HIGHGATE CEMETERY WAS THE SCENE OF A 'VALENTINE'S DAY MASCARA.' EYEWITNESSES REPORT SCENES OF THE ANIMATED DEAD DANCING WITH THE LIVING.

"THE *'GOD'* BAPHOMET, STILL WANTED BY THE POLICE, HAS CLAIMED RESPONSIBILITY."

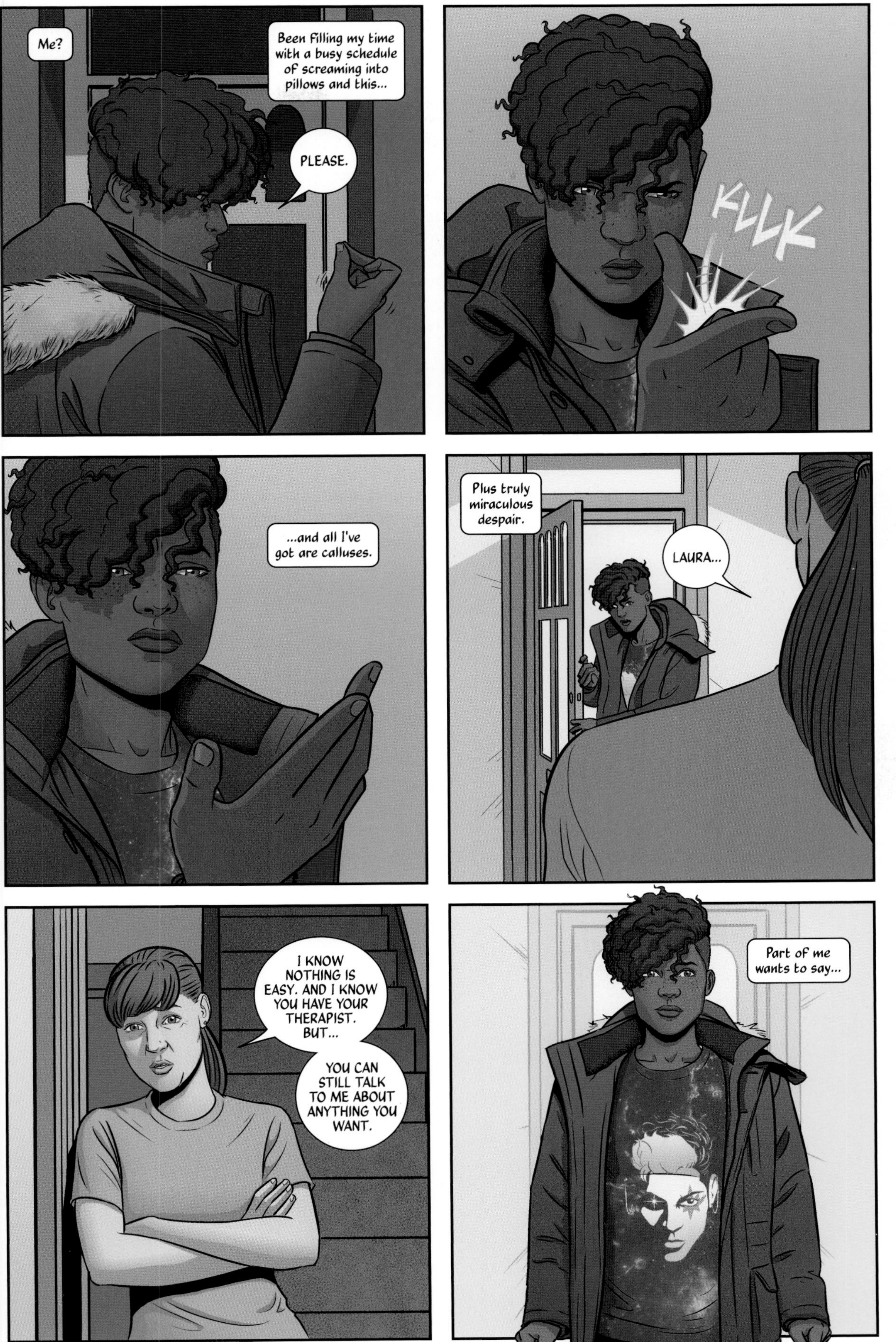
Me?
Been filling my time with a busy schedule of screaming into pillows and this...
PLEASE.
KLLK
...and all I've got are calluses.
Plus truly miraculous despair.
LAURA...
I KNOW NOTHING IS EASY. AND I KNOW YOU HAVE YOUR THERAPIST. BUT...
YOU CAN STILL TALK TO ME ABOUT ANYTHING YOU WANT.
Part of me wants to say...

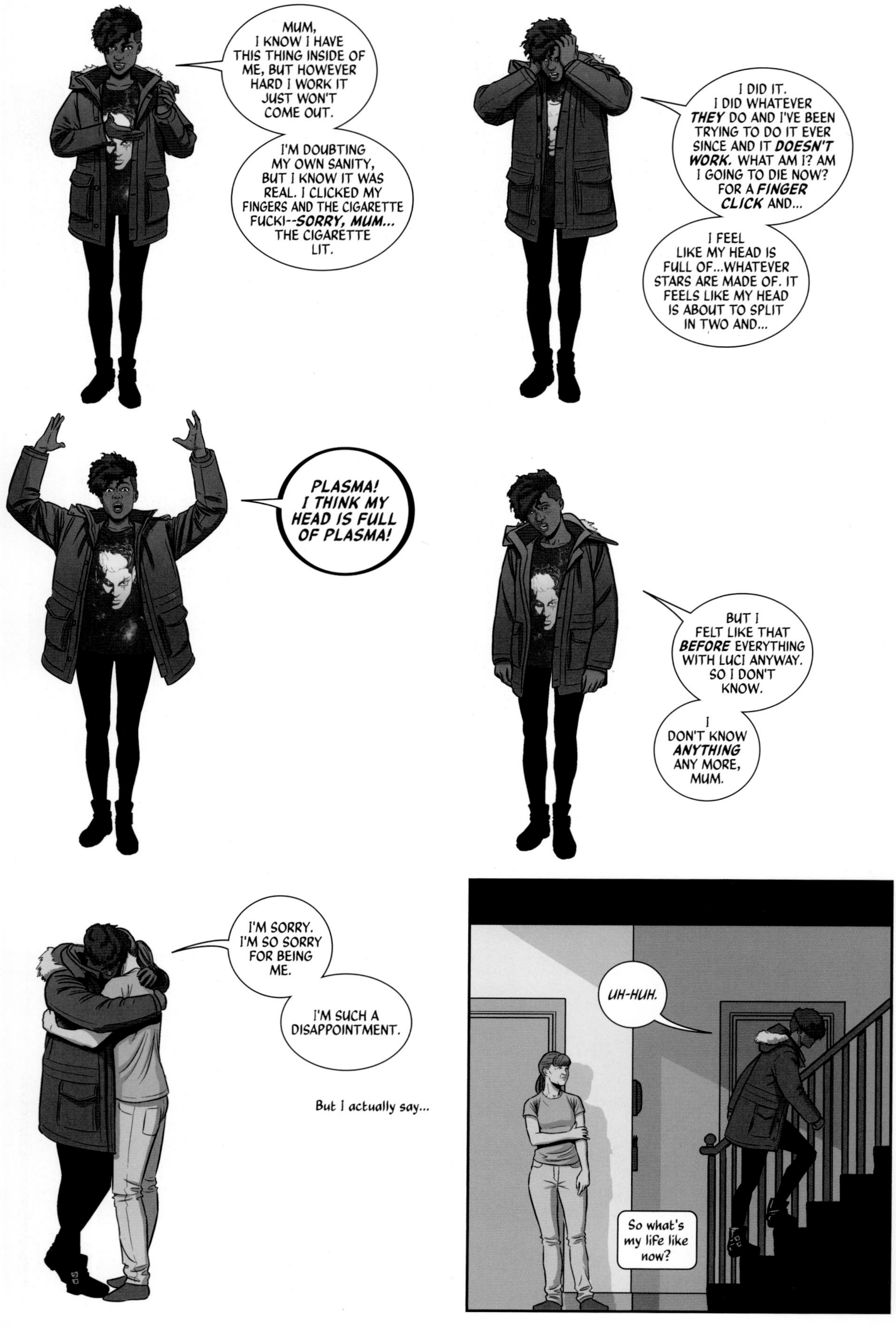
MUM, I KNOW I HAVE THIS THING INSIDE OF ME, BUT HOWEVER HARD I WORK IT JUST WON'T COME OUT.
I'M DOUBTING MY OWN SANITY, BUT I KNOW IT WAS REAL. I CLICKED MY FINGERS AND THE CIGARETTE FUCKI--SORRY, MUM... THE CIGARETTE LIT.
I DID IT. I DID WHATEVER THEY DO AND I'VE BEEN TRYING TO DO IT EVER SINCE AND IT DOESN'T WORK. WHAT AM I? AM I GOING TO DIE NOW? FOR A FINGER CLICK AND...
I FEEL LIKE MY HEAD IS FULL OF...WHATEVER STARS ARE MADE OF. IT FEELS LIKE MY HEAD IS ABOUT TO SPLIT IN TWO AND...
PLASMA! I THINK MY HEAD IS FULL OF PLASMA!
BUT I FELT LIKE THAT BEFORE EVERYTHING WITH LUCI ANYWAY. SO I DON'T KNOW.
I DON'T KNOW ANYTHING ANY MORE, MUM.
I'M SORRY. I'M SO SORRY FOR BEING ME.
I'M SUCH A DISAPPOINTMENT.
But I actually say...
UH-HUH.
So what's my life like now?

THE LIFE OF LAURA WILSON, AGED SEVENTEEN AND THREE QUARTERS.

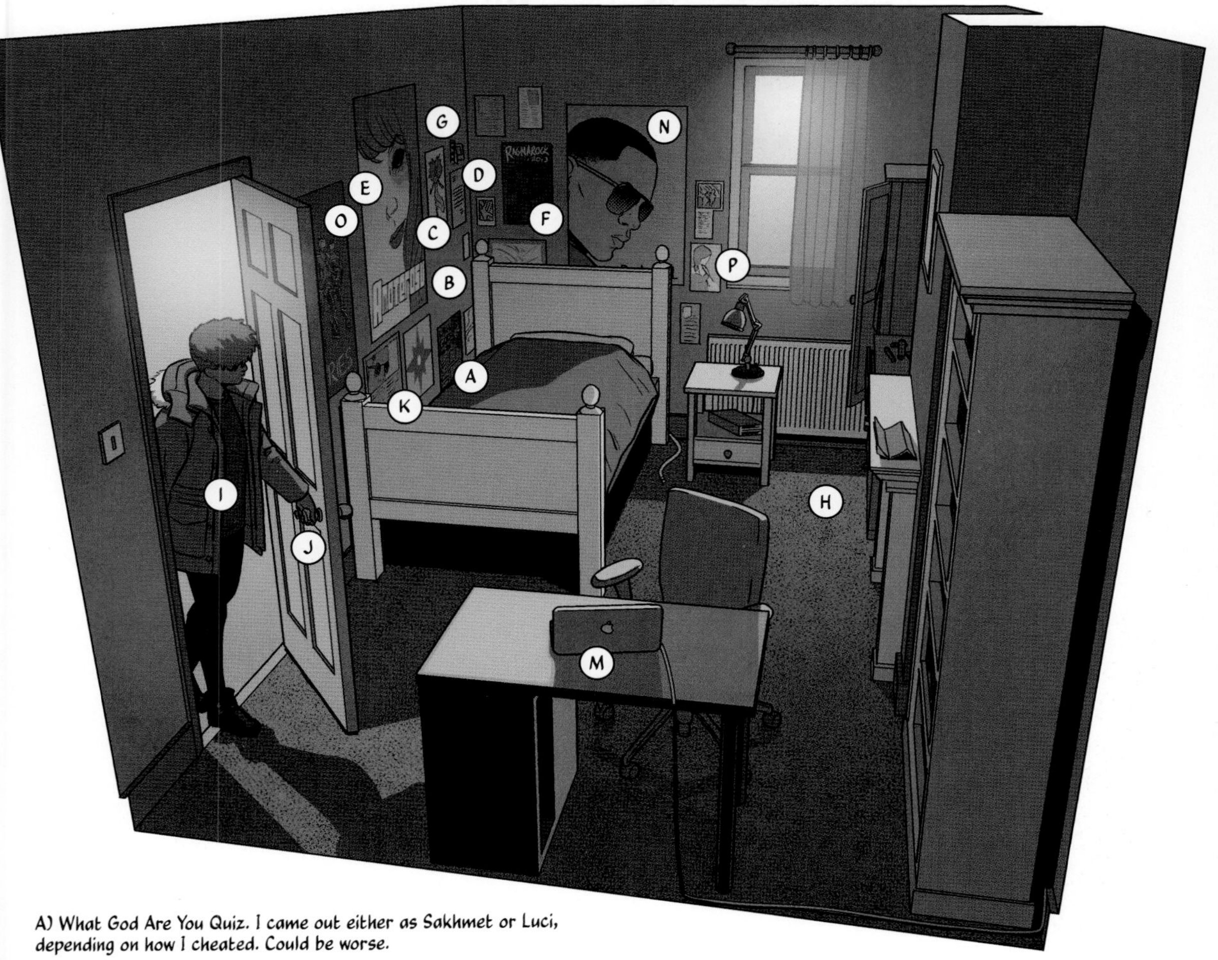
G
N
E
D
O
C
F
B
P
A
K
I
J
H
M

A) What God Are You Quiz. I came out either as Sakhmet or Luci, depending on how I cheated. Could be worse.

B) Suspicious gap. Couldn't bear Luci's poster there. Couldn't bear putting anything in its place.

C) Flyposter. Stolen from down the road near the venue the day before I saw Amaterasu.

D) I wrote to Brunhilde when she was kicked out of The Valkyries. She wrote back. That was kind of amazing.

E) Fan art poster. Bought from the land of online.

F) From last year's Ragnarock. August 15th, so before The Recurrence. Absolutely tiny. I was one of the youngest people there. This year's will be bigger than Glastonbury.

G) Photos of old friends from school. Some have called me. More than I expected. I'm...grateful? I think I am.

H) My floor's messier in real life. Pictured like this as I'm in denial.

I) 17-year-old girl with no life.

J) Unrelentingly unmiraculous fingertips.

K) Handed out to the crowd after Inanna's residency. Mine got crumpled. This has been carefully and lovingly ironed.

L) The cigarette box and the dog-end are hidden here. I can't throw them away, but I don't want mum to think I'm smoking.

M) Second-hand. Or possibly third-hand.

N) Still have a lot of inappropriate naked feelings about Baal. Still hope he isn't the murderer.

O) Valkyries, in their original line-up.

P) I draw the gods occasionally. This is the best I ever managed. It's Sakhmet, though here she looks more like Rihanna.

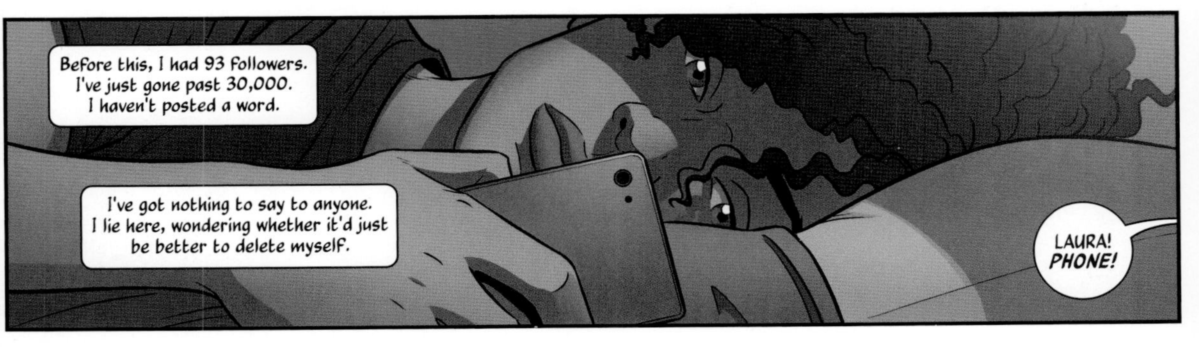
Before this, I had 93 followers. I've just gone past 30,000. I haven't posted a word.
I've got nothing to say to anyone. I lie here, wondering whether it'd just be better to delete myself.
LAURA! PHONE!

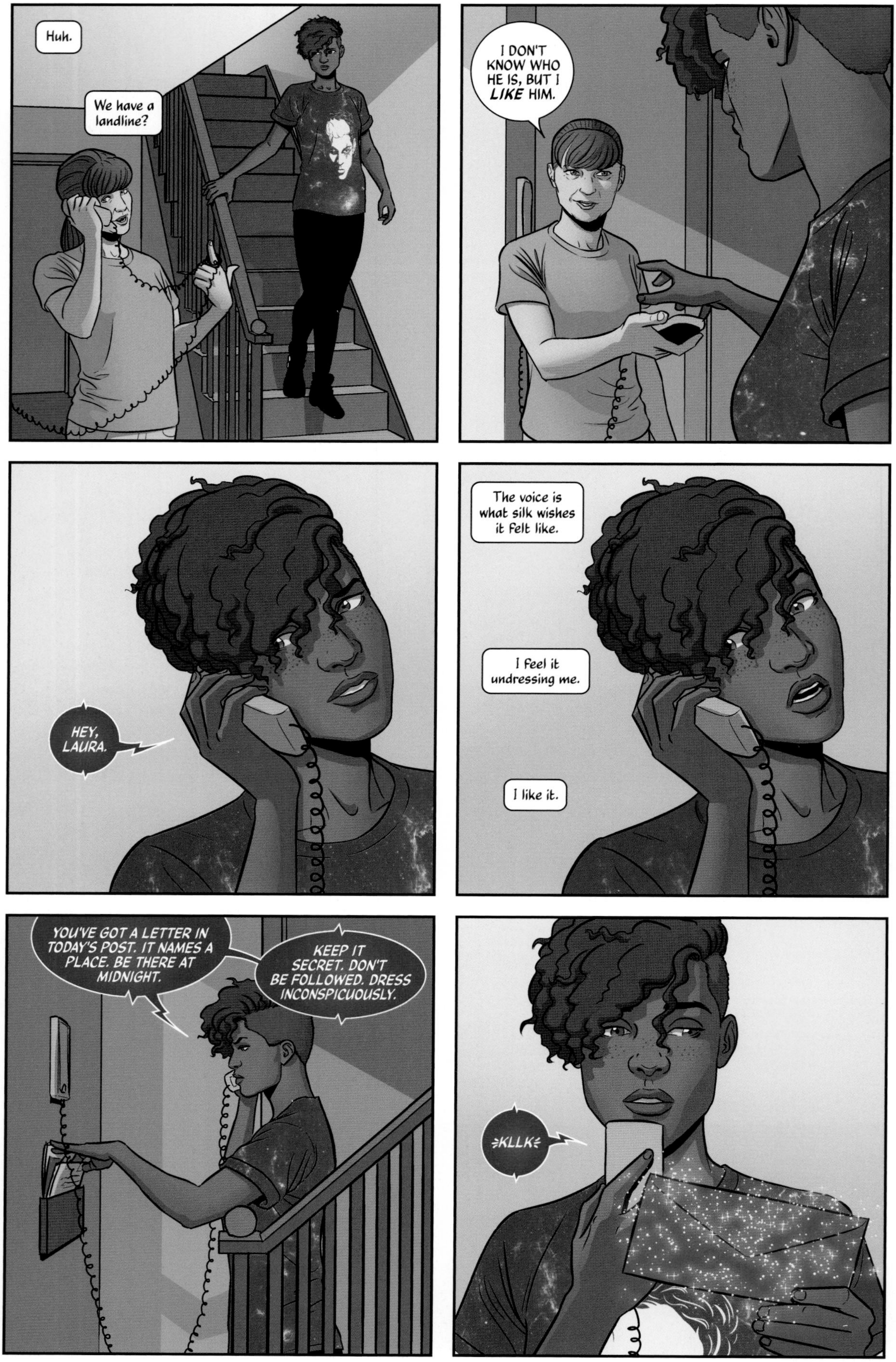
Huh.
We have a landline?
I DON'T KNOW WHO HE IS, BUT I *LIKE* HIM.
HEY, LAURA.
The voice is what silk wishes it felt like.
I feel it undressing me.
I like it.
YOU'VE GOT A LETTER IN TODAY'S POST. IT NAMES A PLACE. BE THERE AT MIDNIGHT.
KEEP IT SECRET. DON'T BE FOLLOWED. DRESS INCONSPICUOUSLY.
KLLK

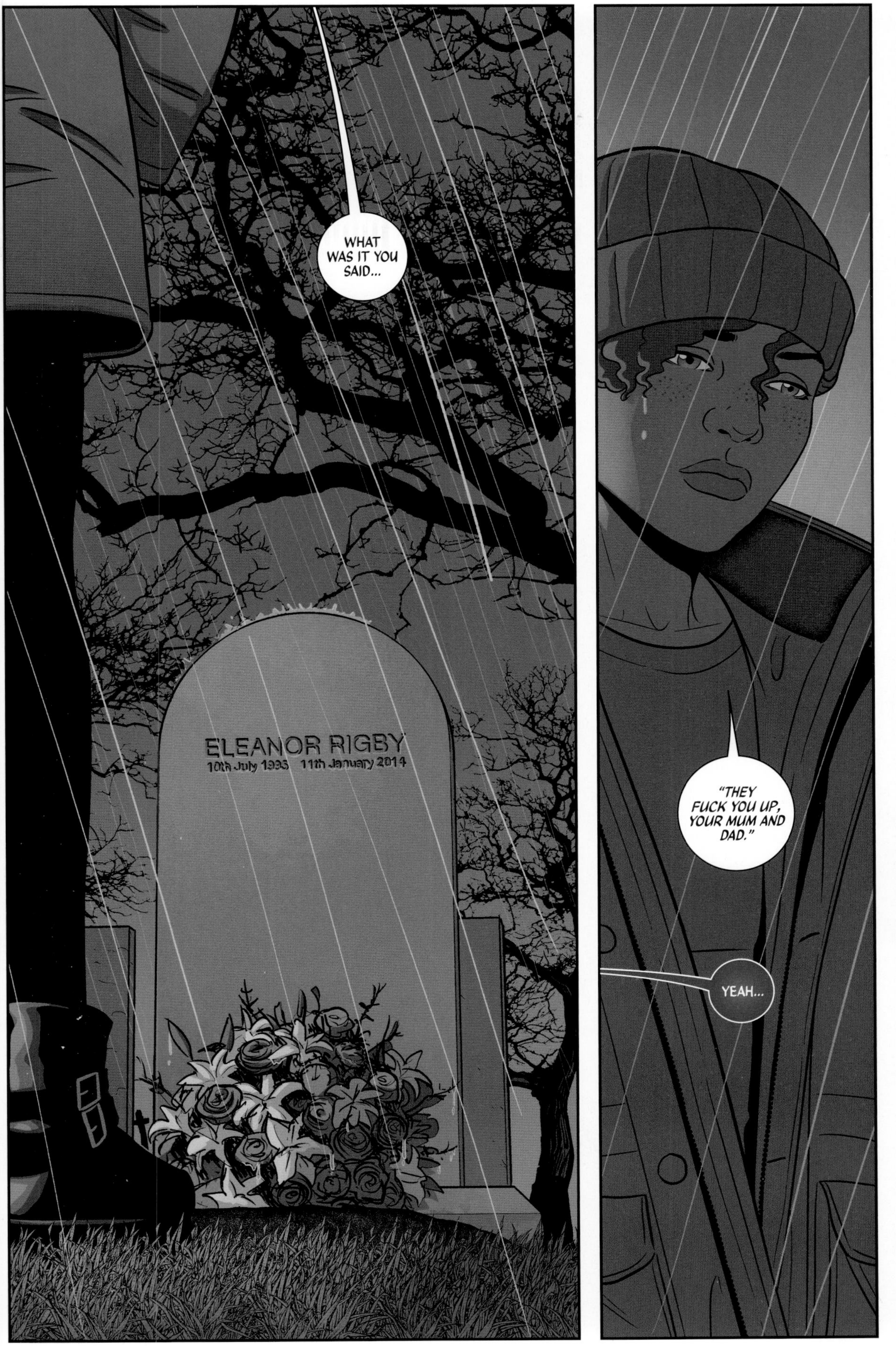
WHAT WAS IT YOU SAID...
ELEANOR RIGBY
10th July 1995 11th January 2014
"THEY FUCK YOU UP, YOUR MUM AND DAD."
YEAH...

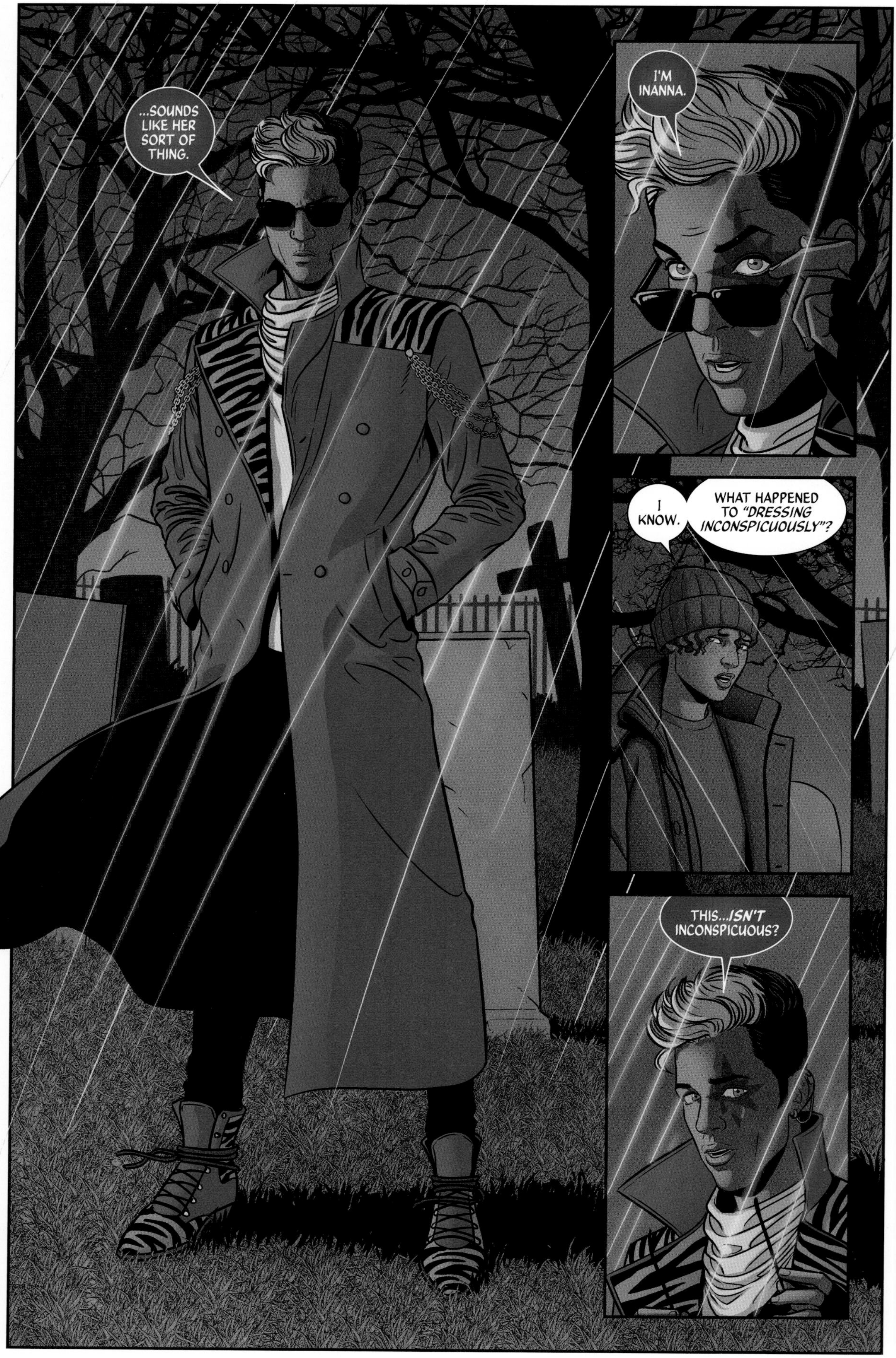
...SOUNDS LIKE HER SORT OF THING.
I'M INANNA.
I KNOW.
WHAT HAPPENED TO *"DRESSING INCONSPICUOUSLY"*?
THIS...***ISN'T*** INCONSPICUOUS?

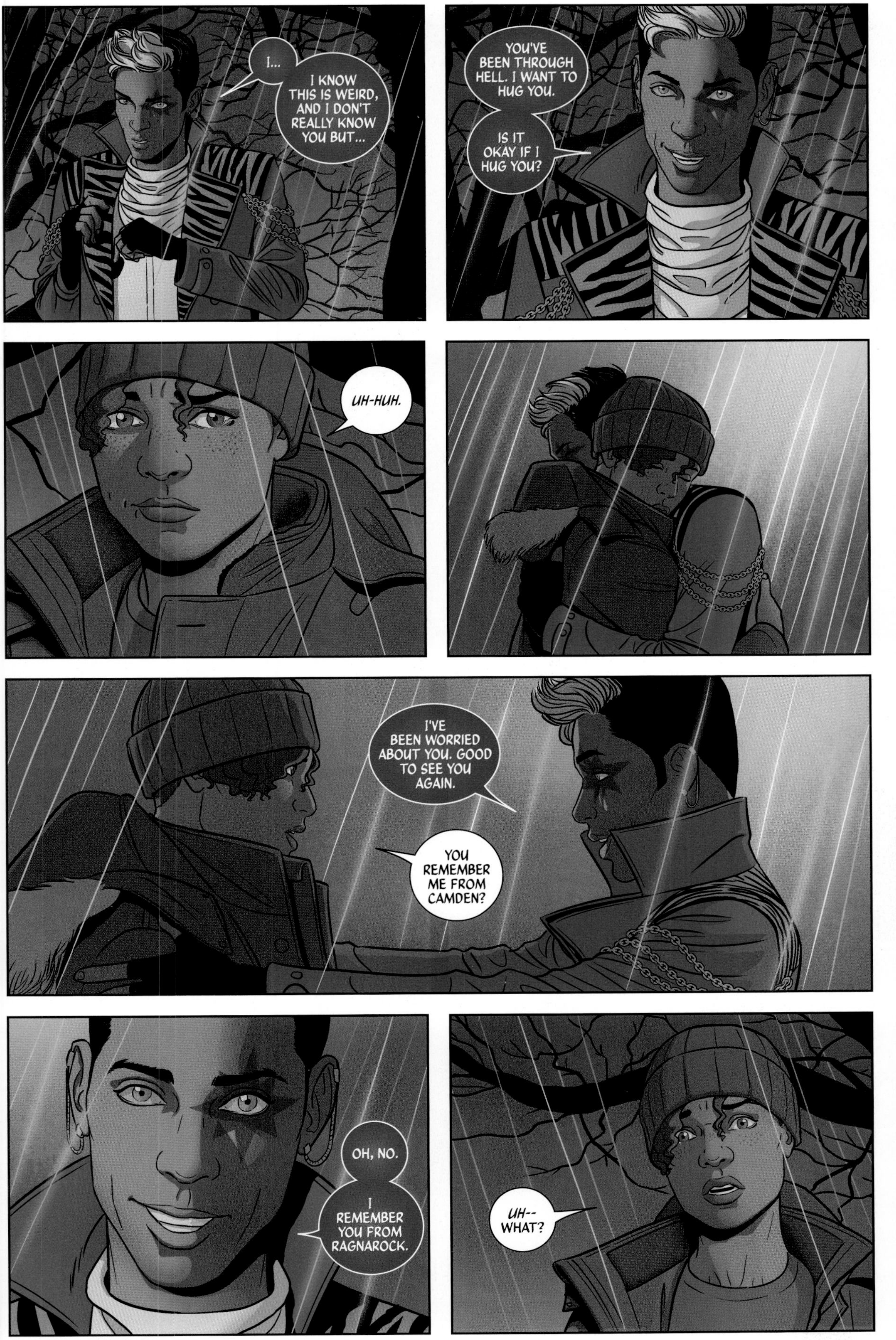
I...
I KNOW THIS IS WEIRD, AND I DON'T REALLY KNOW YOU BUT...
YOU'VE BEEN THROUGH HELL. I WANT TO HUG YOU.
IS IT OKAY IF I HUG YOU?
UH-HUH.
I'VE BEEN WORRIED ABOUT YOU. GOOD TO SEE YOU AGAIN.
YOU REMEMBER ME FROM CAMDEN?
OH, NO.
I REMEMBER YOU FROM RAGNAROCK.
UH-- WHAT?

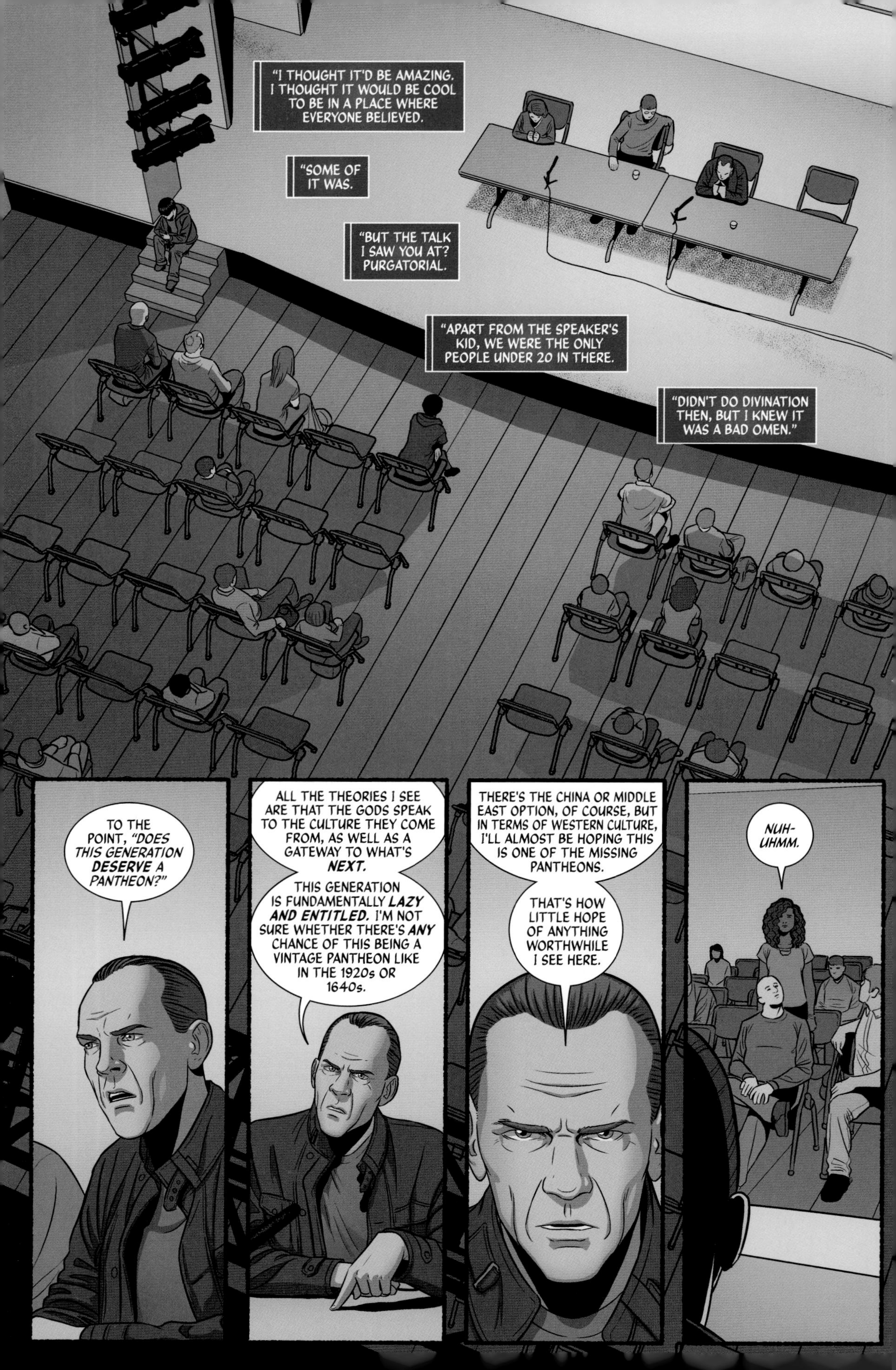
"I THOUGHT IT'D BE AMAZING. I THOUGHT IT WOULD BE COOL TO BE IN A PLACE WHERE EVERYONE BELIEVED.
"SOME OF IT WAS.
"BUT THE TALK I SAW YOU AT? PURGATORIAL.
"APART FROM THE SPEAKER'S KID, WE WERE THE ONLY PEOPLE UNDER 20 IN THERE.
"DIDN'T DO DIVINATION THEN, BUT I KNEW IT WAS A BAD OMEN."
TO THE POINT, *"DOES THIS GENERATION **DESERVE** A PANTHEON?"*
ALL THE THEORIES I SEE ARE THAT THE GODS SPEAK TO THE CULTURE THEY COME FROM, AS WELL AS A GATEWAY TO WHAT'S ***NEXT.***
THIS GENERATION IS FUNDAMENTALLY ***LAZY AND ENTITLED.*** I'M NOT SURE WHETHER THERE'S ***ANY*** CHANCE OF THIS BEING A VINTAGE PANTHEON LIKE IN THE 1920s OR 1640s.
THERE'S THE CHINA OR MIDDLE EAST OPTION, OF COURSE, BUT IN TERMS OF WESTERN CULTURE, I'LL ALMOST BE HOPING THIS IS ONE OF THE MISSING PANTHEONS.
THAT'S HOW LITTLE HOPE OF ANYTHING WORTHWHILE I SEE HERE.
NUH-UHMM.

YOU'RE ONLY SEEING CYCLES. LIKE...WHAT'S HAPPENED *BEFORE*. YOU DON'T KNOW ANYTHING ABOUT WHAT CAN HAPPEN *NOW*.

YOU HAVE NO FAITH. YOU DON'T *BELIEVE*.

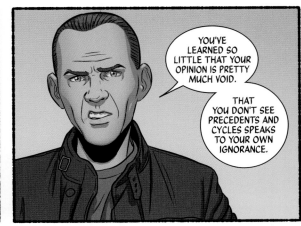

YOU'VE LEARNED SO LITTLE THAT YOUR OPINION IS PRETTY MUCH VOID.

THAT YOU DON'T SEE PRECEDENTS AND CYCLES SPEAKS TO YOUR OWN IGNORANCE.

DO YOU UNDERSTAND WHO YOU'RE TALKING TO? I'VE *ORGANISED* RAGNAROCK FOR THE LAST TEN YEARS.

SOME OF US HERE HAVE SPENT OUR *LIVES* LEARNING ABOUT THIS.

YOU'VE LEARNED SO MUCH YOU KNOW *NOTHING*.

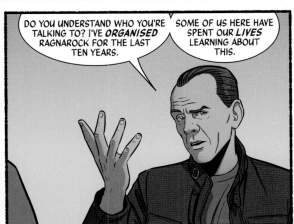

THANKS FOR THE EVIDENCE SUPPORTING MY POSITION. JUST LOOK AT YOU.

YOU DON'T *DESERVE* A PANTHEON.

LET'S TALK IN TWO YEARS.

YOU WERE FEARLESS.

NUH-UH. JUST ANGRY. I WENT OUTSIDE AND STOLE CIGARETTES UNTIL I STOPPED SHAKING. I'D NEVER EVEN SMOKED BEFORE...

...I'M SORRY, I DON'T REMEMBER YOU.

"YOU WOULDN'T THEN. MY GO-TO COSPLAY WAS WALLPAPER.

"EVERYTHING CHANGED AFTER ANANKE'S VISIT..."

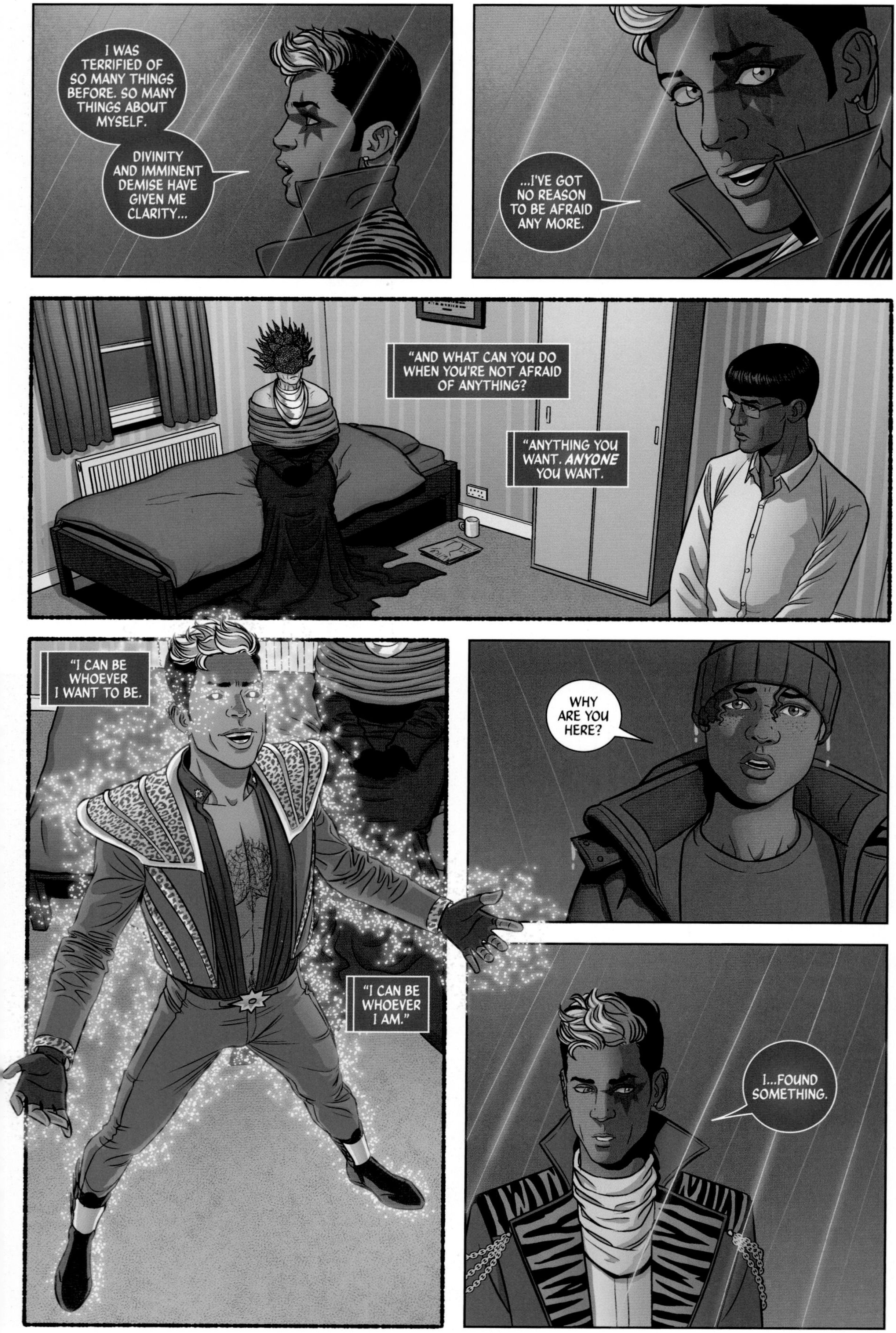

I WAS TERRIFIED OF SO MANY THINGS BEFORE. SO MANY THINGS ABOUT MYSELF.
DIVINITY AND IMMINENT DEMISE HAVE GIVEN ME CLARITY...
...I'VE GOT NO REASON TO BE AFRAID ANY MORE.
"AND WHAT CAN YOU DO WHEN YOU'RE NOT AFRAID OF ANYTHING?
"ANYTHING YOU WANT. ANYONE YOU WANT.
"I CAN BE WHOEVER I WANT TO BE.
"I CAN BE WHOEVER I AM."
WHY ARE YOU HERE?
I...FOUND SOMETHING.

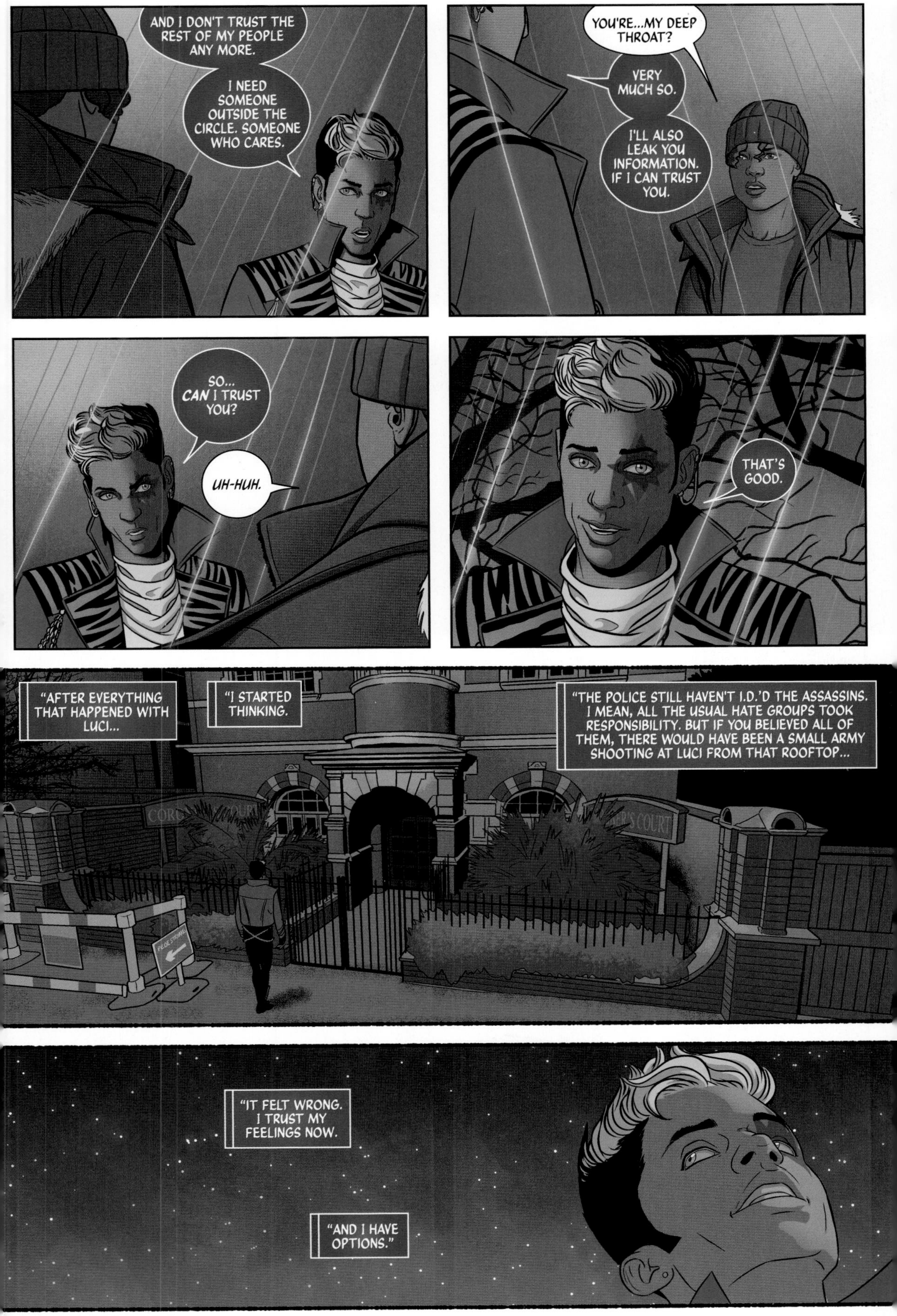
AND I DON'T TRUST THE REST OF MY PEOPLE ANY MORE.
I NEED SOMEONE OUTSIDE THE CIRCLE. SOMEONE WHO CARES.
YOU'RE...MY DEEP THROAT?
VERY MUCH SO.
I'LL ALSO LEAK YOU INFORMATION. IF I CAN TRUST YOU.
SO... CAN I TRUST YOU?
UH-HUH.
THAT'S GOOD.
"AFTER EVERYTHING THAT HAPPENED WITH LUCI...
"I STARTED THINKING.
"THE POLICE STILL HAVEN'T I.D.'D THE ASSASSINS. I MEAN, ALL THE USUAL HATE GROUPS TOOK RESPONSIBILITY. BUT IF YOU BELIEVED ALL OF THEM, THERE WOULD HAVE BEEN A SMALL ARMY SHOOTING AT LUCI FROM THAT ROOFTOP...
"IT FELT WRONG. I TRUST MY FEELINGS NOW.
"AND I HAVE OPTIONS."

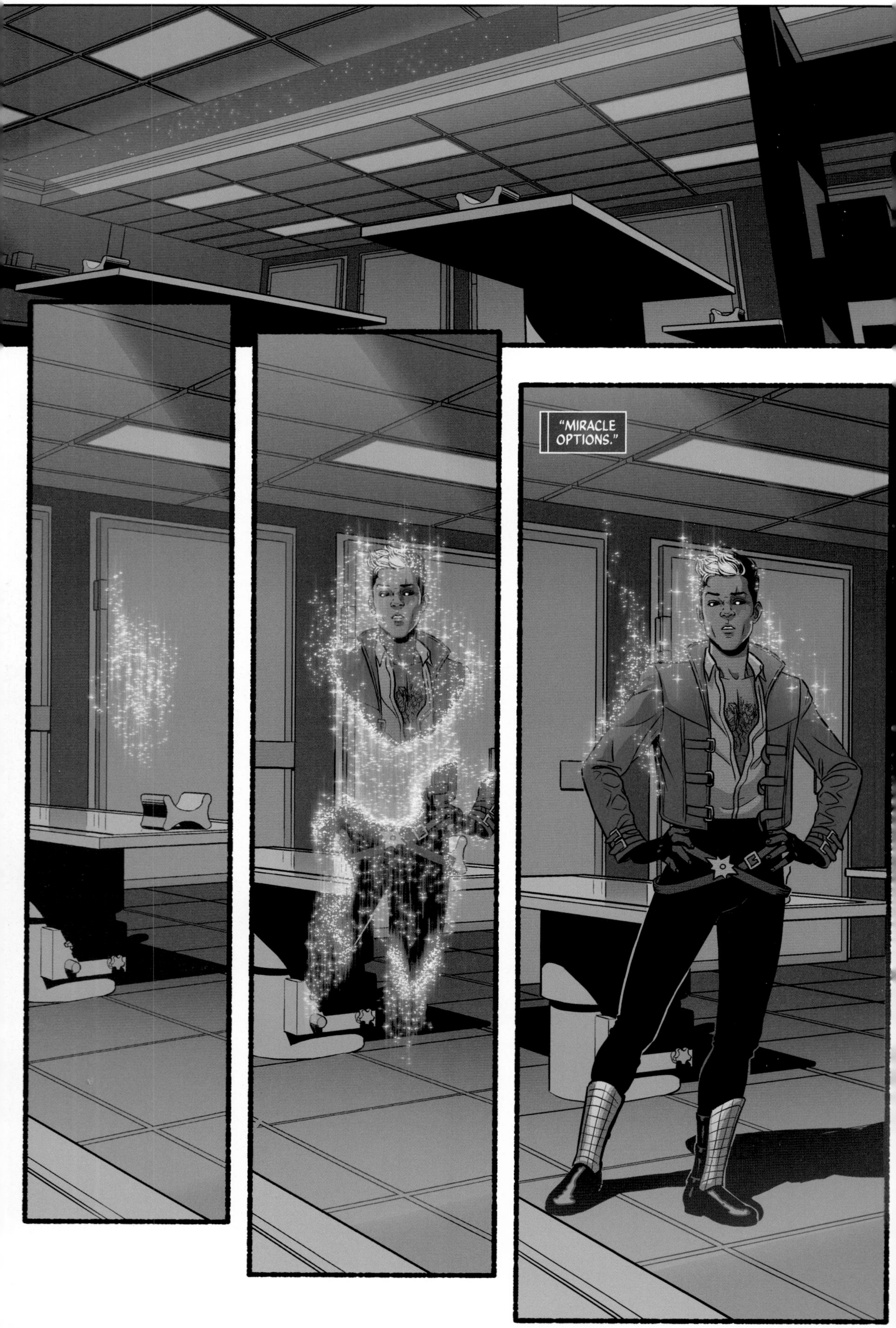
"MIRACLE OPTIONS."

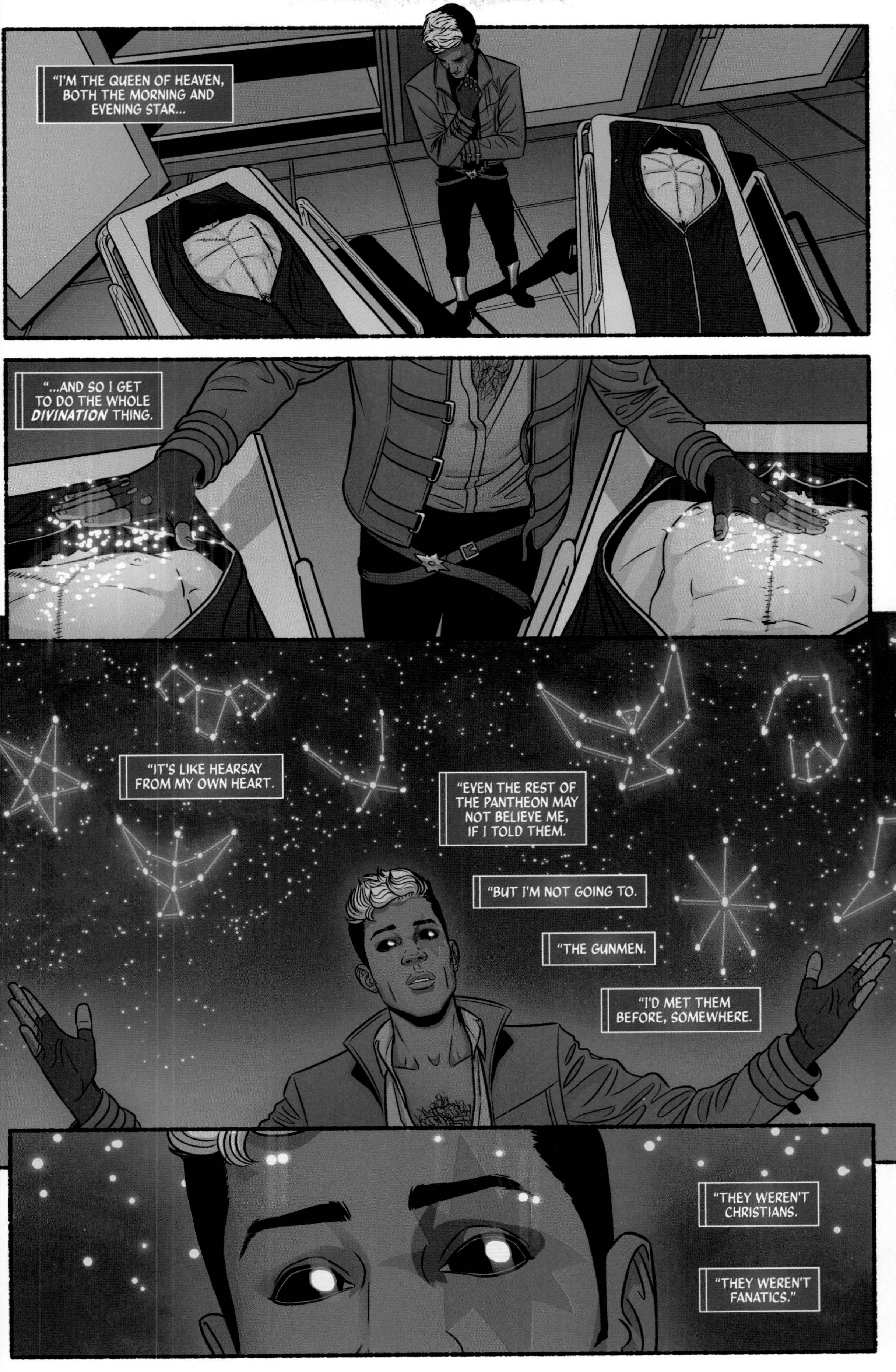
"I'M THE QUEEN OF HEAVEN, BOTH THE MORNING AND EVENING STAR...
"...AND SO I GET TO DO THE WHOLE *DIVINATION* THING.
"IT'S LIKE HEARSAY FROM MY OWN HEART.
"EVEN THE REST OF THE PANTHEON MAY NOT BELIEVE ME, IF I TOLD THEM.
"BUT I'M NOT GOING TO.
"THE GUNMEN.
"I'D MET THEM BEFORE, SOMEWHERE.
"THEY WEREN'T CHRISTIANS.
"THEY WEREN'T FANATICS."

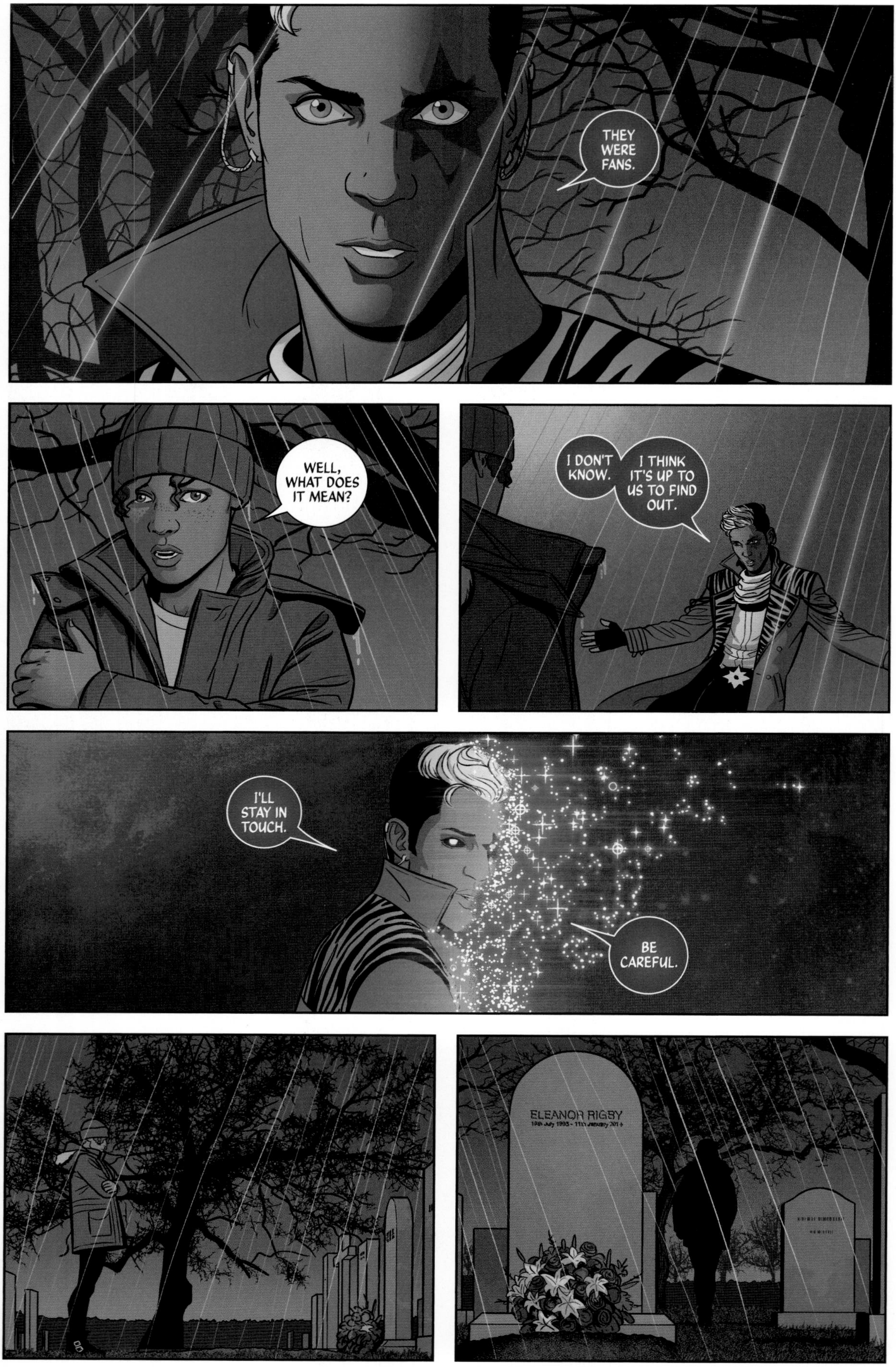
THEY WERE FANS.
WELL, WHAT DOES IT MEAN?
I DON'T KNOW.
I THINK IT'S UP TO US TO FIND OUT.
I'LL STAY IN TOUCH.
BE CAREFUL.
ELEANOR RIGBY

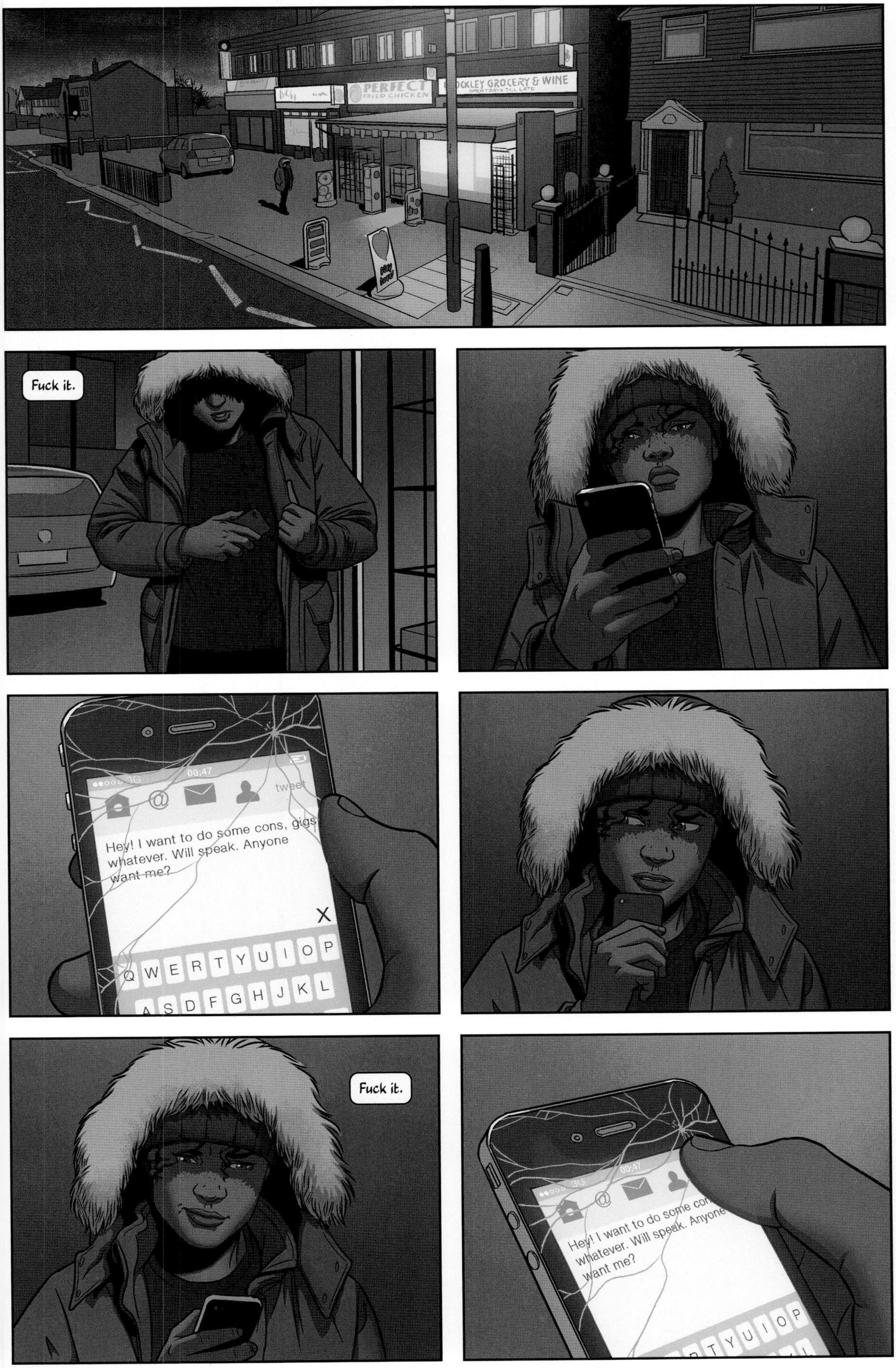PERFECT
FRIED CHICKEN
OCKLEY GROCERY & WINE
OPEN 7 DAYS TILL LATE
Fuck it.
00:47
3G
tweet
Hey! I want to do some cons, gigs, whatever. Will speak. Anyone want me?
X
QWERTYUIOP
ASDFGHJKL
Fuck it.
00:47
3G
Hey! I want to do some con whatever. Will speak. Anyone want me?
RTYUIOP

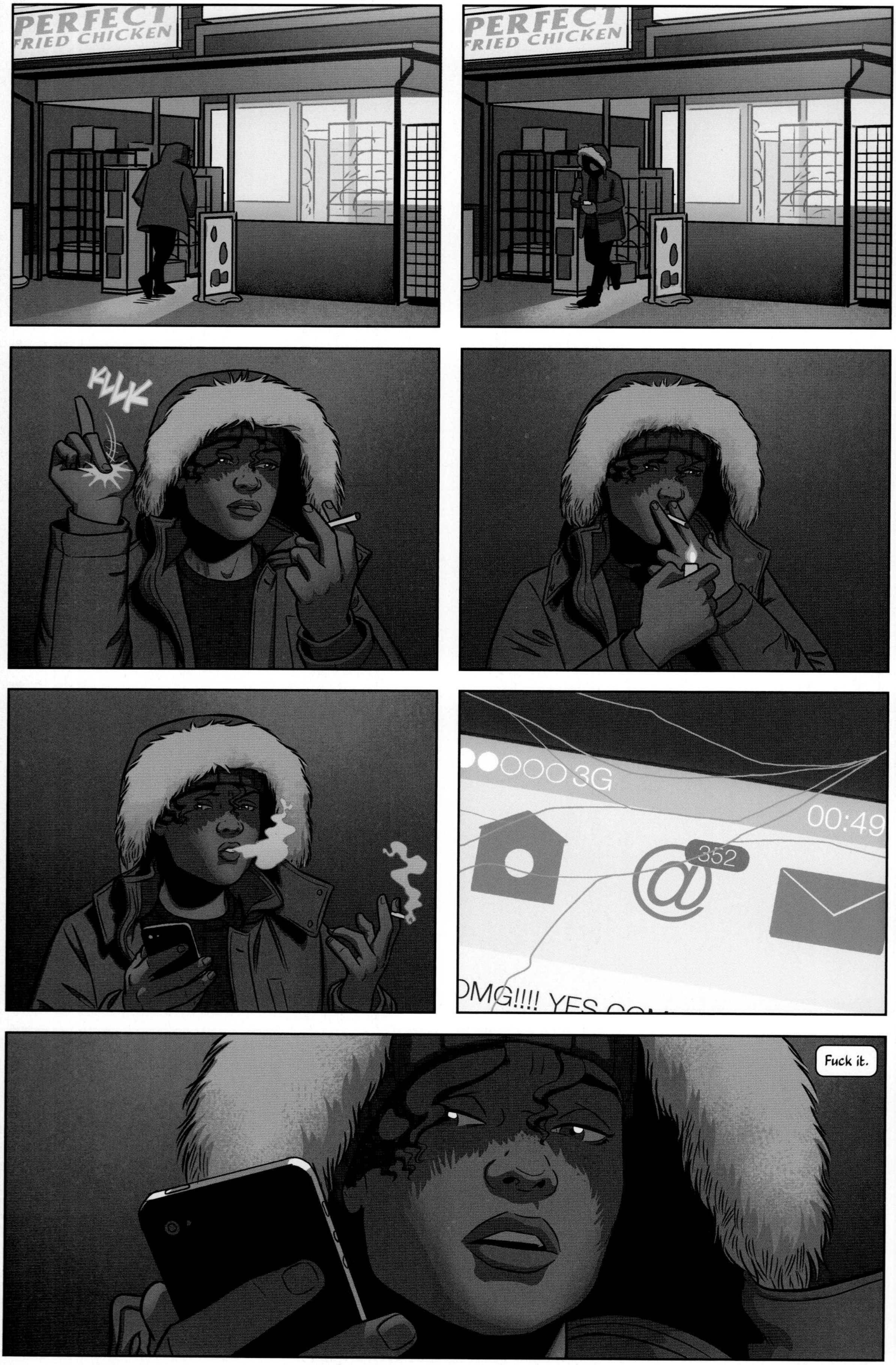
PERFECT
FRIED CHICKEN
PERFECT
FRIED CHICKEN
KLIK
3G
00:49
352
OMG!!!! YES
Fuck it.

ABANDON
ALL HOPE

1 MARCH 2014

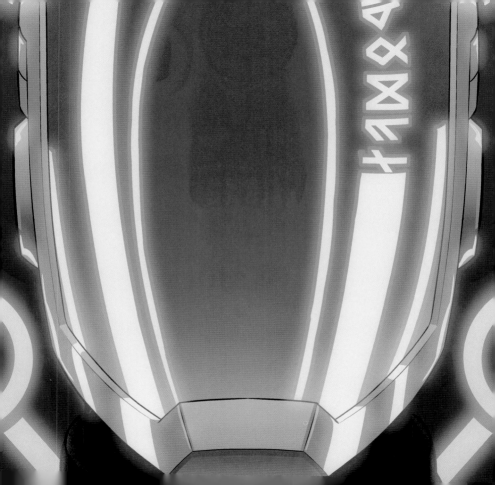

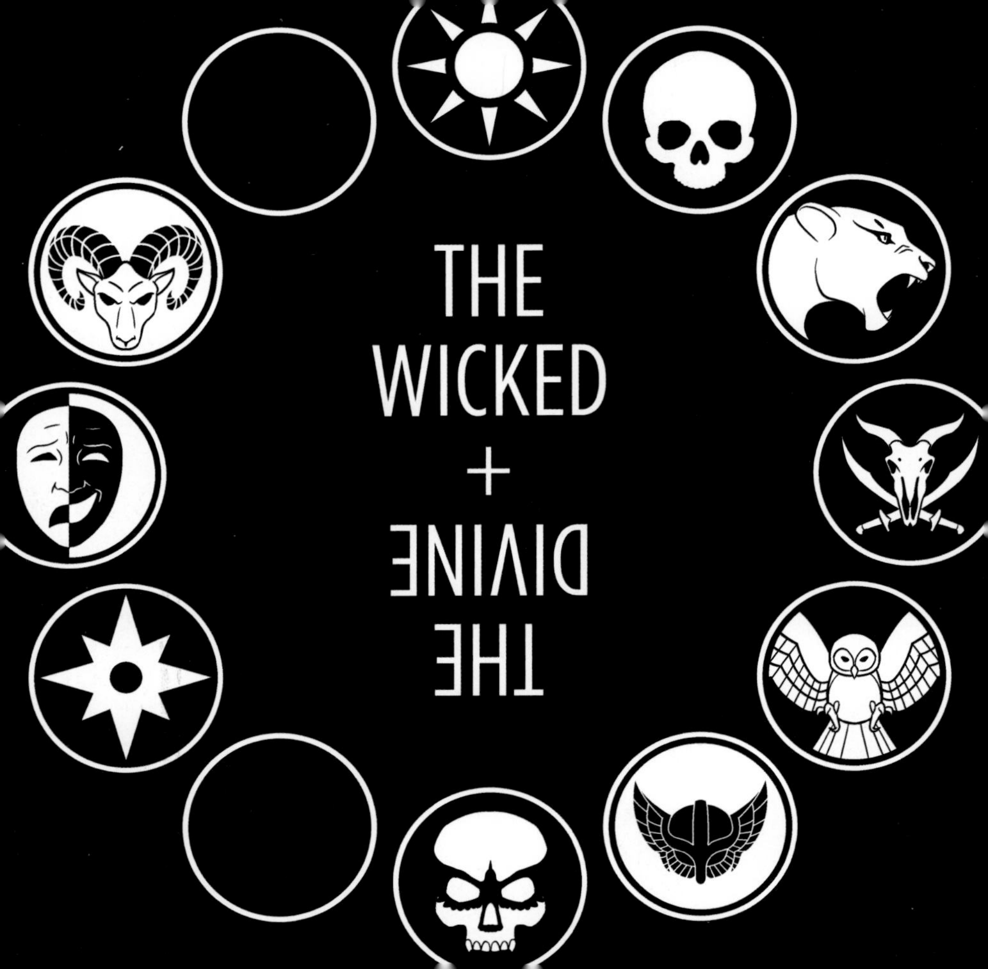
THE
WICKED
+
DIVINE
THE

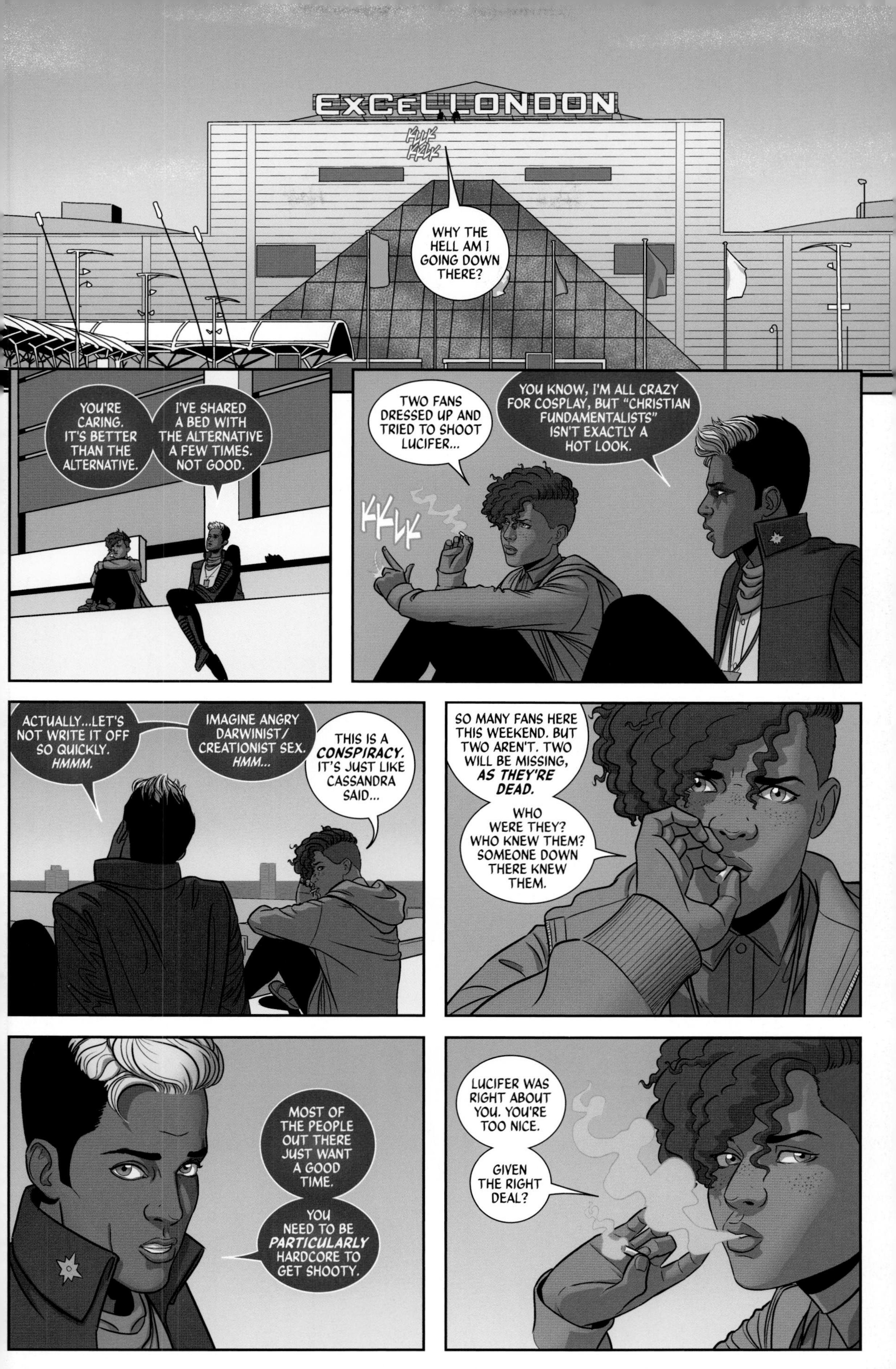
ExCeL LONDON
WHY THE HELL AM I GOING DOWN THERE?
YOU'RE CARING. IT'S BETTER THAN THE ALTERNATIVE.
I'VE SHARED A BED WITH THE ALTERNATIVE A FEW TIMES. NOT GOOD.
TWO FANS DRESSED UP AND TRIED TO SHOOT LUCIFER...
YOU KNOW, I'M ALL CRAZY FOR COSPLAY, BUT "CHRISTIAN FUNDAMENTALISTS" ISN'T EXACTLY A HOT LOOK.
IMAGINE ANGRY DARWINIST/ CREATIONIST SEX. HMM...
ACTUALLY...LET'S NOT WRITE IT OFF SO QUICKLY. HMMM.
THIS IS A CONSPIRACY. IT'S JUST LIKE CASSANDRA SAID...
SO MANY FANS HERE THIS WEEKEND. BUT TWO AREN'T. TWO WILL BE MISSING, AS THEY'RE DEAD.
WHO WERE THEY? WHO KNEW THEM? SOMEONE DOWN THERE KNEW THEM.
MOST OF THE PEOPLE OUT THERE JUST WANT A GOOD TIME.
YOU NEED TO BE PARTICULARLY HARDCORE TO GET SHOOTY.
LUCIFER WAS RIGHT ABOUT YOU. YOU'RE TOO NICE.
GIVEN THE RIGHT DEAL?

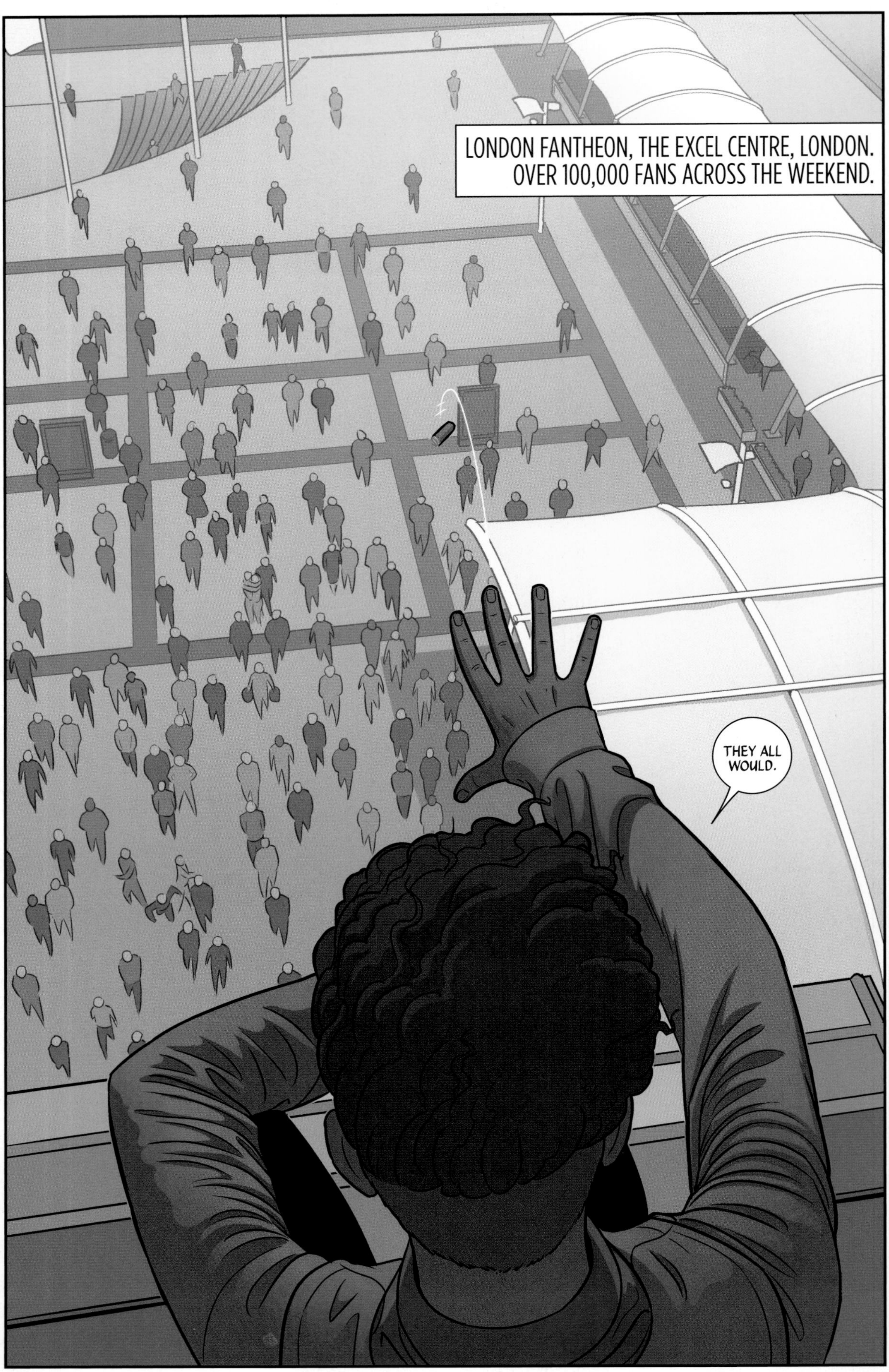
LONDON FANTHEON, THE EXCEL CENTRE, LONDON. OVER 100,000 FANS ACROSS THE WEEKEND.
THEY ALL WOULD.

AWKWARD
CONVERSATION

12 APRIL 2014

CUSTOM HOUSE

Evening Gig Venue

My first autograph of the day

Queue went out the building
First thing I was glad of about this whole thing —
I got to skip.

My twelfth autograph of the day. ☺

the exact point where I decided I'm not signing autographs any more.

ticket sales   online ticket scanners   re-entry

C

Note:
Time slots for Photos With The Stars must be booked online in accordance with London Fantheon Terms & Conditions, in order for sufficient time for positive vetting to take place.

Unvetted applicants will not be admitted to the PWTS venue.

"THE NEXT BEST THING TO GODLINESS"

* They had that Tara poster Luci vandalised in here.
They were treating it like an ICON.
I stayed away.

LONDON
Fantheon ™

They actually had signing times for me on both days.
Nothing about this is not strange.

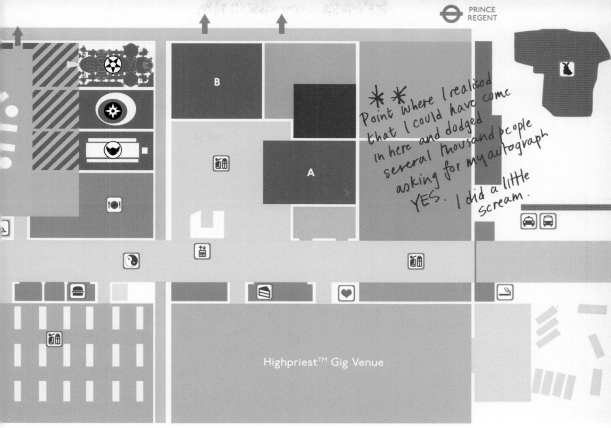

PRINCE REGENT
B
A
Highpriest™ Gig Venue
** Point where I realised that I could have come in here and dodged several thousand people asking for my autograph
YES. I did a little scream.

Luci died three months ago – and they've still using her – CLASSY

- Welcome
- Main Entrance Route
- Shrine
- Cosplay
- God Homage Zone
- Artifacts Of The Gods
- Photos With The Stars
- Highpriest™ Inner Sanctum
- Tranquil Meditation & Trees
- Secure Route
- Security Check
- Panel Room
- Memorabilia
- Press Lounge
- VIP Zone
- Gig Space

- WCs
- Main Circulation
- Food Court
- Fantheon Fanworks
- History Zone
- Outside Broadcast
- Riverside Garden
- Taxi Drop Off
- Changing Rooms
- Business Services
- First Aid & Pharmacy
- Shopping Mall
- Information Centre
- Gods' Private Hotel
- VIP Drop Off
- External Area
- Family Space (becomes Recovery Room from 7pm onwards)

- Fire Exit
- Meeting Point
- God, I Need A Coffee
- Hamaterasu Sandwiches
- Baal-You-Can-Eat-Buffet
- Inanna and Out Burgers
- Amateragu Italian
- Bap-O-Meat
- The Val-Cakery
- Retail Area
- Lifts & Stairs
- Style Council
- Defibrillator
- Drinking Water
- Smoking Area
- ATM

2015 art & design: alison sampson
www.alisonsampsonart.tumblr.com

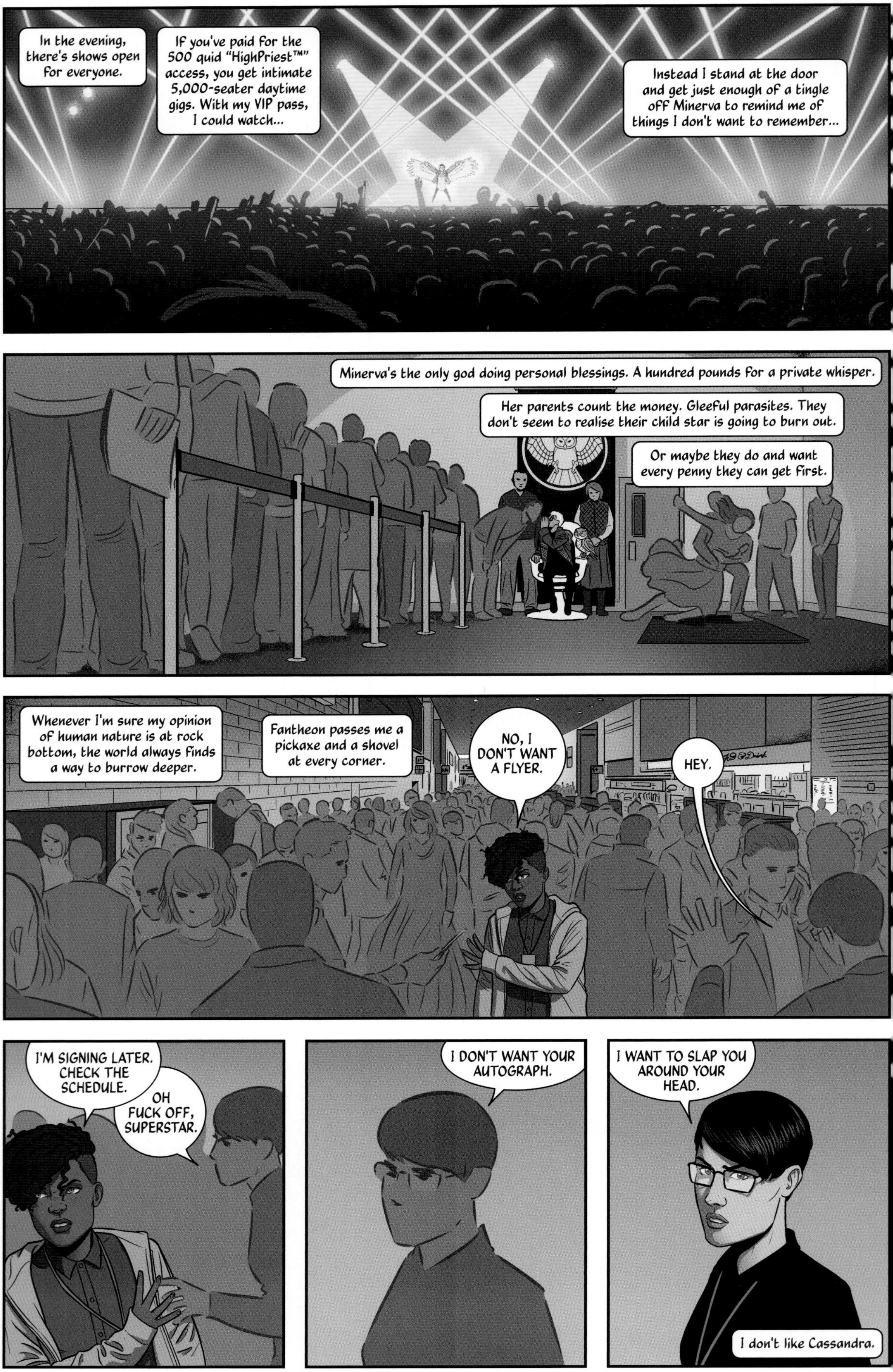
In the evening, there's shows open for everyone.
If you've paid for the 500 quid "HighPriest™" access, you get intimate 5,000-seater daytime gigs. With my VIP pass, I could watch...
Instead I stand at the door and get just enough of a tingle off Minerva to remind me of things I don't want to remember...
Minerva's the only god doing personal blessings. A hundred pounds for a private whisper.
Her parents count the money. Gleeful parasites. They don't seem to realise their child star is going to burn out.
Or maybe they do and want every penny they can get first.
Whenever I'm sure my opinion of human nature is at rock bottom, the world always finds a way to burrow deeper.
Fantheon passes me a pickaxe and a shovel at every corner.
NO, I DON'T WANT A FLYER.
HEY.
I'M SIGNING LATER. CHECK THE SCHEDULE.
OH FUCK OFF, SUPERSTAR.
I DON'T WANT YOUR AUTOGRAPH.
I WANT TO SLAP YOU AROUND YOUR HEAD.
I don't like Cassandra.

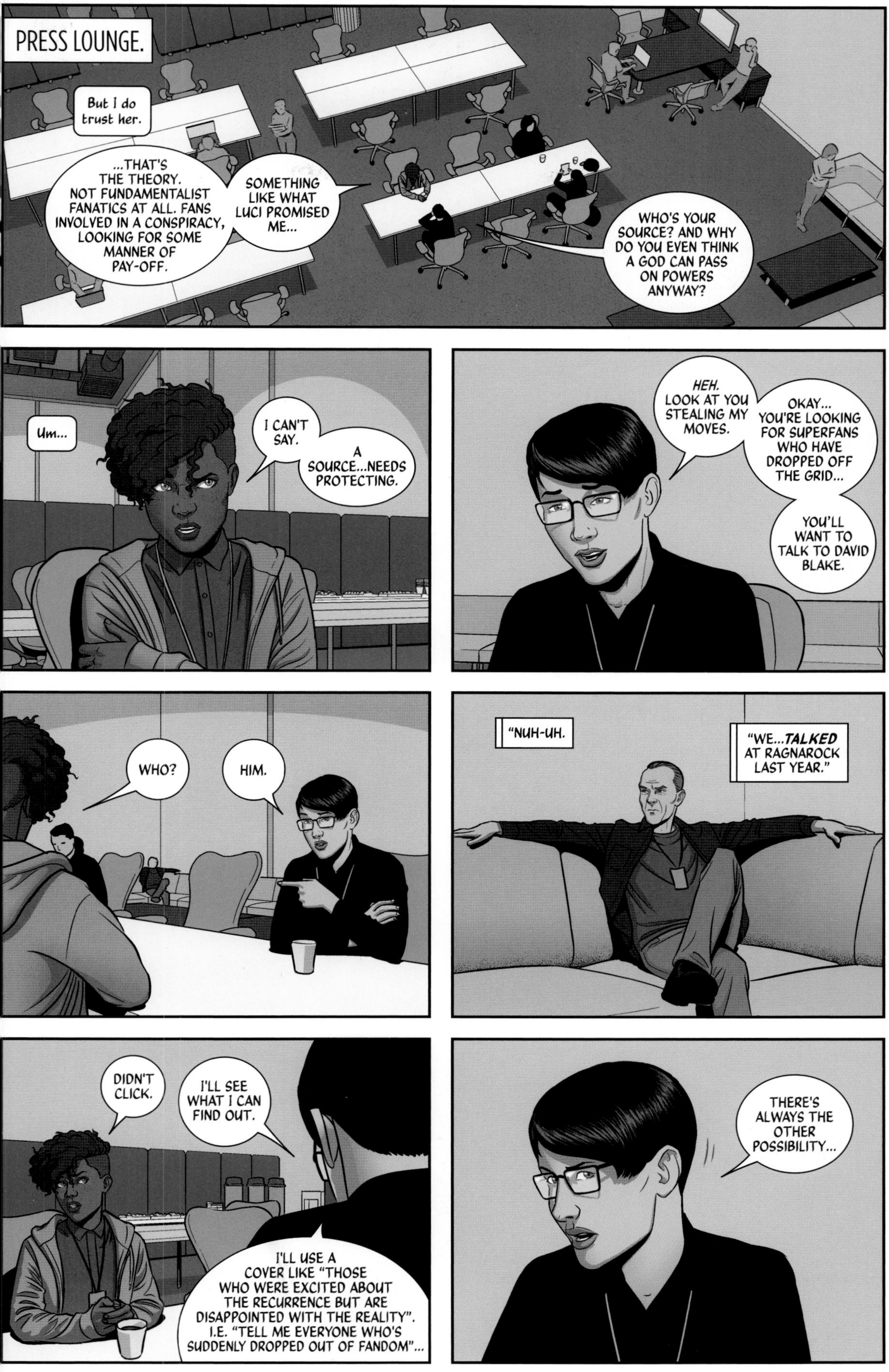
PRESS LOUNGE.
But I do trust her.
...THAT'S THE THEORY. NOT FUNDAMENTALIST FANATICS AT ALL. FANS INVOLVED IN A CONSPIRACY, LOOKING FOR SOME MANNER OF PAY-OFF.
SOMETHING LIKE WHAT LUCI PROMISED ME...
WHO'S YOUR SOURCE? AND WHY DO YOU EVEN THINK A GOD CAN PASS ON POWERS ANYWAY?
Um...
I CAN'T SAY.
A SOURCE...NEEDS PROTECTING.
HEH. LOOK AT YOU STEALING MY MOVES.
OKAY... YOU'RE LOOKING FOR SUPERFANS WHO HAVE DROPPED OFF THE GRID...
YOU'LL WANT TO TALK TO DAVID BLAKE.
WHO?
HIM.
"NUH-UH.
"WE...TALKED AT RAGNAROCK LAST YEAR."
DIDN'T CLICK.
I'LL SEE WHAT I CAN FIND OUT.
I'LL USE A COVER LIKE "THOSE WHO WERE EXCITED ABOUT THE RECURRENCE BUT ARE DISAPPOINTED WITH THE REALITY". I.E. "TELL ME EVERYONE WHO'S SUDDENLY DROPPED OUT OF FANDOM"...
THERE'S ALWAYS THE OTHER POSSIBILITY...

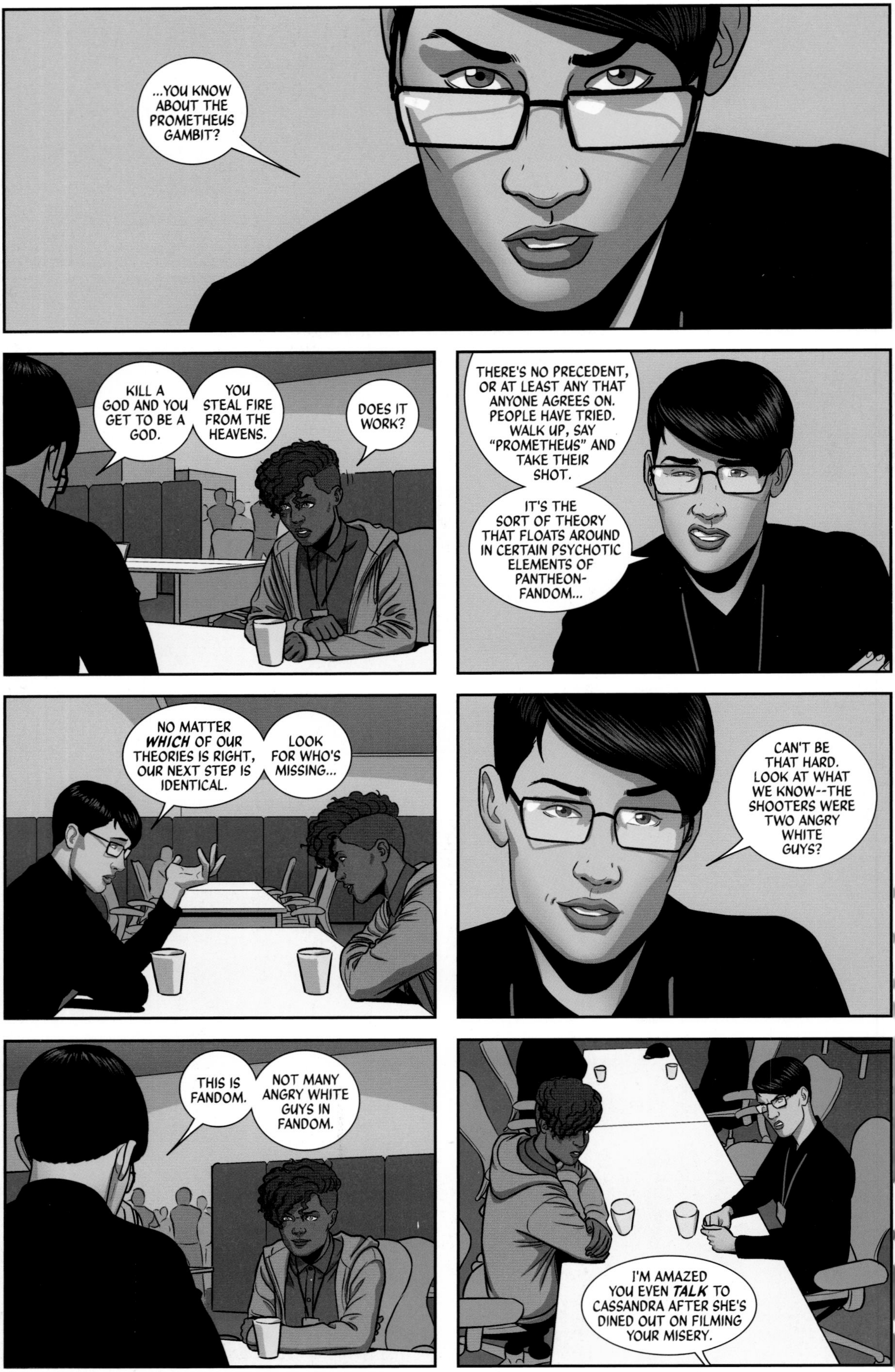
...YOU KNOW ABOUT THE PROMETHEUS GAMBIT?
KILL A GOD AND YOU GET TO BE A GOD.
YOU STEAL FIRE FROM THE HEAVENS.
DOES IT WORK?
THERE'S NO PRECEDENT, OR AT LEAST ANY THAT ANYONE AGREES ON. PEOPLE HAVE TRIED. WALK UP, SAY "PROMETHEUS" AND TAKE THEIR SHOT.
IT'S THE SORT OF THEORY THAT FLOATS AROUND IN CERTAIN PSYCHOTIC ELEMENTS OF PANTHEON-FANDOM...
NO MATTER *WHICH* OF OUR THEORIES IS RIGHT, OUR NEXT STEP IS IDENTICAL.
LOOK FOR WHO'S MISSING...
CAN'T BE THAT HARD. LOOK AT WHAT WE KNOW--THE SHOOTERS WERE TWO ANGRY WHITE GUYS?
THIS IS FANDOM.
NOT MANY ANGRY WHITE GUYS IN FANDOM.
I'M AMAZED YOU EVEN *TALK* TO CASSANDRA AFTER SHE'S DINED OUT ON FILMING YOUR MISERY.

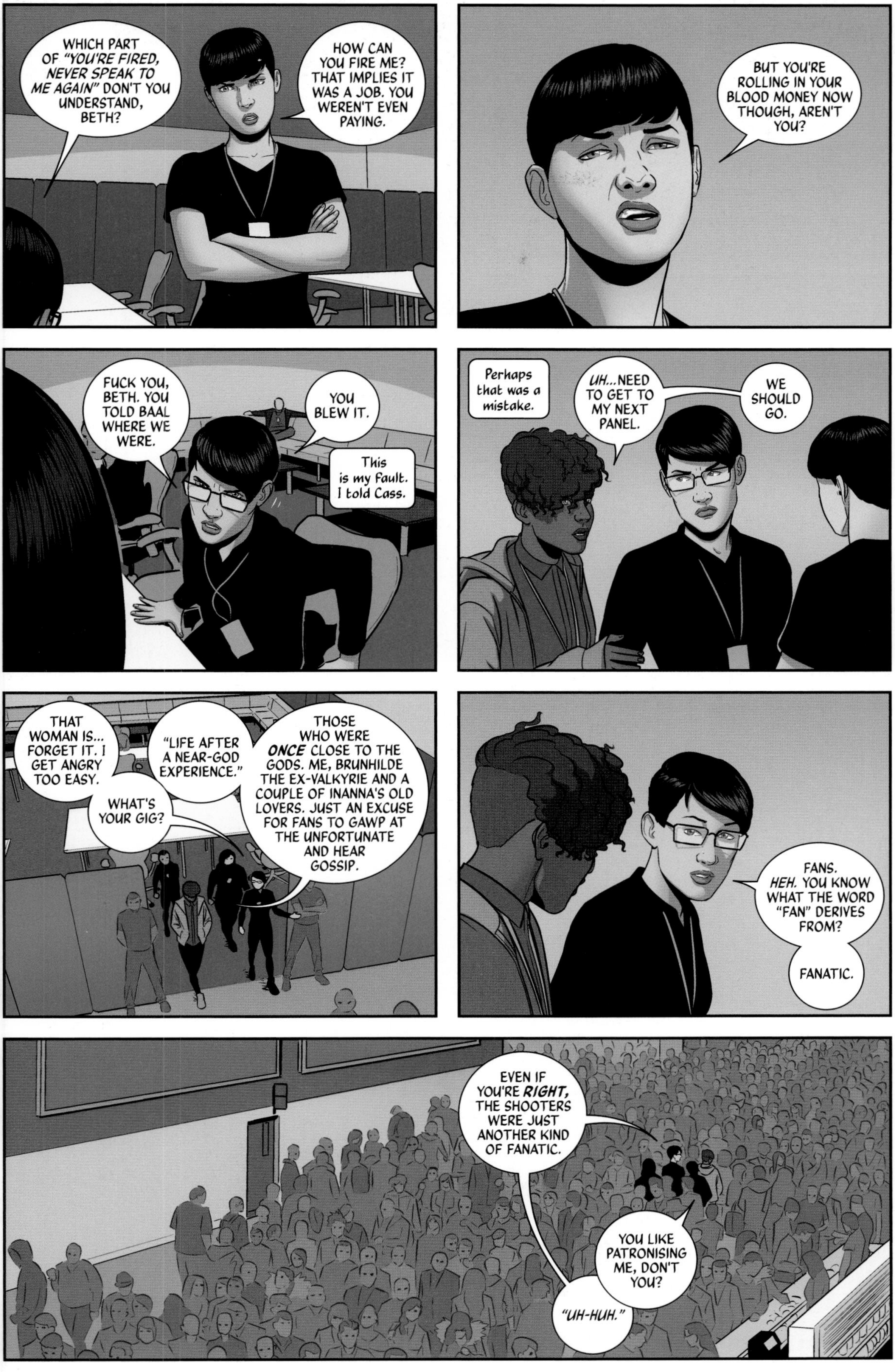
WHICH PART OF "YOU'RE FIRED, NEVER SPEAK TO ME AGAIN" DON'T YOU UNDERSTAND, BETH?
HOW CAN YOU FIRE ME? THAT IMPLIES IT WAS A JOB. YOU WEREN'T EVEN PAYING.
BUT YOU'RE ROLLING IN YOUR BLOOD MONEY NOW THOUGH, AREN'T YOU?
FUCK YOU, BETH. YOU TOLD BAAL WHERE WE WERE.
YOU BLEW IT.
This is my fault. I told Cass.
Perhaps that was a mistake.
UH...NEED TO GET TO MY NEXT PANEL.
WE SHOULD GO.
THAT WOMAN IS... FORGET IT. I GET ANGRY TOO EASY.
WHAT'S YOUR GIG?
"LIFE AFTER A NEAR-GOD EXPERIENCE."
THOSE WHO WERE ONCE CLOSE TO THE GODS. ME, BRUNHILDE THE EX-VALKYRIE AND A COUPLE OF INANNA'S OLD LOVERS. JUST AN EXCUSE FOR FANS TO GAWP AT THE UNFORTUNATE AND HEAR GOSSIP.
FANS. HEH. YOU KNOW WHAT THE WORD "FAN" DERIVES FROM?
FANATIC.
EVEN IF YOU'RE RIGHT, THE SHOOTERS WERE JUST ANOTHER KIND OF FANATIC.
YOU LIKE PATRONISING ME, DON'T YOU?
"UH-HUH."

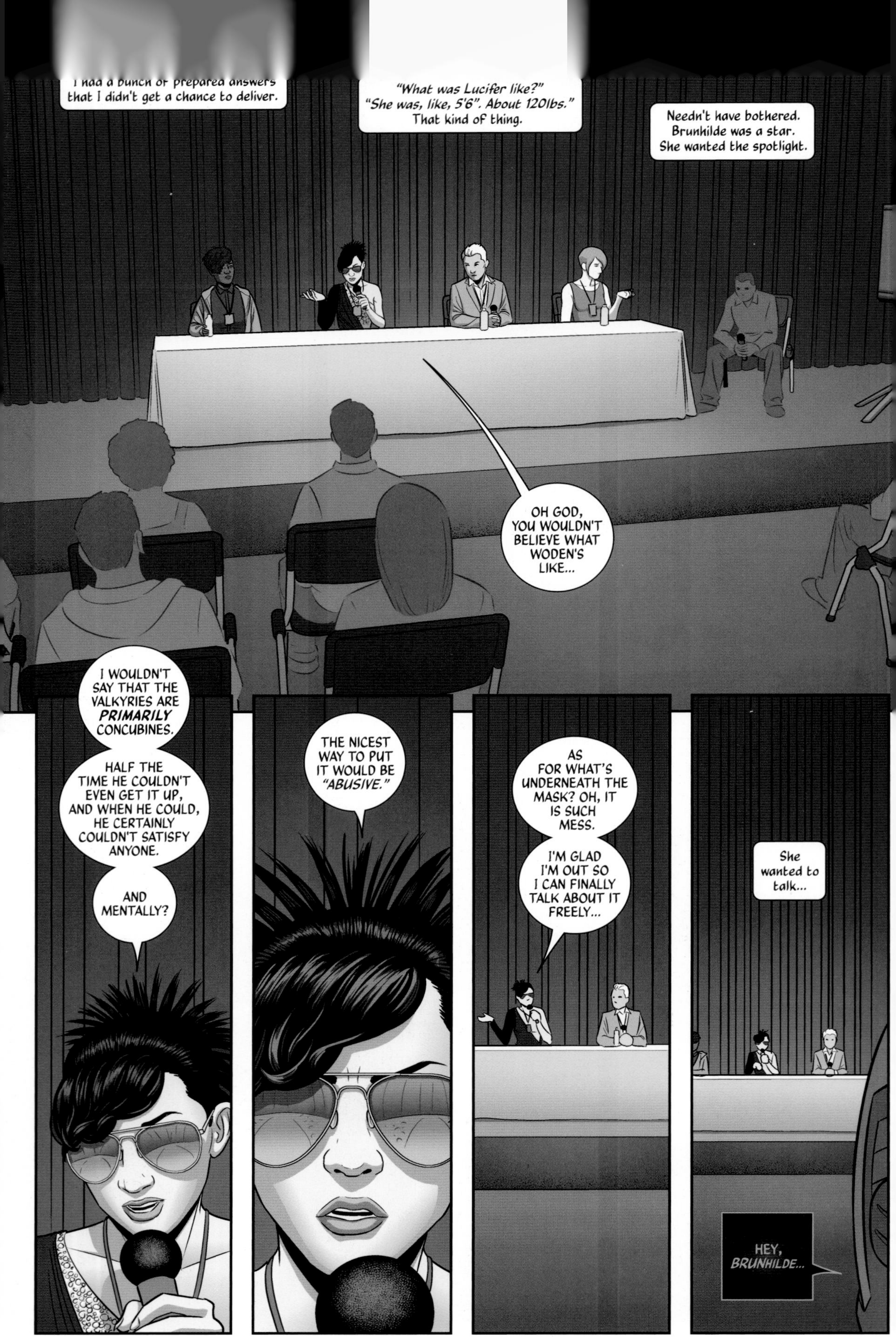
I had a bunch of prepared answers
that I didn't get a chance to deliver.
"What was Lucifer like?"
"She was, like, 5'6". About 120lbs."
That kind of thing.
Needn't have bothered.
Brunhilde was a star.
She wanted the spotlight.
OH GOD, YOU WOULDN'T BELIEVE WHAT WODEN'S LIKE...
I WOULDN'T SAY THAT THE VALKYRIES ARE *PRIMARILY* CONCUBINES.
HALF THE TIME HE COULDN'T EVEN GET IT UP, AND WHEN HE COULD, HE CERTAINLY COULDN'T SATISFY ANYONE.
AND MENTALLY?
THE NICEST WAY TO PUT IT WOULD BE *"ABUSIVE."*
AS FOR WHAT'S UNDERNEATH THE MASK? OH, IT IS SUCH MESS.
I'M GLAD I'M OUT SO I CAN FINALLY TALK ABOUT IT FREELY...
She wanted to talk...
HEY, *BRUNHILDE*...

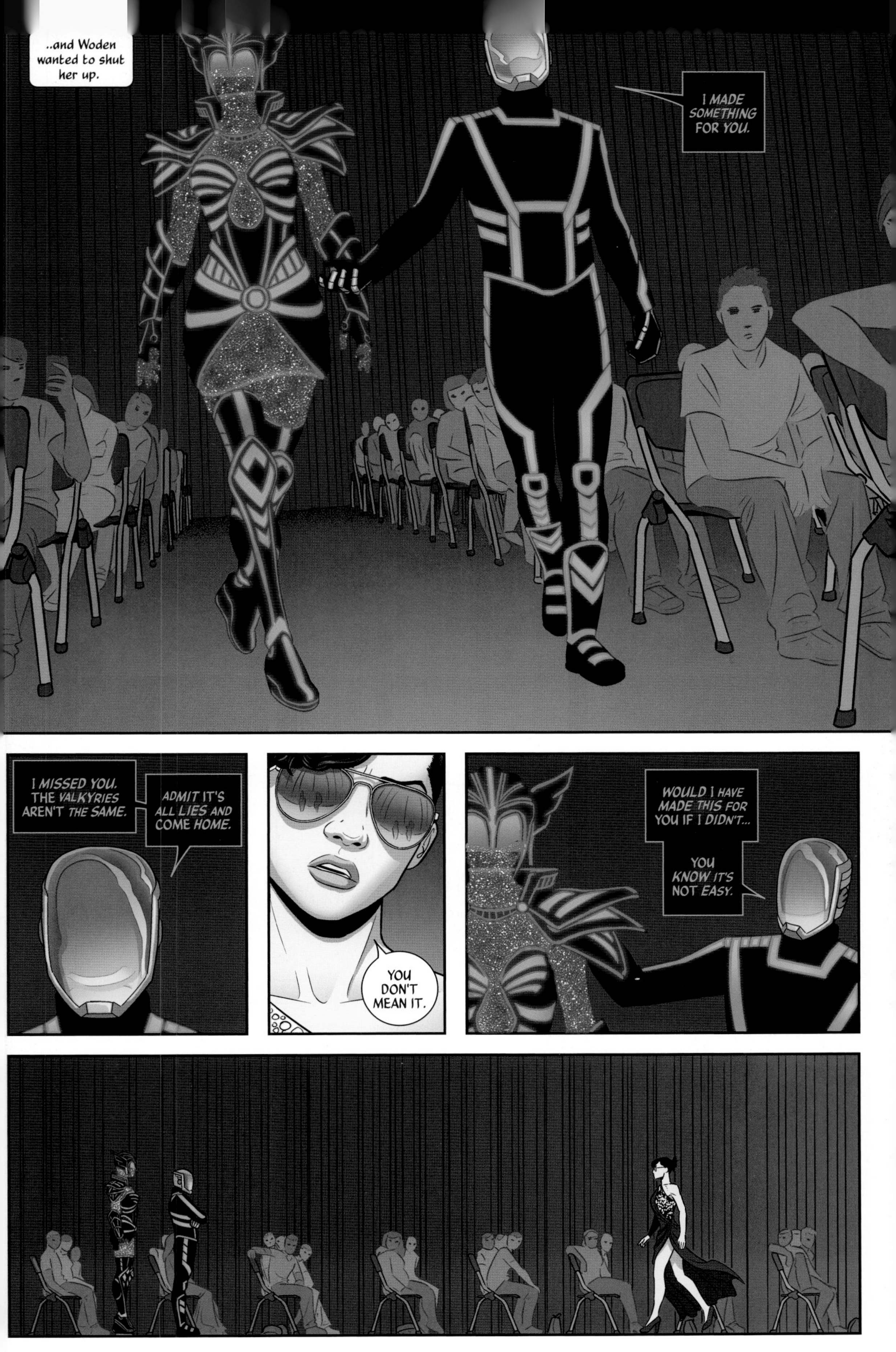
..and Woden wanted to shut her up.
I MADE SOMETHING FOR YOU.
I MISSED YOU. THE VALKYRIES AREN'T THE SAME.
ADMIT IT'S ALL LIES AND COME HOME.
YOU DON'T MEAN IT.
WOULD I HAVE MADE THIS FOR YOU IF I DIDN'T...
YOU KNOW IT'S NOT EASY.

...DOES IT HAVE TO BE HERE?

IT DOES.

YOU *KNOW* I *LOVE* YOU, BUT I *DON'T EXACTLY TRUST* YOU *ANY* MORE.

IT WAS ALL LIES.

EVERY WORD OF IT.

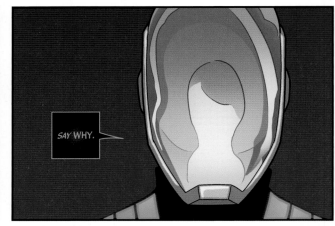

SAY WHY.

I WANTED TO GET BACK AT YOU FOR KICKING ME OUT.

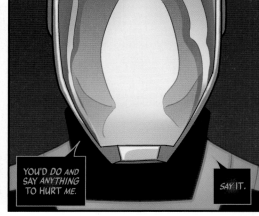

YOU'D *DO* AND SAY *ANYTHING* TO HURT *ME.*

SAY IT.

I'D DO AND SAY ANYTHING.

IT'S ALL I HAVE LEFT.

THANK YOU.

KLLK

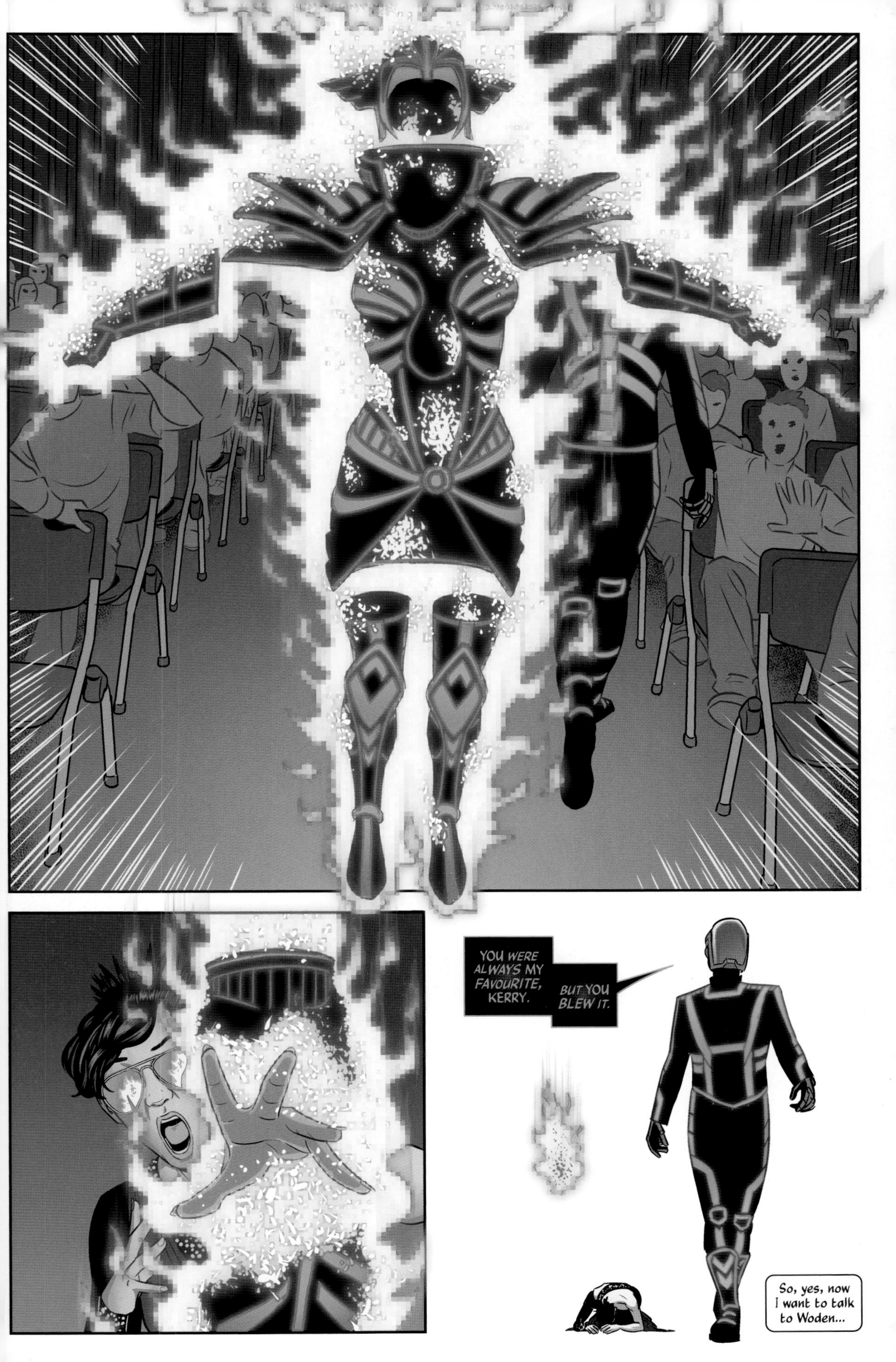
YOU WERE ALWAYS MY FAVOURITE, KERRY.
BUT YOU BLEW IT.
So, yes, now I want to talk to Woden...

...but so does Inanna. In private. Angrily.

I'm left outside passing the time with VIP-level harassment.

NO, YOU CAN'T BUY MY PHONE!

YOU HEARD THE GIRL. LEAVE HER ALONE.

My Crush...

SO, HOW'S SATAN'S LITTLE HELPER?

...crushed.

HEY, I DIDN'T MEAN--

FORGET IT.

WODEN... I WAS WONDERING....

NO, YOU DON'T HAVE WHAT IT TAKES TO BE A VALKYRIE.

BECAUSE I'M NOT OVER 5'8" AND ASIAN?

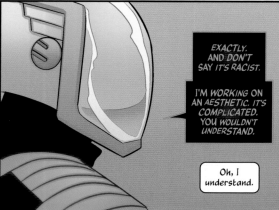

EXACTLY. AND DON'T SAY IT'S RACIST.

I'M WORKING ON AN AESTHETIC. IT'S COMPLICATED. YOU WOULDN'T UNDERSTAND.

Oh, I understand.

It's a racist aesthetic of girls you want to fuck.

I WANTED TO TALK ABOUT BRUNHILDE.

WASN'T THAT...A BIT STRONG?

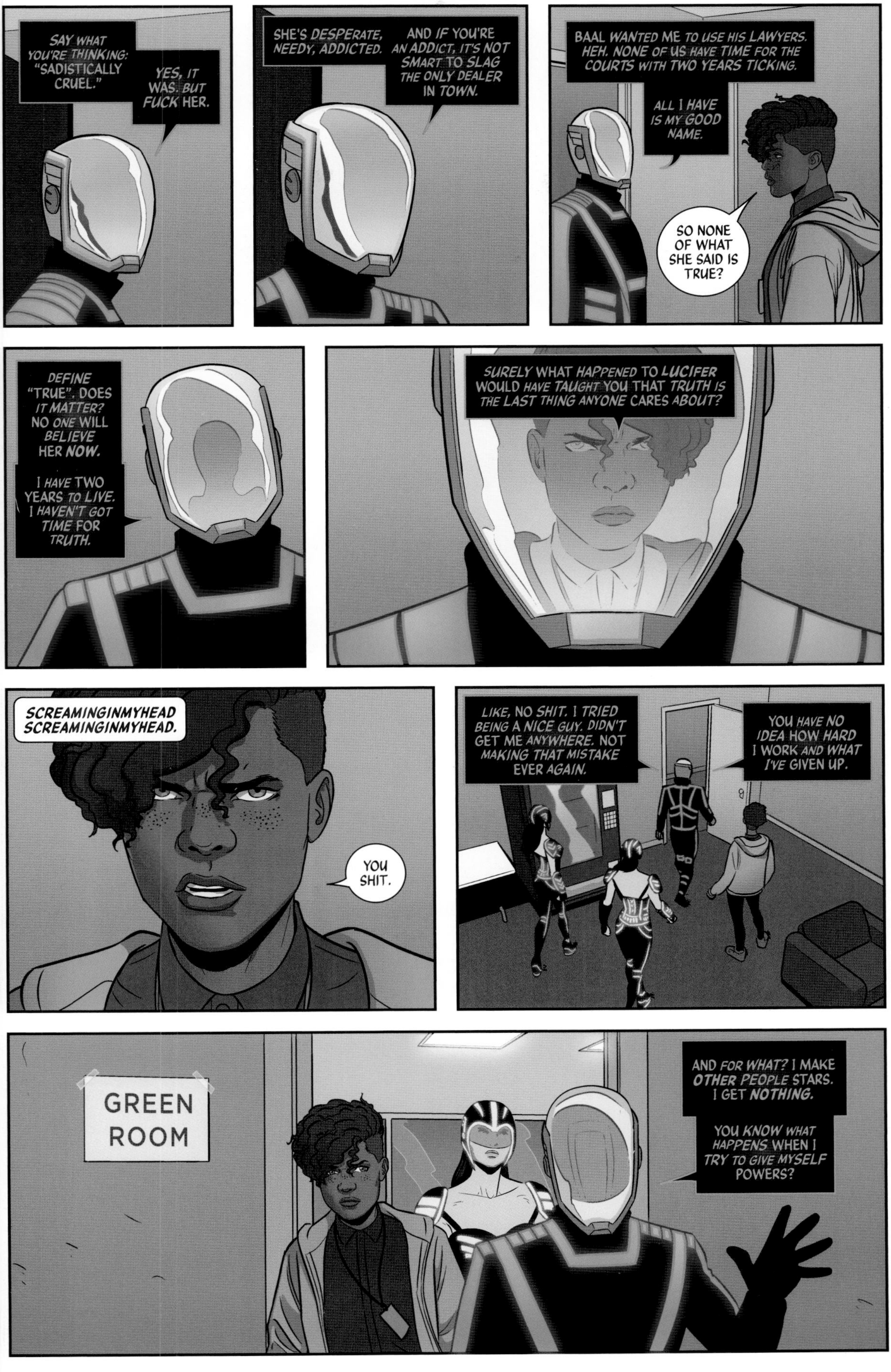
SAY WHAT YOU'RE THINKING: "SADISTICALLY CRUEL."
YES, IT WAS. BUT FUCK HER.
SHE'S DESPERATE, NEEDY, ADDICTED.
AND IF YOU'RE AN ADDICT, IT'S NOT SMART TO SLAG THE ONLY DEALER IN TOWN.
BAAL WANTED ME TO USE HIS LAWYERS. HEH. NONE OF US HAVE TIME FOR THE COURTS WITH TWO YEARS TICKING.
ALL I HAVE IS MY GOOD NAME.
SO NONE OF WHAT SHE SAID IS TRUE?
DEFINE "TRUE". DOES IT MATTER? NO ONE WILL BELIEVE HER NOW.
I HAVE TWO YEARS TO LIVE. I HAVEN'T GOT TIME FOR TRUTH.
SURELY WHAT HAPPENED TO LUCIFER WOULD HAVE TAUGHT YOU THAT TRUTH IS THE LAST THING ANYONE CARES ABOUT?
SCREAMINGINMYHEAD SCREAMINGINMYHEAD.
YOU SHIT.
LIKE, NO SHIT. I TRIED BEING A NICE GUY. DIDN'T GET ME ANYWHERE. NOT MAKING THAT MISTAKE EVER AGAIN.
YOU HAVE NO IDEA HOW HARD I WORK AND WHAT I'VE GIVEN UP.
GREEN ROOM
AND FOR WHAT? I MAKE OTHER PEOPLE STARS. I GET NOTHING.
YOU KNOW WHAT HAPPENS WHEN I TRY TO GIVE MYSELF POWERS?

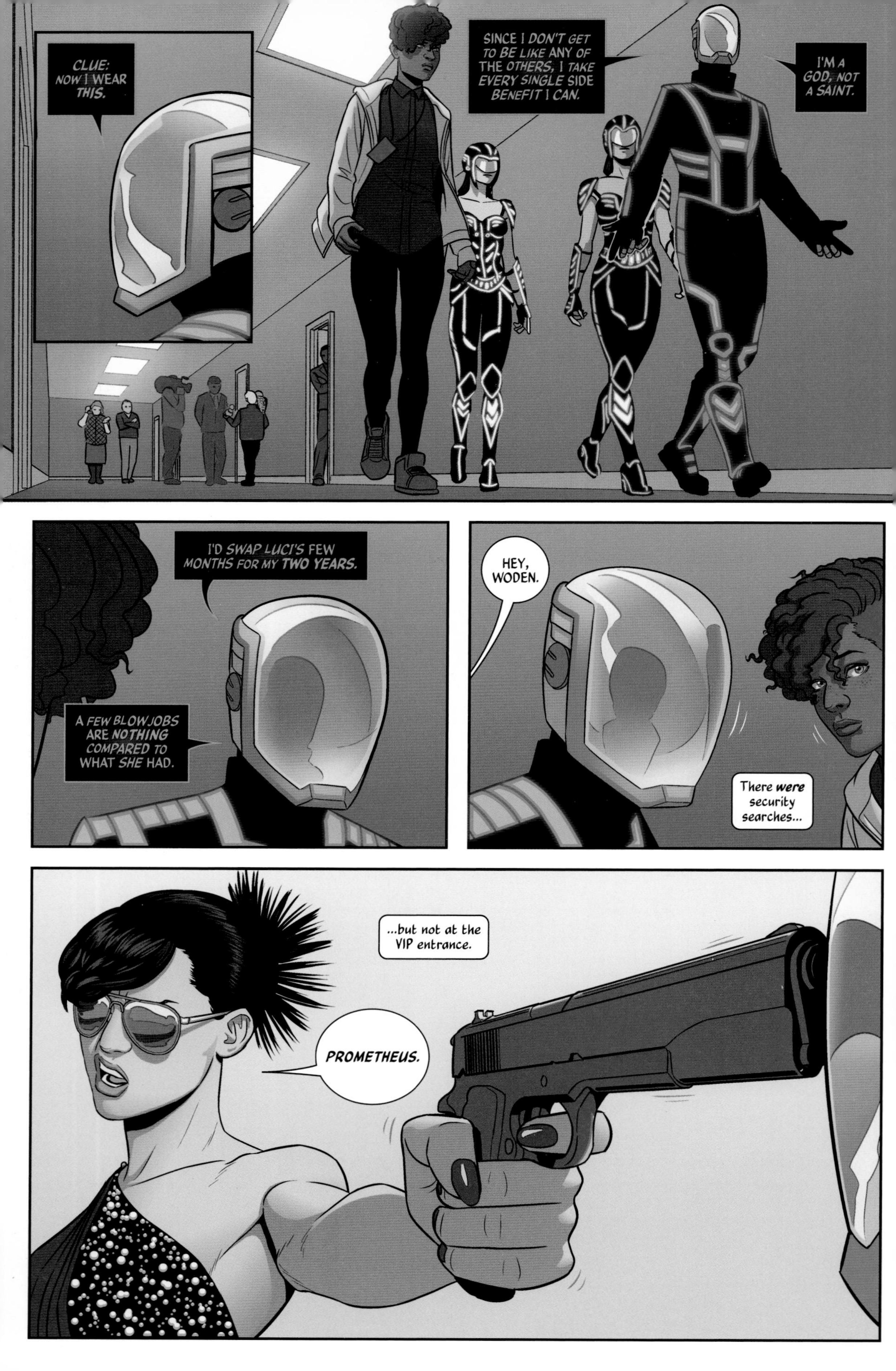
CLUE: NOW I WEAR THIS.
SINCE I DON'T GET TO BE LIKE ANY OF THE OTHERS, I TAKE EVERY SINGLE SIDE BENEFIT I CAN.
I'M A GOD, NOT A SAINT.
I'D SWAP LUCI'S FEW MONTHS FOR MY TWO YEARS.
A FEW BLOWJOBS ARE NOTHING COMPARED TO WHAT SHE HAD.
HEY, WODEN.
There were security searches...
...but not at the VIP entrance.
PROMETHEUS.

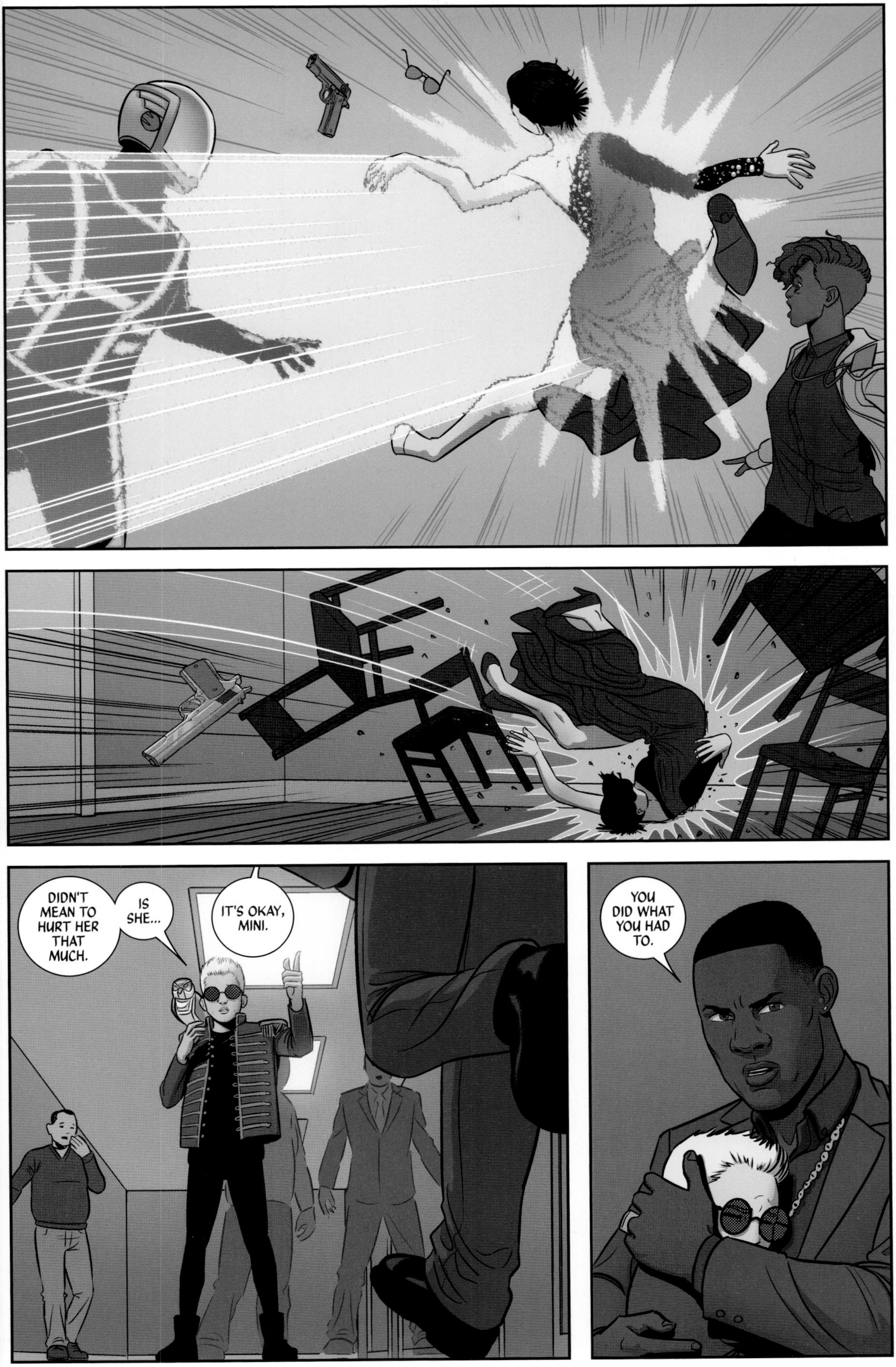
DIDN'T MEAN TO HURT HER THAT MUCH.
IS SHE...
IT'S OKAY, MINI.
YOU DID WHAT YOU HAD TO.

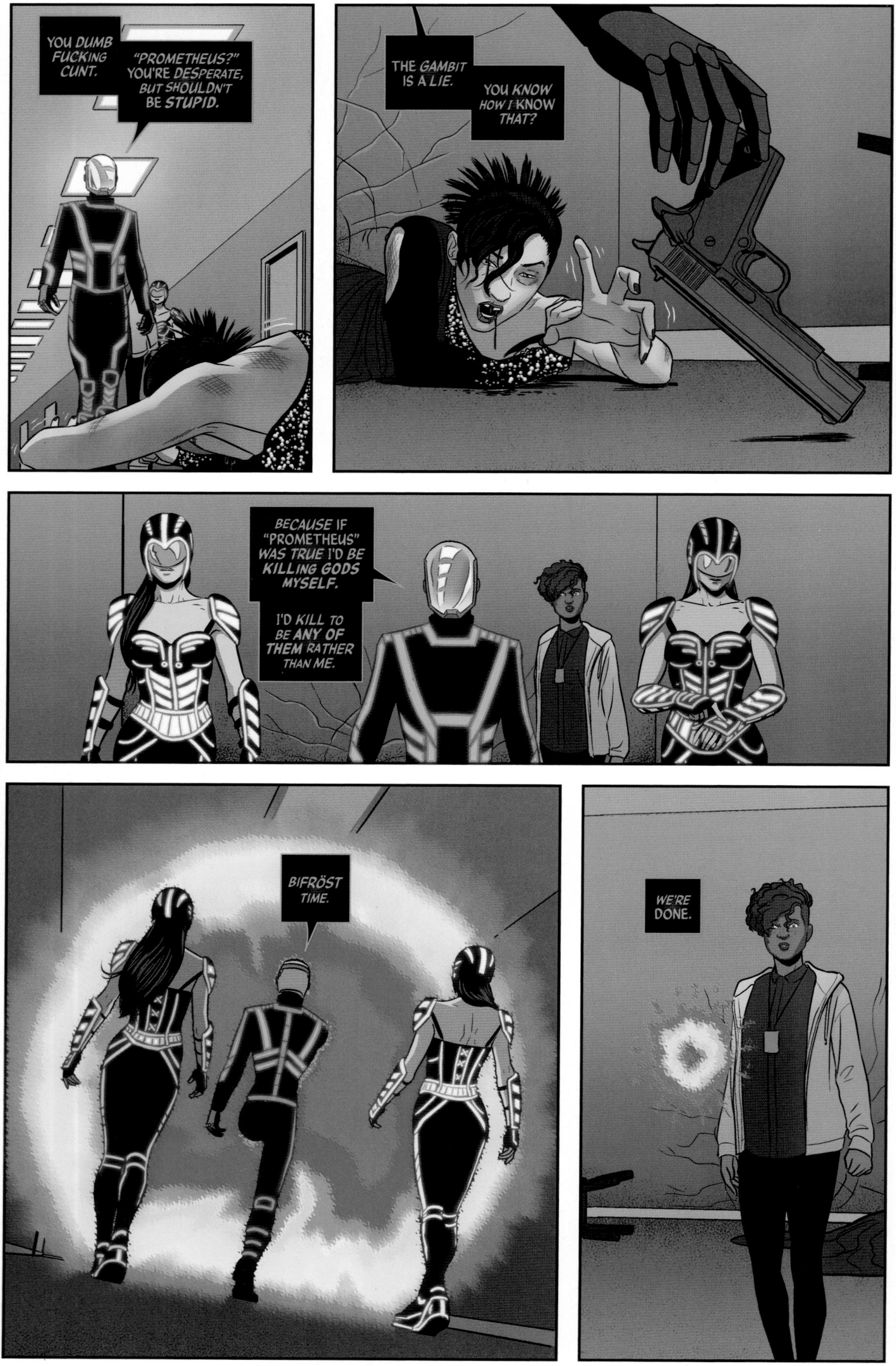

YOU DUMB FUCKING CUNT.
"PROMETHEUS?" YOU'RE DESPERATE, BUT SHOULDN'T BE STUPID.
THE GAMBIT IS A LIE.
YOU KNOW HOW I KNOW THAT?
BECAUSE IF "PROMETHEUS" WAS TRUE I'D BE KILLING GODS MYSELF.
I'D KILL TO BE ANY OF THEM RATHER THAN ME.
BIFRÖST TIME.
WE'RE DONE.

BAD
COMPANY

13 APRIL 2014

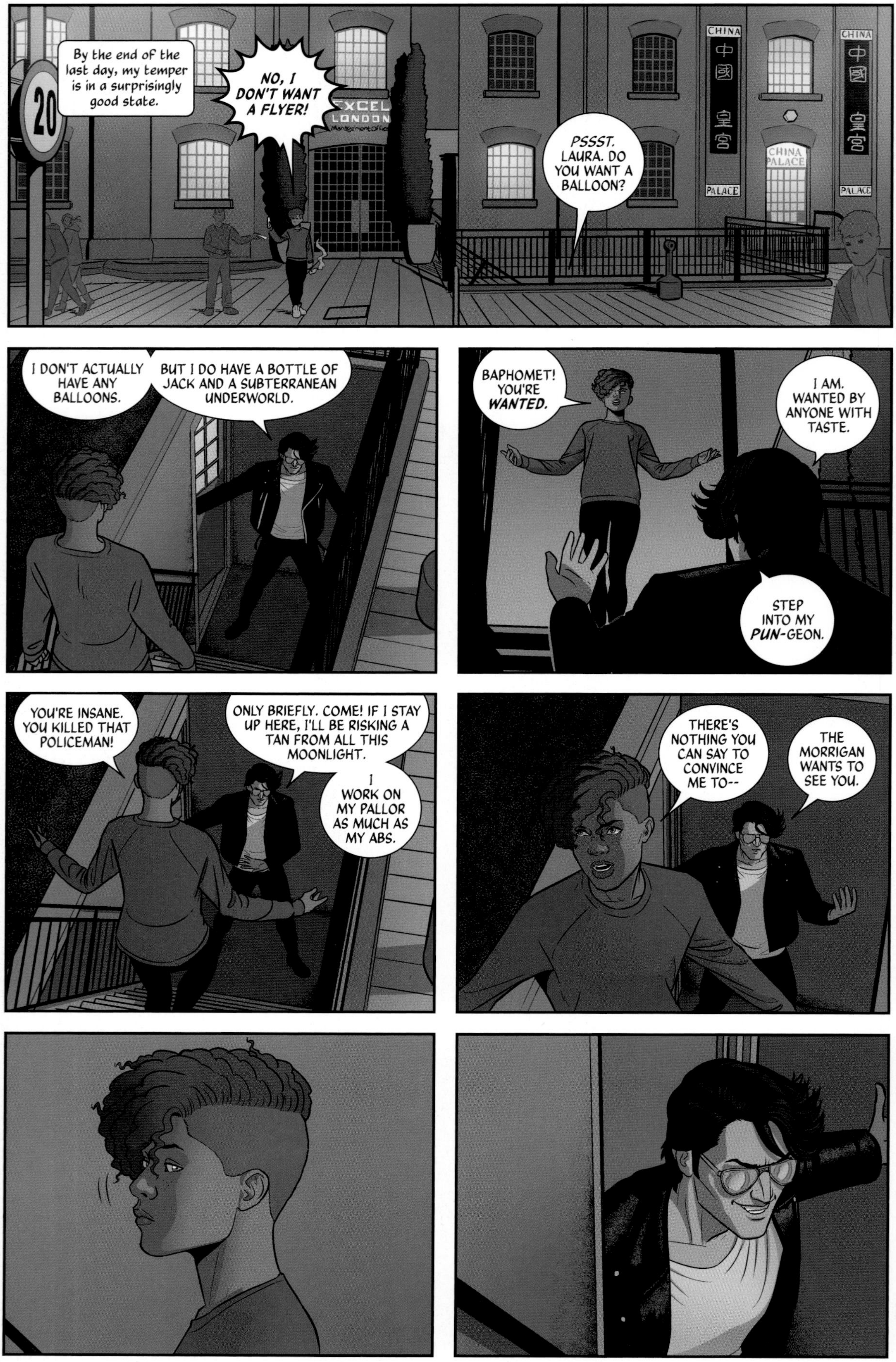

By the end of the last day, my temper is in a surprisingly good state.
NO, I DON'T WANT A FLYER!
20
CHINA 中國 皇宮 PALACE
PSSST. LAURA. DO YOU WANT A BALLOON?
I DON'T ACTUALLY HAVE ANY BALLOONS.
BUT I DO HAVE A BOTTLE OF JACK AND A SUBTERRANEAN UNDERWORLD.
BAPHOMET! YOU'RE *WANTED.*
I AM. WANTED BY ANYONE WITH TASTE.
STEP INTO MY *PUN*-GEON.
YOU'RE INSANE. YOU KILLED THAT POLICEMAN!
ONLY BRIEFLY. COME! IF I STAY UP HERE, I'LL BE RISKING A TAN FROM ALL THIS MOONLIGHT.
I WORK ON MY PALLOR AS MUCH AS MY ABS.
THERE'S NOTHING YOU CAN SAY TO CONVINCE ME TO--
THE MORRIGAN WANTS TO SEE YOU.

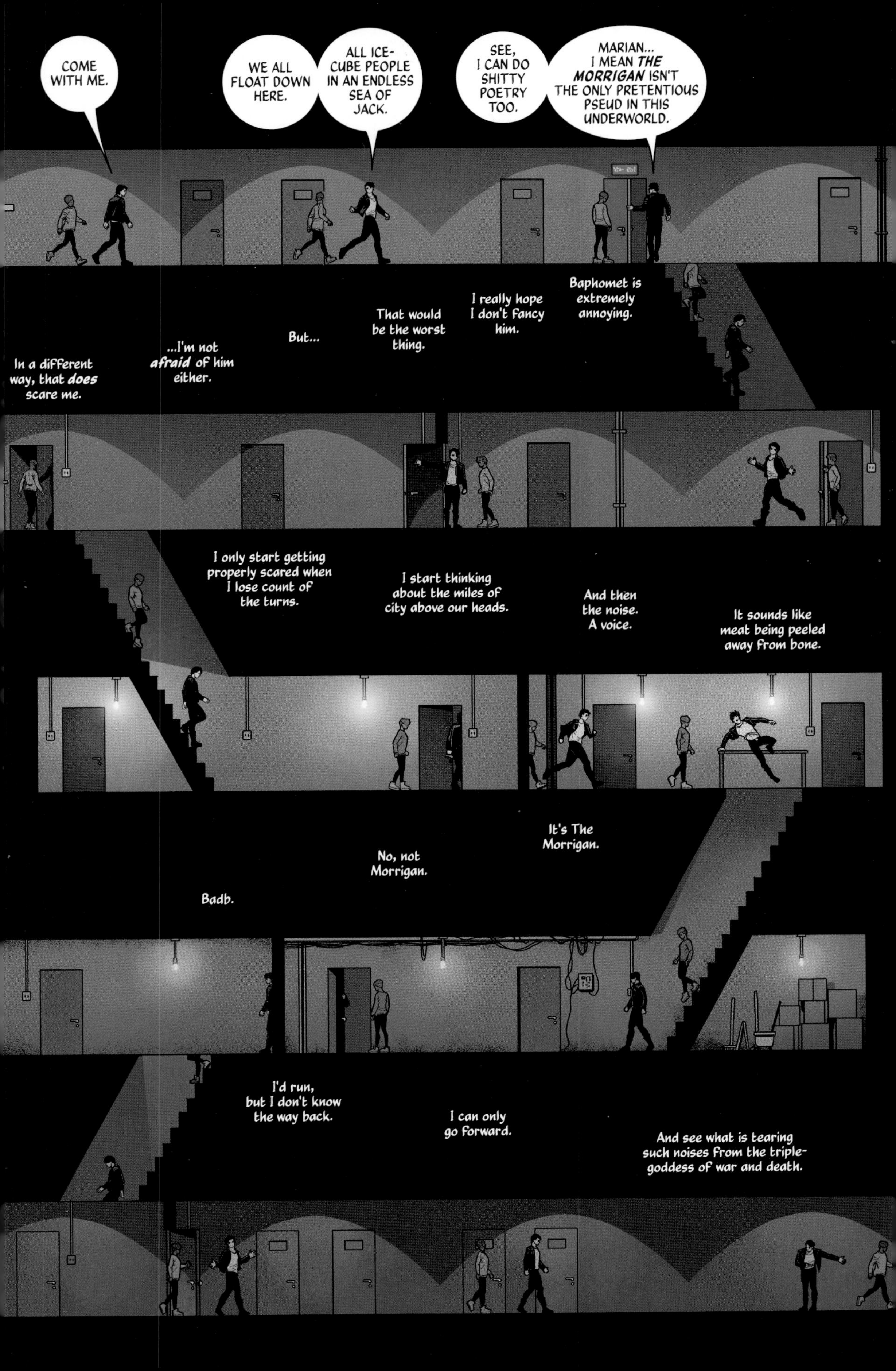
COME WITH ME.
WE ALL FLOAT DOWN HERE.
ALL ICE-CUBE PEOPLE IN AN ENDLESS SEA OF JACK.
SEE, I CAN DO SHITTY POETRY TOO.
MARIAN... I MEAN ***THE MORRIGAN*** ISN'T THE ONLY PRETENTIOUS PSEUD IN THIS UNDERWORLD.
Baphomet is extremely annoying.
I really hope I don't fancy him.
That would be the worst thing.
But...
...I'm not ***afraid*** of him either.
In a different way, that ***does*** scare me.
I only start getting properly scared when I lose count of the turns.
I start thinking about the miles of city above our heads.
And then the noise. A voice.
It sounds like meat being peeled away from bone.
It's The Morrigan.
No, not Morrigan.
Badb.
I'd run, but I don't know the way back.
I can only go forward.
And see what is tearing such noises from the triple-goddess of war and death.

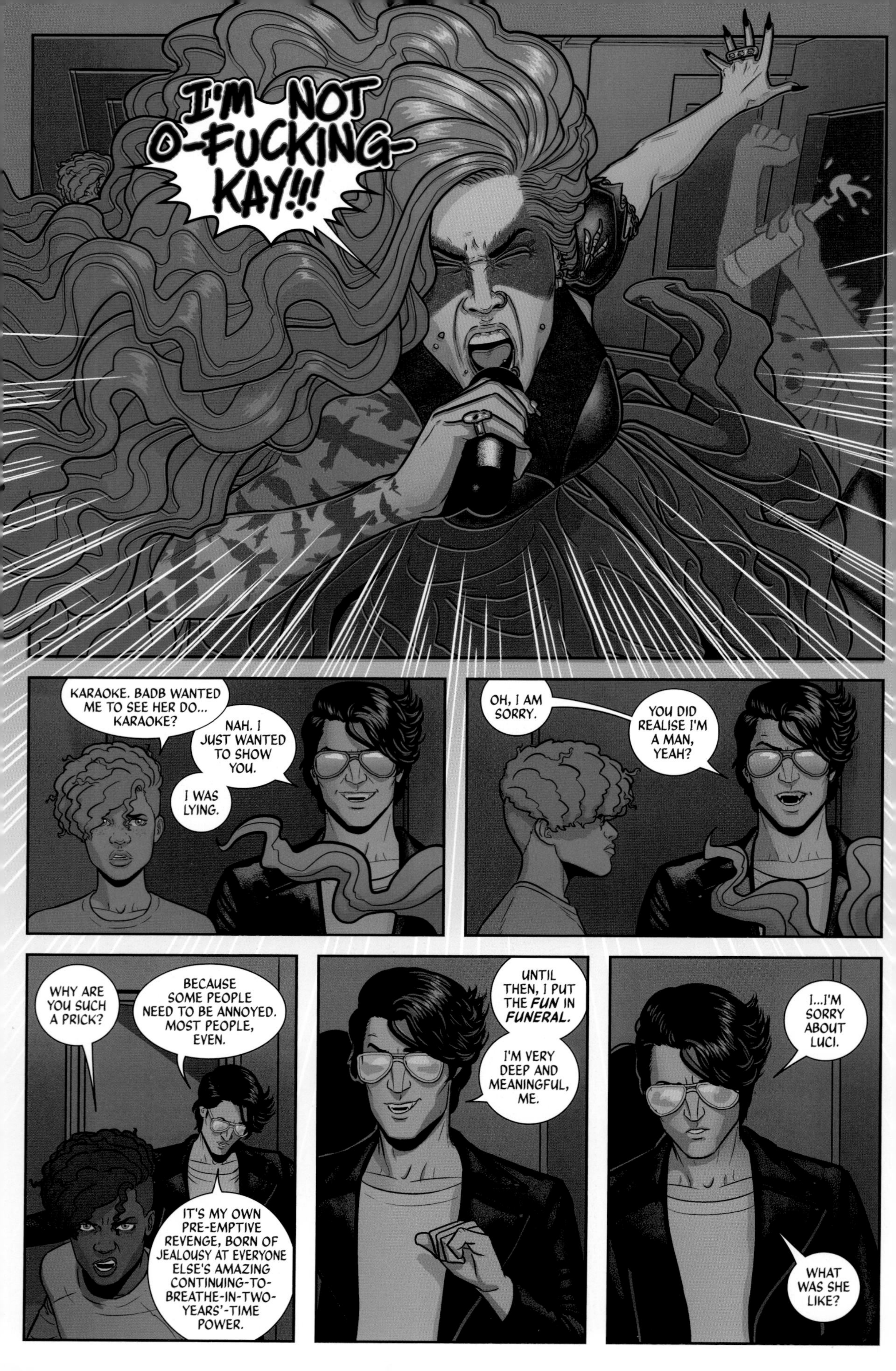
I'M NOT O-FUCKING-KAY!!!
KARAOKE. BADB WANTED ME TO SEE HER DO... KARAOKE?
NAH. I JUST WANTED TO SHOW YOU.
I WAS LYING.
OH, I AM SORRY.
YOU DID REALISE I'M A MAN, YEAH?
WHY ARE YOU SUCH A PRICK?
BECAUSE SOME PEOPLE NEED TO BE ANNOYED. MOST PEOPLE, EVEN.
IT'S MY OWN PRE-EMPTIVE REVENGE, BORN OF JEALOUSY AT EVERYONE ELSE'S AMAZING CONTINUING-TO-BREATHE-IN-TWO-YEARS'-TIME POWER.
UNTIL THEN, I PUT THE FUN IN FUNERAL.
I'M VERY DEEP AND MEANINGFUL, ME.
I...I'M SORRY ABOUT LUCI.
WHAT WAS SHE LIKE?

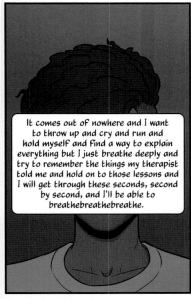

It comes out of nowhere and I want to throw up and cry and run and hold myself and find a way to explain everything but I just breathe deeply and try to remember the things my therapist told me and hold on to those lessons and I will get through these seconds, second by second, and I'll be able to breathebreathebreathe.

I HAVE TO GO.

LAURA. STOP.

YES, I LIED TO GET YOU DOWN HERE.

YOU'RE IN HELL. YOU NEED COMPANY.

MORRIGAN AND I AREN'T *GOOD* COMPANY.

BUT WE'RE GOOD *BAD* COMPANY.

AND WE'VE BEEN THERE.

I CAN'T SAY I CARE, BUT I DO UNDERSTAND.

PLUS-- I WASN'T LYING ABOUT THE JACK.

I can't think of a reason to say no.

It ends up being an awful evening.

I love it.

I don't want it to ever end.

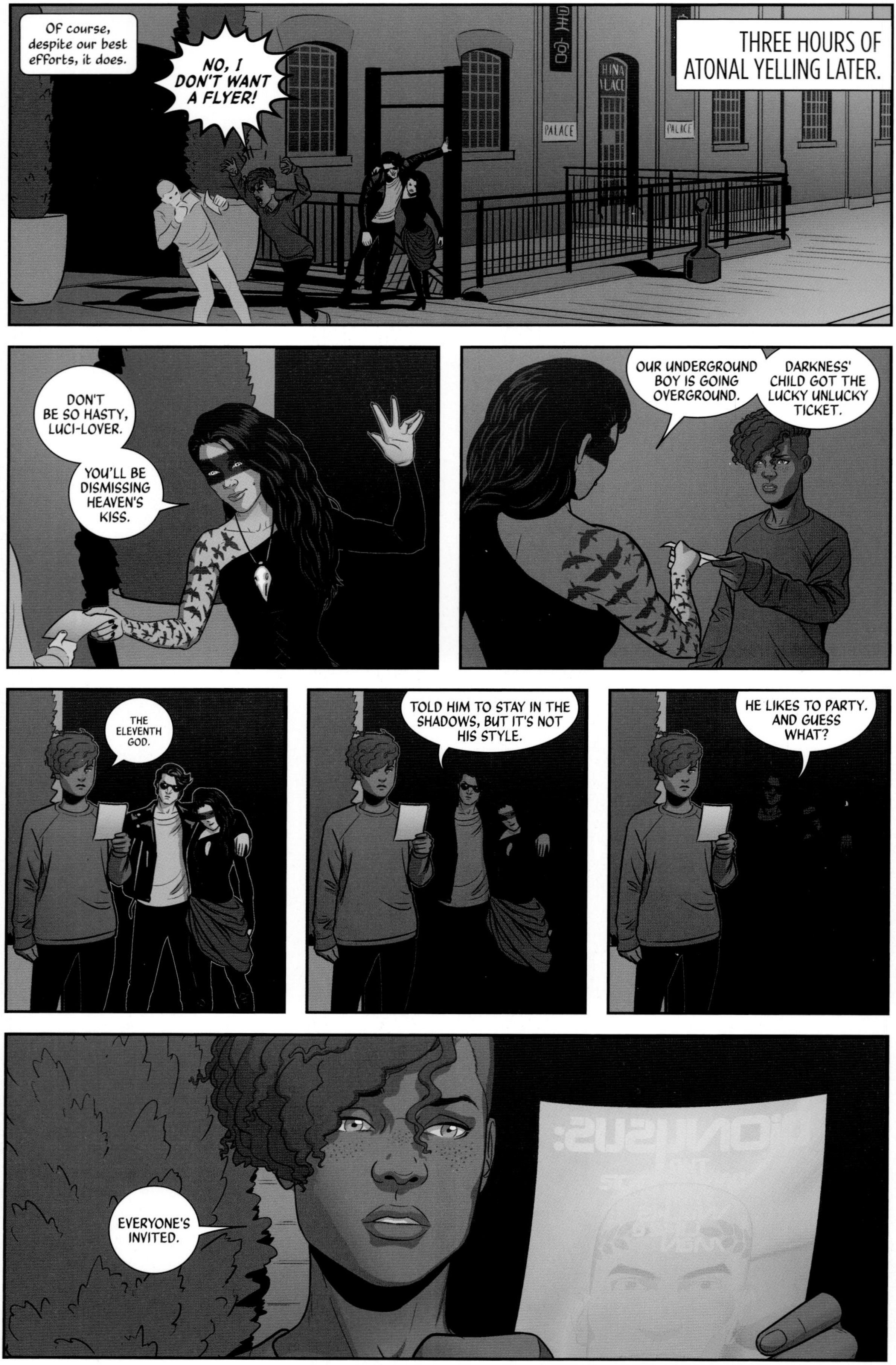
Of course, despite our best efforts, it does.
THREE HOURS OF ATONAL YELLING LATER.
NO, I DON'T WANT A FLYER!
PALACE
PALACE
DON'T BE SO HASTY, LUCI-LOVER.
YOU'LL BE DISMISSING HEAVEN'S KISS.
OUR UNDERGROUND BOY IS GOING OVERGROUND.
DARKNESS' CHILD GOT THE LUCKY UNLUCKY TICKET.
THE ELEVENTH GOD.
TOLD HIM TO STAY IN THE SHADOWS, BUT IT'S NOT HIS STYLE.
HE LIKES TO PARTY. AND GUESS WHAT?
EVERYONE'S INVITED.

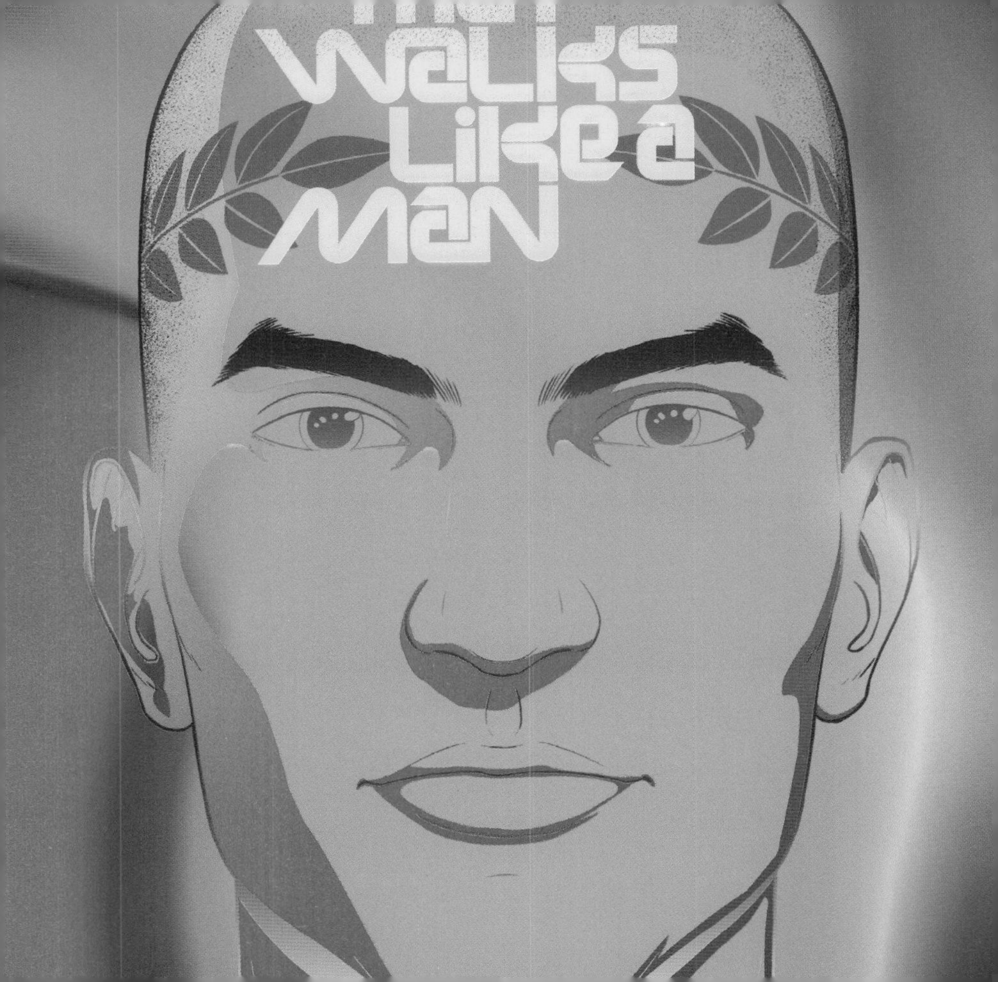
Walks
Like a
Man

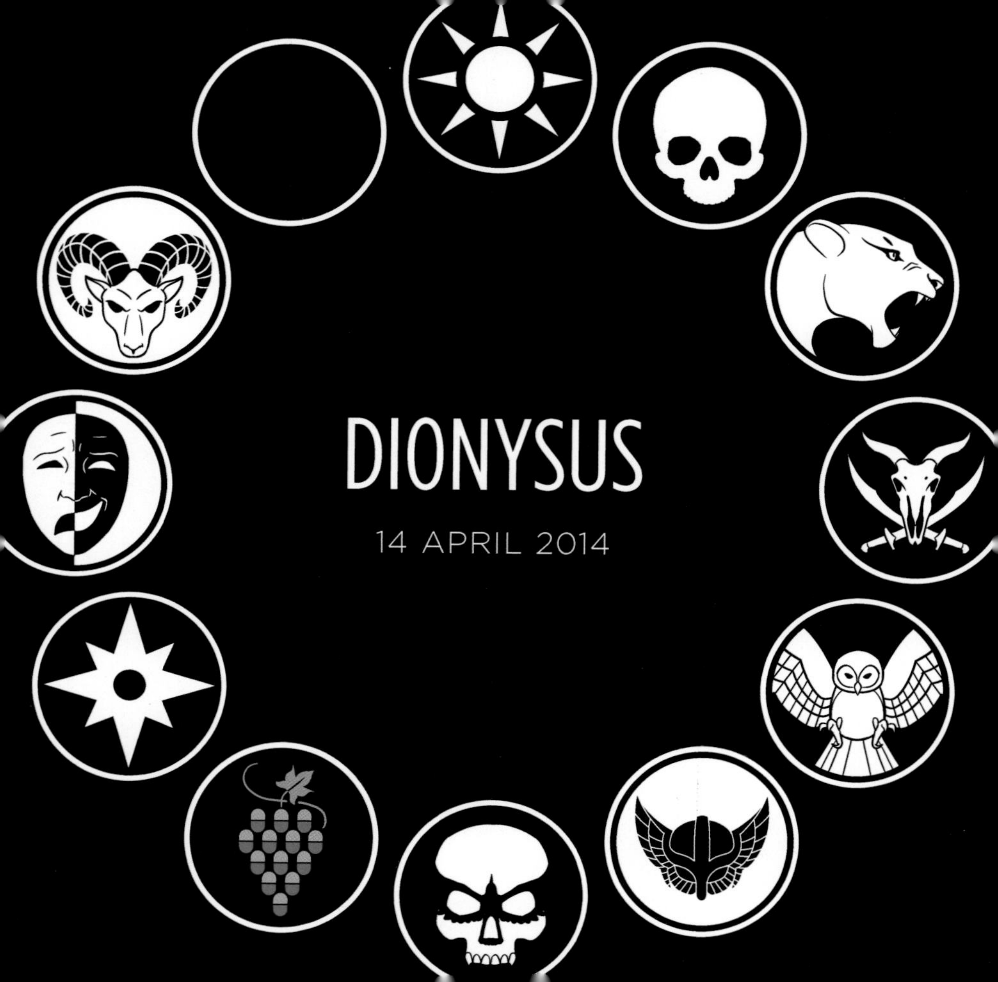
DIONYSUS
14 APRIL 2014

THE
WICKED
+
THE DIVINE

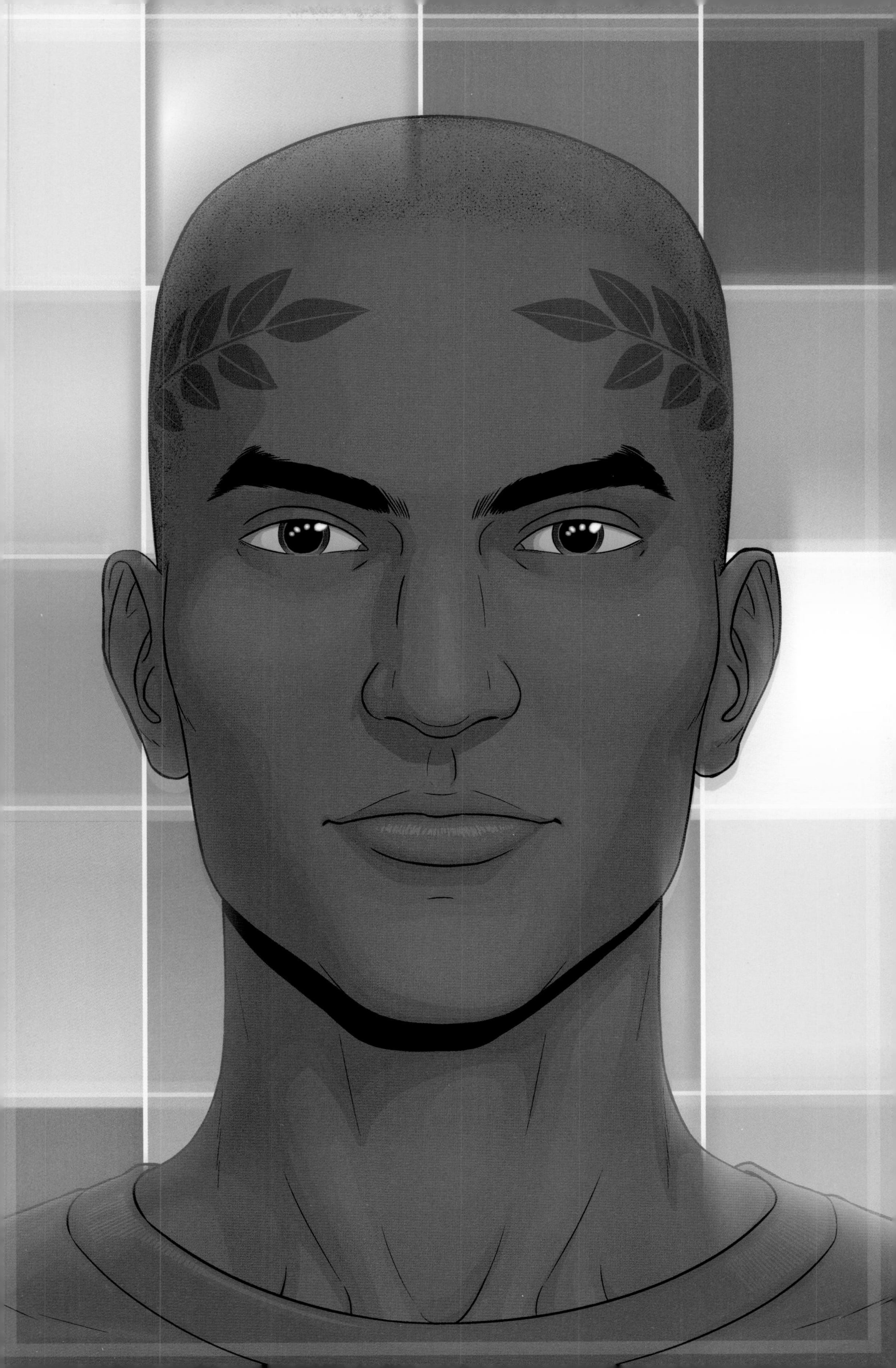

THE WICKED + THE DIVINE

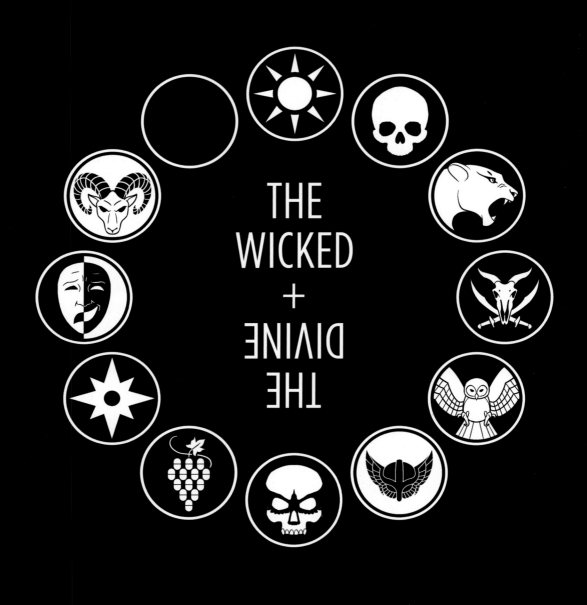

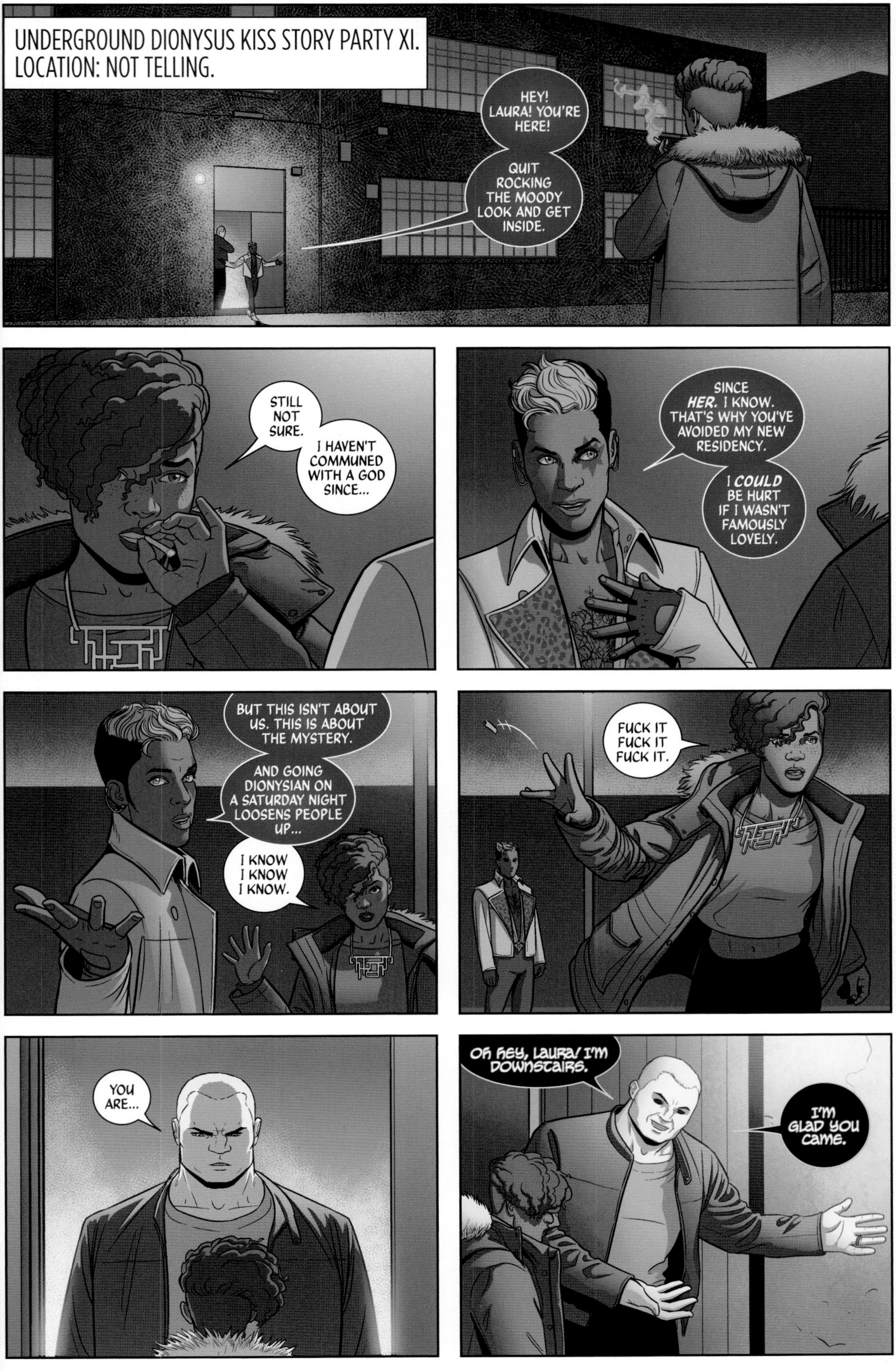
UNDERGROUND DIONYSUS KISS STORY PARTY XI. LOCATION: NOT TELLING.
HEY! LAURA! YOU'RE HERE!
QUIT ROCKING THE MOODY LOOK AND GET INSIDE.
STILL NOT SURE.
I HAVEN'T COMMUNED WITH A GOD SINCE...
SINCE HER. I KNOW. THAT'S WHY YOU'VE AVOIDED MY NEW RESIDENCY.
I COULD BE HURT IF I WASN'T FAMOUSLY LOVELY.
BUT THIS ISN'T ABOUT US. THIS IS ABOUT THE MYSTERY.
AND GOING DIONYSIAN ON A SATURDAY NIGHT LOOSENS PEOPLE UP...
I KNOW I KNOW I KNOW.
FUCK IT FUCK IT FUCK IT.
YOU ARE...
OH HEY, LAURA! I'M DOWNSTAIRS.
I'M GLAD YOU CAME.

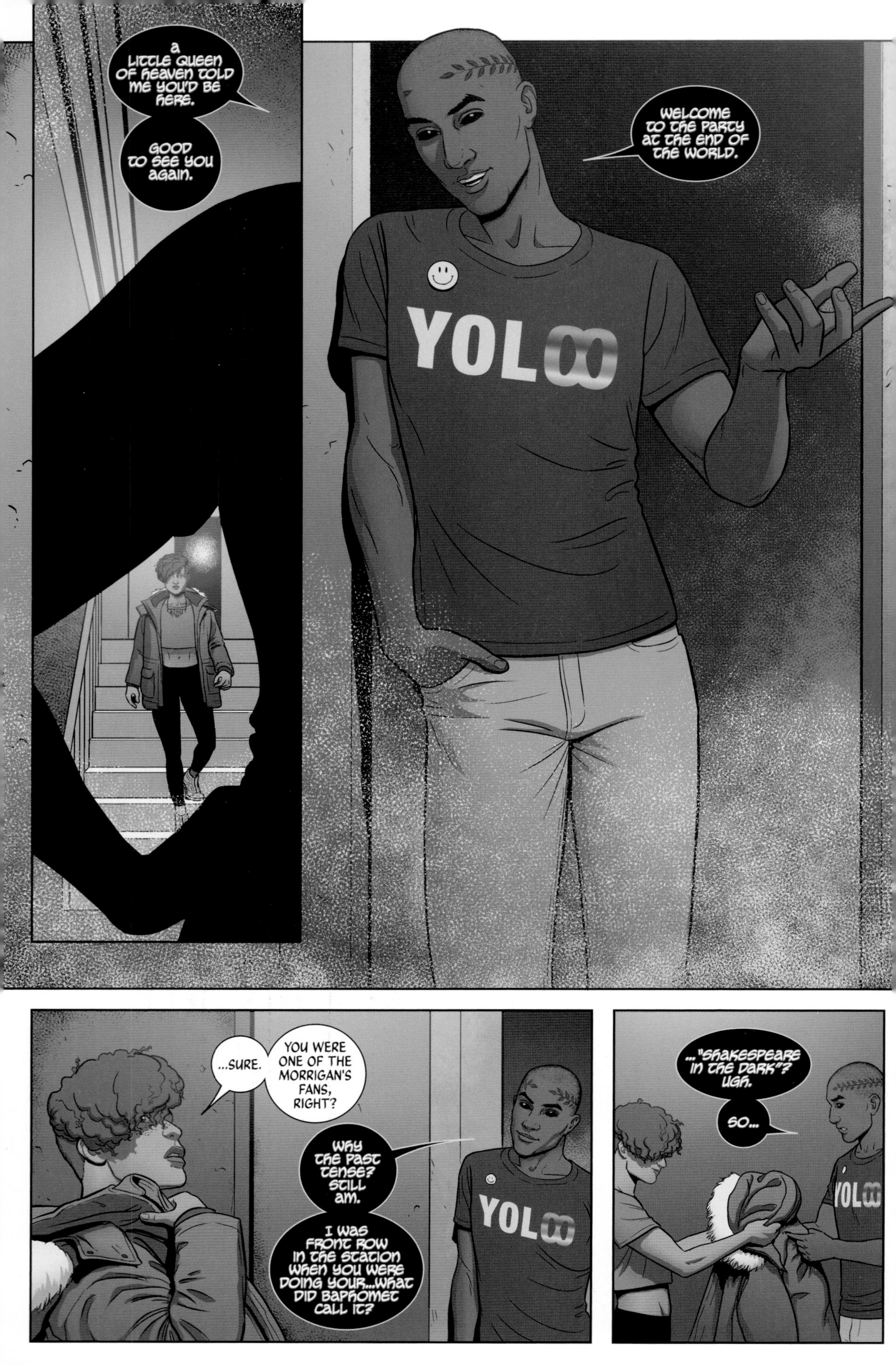
A LITTLE QUEEN OF HEAVEN TOLD ME YOU'D BE HERE.
GOOD TO SEE YOU AGAIN.
WELCOME TO THE PARTY AT THE END OF THE WORLD.
YOL∞
...SURE.
YOU WERE ONE OF THE MORRIGAN'S FANS, RIGHT?
WHY THE PAST TENSE? STILL AM.
I WAS FRONT ROW IN THE STATION WHEN YOU WERE DOING YOUR...WHAT DID BAPHOMET CALL IT?
YOL∞
..."SHAKESPEARE IN THE DARK"? UGH.
SO...
YOL∞

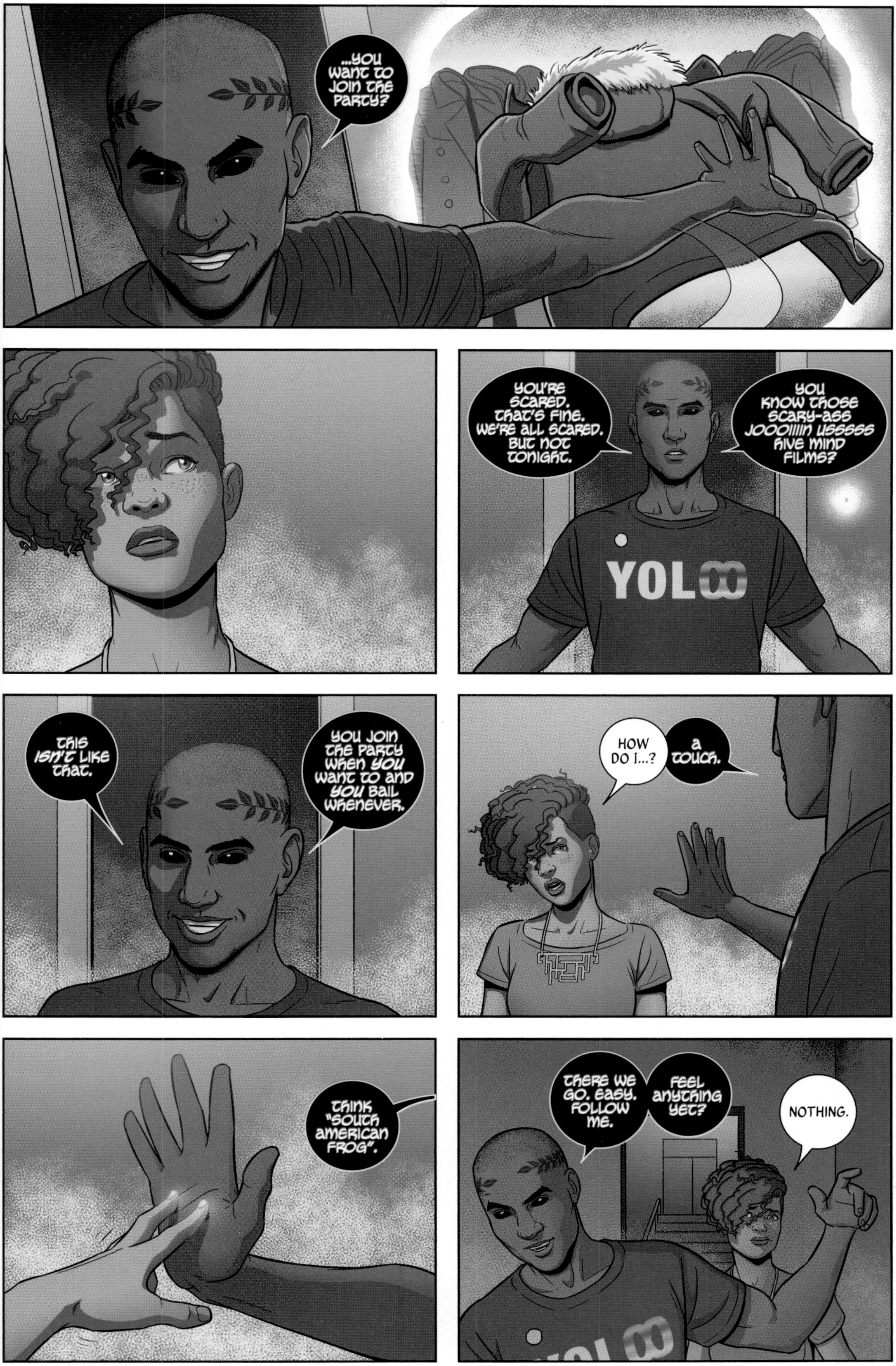
...YOU WANT TO JOIN THE PARTY?
YOU'RE SCARED. THAT'S FINE. WE'RE ALL SCARED. BUT NOT TONIGHT.
YOU KNOW THOSE SCARY-ASS JOOOIIIIN USSSSS HIVE MIND FILMS?
YOL∞
THIS ISN'T LIKE THAT.
YOU JOIN THE PARTY WHEN YOU WANT TO AND YOU BAIL WHENEVER.
HOW DO I...?
A TOUCH.
THINK "SOUTH AMERICAN FROG".
THERE WE GO. EASY. FOLLOW ME.
FEEL ANYTHING YET?
NOTHING.

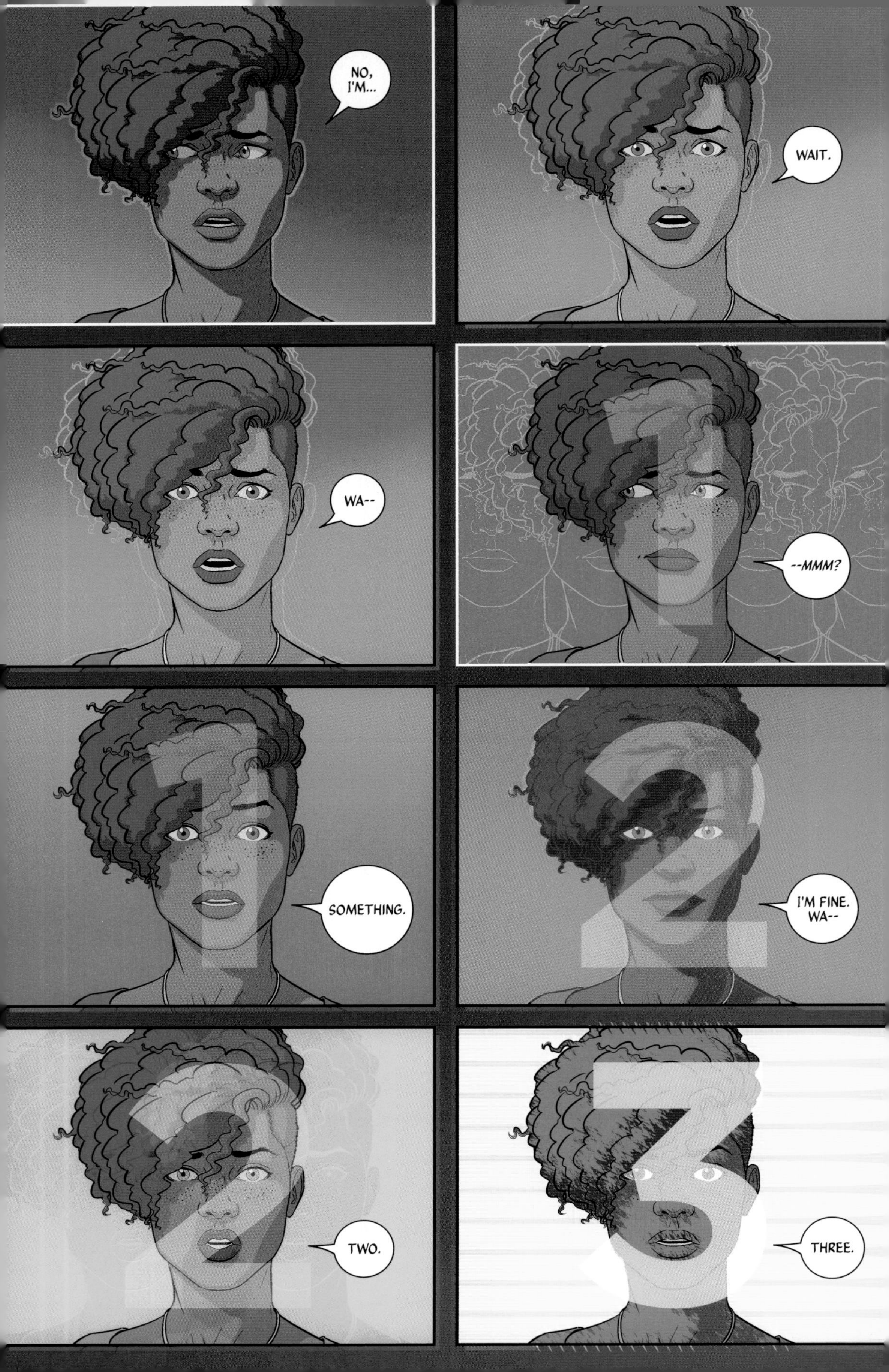
NO, I'M...
WAIT.
WA--
--MMM?
SOMETHING.
I'M FINE. WA--
TWO.
THREE.

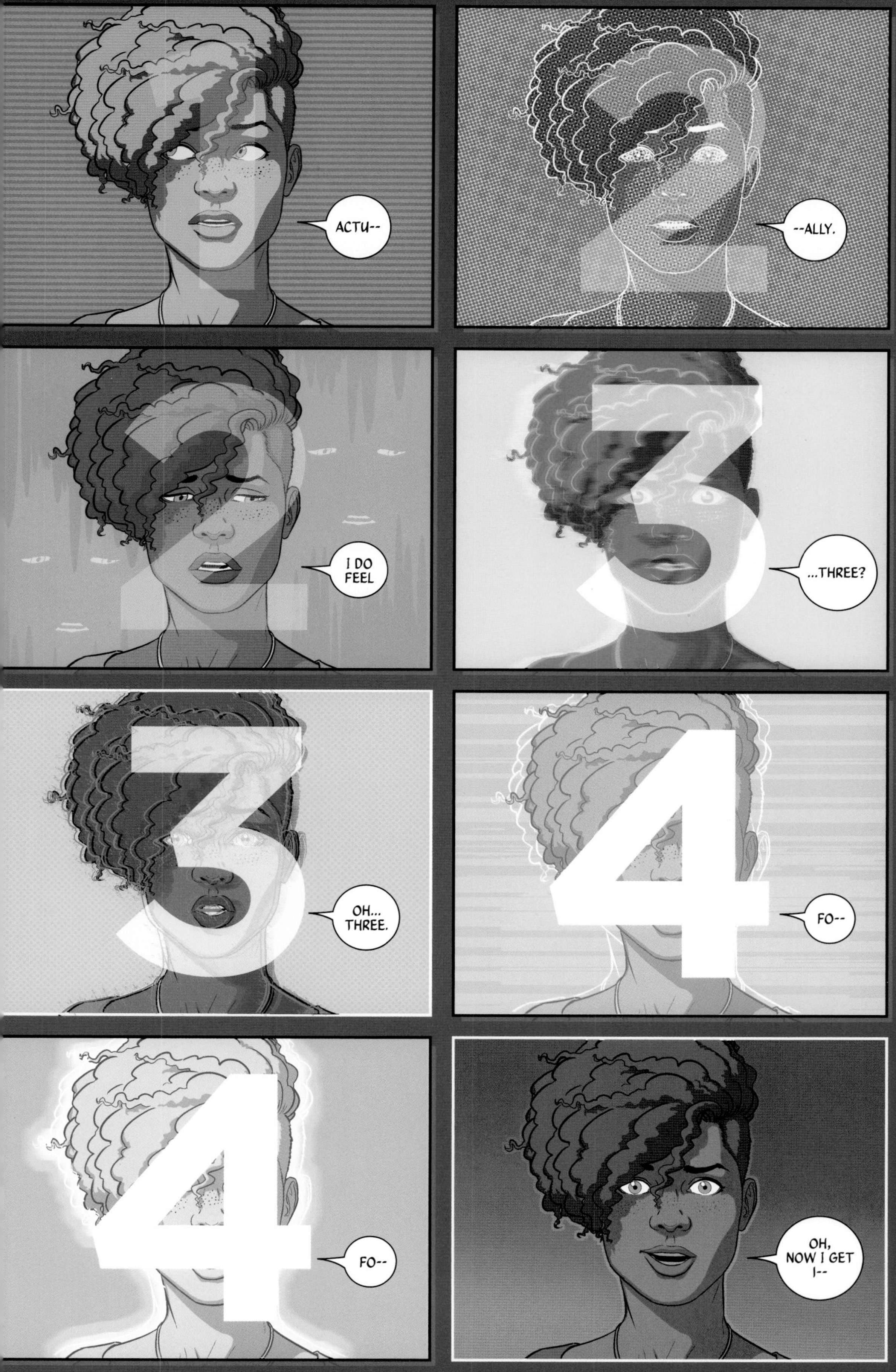
ACTU--
--ALLY.
I DO FEEL
...THREE?
OH... THREE.
FO--
FO--
OH, NOW I GET I--

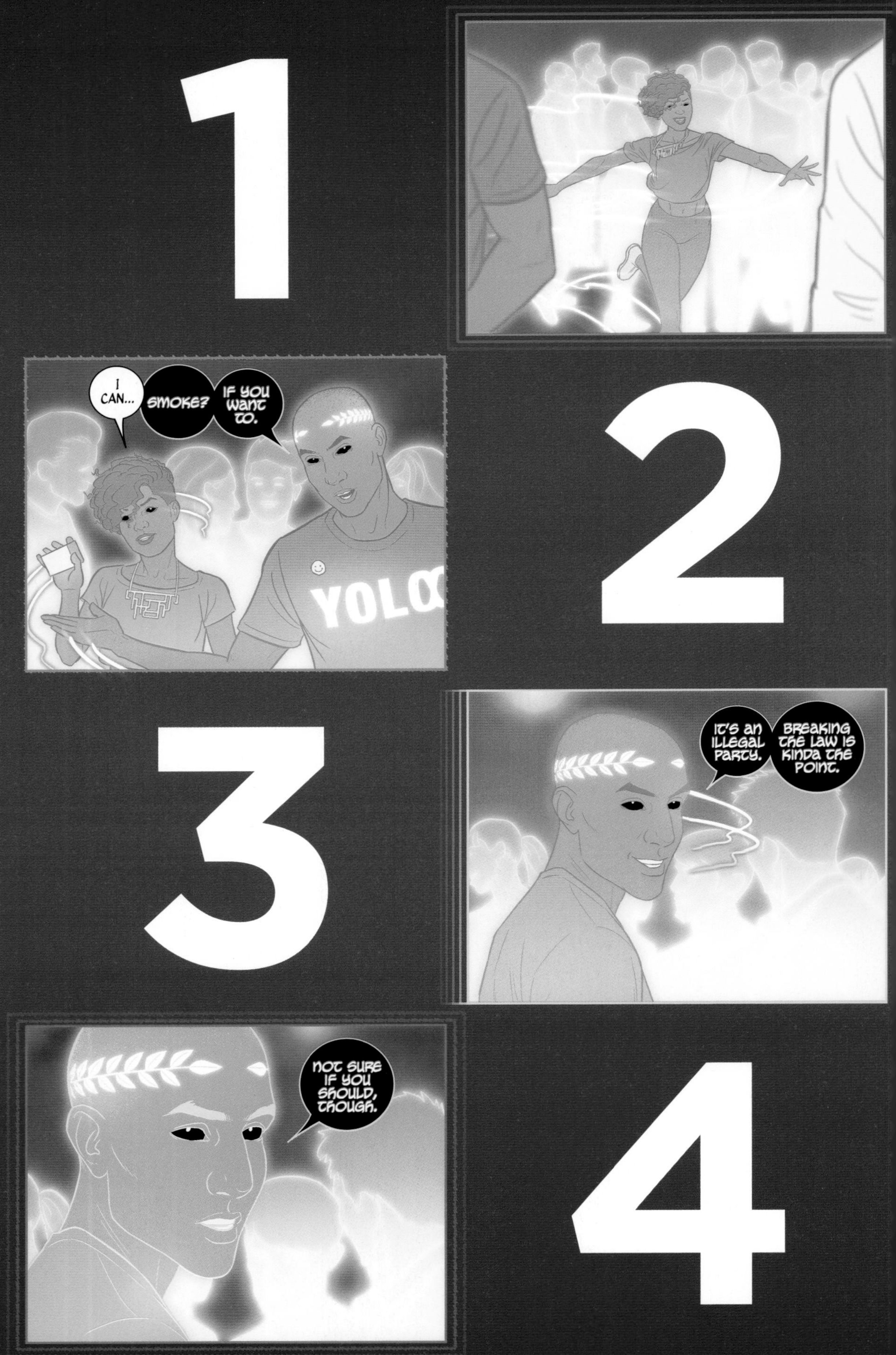
1
I CAN...
SMOKE?
IF YOU WANT TO.
2
3
IT'S AN ILLEGAL PARTY.
BREAKING THE LAW IS KINDA THE POINT.
NOT SURE IF YOU SHOULD, THOUGH.
4

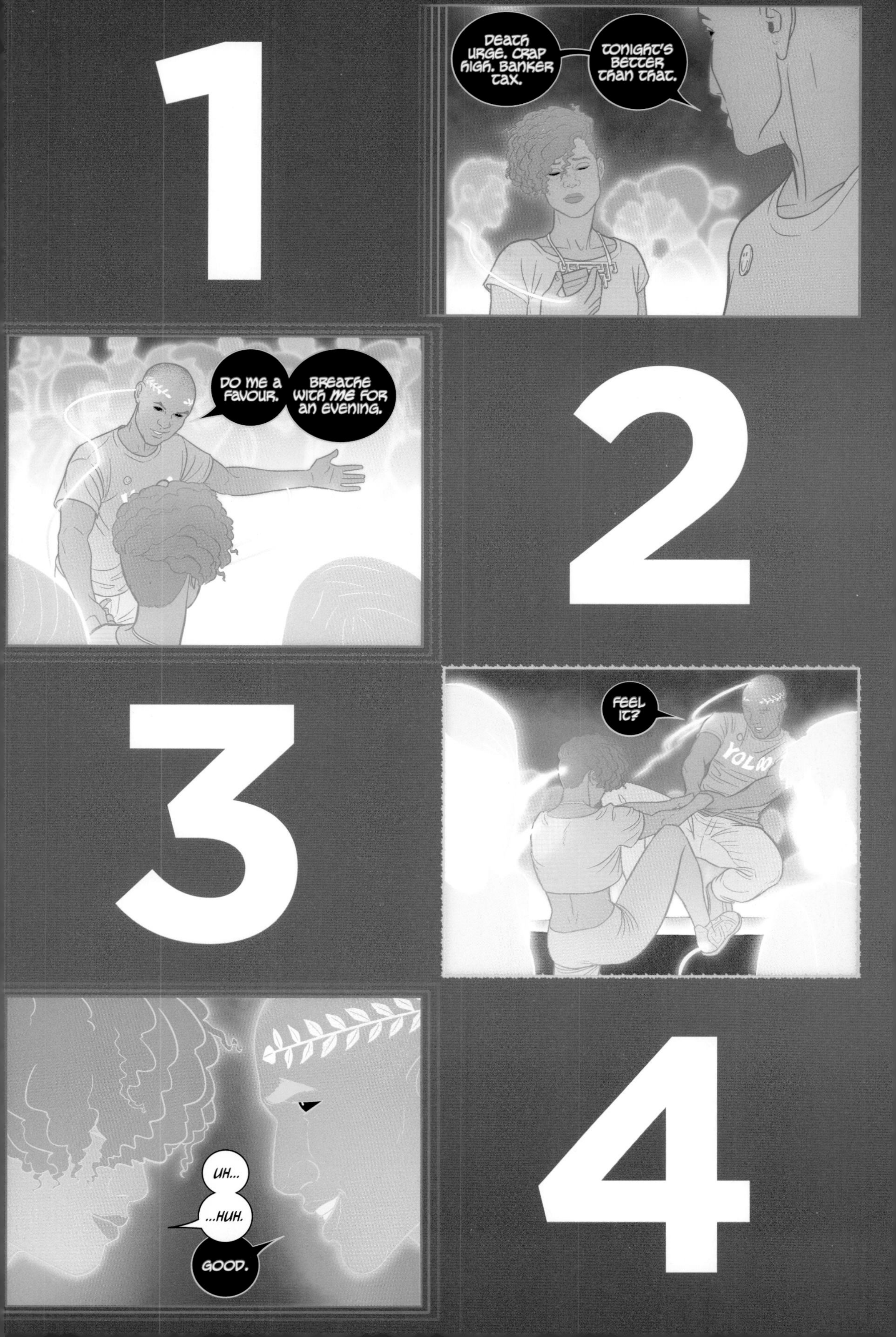
1
DEATH URGE. CRAP HIGH. BANKER TAX.
TONIGHT'S BETTER THAN THAT.
DO ME A FAVOUR.
BREATHE WITH *ME* FOR AN EVENING.
2
3
FEEL IT?
UH...
...HUH.
GOOD.
4

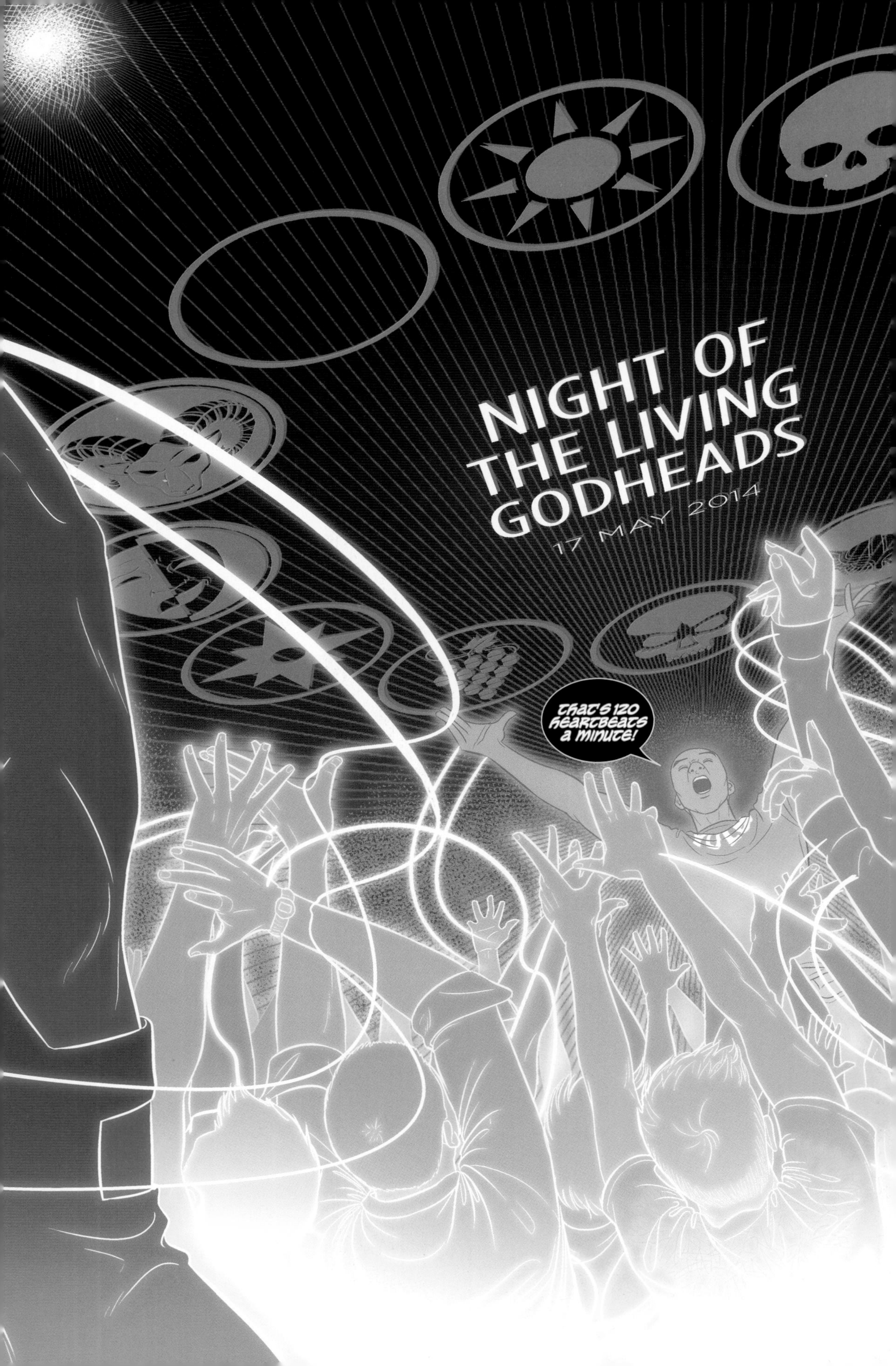
NIGHT OF THE LIVING GODHEADS
17 MAY 2014
THAT'S 120 HEARTBEATS A MINUTE!

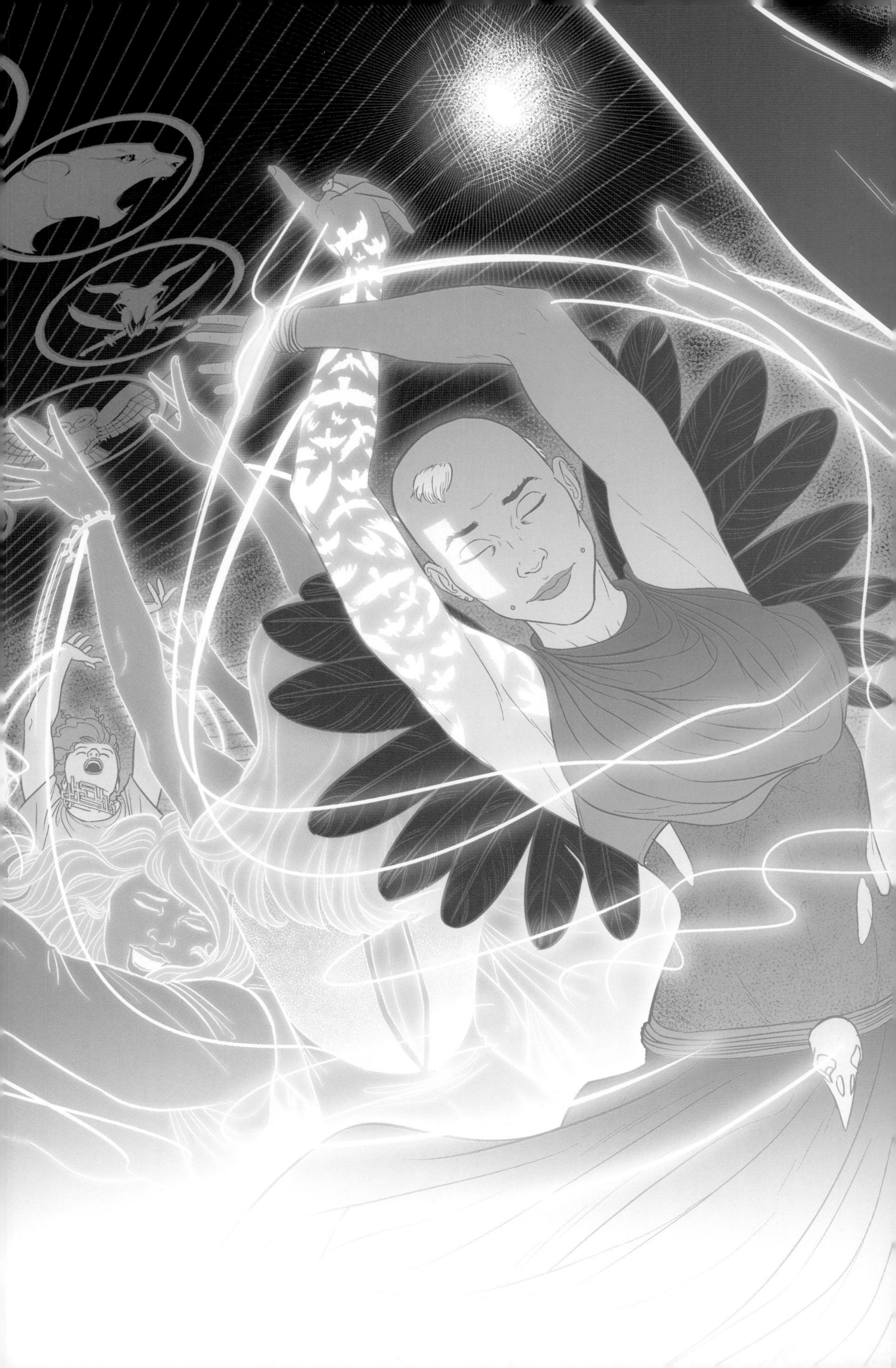

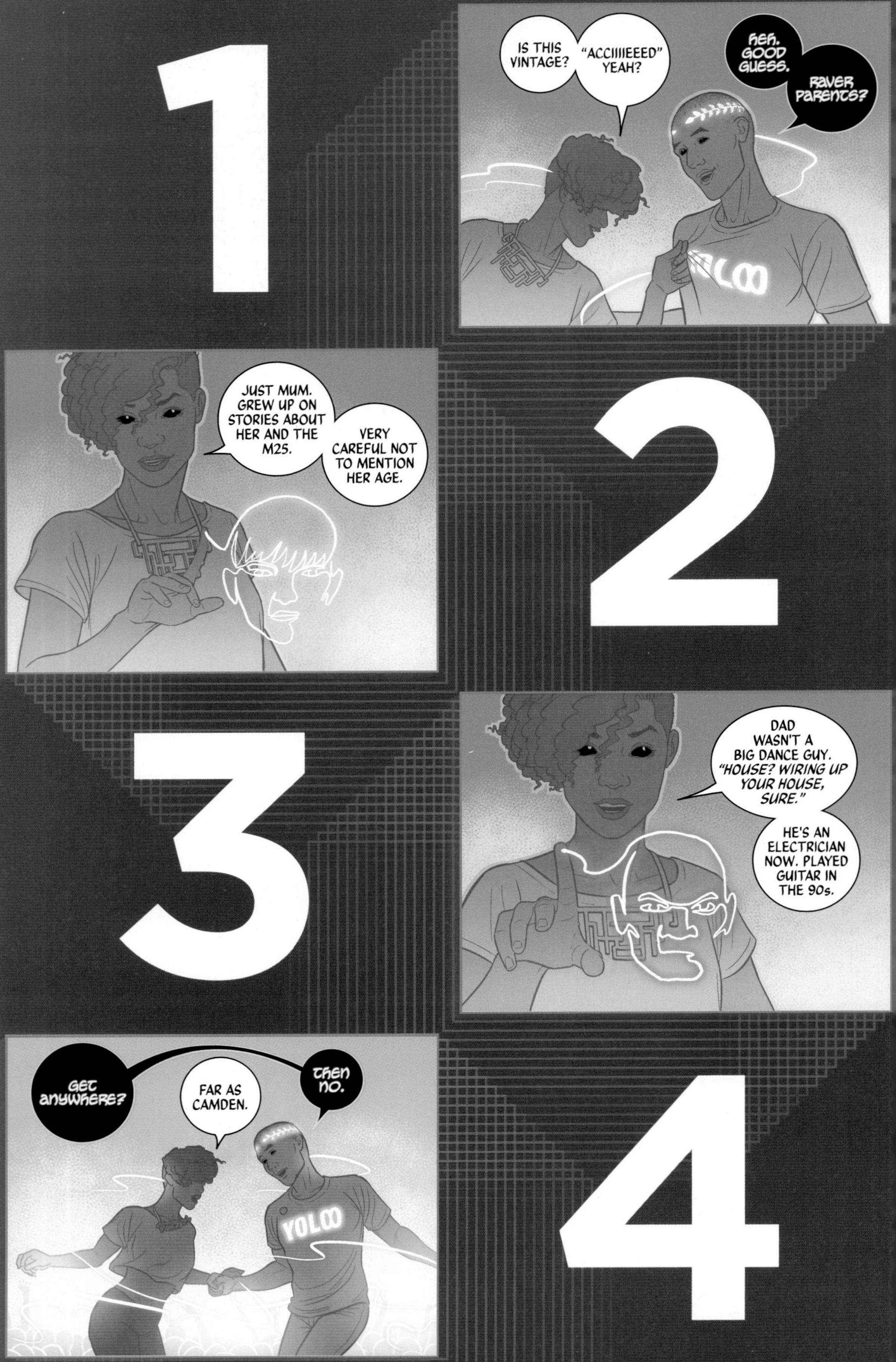
1
IS THIS VINTAGE?
"ACCIIIIEEED" YEAH?
HEH. GOOD GUESS.
RAVER PARENTS?
YOLOO
2
JUST MUM. GREW UP ON STORIES ABOUT HER AND THE M25.
VERY CAREFUL NOT TO MENTION HER AGE.
3
DAD WASN'T A BIG DANCE GUY. "HOUSE? WIRING UP YOUR HOUSE, SURE."
HE'S AN ELECTRICIAN NOW. PLAYED GUITAR IN THE 90s.
4
GET ANYWHERE?
FAR AS CAMDEN.
THEN NO.
YOLOO

1

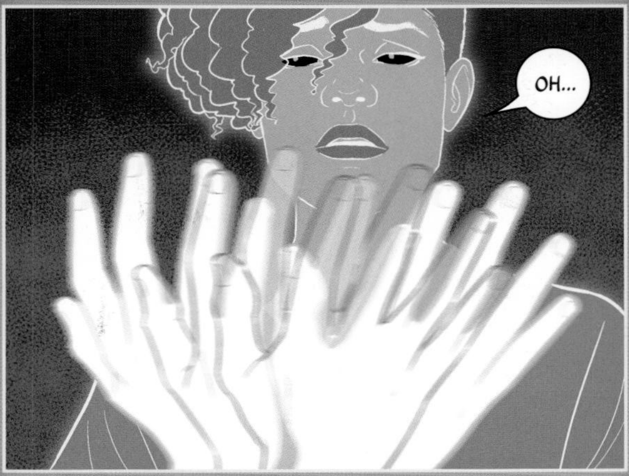
OH...

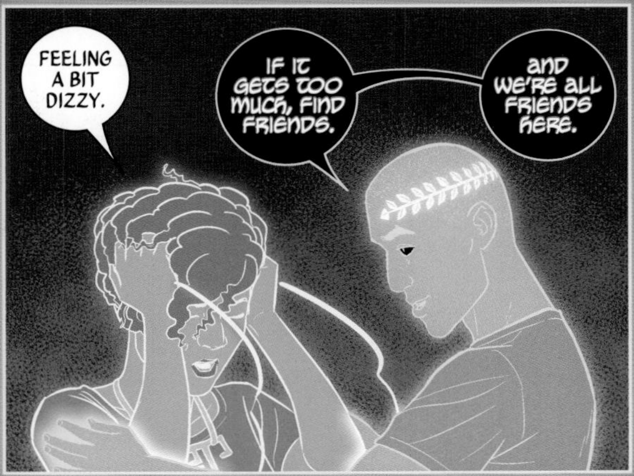
FEELING A BIT DIZZY.
IF IT GETS TOO MUCH, FIND FRIENDS.
AND WE'RE ALL FRIENDS HERE.

2

3

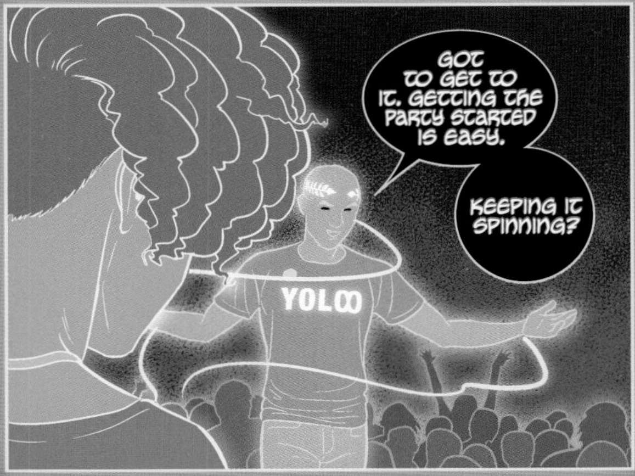
GOT TO GET TO IT. GETTING THE PARTY STARTED IS EASY.
KEEPING IT SPINNING?
YOLO∞

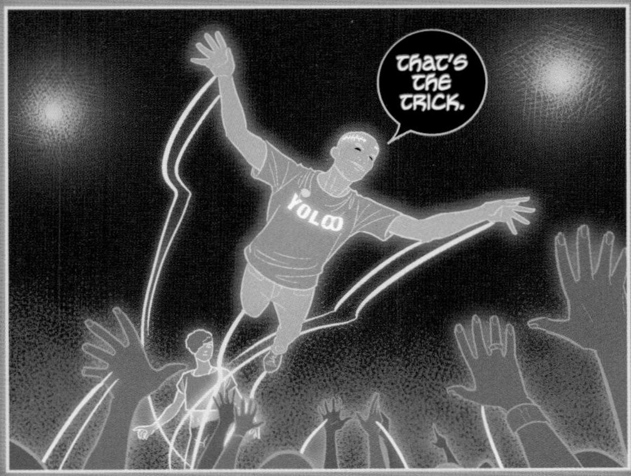
THAT'S THE TRICK.
YOLO∞

4

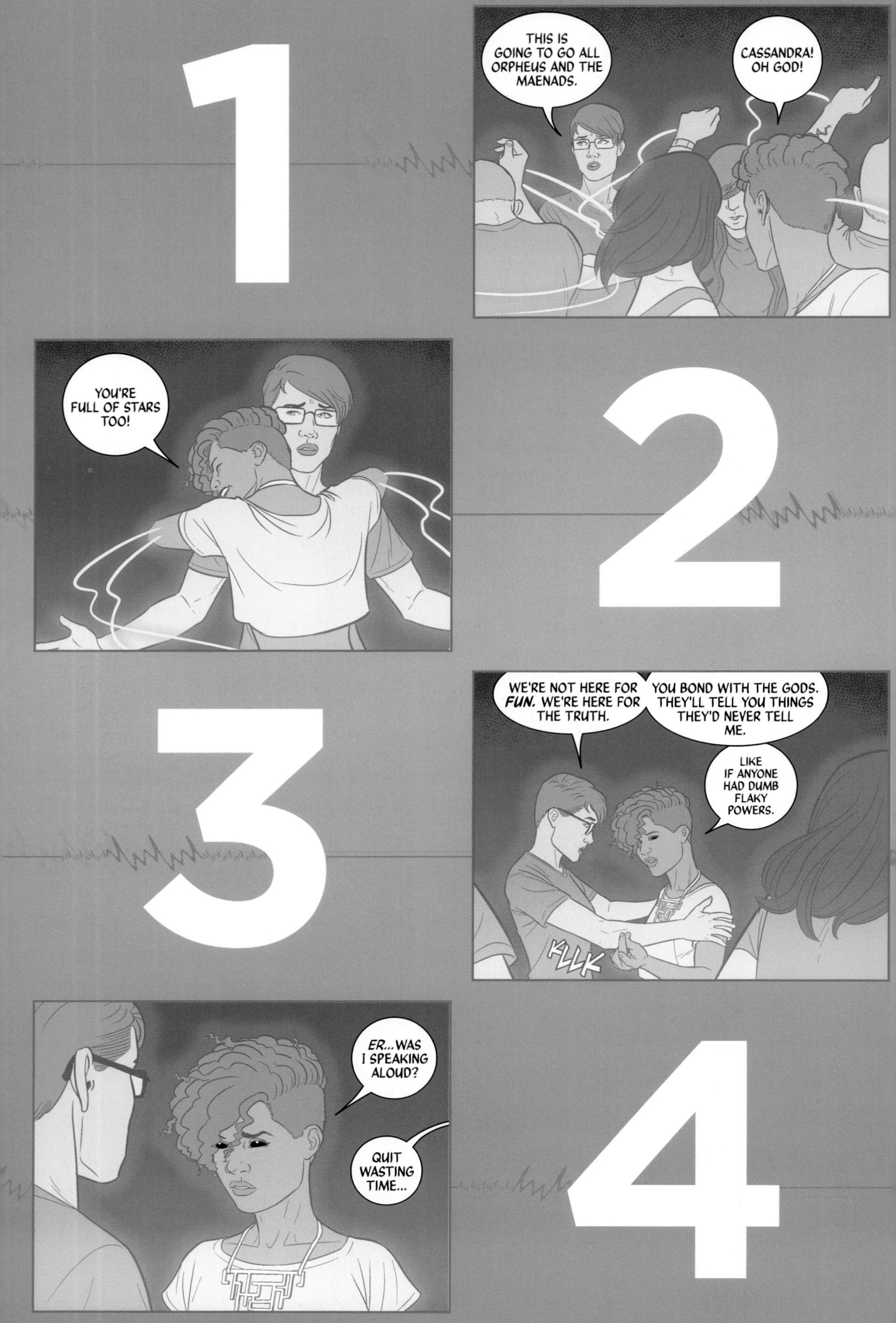
1
THIS IS GOING TO GO ALL ORPHEUS AND THE MAENADS.
CASSANDRA! OH GOD!
YOU'RE FULL OF STARS TOO!
2
3
WE'RE NOT HERE FOR *FUN.* WE'RE HERE FOR THE TRUTH.
YOU BOND WITH THE GODS. THEY'LL TELL YOU THINGS THEY'D NEVER TELL ME.
LIKE IF ANYONE HAD DUMB FLAKY POWERS.
KLLK
ER... WAS I SPEAKING ALOUD?
QUIT WASTING TIME...
4

1

I'M PRETTY SURE 50% OF YOU WANT TO HIT THE FLOOR.

NO. I DON'T DANCE.

2

3

THERE'S NO MUSIC! I REPEAT! NO MUSIC!
WHAT ARE YOU ALL FUCKING DANCING TO?!

I WATCH.

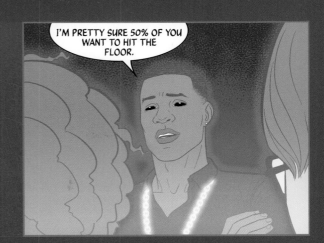

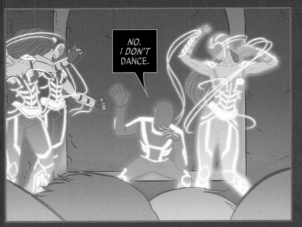

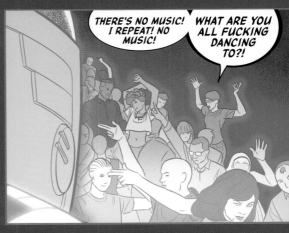

4

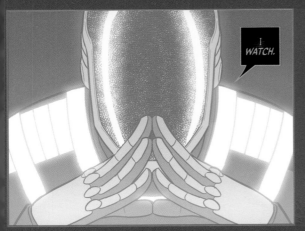

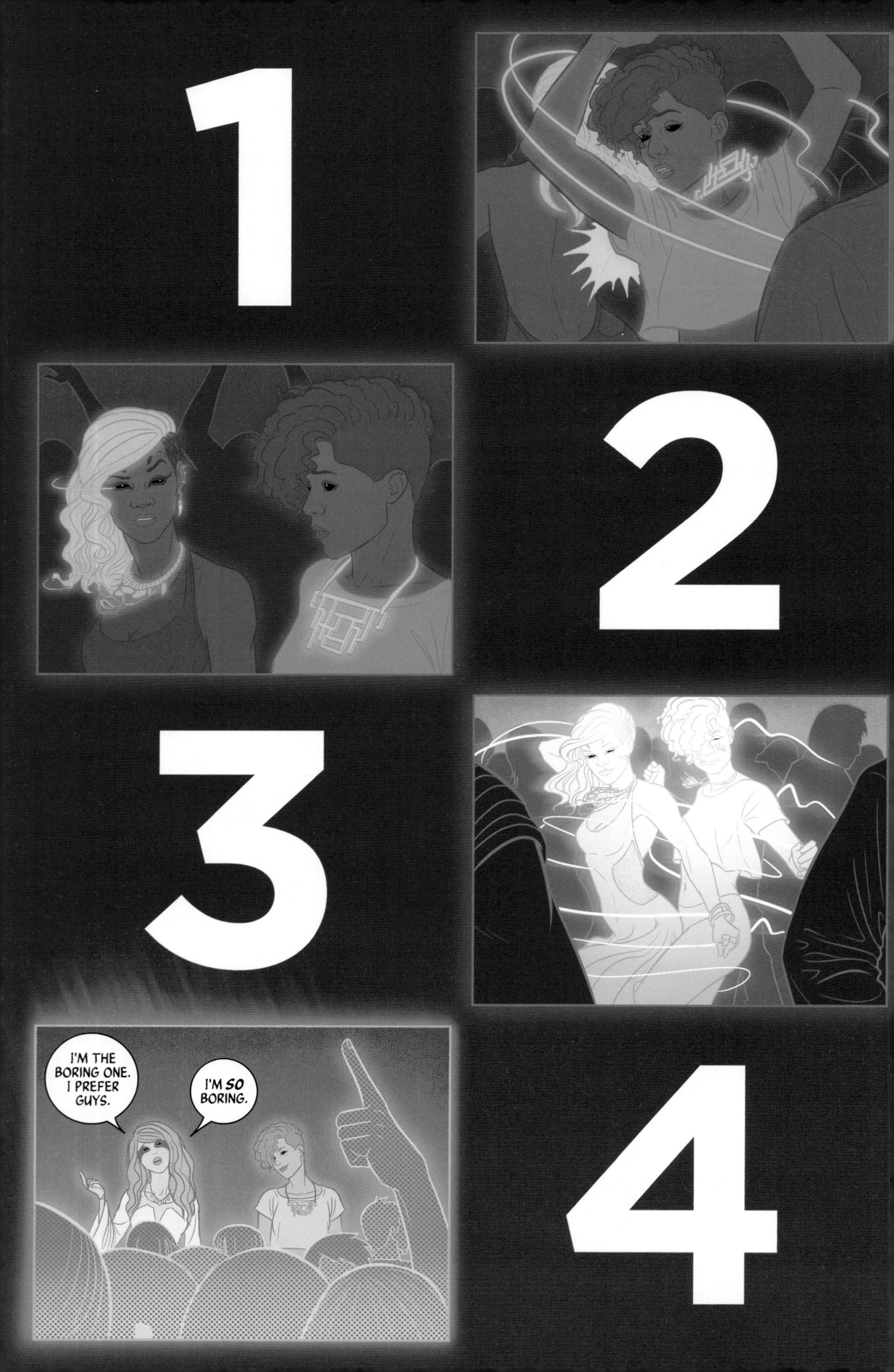
1
2
3
I'M THE BORING ONE. I PREFER GUYS.
I'M SO BORING.
4

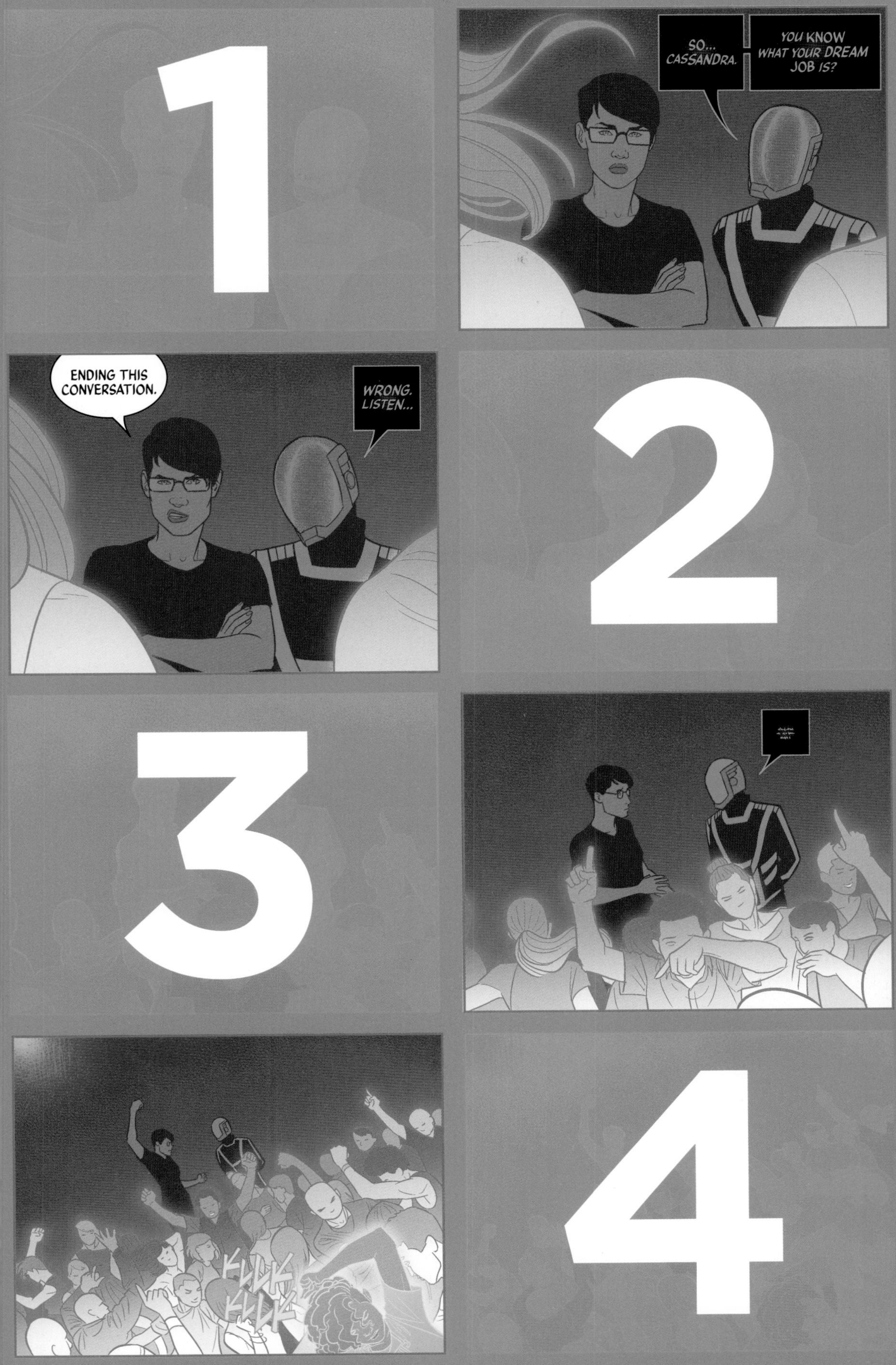
1
SO... CASSANDRA.
YOU KNOW WHAT YOUR DREAM JOB IS?
ENDING THIS CONVERSATION.
WRONG. LISTEN...
2
3
4
KLLK
KLLK

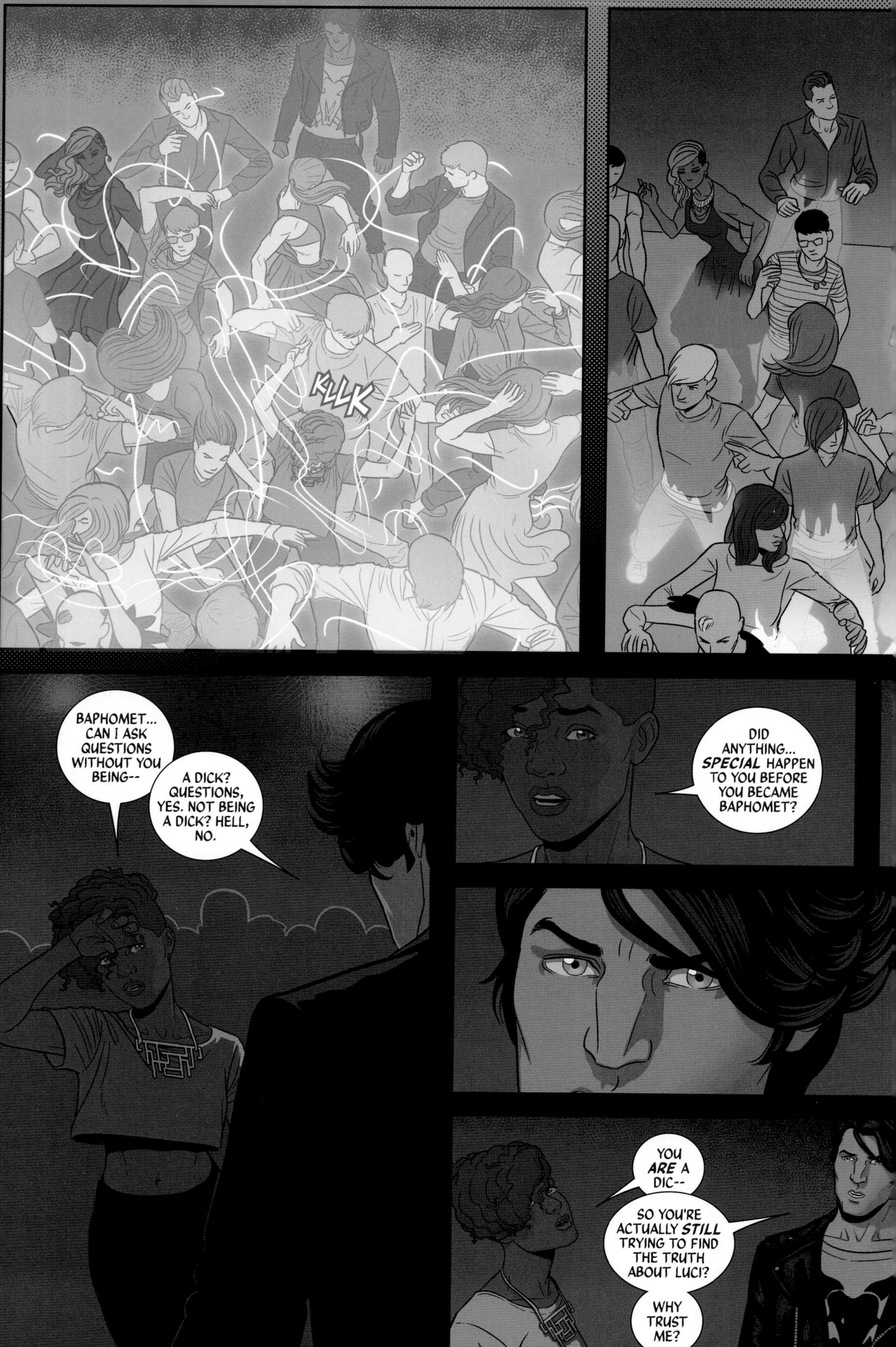
KLLK
BAPHOMET... CAN I ASK QUESTIONS WITHOUT YOU BEING--
A DICK? QUESTIONS, YES. NOT BEING A DICK? HELL, NO.
DID ANYTHING... SPECIAL HAPPEN TO YOU BEFORE YOU BECAME BAPHOMET?
YOU ARE A DIC--
SO YOU'RE ACTUALLY STILL TRYING TO FIND THE TRUTH ABOUT LUCI?
WHY TRUST ME?

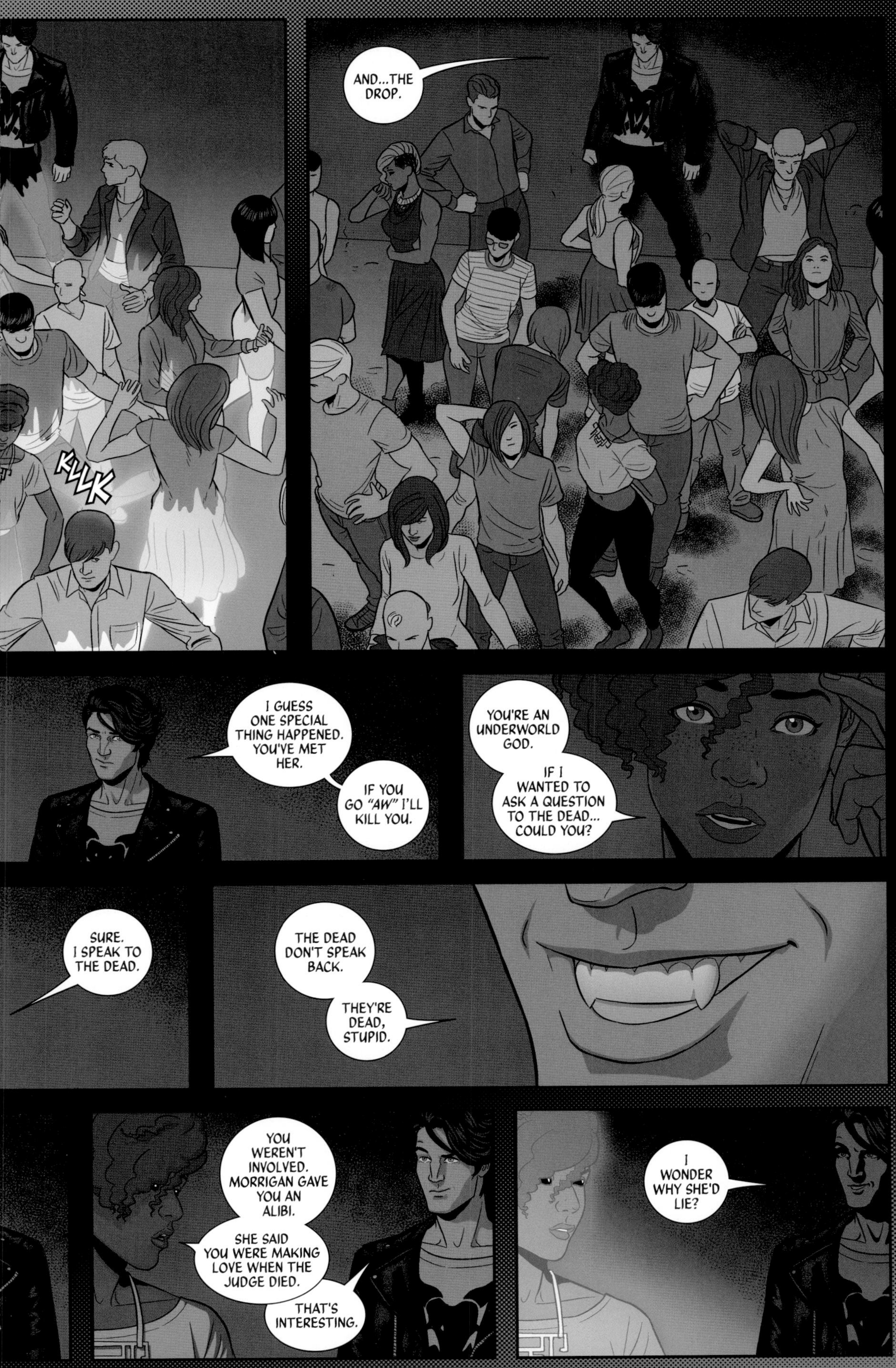
KLLK
AND...THE DROP.
I GUESS ONE SPECIAL THING HAPPENED. YOU'VE MET HER.
IF YOU GO "AW" I'LL KILL YOU.
YOU'RE AN UNDERWORLD GOD.
IF I WANTED TO ASK A QUESTION TO THE DEAD... COULD YOU?
SURE. I SPEAK TO THE DEAD.
THE DEAD DON'T SPEAK BACK.
THEY'RE DEAD, STUPID.
YOU WEREN'T INVOLVED. MORRIGAN GAVE YOU AN ALIBI.
SHE SAID YOU WERE MAKING LOVE WHEN THE JUDGE DIED.
THAT'S INTERESTING.
I WONDER WHY SHE'D LIE?

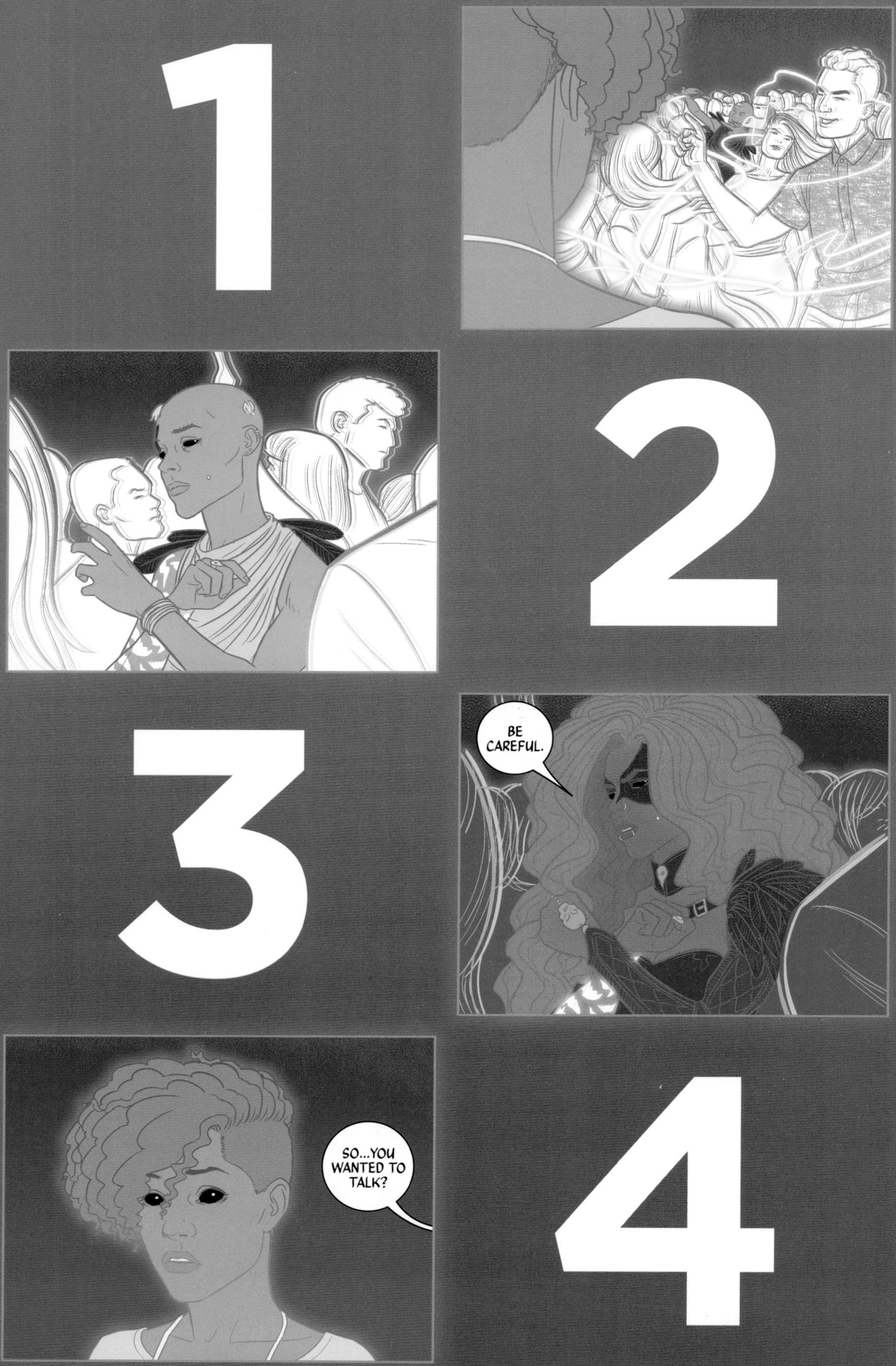
1
2
3
BE CAREFUL.
SO...YOU WANTED TO TALK?
4

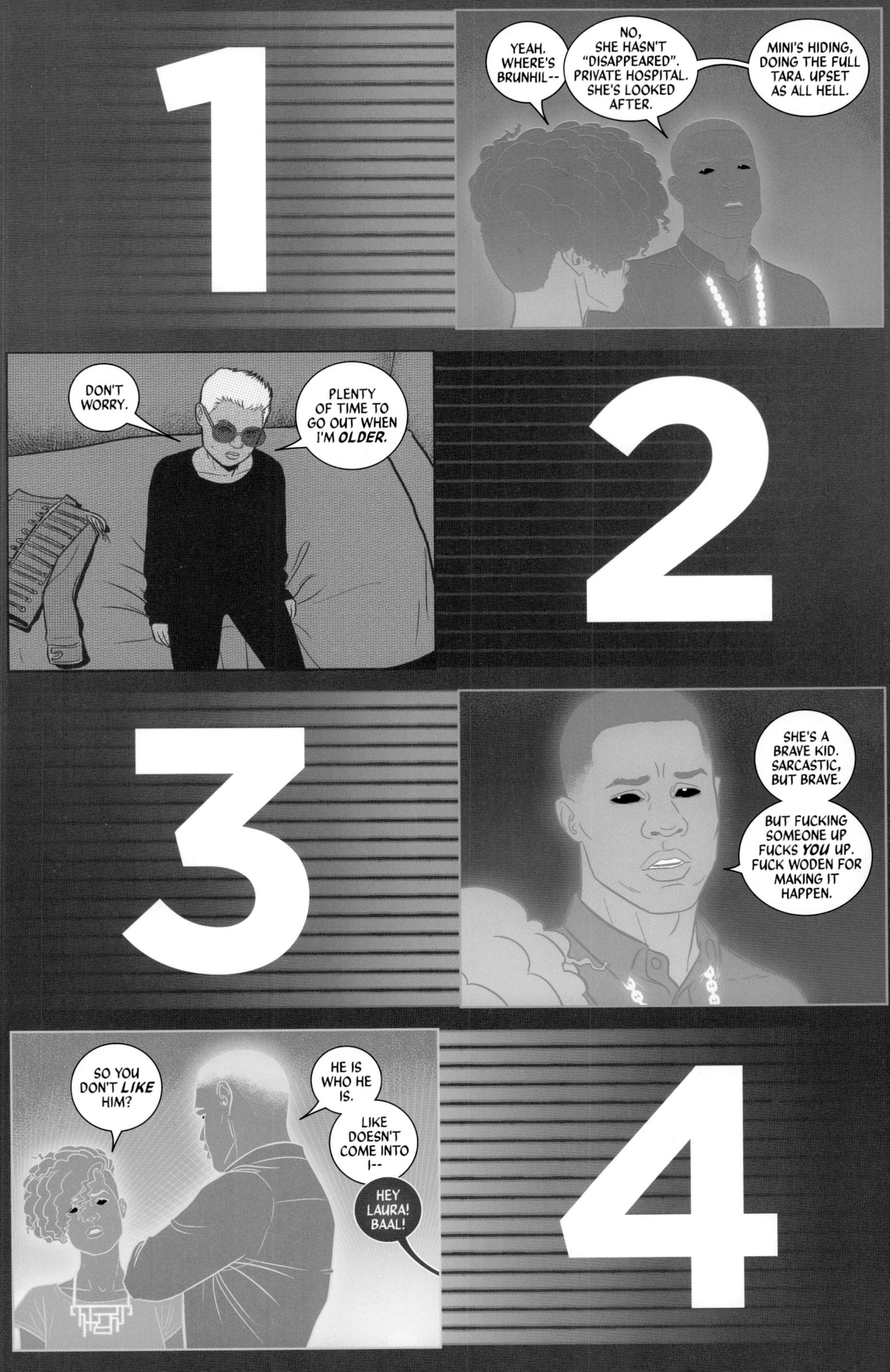
1
YEAH. WHERE'S BRUNHIL--
NO, SHE HASN'T "DISAPPEARED". PRIVATE HOSPITAL. SHE'S LOOKED AFTER.
MINI'S HIDING, DOING THE FULL TARA. UPSET AS ALL HELL.
DON'T WORRY.
PLENTY OF TIME TO GO OUT WHEN I'M *OLDER.*
2
3
SHE'S A BRAVE KID. SARCASTIC, BUT BRAVE.
BUT FUCKING SOMEONE UP FUCKS *YOU* UP. FUCK WODEN FOR MAKING IT HAPPEN.
SO YOU DON'T *LIKE* HIM?
HE IS WHO HE IS.
LIKE DOESN'T COME INTO I--
HEY LAURA! BAAL!
4

1

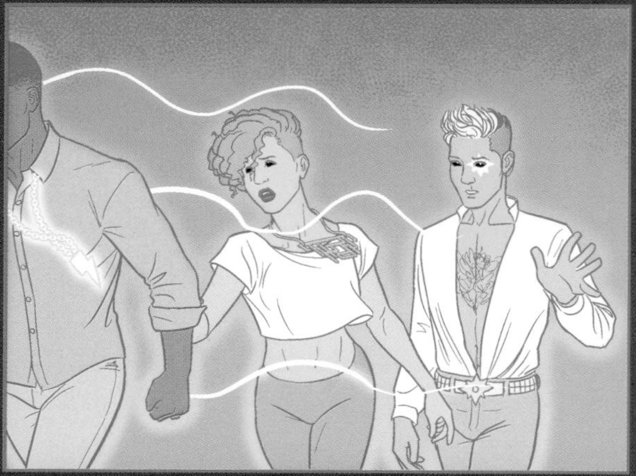

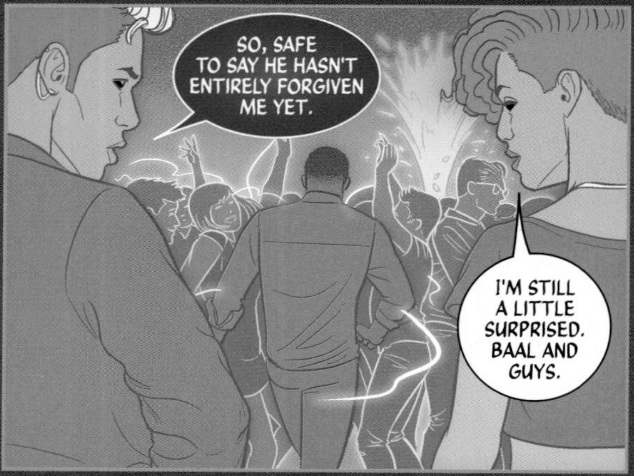
SO, SAFE TO SAY HE HASN'T ENTIRELY FORGIVEN ME YET.
I'M STILL A LITTLE SURPRISED. BAAL AND GUYS.

2

3

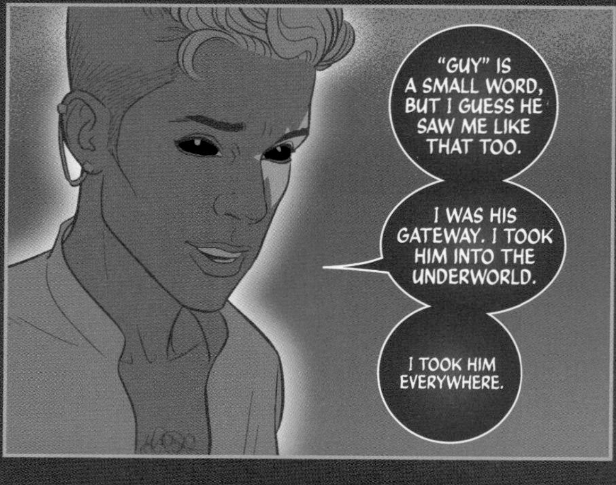
"GUY" IS A SMALL WORD, BUT I GUESS HE SAW ME LIKE THAT TOO.
I WAS HIS GATEWAY. I TOOK HIM INTO THE UNDERWORLD.
I TOOK HIM EVERYWHERE.

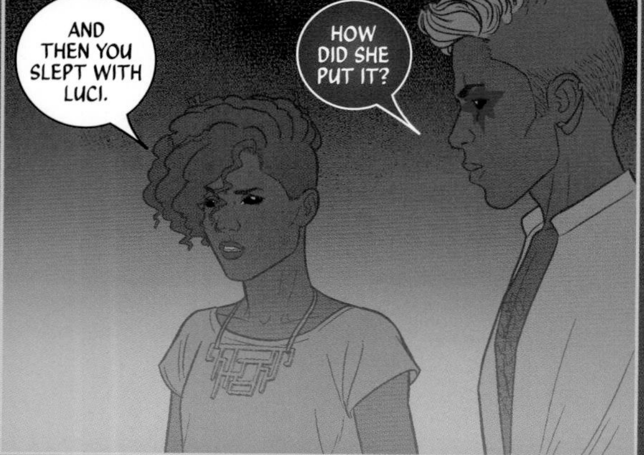
AND THEN YOU SLEPT WITH LUCI.
HOW DID SHE PUT IT?

4

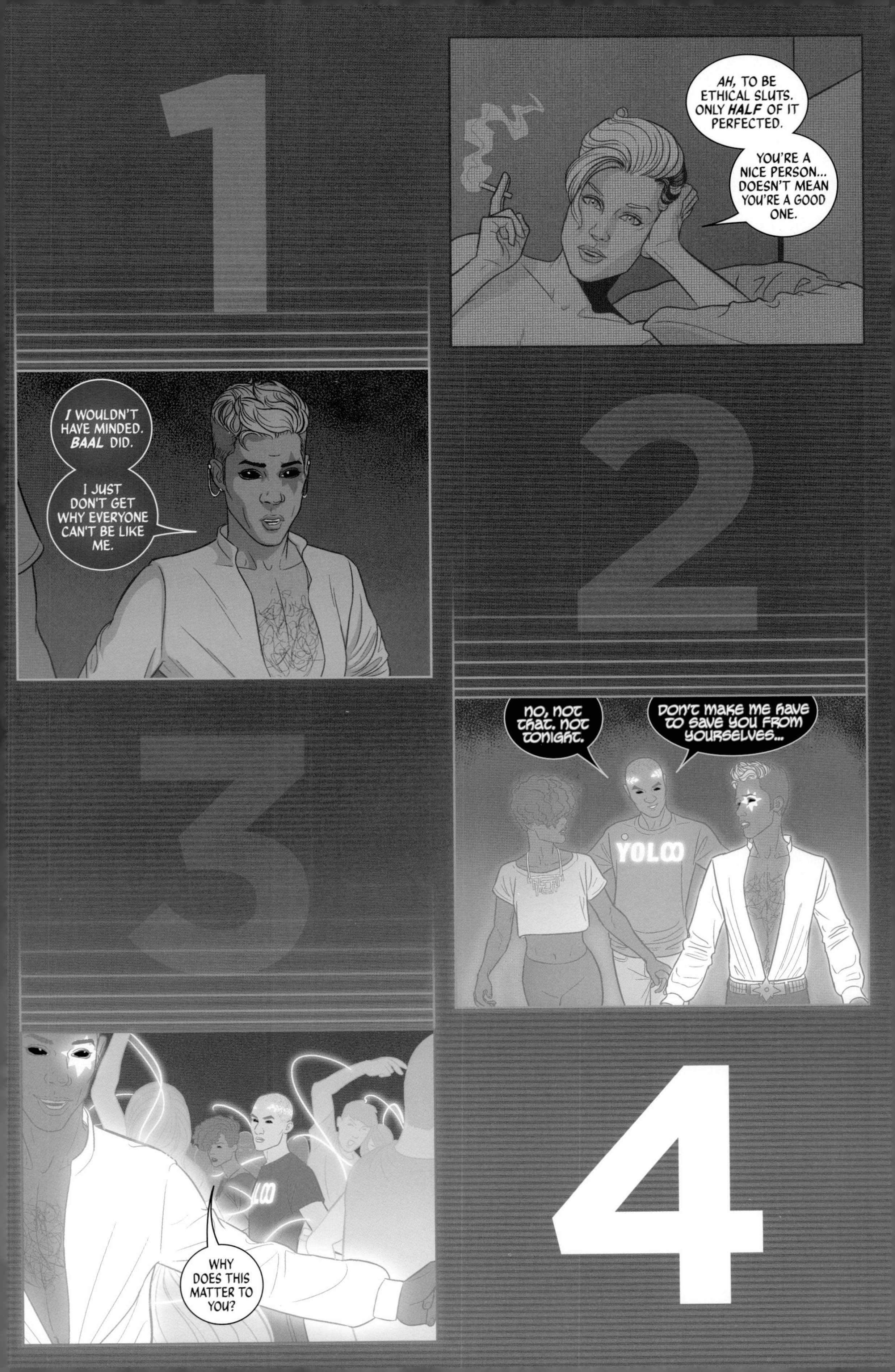
1
AH, TO BE ETHICAL SLUTS. ONLY HALF OF IT PERFECTED.
YOU'RE A NICE PERSON... DOESN'T MEAN YOU'RE A GOOD ONE.
I WOULDN'T HAVE MINDED. BAAL DID.
I JUST DON'T GET WHY EVERYONE CAN'T BE LIKE ME.
2
3
NO, NOT THAT. NOT TONIGHT.
DON'T MAKE ME HAVE TO SAVE YOU FROM YOURSELVES...
YOLO∞
WHY DOES THIS MATTER TO YOU?
4

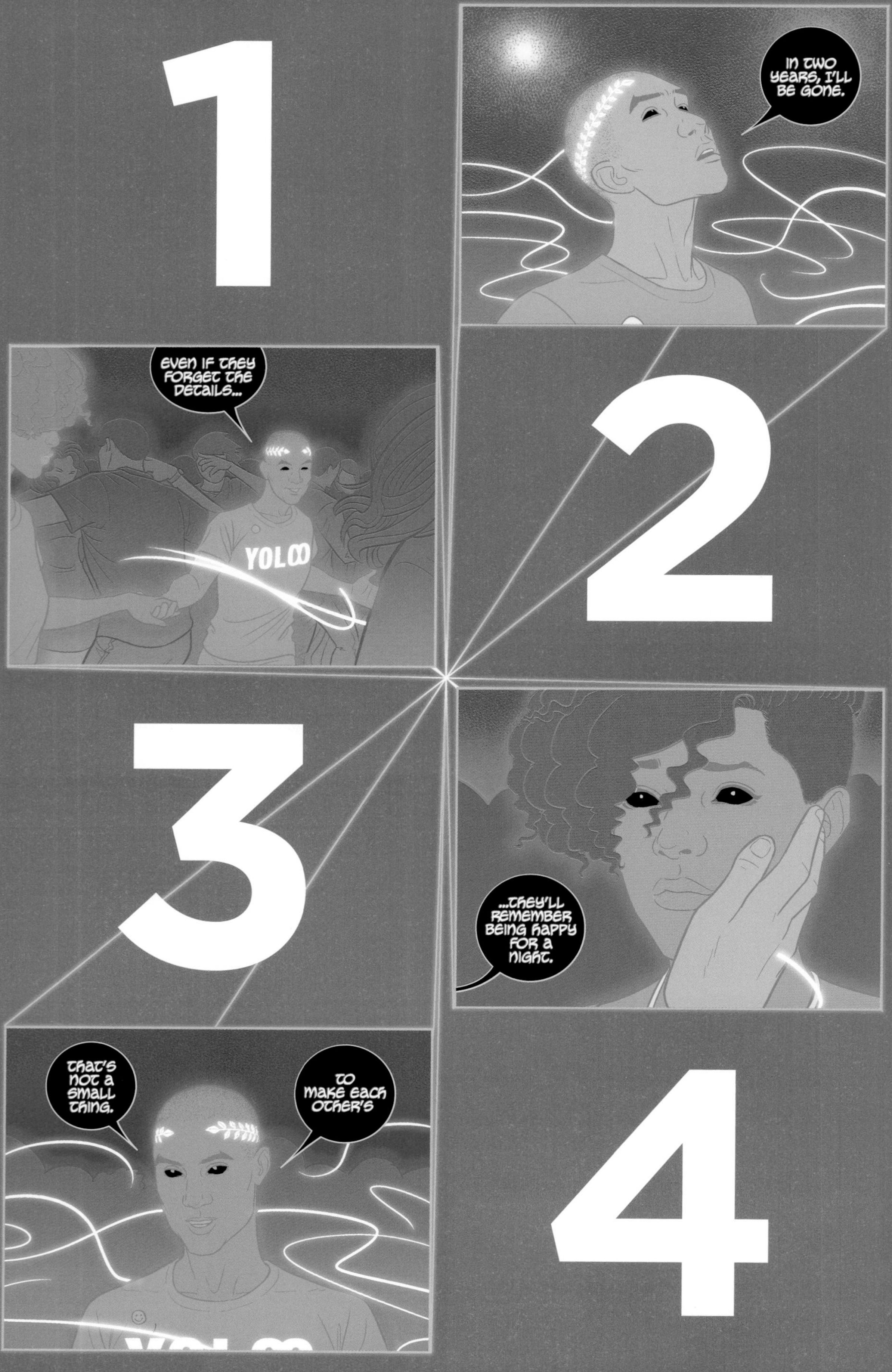
1
IN TWO YEARS, I'LL BE GONE.
2
EVEN IF THEY FORGET THE DETAILS...
YOLO∞
3
...THEY'LL REMEMBER BEING HAPPY FOR A NIGHT.
THAT'S NOT A SMALL THING.
TO MAKE EACH OTHER'S
4

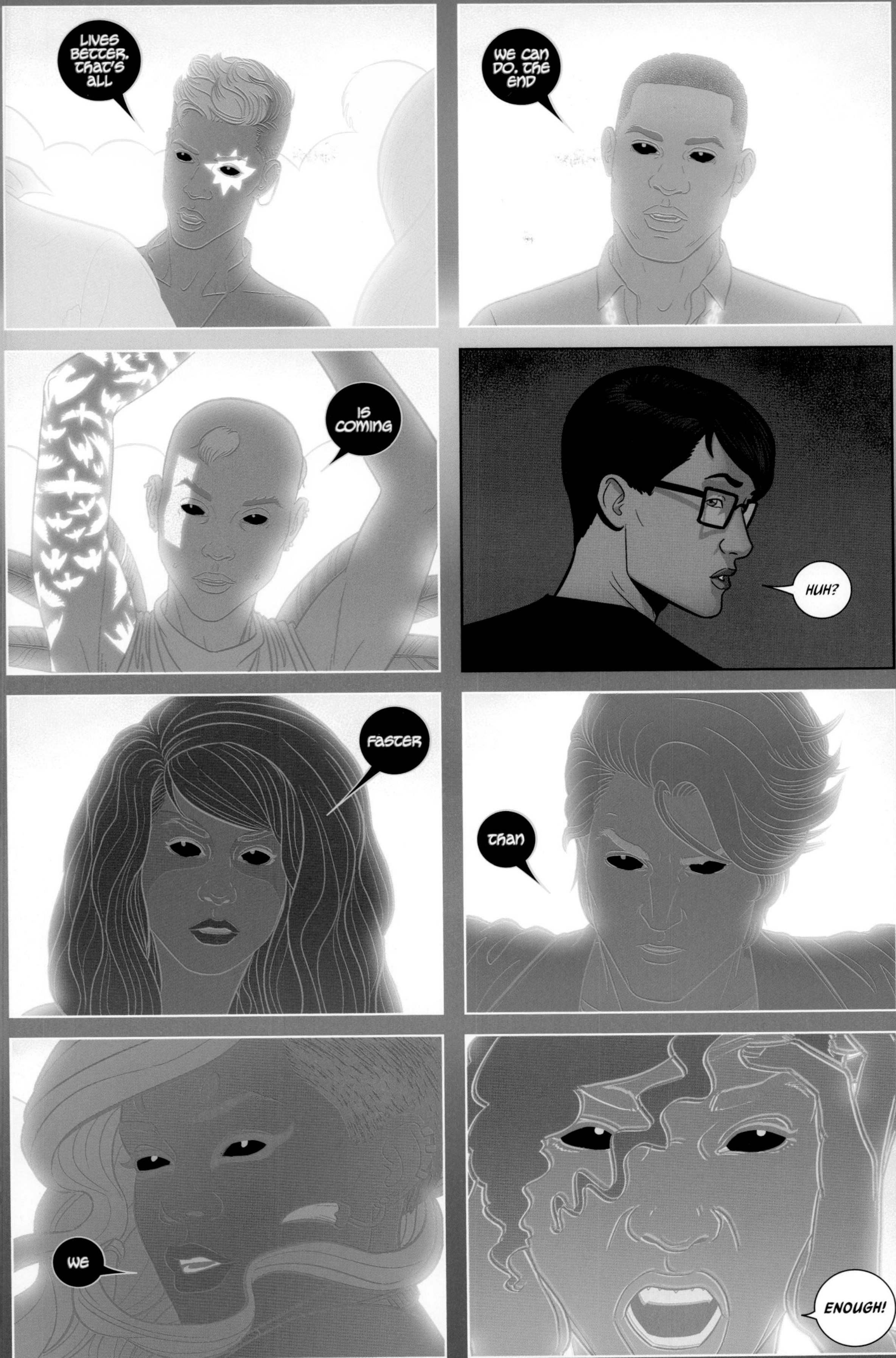
LIVES BETTER. THAT'S ALL
WE CAN DO. THE END
IS COMING
HUH?
FASTER
THAN
WE
ENOUGH!

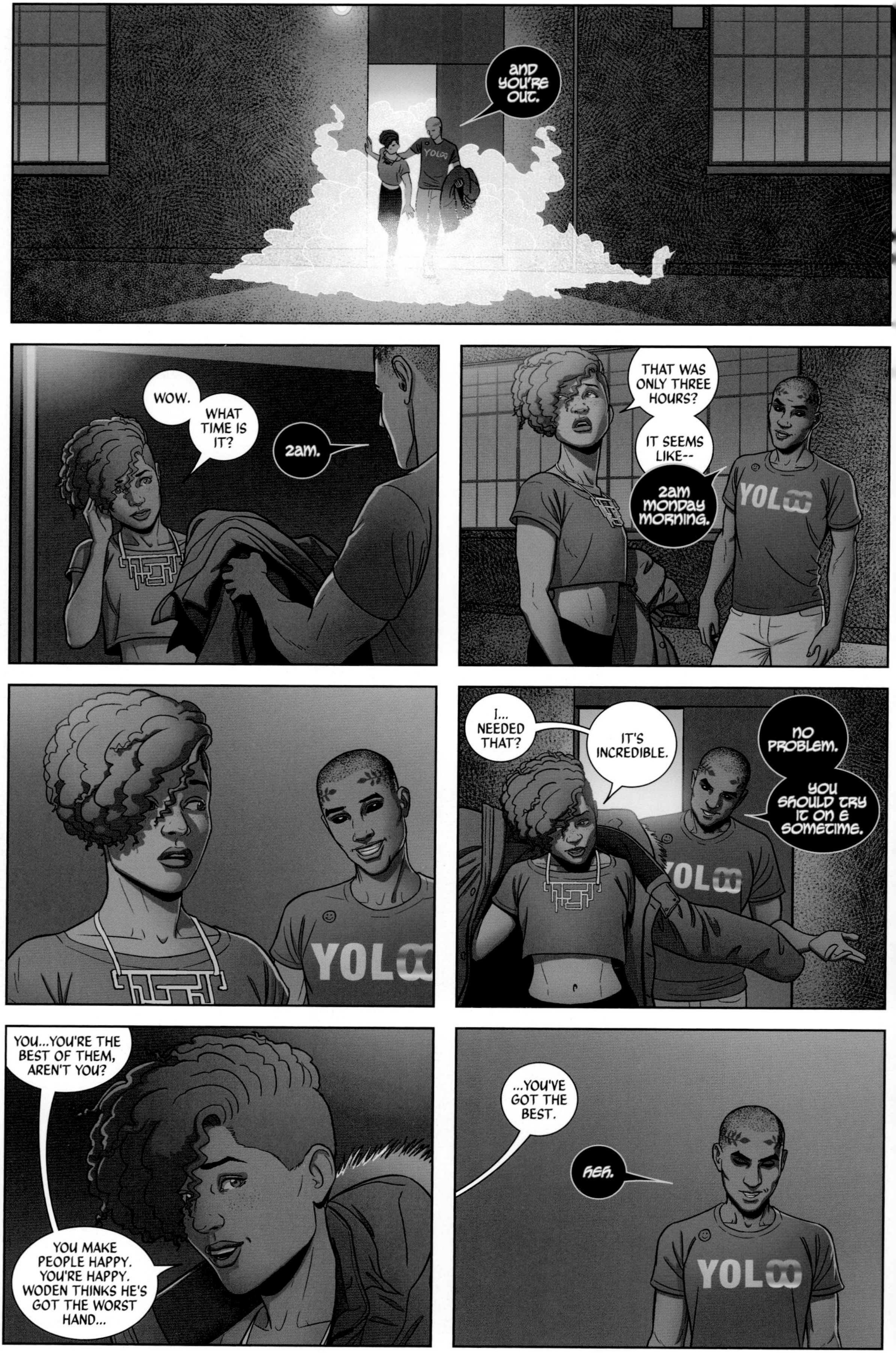
and you're out.
WOW.
WHAT TIME IS IT?
2am.
THAT WAS ONLY THREE HOURS?
IT SEEMS LIKE--
2am monday morning.
I... NEEDED THAT?
IT'S INCREDIBLE.
no problem.
you should try it on e sometime.
YOU...YOU'RE THE BEST OF THEM, AREN'T YOU?
YOU MAKE PEOPLE HAPPY. YOU'RE HAPPY. WODEN THINKS HE'S GOT THE WORST HAND...
...YOU'VE GOT THE BEST.
HER.

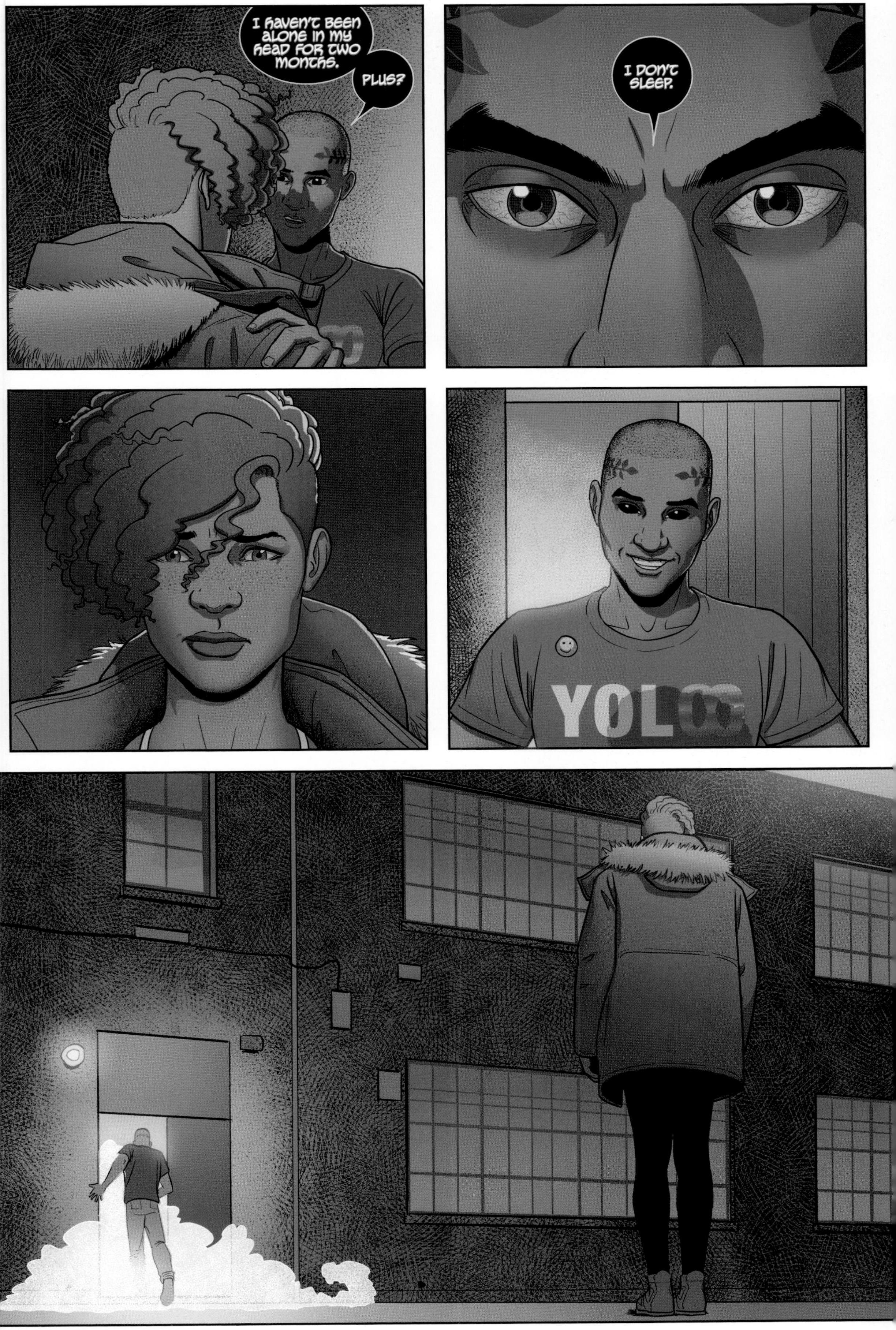
I HAVEN'T BEEN ALONE IN MY HEAD FOR TWO MONTHS.
PLUS?
I DON'T SLEEP.
YOLO

NEVER GOING TO
BE ALONE AGAIN

19 MAY 2014

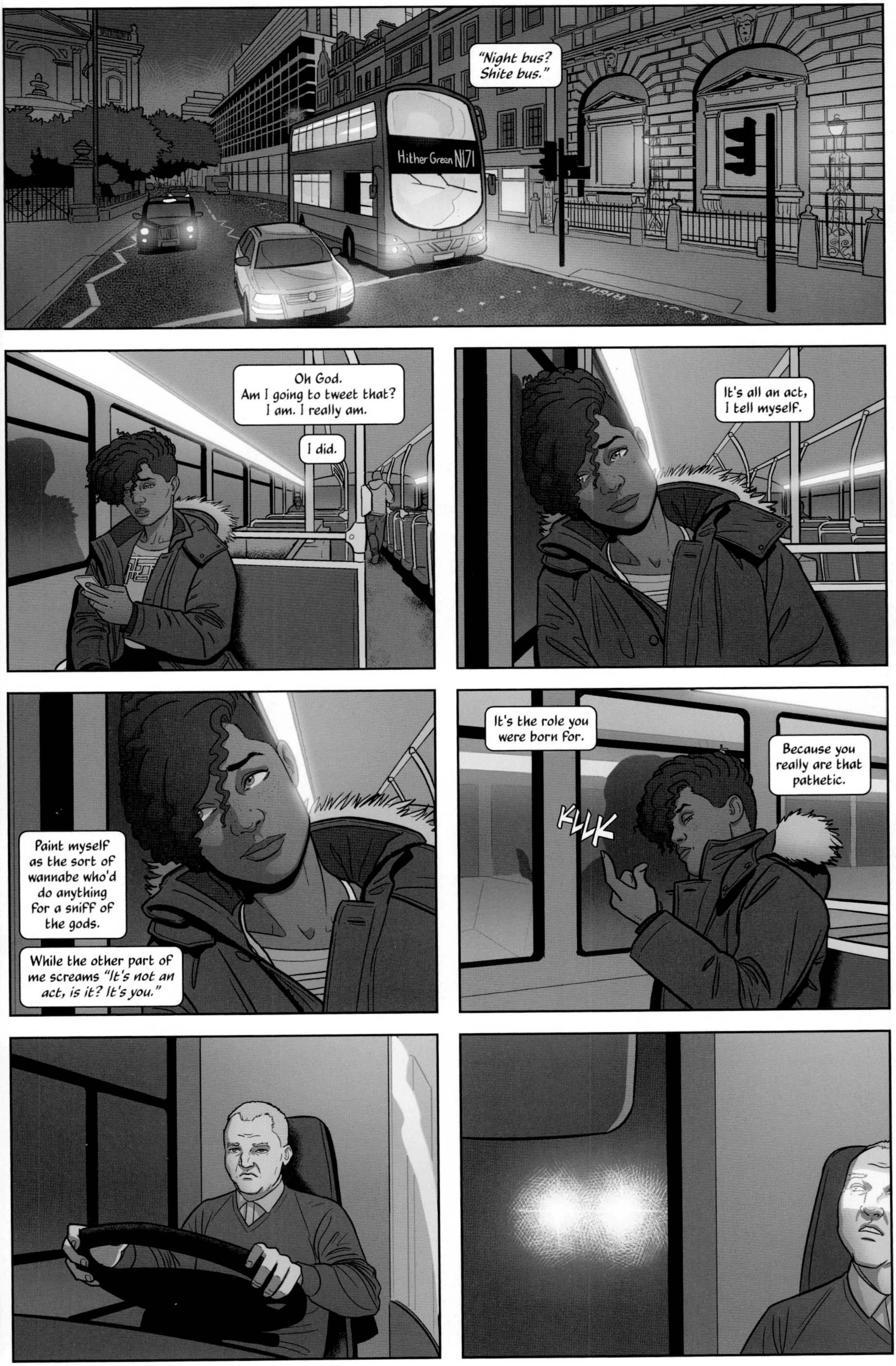
"Night bus? Shite bus."
Hither Green N171
Oh God. Am I going to tweet that? I am. I really am.
I did.
It's all an act, I tell myself.
Paint myself as the sort of wannabe who'd do anything for a sniff of the gods.
While the other part of me screams "It's not an act, is it? It's you."
It's the role you were born for.
Because you really are that pathetic.
KLLK

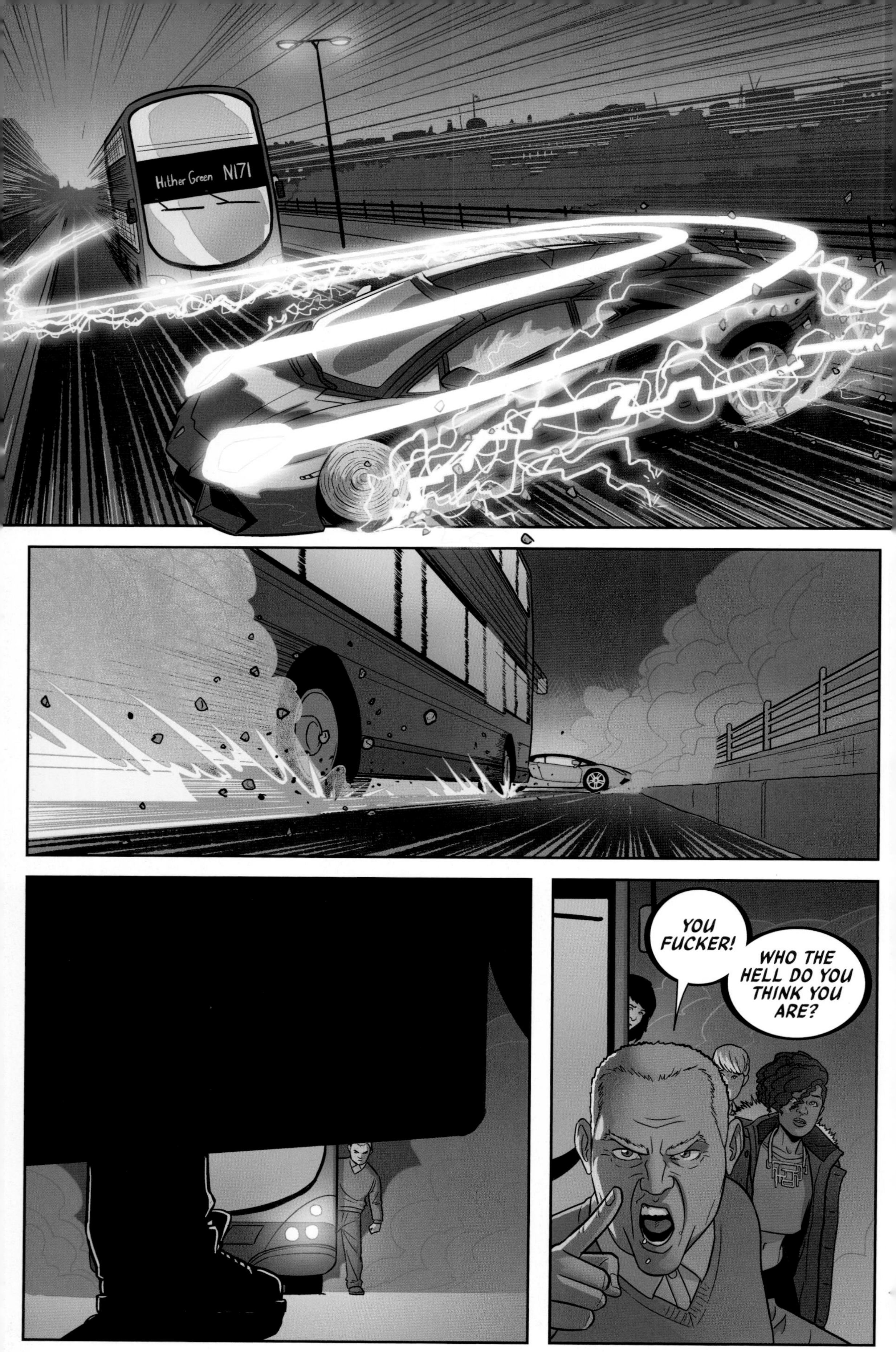
Hither Green N171
YOU FUCKER!
WHO THE HELL DO YOU THINK YOU ARE?

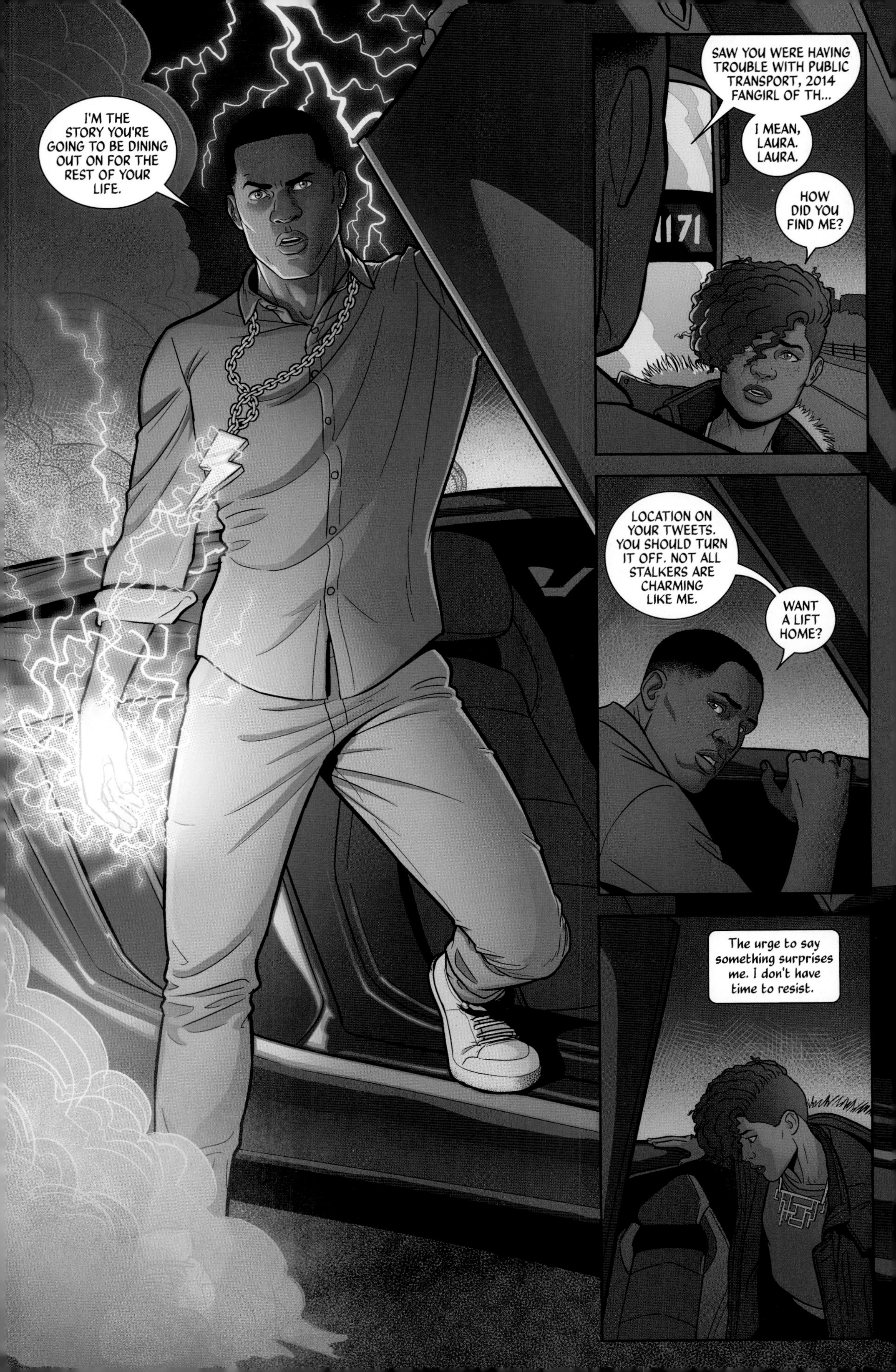
I'M THE STORY YOU'RE GOING TO BE DINING OUT ON FOR THE REST OF YOUR LIFE.
SAW YOU WERE HAVING TROUBLE WITH PUBLIC TRANSPORT, 2014 FANGIRL OF TH...
I MEAN, LAURA. LAURA.
HOW DID YOU FIND ME?
LOCATION ON YOUR TWEETS. YOU SHOULD TURN IT OFF. NOT ALL STALKERS ARE CHARMING LIKE ME.
WANT A LIFT HOME?
The urge to say something surprises me. I don't have time to resist.

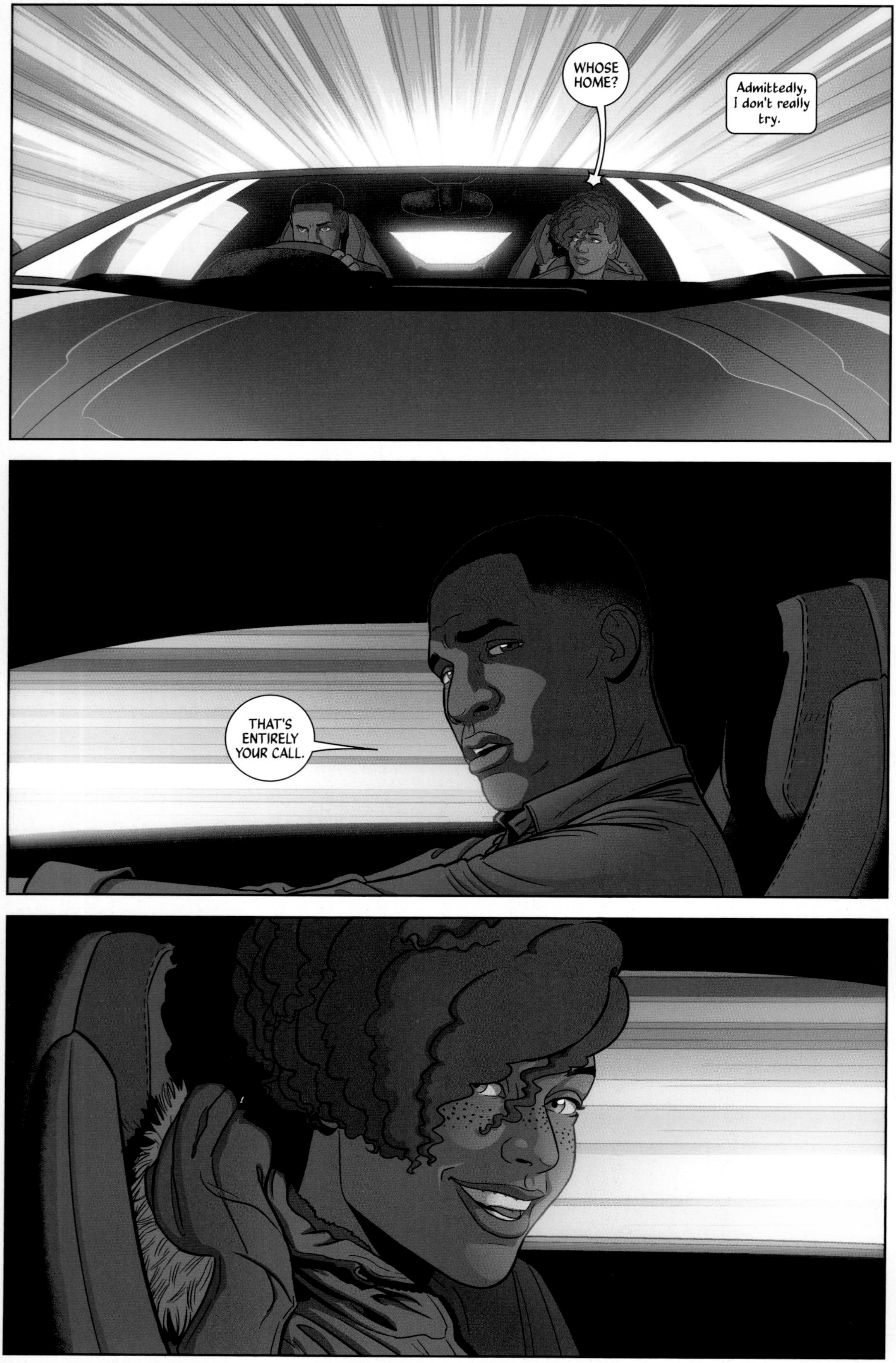
WHOSE HOME?
Admittedly, I don't really try.
THAT'S ENTIRELY YOUR CALL.

UH-HUH

19 MAY 2014

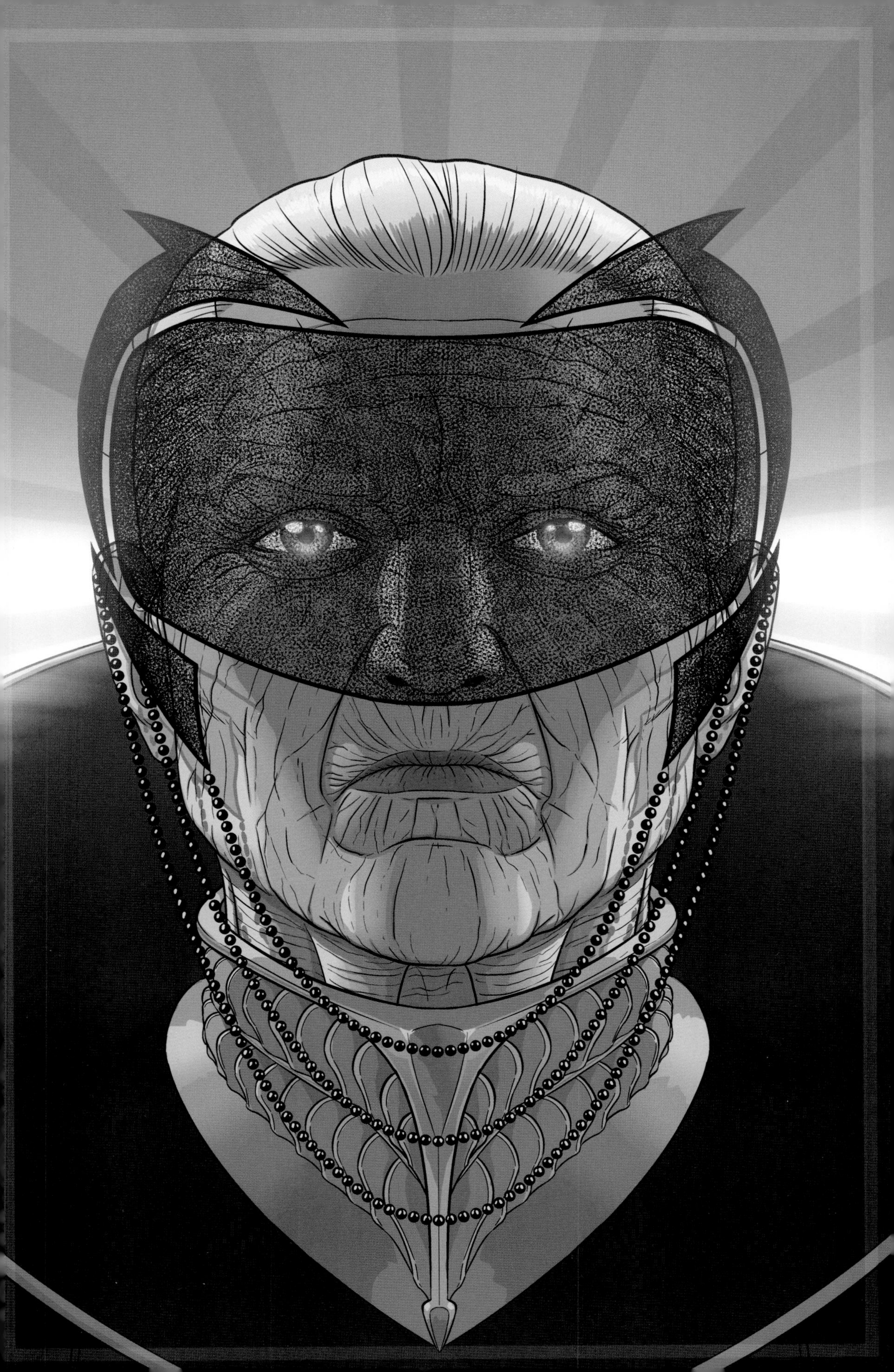

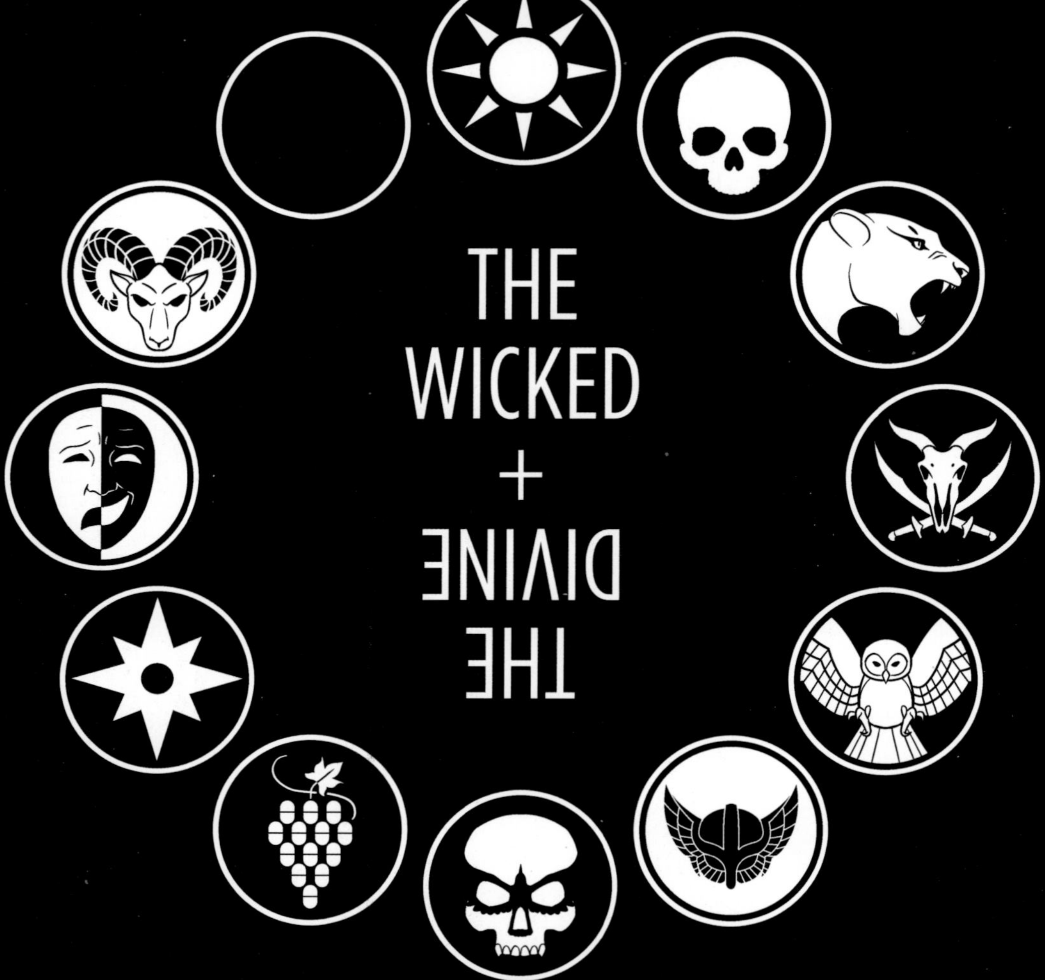
THE
WICKED
+
THE
DIVINE

BROCKLEY, SOUTH LONDON.

LAURA SHOULD BE HOME FOR DINNER.

WHY SO SURE?

SHE'S ON THE TELEVISION AGAIN.

SHE JUST LEFT THAT INANNA GUY'S PLACE.

INANNA RESIDENCY ENTERS SECOND MONTH

THAT'S GREAT. PLENTY OF TIME.

SHE PROMISED. GOOD GIRL.

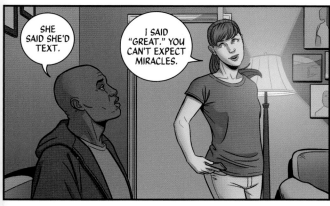

SHE SAID SHE'D TEXT.

I SAID "GREAT." YOU CAN'T EXPECT MIRACLES.

THE EAST LONDON LINE IS DOWN AGAIN. SHE'D BE BETTER OFF GOING THROUGH CENTRAL.

I'LL TEXT HER.

WILL SHE THINK I'M WORRYING?

YOU *ARE* WORRYING.

SOMEONE HAS TO.

I LOOK AT THEM ALL AND THINK...

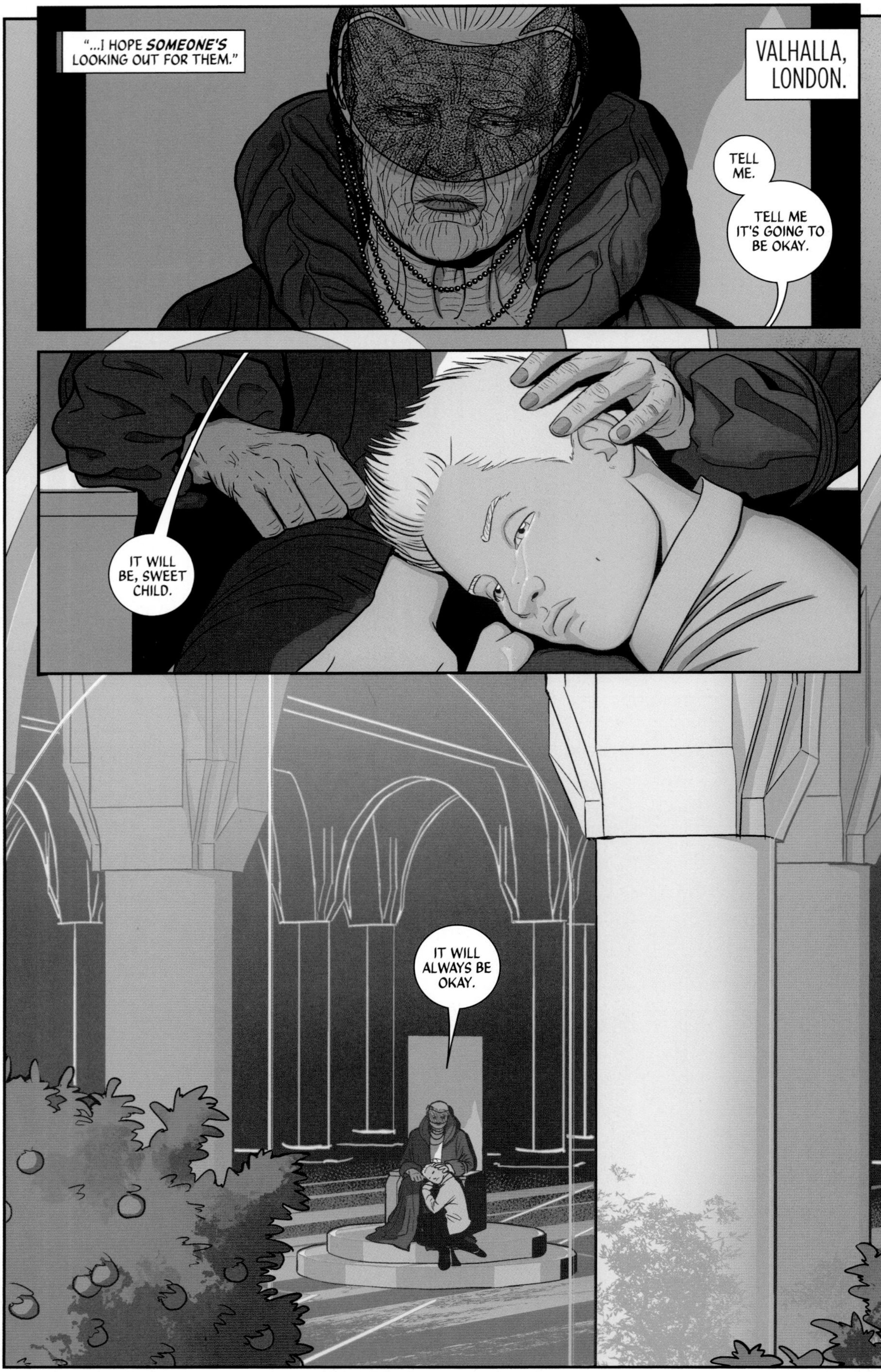
"...I HOPE SOMEONE'S LOOKING OUT FOR THEM."
VALHALLA, LONDON.
TELL ME.
TELL ME IT'S GOING TO BE OKAY.
IT WILL BE, SWEET CHILD.
IT WILL ALWAYS BE OKAY.

THIS IS A GIFT

28 JUNE 2014

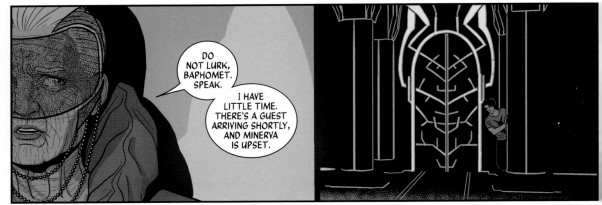

DO NOT LURK, BAPHOMET. SPEAK.

I HAVE LITTLE TIME. THERE'S A GUEST ARRIVING SHORTLY, AND MINERVA IS UPSET.

LUCIFER'S FRIEND...SHE WAS ASKING ALL SORTS OF QUESTIONS THAT HAVE BEEN NAGGING AT ME. LIKE, *STRANGE* QUESTIONS.

SHE ALSO SAID THE MORRIGAN GAVE ME...AN ALIBI. FOR THE JUDGE.

BUT IT'S NOT TRUE.

I'M SURE SHE HAD HER REASONS.

BUT WHY LIE? I HAVEN'T KILLED ANYONE.

SO YOU SAY.

WHAT'S WRONG WITH SHIRLEY TEMPLE?

I'M GOING TO DIE. WE'RE ALL GOING TO DIE.

SO LOSE YOUR SARCASM, WHEN YOU'RE JUST WORM-FOOD!

WE ALL ARE, AND--

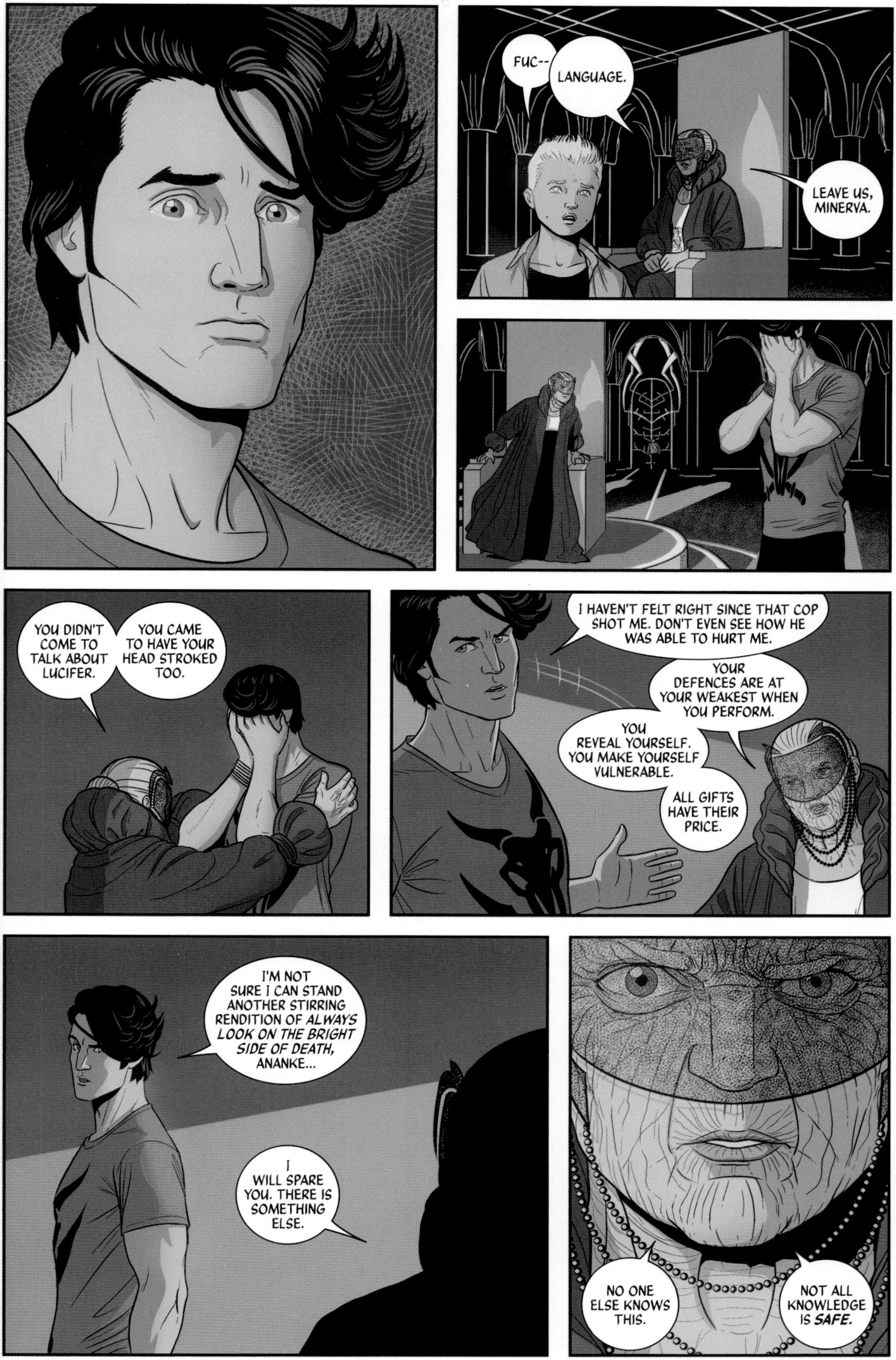
FUC--
LANGUAGE.
LEAVE US, MINERVA.
YOU DIDN'T COME TO TALK ABOUT LUCIFER.
YOU CAME TO HAVE YOUR HEAD STROKED TOO.
I HAVEN'T FELT RIGHT SINCE THAT COP SHOT ME. DON'T EVEN SEE HOW HE WAS ABLE TO HURT ME.
YOUR DEFENCES ARE AT YOUR WEAKEST WHEN YOU PERFORM.
YOU REVEAL YOURSELF. YOU MAKE YOURSELF VULNERABLE.
ALL GIFTS HAVE THEIR PRICE.
I'M NOT SURE I CAN STAND ANOTHER STIRRING RENDITION OF *ALWAYS LOOK ON THE BRIGHT SIDE OF DEATH*, ANANKE...
I WILL SPARE YOU. THERE IS SOMETHING ELSE.
NO ONE ELSE KNOWS THIS.
NOT ALL KNOWLEDGE IS ***SAFE.***

THAT'S WHY I DISMISSED MINERVA. HER MORAL COMPASS IS NOT DEVELOPED. THE YOUNGEST ARE MOST LIKELY TO ACT OUT, IN MY EXPERIENCE.

I WOULD RATHER NONE OF YOU KNOW...BUT YOU ARE *YOU,* AND NO FOOL.

YOU ARE EXPLORING YOUR DIVINITY. YOU COULD EASILY CHANCE UPON IT YOURSELF. AND AS THE FEAR IS HEAVY UPON YOU, YOU COULD BE TEMPTED...

WHAT ARE YOU TALKING ABOUT?

THE PROMETHEUS GAMBIT. THE IDEA THAT A MORTAL MAY KILL A GOD TO STEAL THEIR POWERS IS A LIE. IT DOESN'T WORK. WISHFUL THINKING FOR THE IMMORAL AND GREEDY.

A *DEATH GOD* KILLING A GOD, HOWEVER?

YOU COULD TEAR A FEW MORE YEARS FOR YOURSELF.

THEIR LIFE FOR YOUR LIFE.

NOW HEED MY WORDS, BAPHOMET.

ONLY YOU KNOW THIS. IF A GOD IS MURDERED, *I WILL HUNT YOU DOWN.*

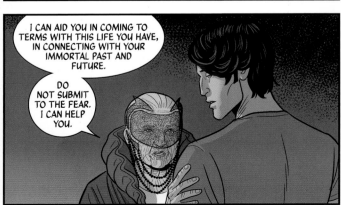

I CAN AID YOU IN COMING TO TERMS WITH THIS LIFE YOU HAVE, IN CONNECTING WITH YOUR IMMORTAL PAST AND FUTURE.

DO NOT SUBMIT TO THE FEAR. I CAN HELP YOU.

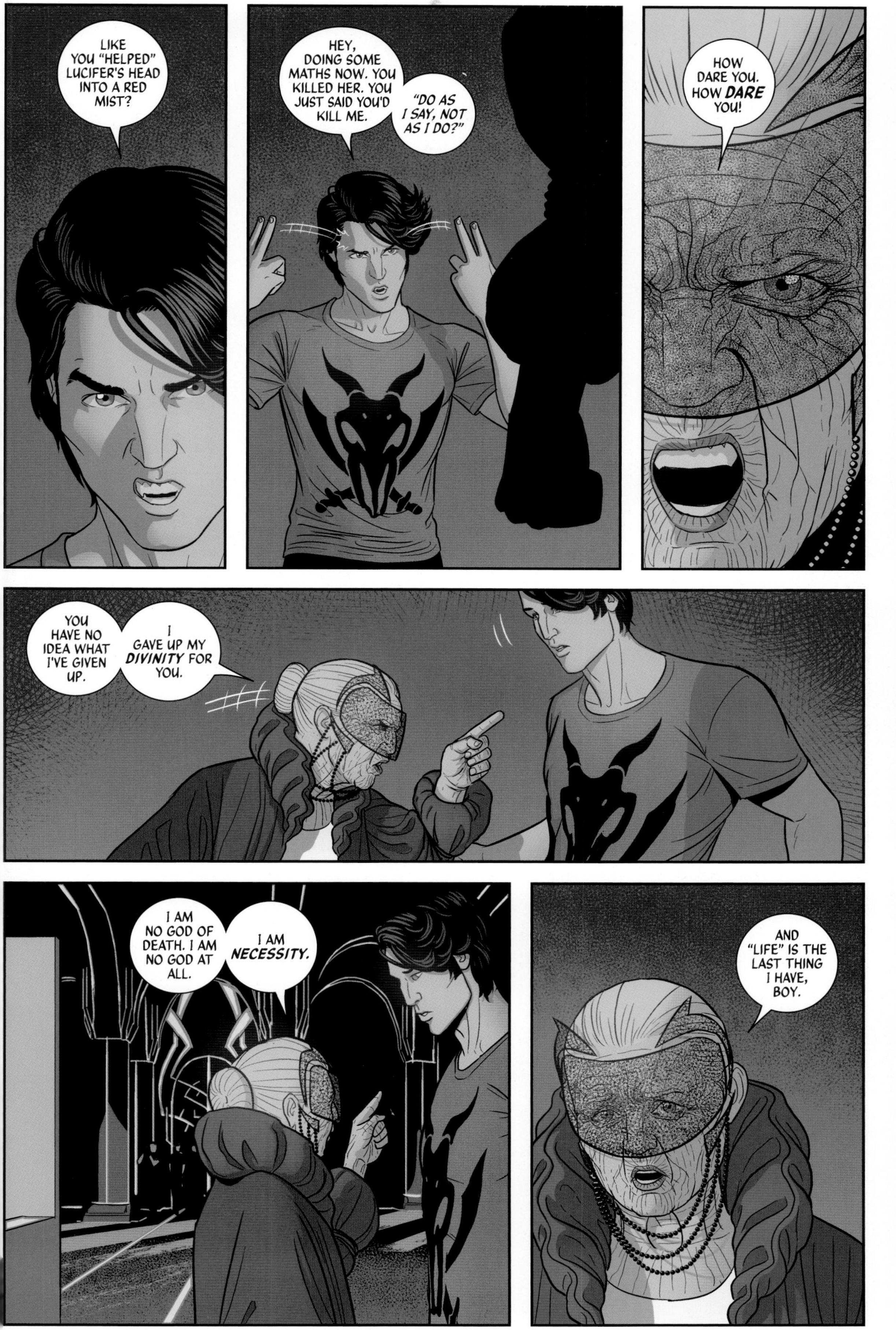
LIKE YOU "HELPED" LUCIFER'S HEAD INTO A RED MIST?
HEY, DOING SOME MATHS NOW. YOU KILLED HER. YOU JUST SAID YOU'D KILL ME.
"DO AS I SAY, NOT AS I DO?"
HOW DARE YOU. HOW *DARE* YOU!
YOU HAVE NO IDEA WHAT I'VE GIVEN UP.
I GAVE UP MY *DIVINITY* FOR YOU.
I AM NO GOD OF DEATH. I AM NO GOD AT ALL.
I AM *NECESSITY.*
AND "LIFE" IS THE LAST THING I HAVE, BOY.

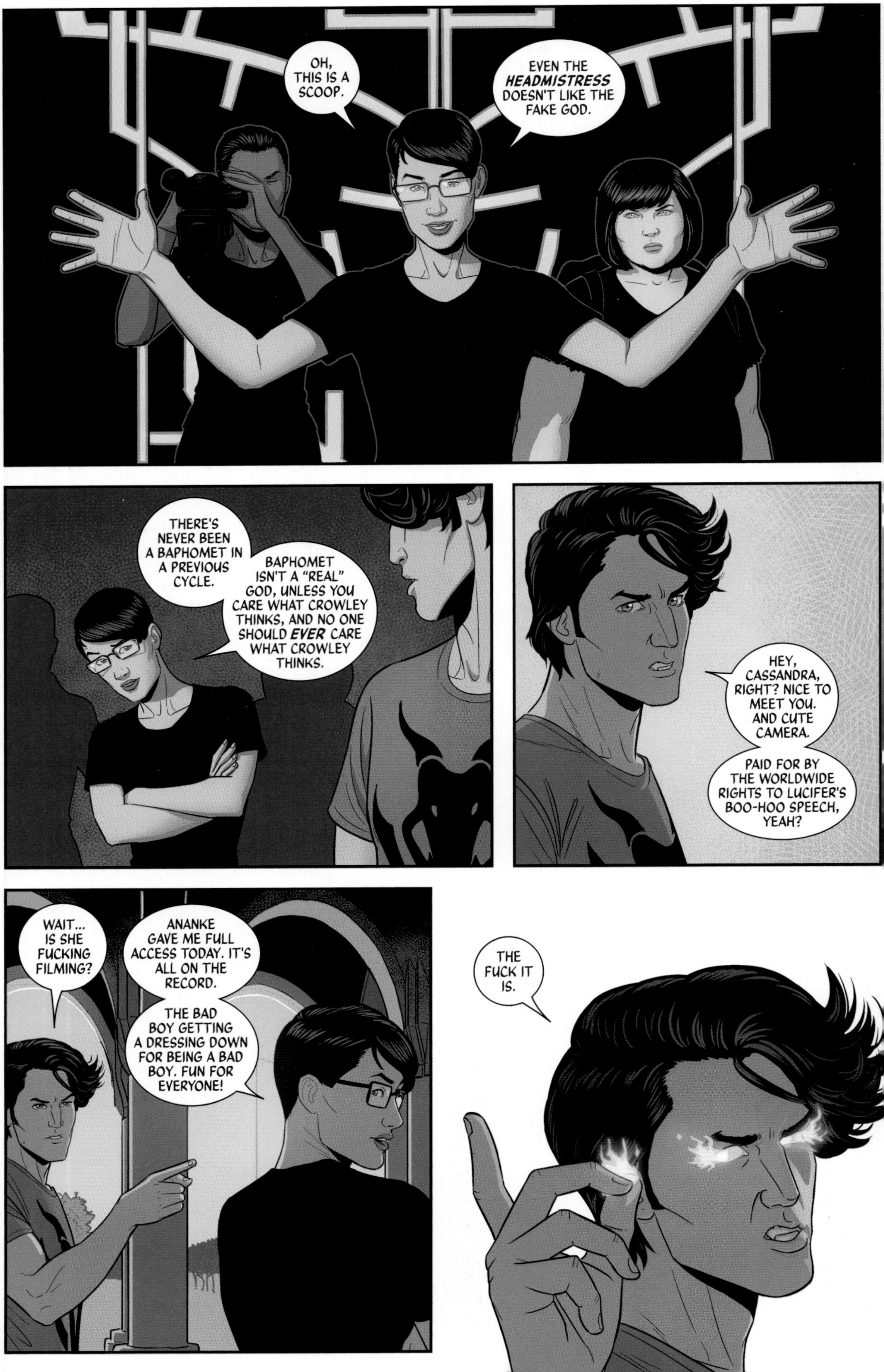
OH, THIS IS A SCOOP.
EVEN THE ***HEADMISTRESS*** DOESN'T LIKE THE FAKE GOD.
THERE'S NEVER BEEN A BAPHOMET IN A PREVIOUS CYCLE.
BAPHOMET ISN'T A "REAL" GOD, UNLESS YOU CARE WHAT CROWLEY THINKS, AND NO ONE SHOULD ***EVER*** CARE WHAT CROWLEY THINKS.
HEY, CASSANDRA, RIGHT? NICE TO MEET YOU. AND CUTE CAMERA.
PAID FOR BY THE WORLDWIDE RIGHTS TO LUCIFER'S BOO-HOO SPEECH, YEAH?
WAIT... IS SHE FUCKING FILMING?
ANANKE GAVE ME FULL ACCESS TODAY. IT'S ALL ON THE RECORD.
THE BAD BOY GETTING A DRESSING DOWN FOR BEING A BAD BOY. FUN FOR EVERYONE!
THE FUCK IT IS.

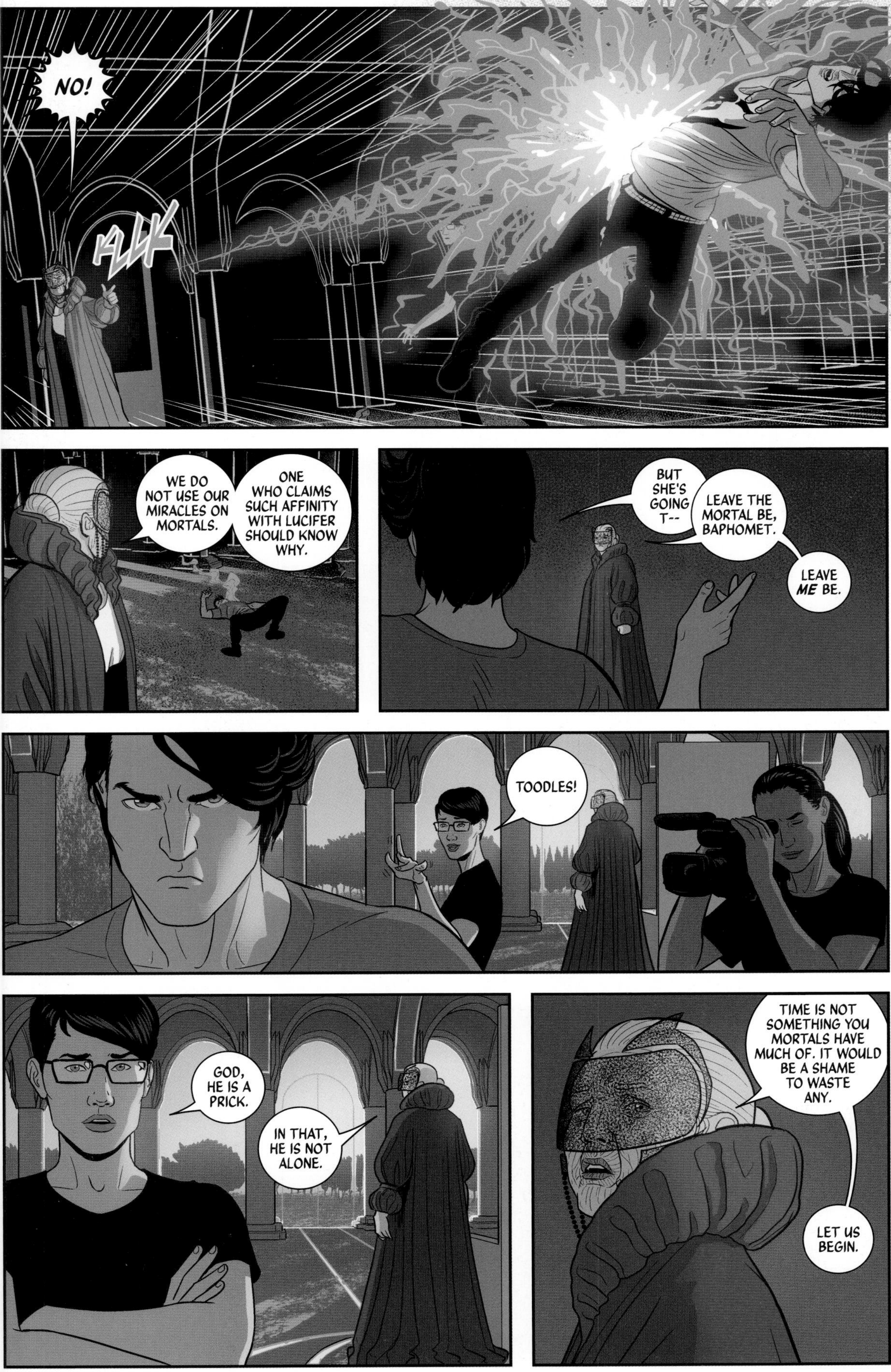
NO!
KLLK
WE DO NOT USE OUR MIRACLES ON MORTALS.
ONE WHO CLAIMS SUCH AFFINITY WITH LUCIFER SHOULD KNOW WHY.
BUT SHE'S GOING T--
LEAVE THE MORTAL BE, BAPHOMET.
LEAVE *ME* BE.
TOODLES!
GOD, HE IS A PRICK.
IN THAT, HE IS NOT ALONE.
TIME IS NOT SOMETHING YOU MORTALS HAVE MUCH OF. IT WOULD BE A SHAME TO WASTE ANY.
LET US BEGIN.

FEAR
AND LOATHING
IN ETERNITY

28 JUNE 2014

FIRST QUESTION. WHY AN INTERVIEW?

WODEN TOLD ME YOU WANTED TO TALK. YOU *NEVER* TALK. YOU'RE BARELY A GHOST IN THE LITERATURE. YOU'RE THIS BIG EXCITING MYSTERY AND YOU SPEAK TO ME NOW... WHY?

YOU ARE RESEARCHING THE CIRCUMSTANCES OF LUCIFER'S DEATH.

I WANT TO HELP YOU.

WAIT. HOW DID YOU--

I DIDN'T. I DO NOW.

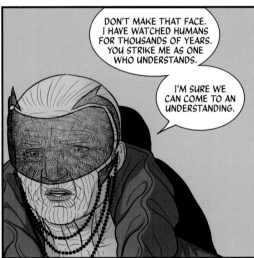

DON'T MAKE THAT FACE. I HAVE WATCHED HUMANS FOR THOUSANDS OF YEARS. YOU STRIKE ME AS ONE WHO UNDERSTANDS.

I'M SURE WE CAN COME TO AN UNDERSTANDING.

OKAY. SERIOUSLY, YOU'RE "IMMORTAL"? PROVE IT.

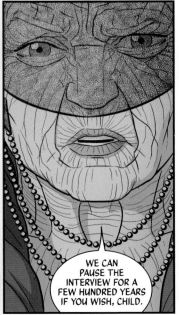

WE CAN PAUSE THE INTERVIEW FOR A FEW HUNDRED YEARS IF YOU WISH, CHILD.

DON'T PATRONISE ME. YOU CAN'T EXPECT ANYONE TO ACCEPT THAT. GIVE US SOME PROOF OF...

WHAT? TELL YOU HOW NAPOLEON LIKED TO EAT HIS EGGS OR WHAT THE SUN LOOKED LIKE RISING OVER THE COLOSSUS OF RHODES? THAT GRAPES PLUCKED FROM THE HANGING GARDENS WERE INFERIOR TO THOSE IN YOUR LOCAL GROCER'S?

THIS IS NOT THAT KIND OF STORY.

MINE IS A LONELIER STORY THAN THAT.

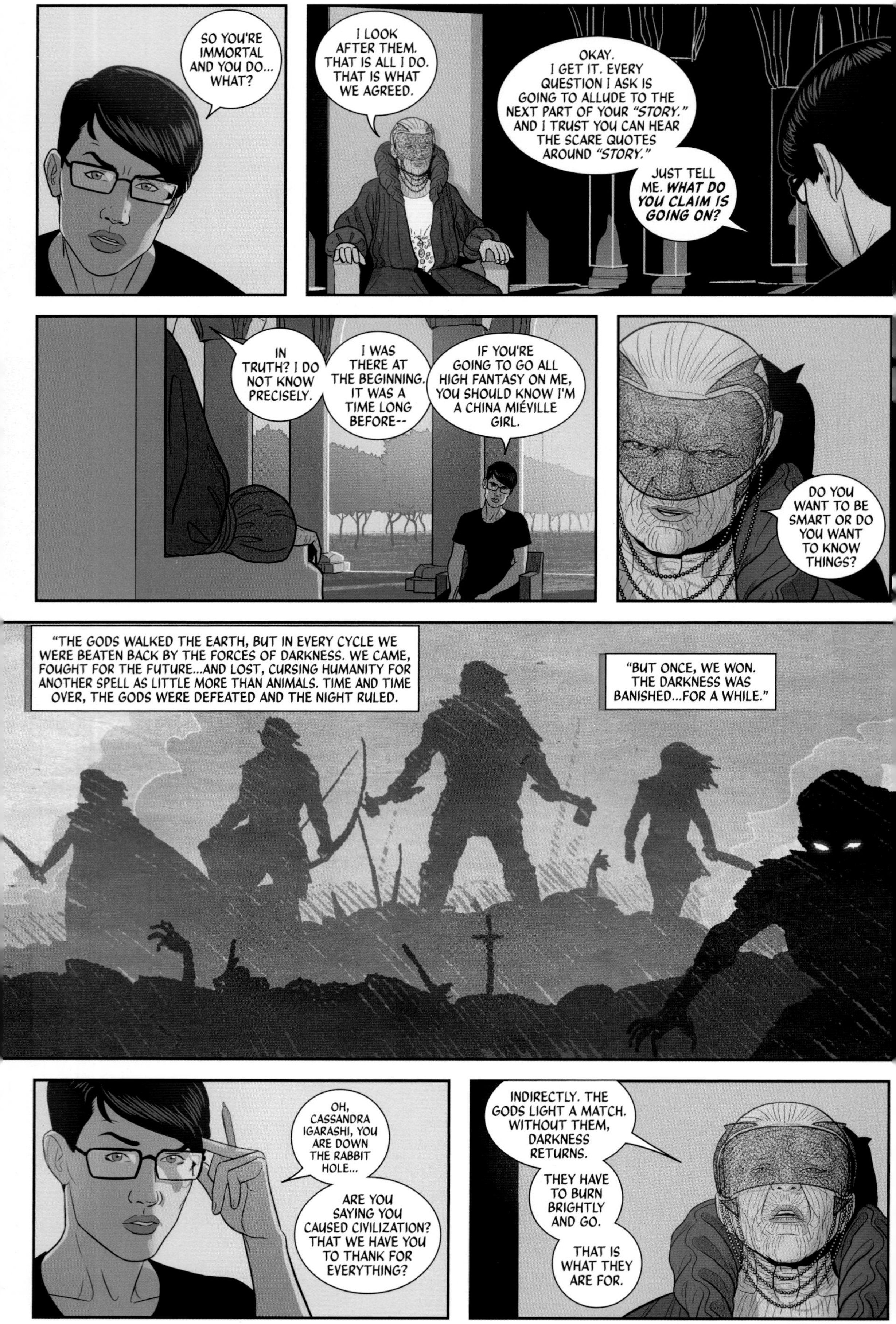
SO YOU'RE IMMORTAL AND YOU DO... WHAT?
I LOOK AFTER THEM. THAT IS ALL I DO. THAT IS WHAT WE AGREED.
OKAY. I GET IT. EVERY QUESTION I ASK IS GOING TO ALLUDE TO THE NEXT PART OF YOUR "STORY." AND I TRUST YOU CAN HEAR THE SCARE QUOTES AROUND "STORY."
JUST TELL ME. WHAT DO YOU CLAIM IS GOING ON?
IN TRUTH? I DO NOT KNOW PRECISELY.
I WAS THERE AT THE BEGINNING. IT WAS A TIME LONG BEFORE--
IF YOU'RE GOING TO GO ALL HIGH FANTASY ON ME, YOU SHOULD KNOW I'M A CHINA MIÉVILLE GIRL.
DO YOU WANT TO BE SMART OR DO YOU WANT TO KNOW THINGS?
"THE GODS WALKED THE EARTH, BUT IN EVERY CYCLE WE WERE BEATEN BACK BY THE FORCES OF DARKNESS. WE CAME, FOUGHT FOR THE FUTURE...AND LOST, CURSING HUMANITY FOR ANOTHER SPELL AS LITTLE MORE THAN ANIMALS. TIME AND TIME OVER, THE GODS WERE DEFEATED AND THE NIGHT RULED.
"BUT ONCE, WE WON. THE DARKNESS WAS BANISHED...FOR A WHILE."
OH, CASSANDRA IGARASHI, YOU ARE DOWN THE RABBIT HOLE...
ARE YOU SAYING YOU CAUSED CIVILIZATION? THAT WE HAVE YOU TO THANK FOR EVERYTHING?
INDIRECTLY. THE GODS LIGHT A MATCH. WITHOUT THEM, DARKNESS RETURNS.
THEY HAVE TO BURN BRIGHTLY AND GO.
THAT IS WHAT THEY ARE FOR.

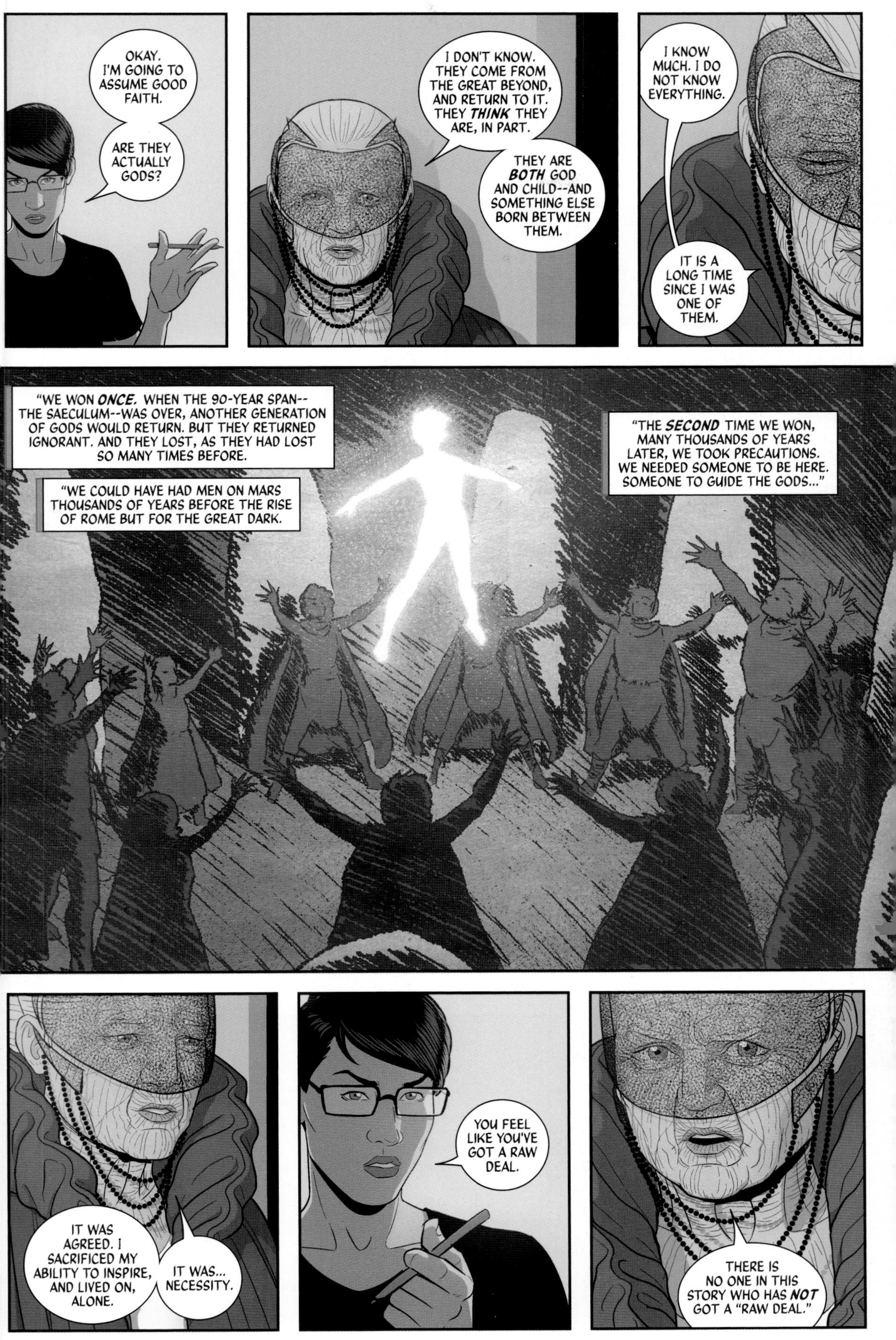
OKAY. I'M GOING TO ASSUME GOOD FAITH.
ARE THEY ACTUALLY GODS?
I DON'T KNOW. THEY COME FROM THE GREAT BEYOND, AND RETURN TO IT. THEY *THINK* THEY ARE, IN PART.
THEY ARE *BOTH* GOD AND CHILD--AND SOMETHING ELSE BORN BETWEEN THEM.
I KNOW MUCH. I DO NOT KNOW EVERYTHING.
IT IS A LONG TIME SINCE I WAS ONE OF THEM.
"WE WON *ONCE.* WHEN THE 90-YEAR SPAN--THE SAECULUM--WAS OVER, ANOTHER GENERATION OF GODS WOULD RETURN. BUT THEY RETURNED IGNORANT. AND THEY LOST, AS THEY HAD LOST SO MANY TIMES BEFORE.
"WE COULD HAVE HAD MEN ON MARS THOUSANDS OF YEARS BEFORE THE RISE OF ROME BUT FOR THE GREAT DARK.
"THE *SECOND* TIME WE WON, MANY THOUSANDS OF YEARS LATER, WE TOOK PRECAUTIONS. WE NEEDED SOMEONE TO BE HERE. SOMEONE TO GUIDE THE GODS..."
IT WAS AGREED. I SACRIFICED MY ABILITY TO INSPIRE, AND LIVED ON, ALONE.
IT WAS... NECESSITY.
YOU FEEL LIKE YOU'VE GOT A RAW DEAL.
THERE IS NO ONE IN THIS STORY WHO HAS *NOT* GOT A "RAW DEAL."

BUT IT CAN BE--LET US SAY IT HAS BEEN A BAD CENTURY FOR ME. SO MUCH CHANGE. I'VE FELT OLDER THAN I EVER HAVE.

I WAS WEAK. I TALKED TO ANOTHER MORTAL...

...GAVE A DRUNKEN DIATRIBE, IF TRUTH BE TOLD...

...IN THE 1940s. TO A MAN CALLED GRAVES.

ROBERT... GRAVES. *"THE WHITE GODDESS"?*

YOU'RE SAYING THAT *YOU* INSPIRED *THE WHITE GODDESS?*

I SHARED SOME THOUGHTS. HE GOT THE GENERAL GIST.

YOU'VE READ THE BOOK, I TAKE IT. DID YOU UNDERSTAND?

YES, OF COURSE.

I DOUBT IT. YOU'RE GOOD AT BEING CRITICAL... BUT YOU'RE NOT EXACTLY A GOOD CRITIC.

FUCK YOU--

IS WHAT YOU SAY TO OTHERS. YOU DISMISS WHAT OTHERS FEEL IN THE PRESENCE OF THE GODS.

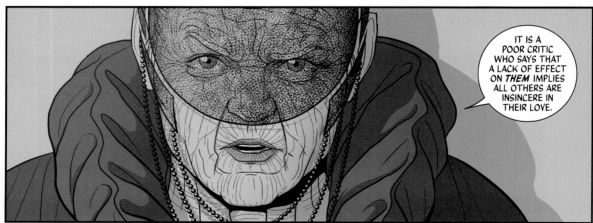

IT IS A POOR CRITIC WHO SAYS THAT A LACK OF EFFECT ON *THEM* IMPLIES ALL OTHERS ARE INSINCERE IN THEIR LOVE.

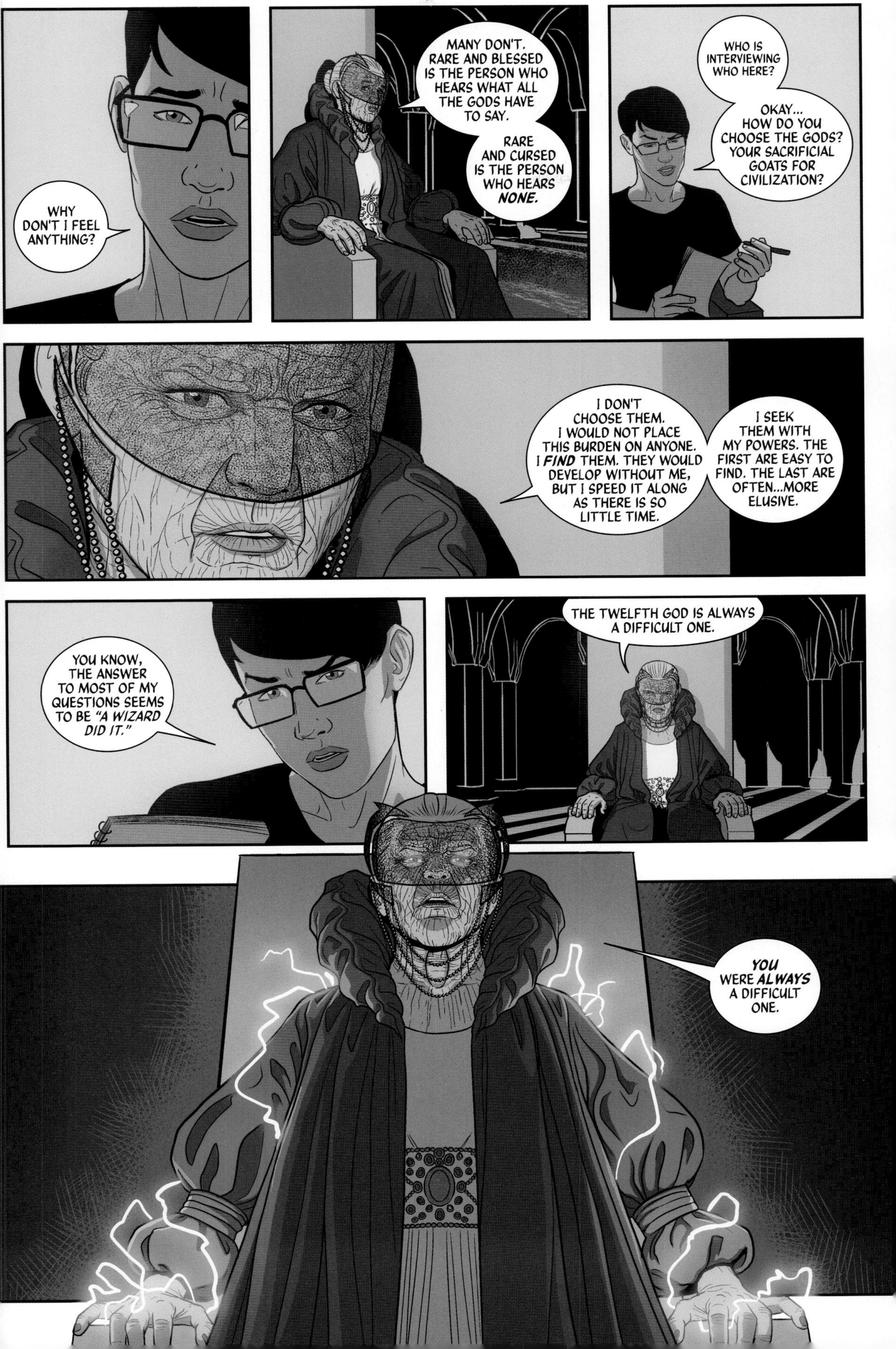
WHY DON'T I FEEL ANYTHING?
MANY DON'T. RARE AND BLESSED IS THE PERSON WHO HEARS WHAT ALL THE GODS HAVE TO SAY.
RARE AND CURSED IS THE PERSON WHO HEARS *NONE.*
WHO IS INTERVIEWING WHO HERE?
OKAY... HOW DO YOU CHOOSE THE GODS? YOUR SACRIFICIAL GOATS FOR CIVILIZATION?
I DON'T CHOOSE THEM. I WOULD NOT PLACE THIS BURDEN ON ANYONE. I ***FIND*** THEM. THEY WOULD DEVELOP WITHOUT ME, BUT I SPEED IT ALONG AS THERE IS SO LITTLE TIME.
I SEEK THEM WITH MY POWERS. THE FIRST ARE EASY TO FIND. THE LAST ARE OFTEN...MORE ELUSIVE.
YOU KNOW, THE ANSWER TO MOST OF MY QUESTIONS SEEMS TO BE *"A WIZARD DID IT."*
THE TWELFTH GOD IS ALWAYS A DIFFICULT ONE.
YOU WERE ***ALWAYS*** A DIFFICULT ONE.

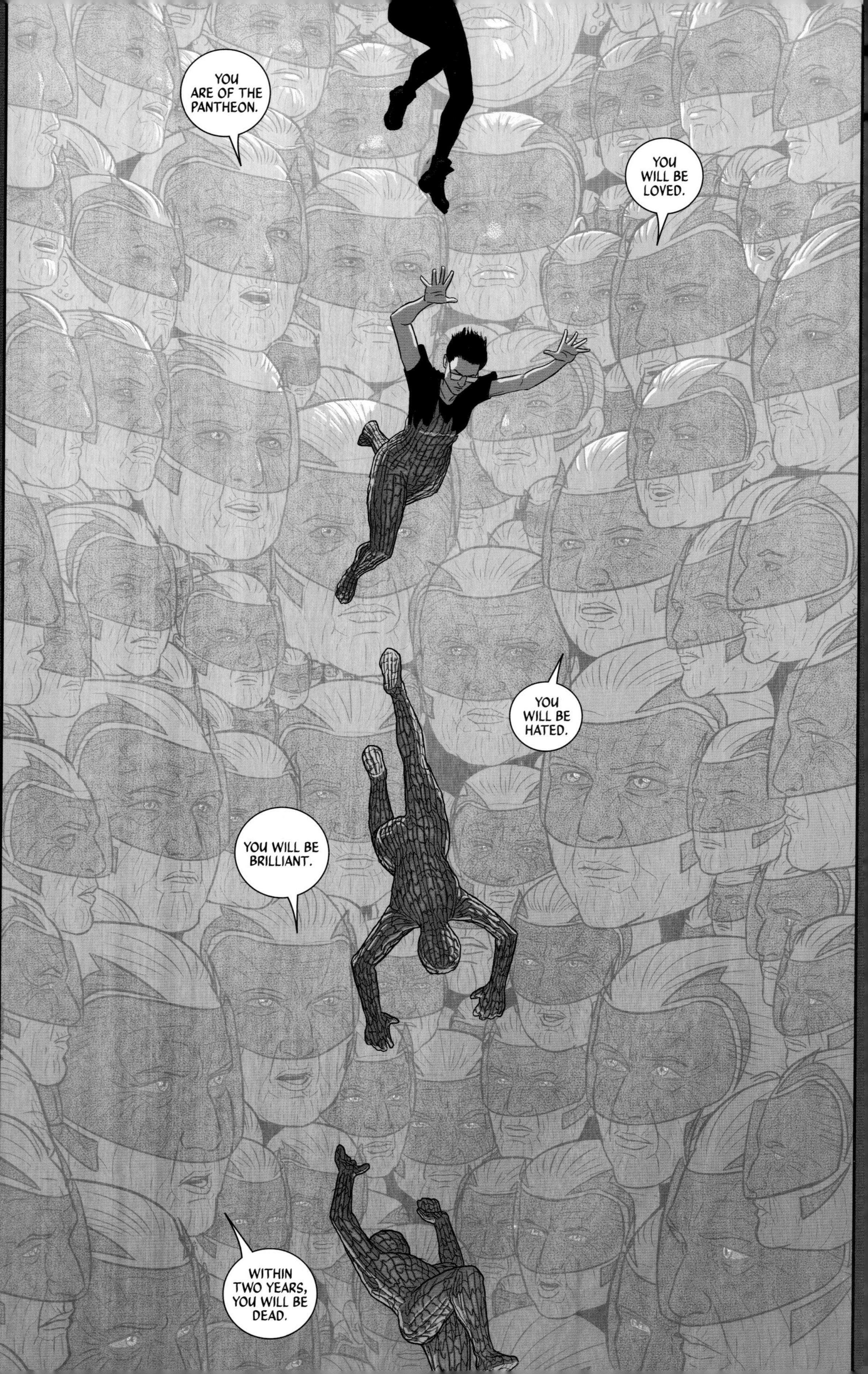
YOU ARE OF THE PANTHEON.
YOU WILL BE LOVED.
YOU WILL BE HATED.
YOU WILL BE BRILLIANT.
WITHIN TWO YEARS, YOU WILL BE DEAD.

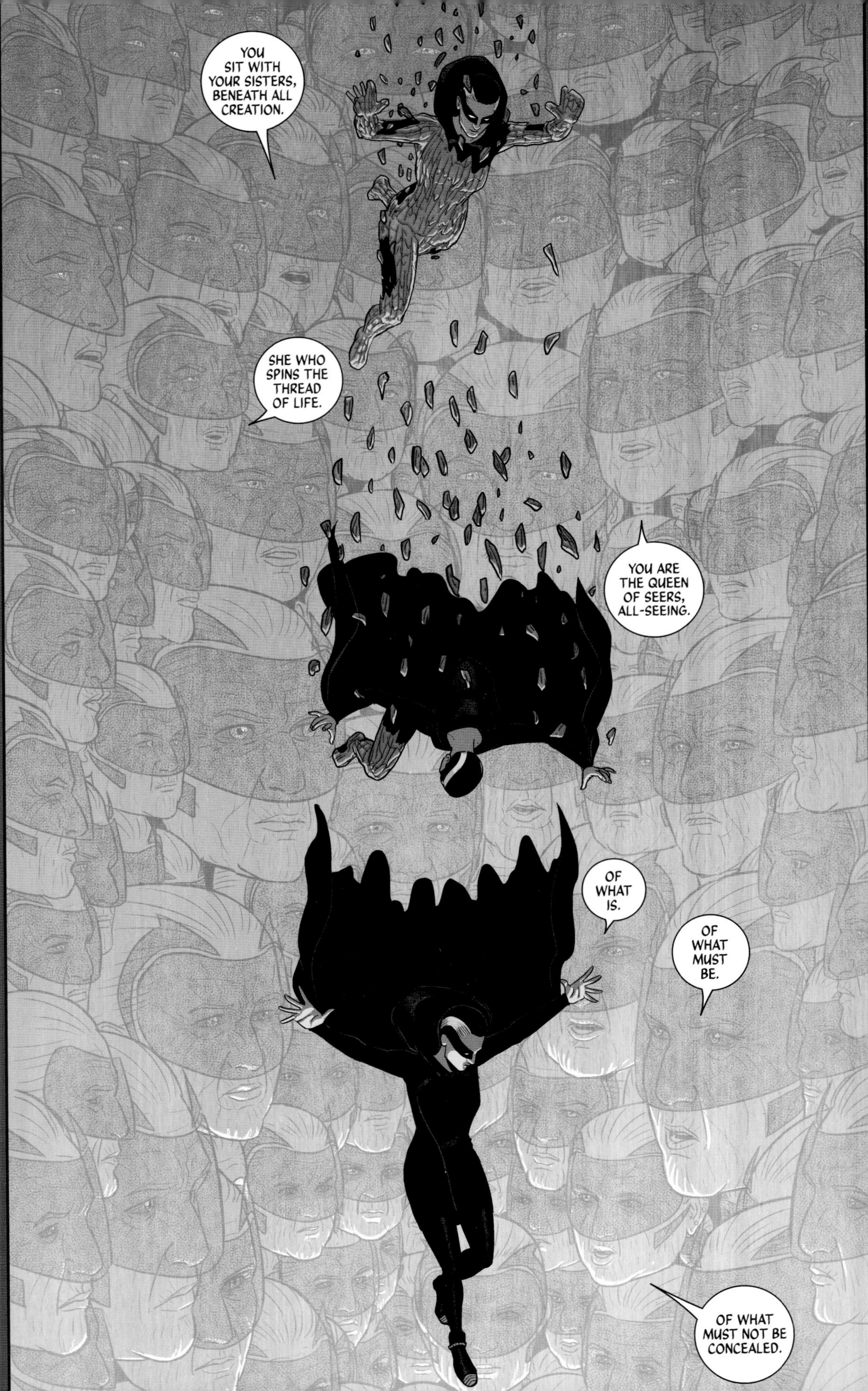
YOU SIT WITH YOUR SISTERS, BENEATH ALL CREATION.
SHE WHO SPINS THE THREAD OF LIFE.
YOU ARE THE QUEEN OF SEERS, ALL-SEEING.
OF WHAT IS.
OF WHAT MUST BE.
OF WHAT MUST NOT BE CONCEALED.

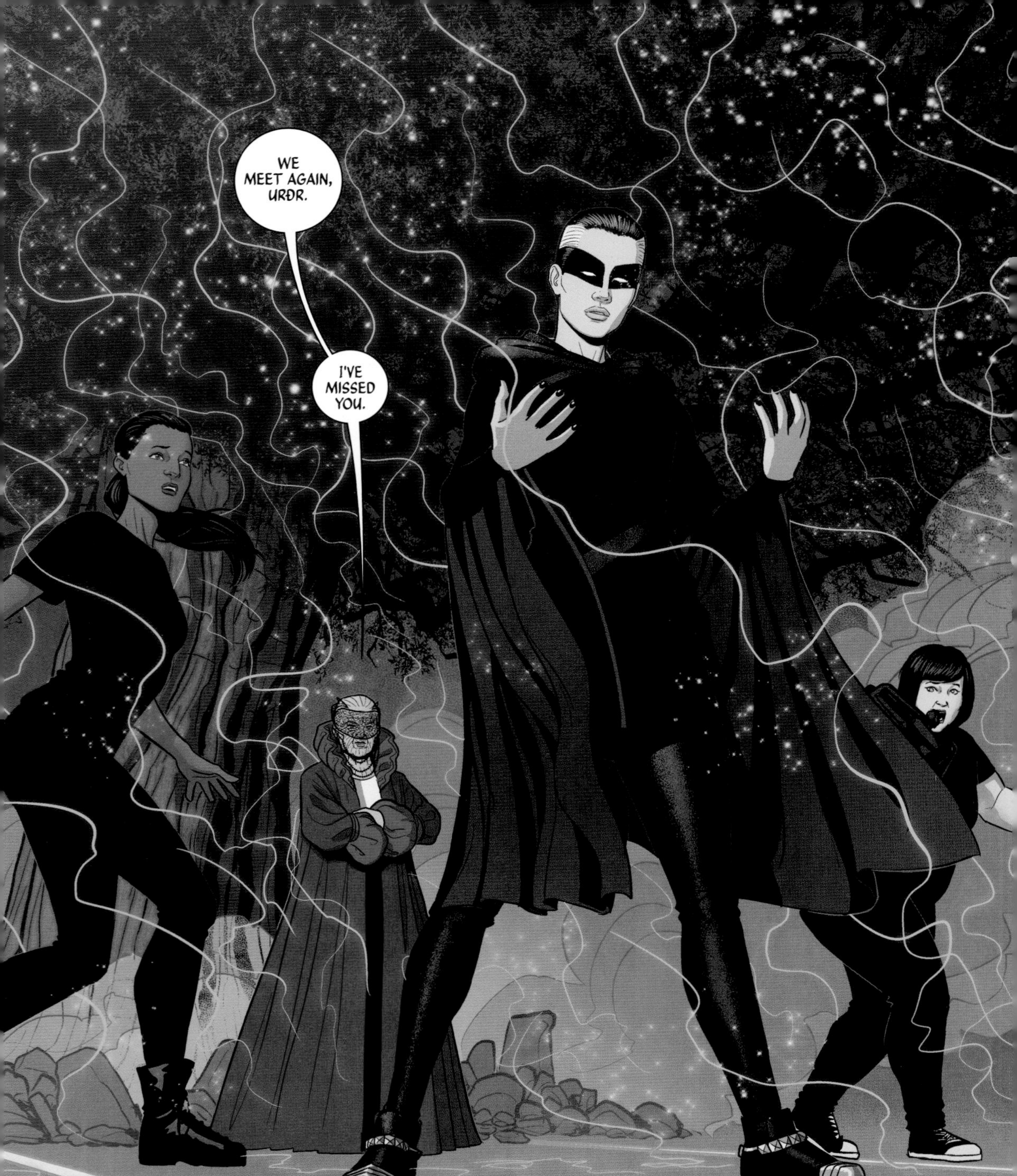
WE MEET AGAIN, URÐR.
I'VE MISSED YOU.

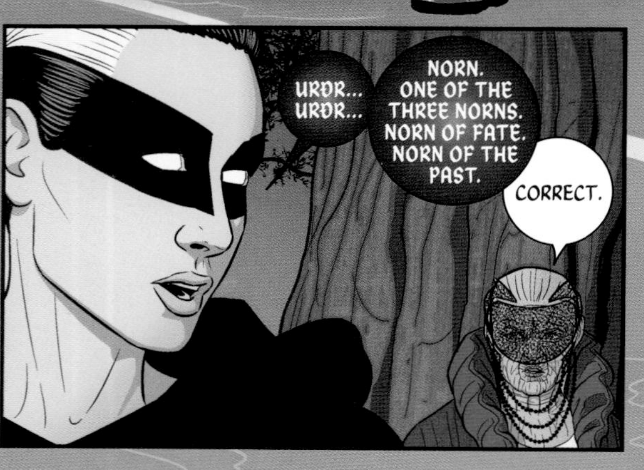
URÐR... URÐR...
NORN. ONE OF THE THREE NORNS. NORN OF FATE. NORN OF THE PAST.
CORRECT.

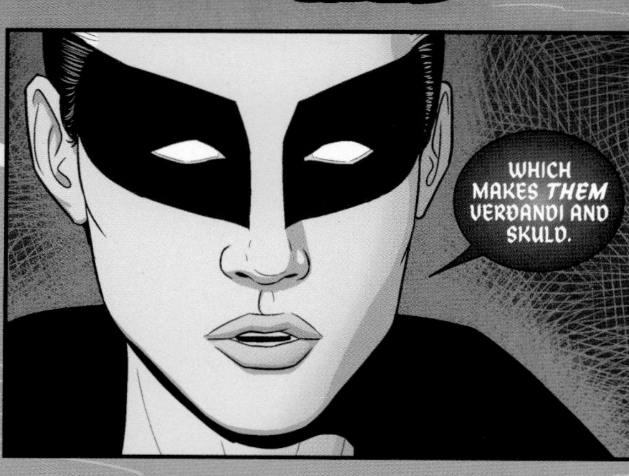
WHICH MAKES THEM VERÐANDI AND SKULD.

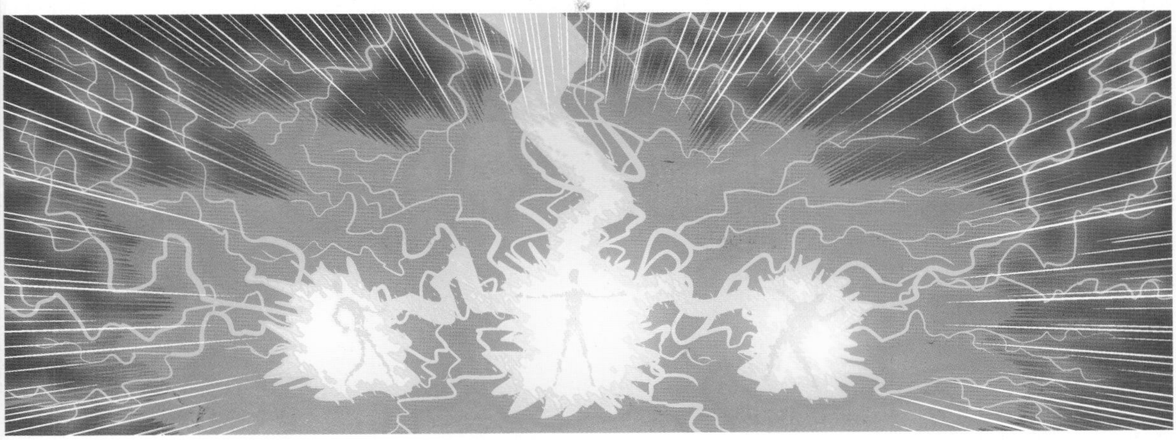

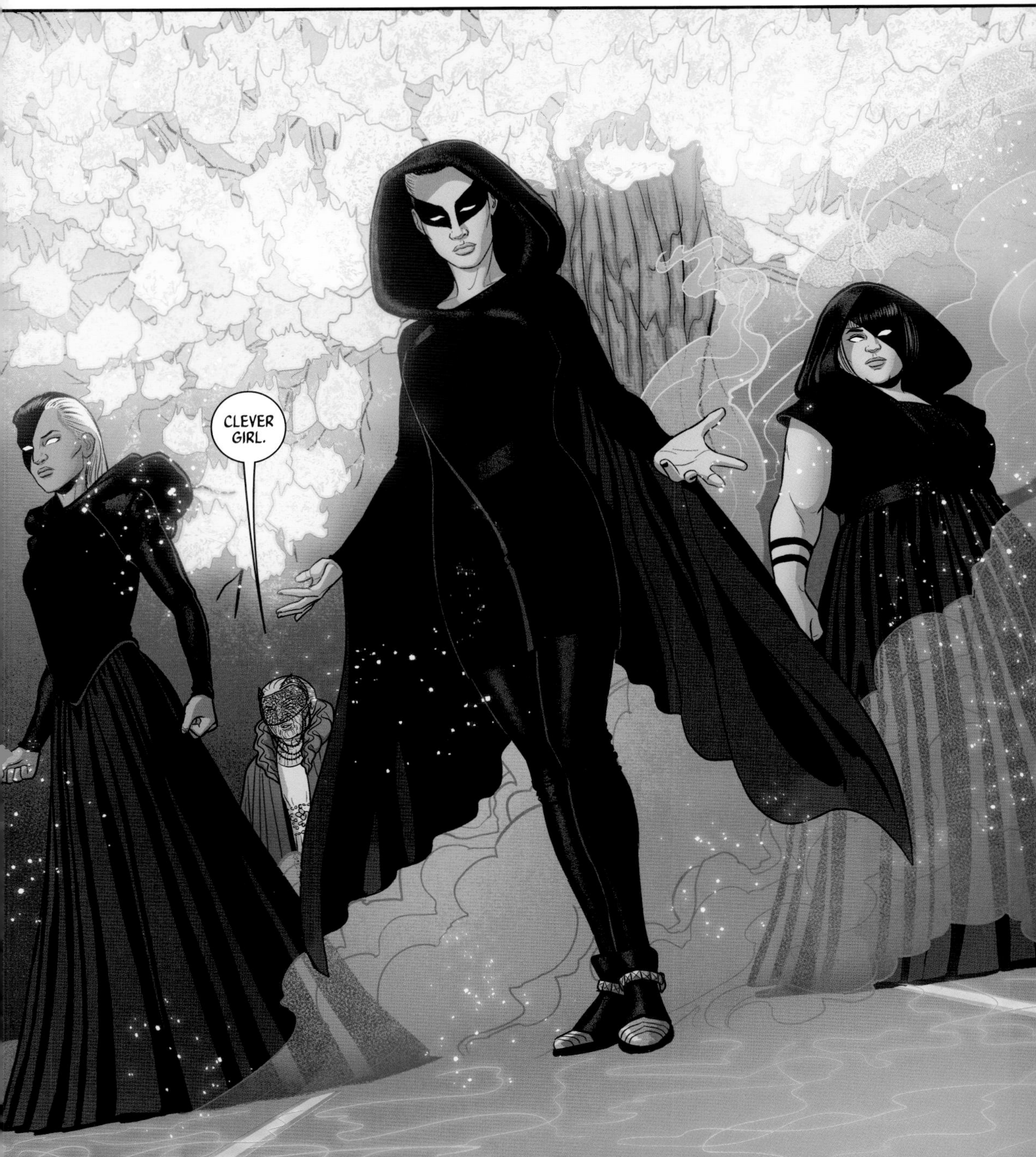
CLEVER GIRL.

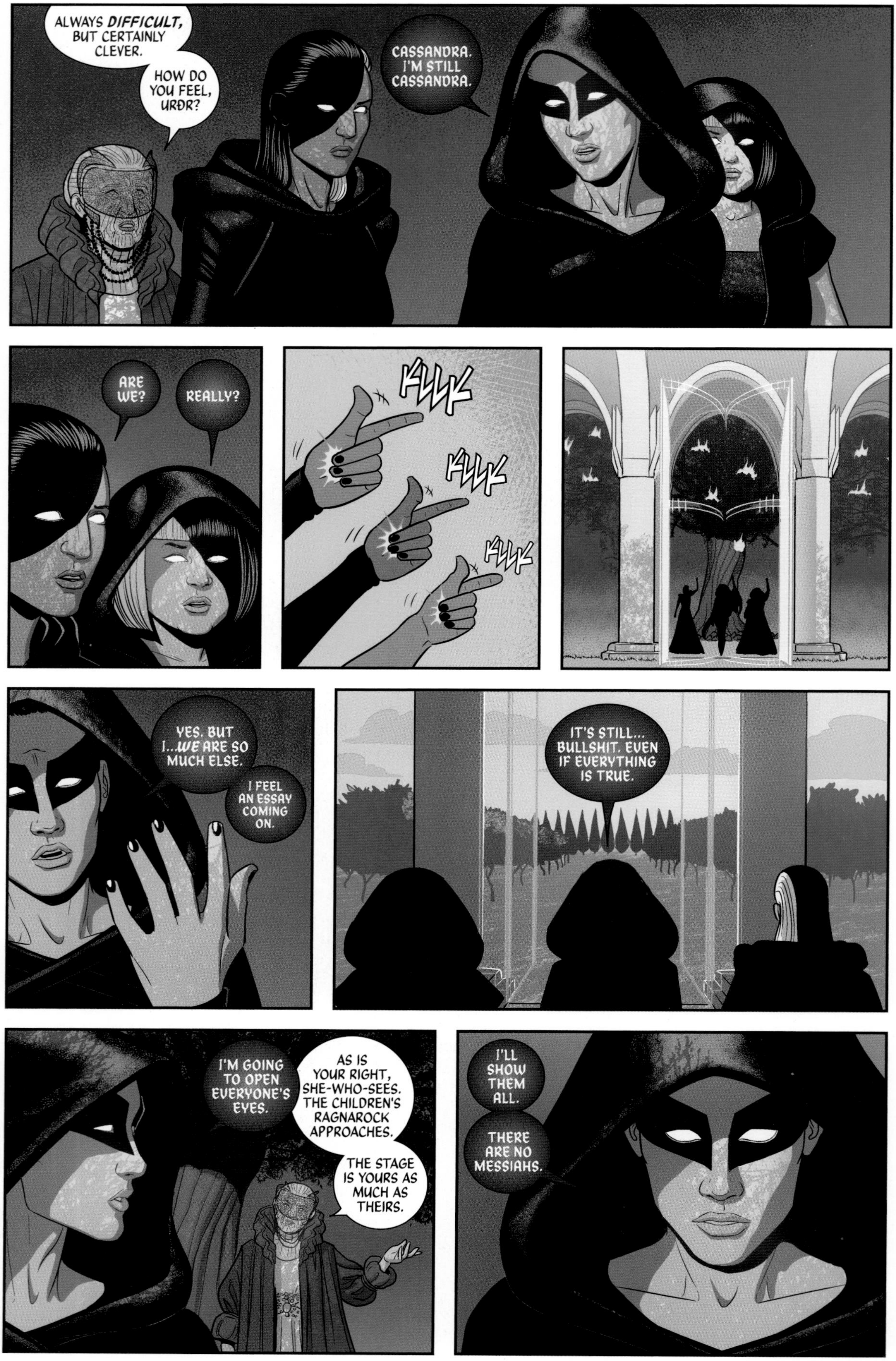
ALWAYS DIFFICULT, BUT CERTAINLY CLEVER.
HOW DO YOU FEEL, URÐR?
CASSANDRA. I'M STILL CASSANDRA.
ARE WE?
REALLY?
KLLK
KLLK
KLLK
YES. BUT I...WE ARE SO MUCH ELSE.
I FEEL AN ESSAY COMING ON.
IT'S STILL... BULLSHIT. EVEN IF EVERYTHING IS TRUE.
I'M GOING TO OPEN EVERYONE'S EYES.
AS IS YOUR RIGHT, SHE-WHO-SEES. THE CHILDREN'S RAGNAROCK APPROACHES.
THE STAGE IS YOURS AS MUCH AS THEIRS.
I'LL SHOW THEM ALL.
THERE ARE NO MESSIAHS.

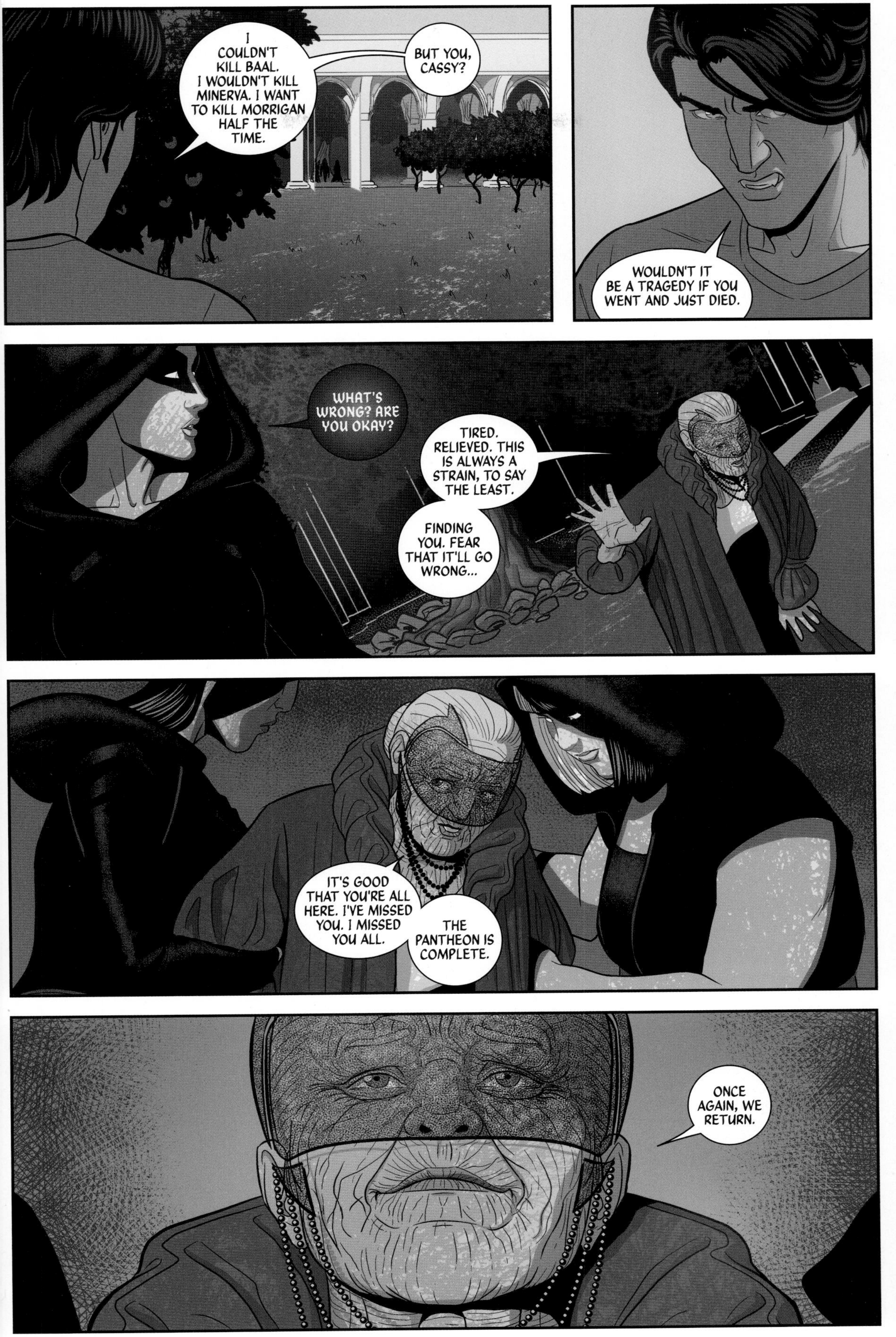
I COULDN'T KILL BAAL. I WOULDN'T KILL MINERVA. I WANT TO KILL MORRIGAN HALF THE TIME.
BUT YOU, CASSY?
WOULDN'T IT BE A TRAGEDY IF YOU WENT AND JUST DIED.
WHAT'S WRONG? ARE YOU OKAY?
TIRED. RELIEVED. THIS IS ALWAYS A STRAIN, TO SAY THE LEAST.
FINDING YOU. FEAR THAT IT'LL GO WRONG...
IT'S GOOD THAT YOU'RE ALL HERE. I'VE MISSED YOU. I MISSED YOU ALL.
THE PANTHEON IS COMPLETE.
ONCE AGAIN, WE RETURN.

THE NORNS

28 JUNE 2014

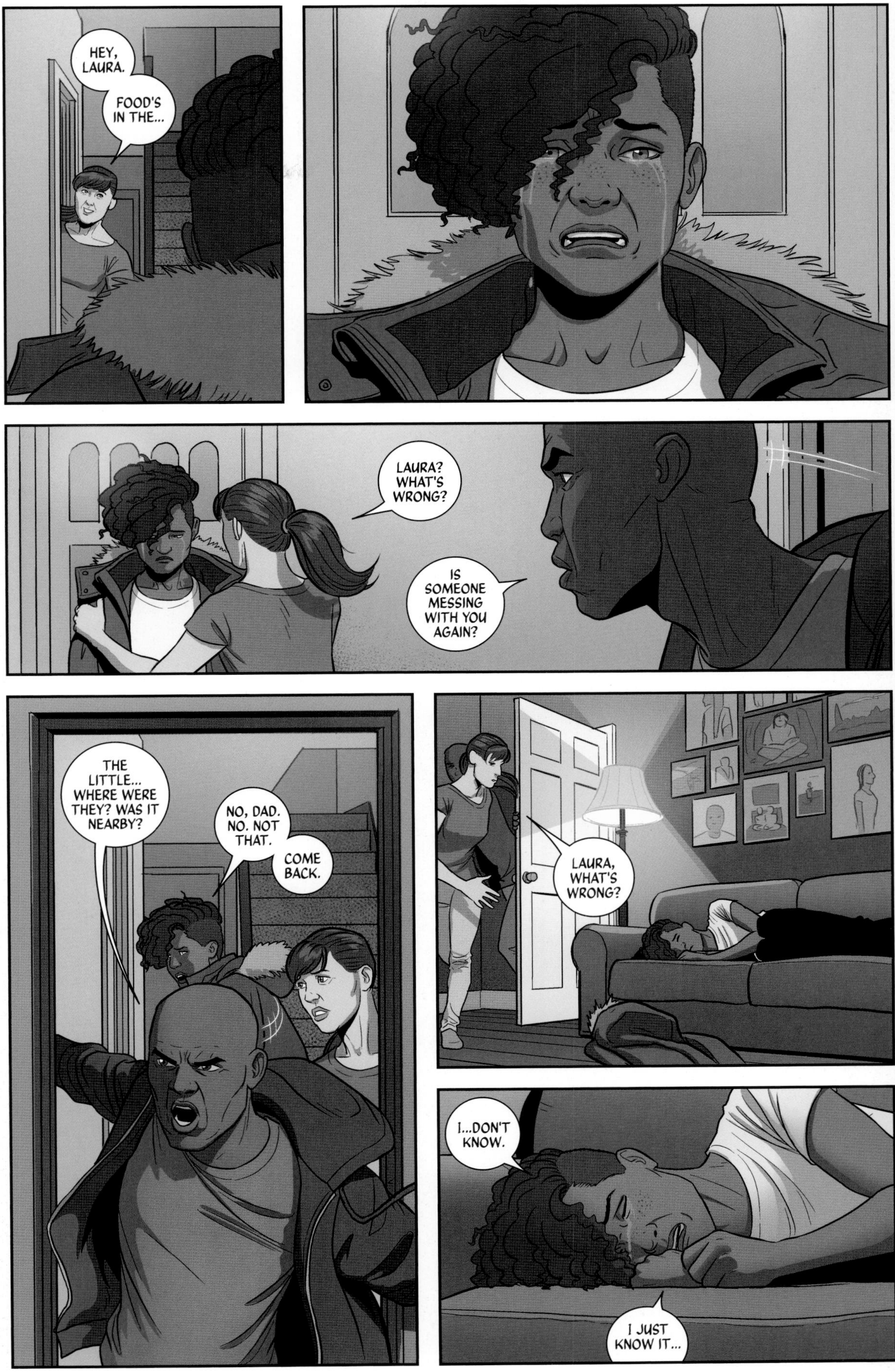
HEY, LAURA.
FOOD'S IN THE...
LAURA? WHAT'S WRONG?
IS SOMEONE MESSING WITH YOU AGAIN?
THE LITTLE... WHERE WERE THEY? WAS IT NEARBY?
NO, DAD. NO. NOT THAT.
COME BACK.
LAURA, WHAT'S WRONG?
I...DON'T KNOW.
I JUST KNOW IT...

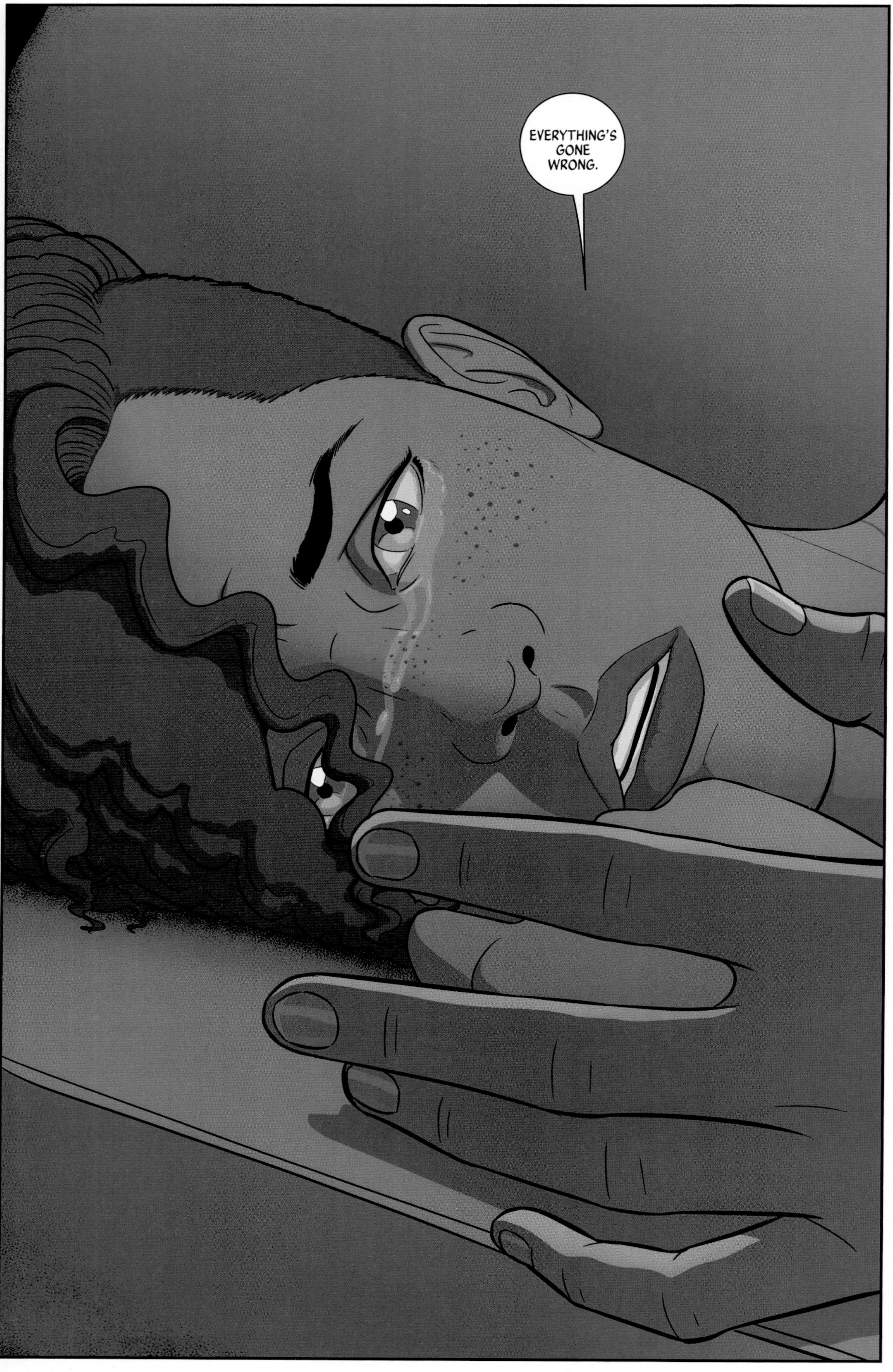
EVERYTHING'S GONE WRONG.

YOU ARE
CORDIALLY INVITED
TO THE DEATH OF
YOUR DREAMS

28 JUNE 2014

10

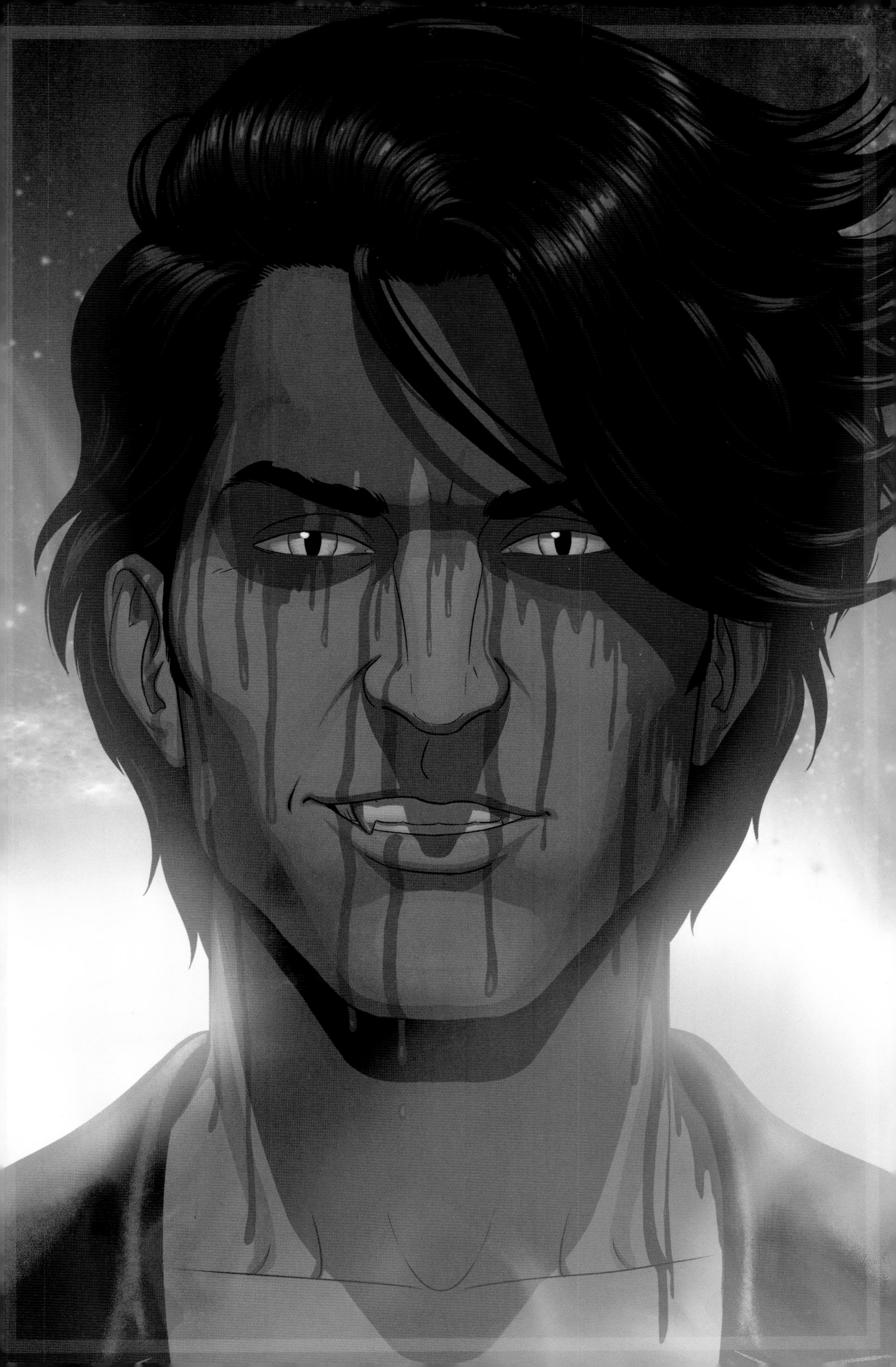

THE
WICKED
+
ƎNIVIᗡ
ƎHT

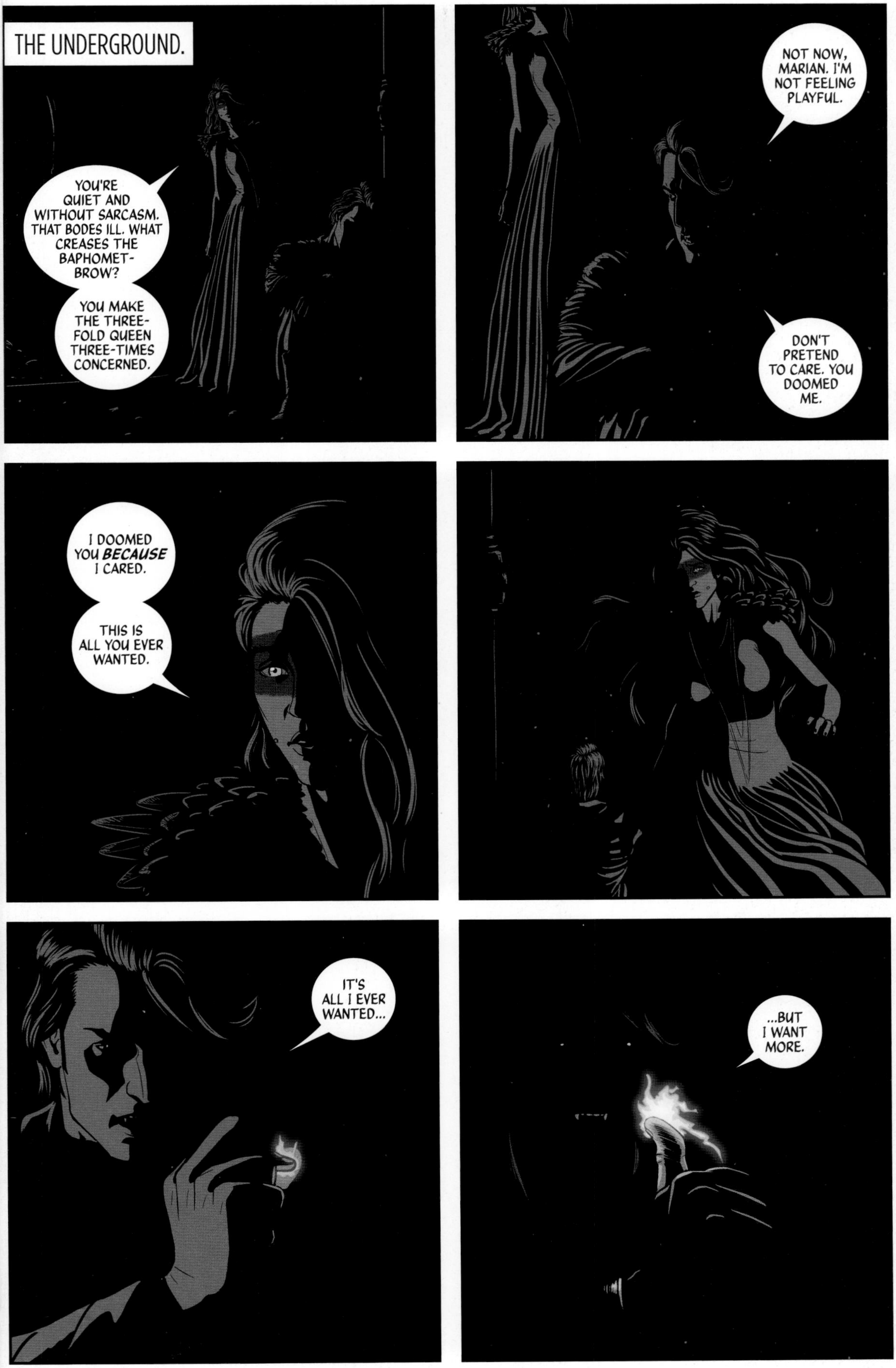

THE UNDERGROUND.
YOU'RE QUIET AND WITHOUT SARCASM. THAT BODES ILL. WHAT CREASES THE BAPHOMET-BROW?
YOU MAKE THE THREE-FOLD QUEEN THREE-TIMES CONCERNED.
NOT NOW, MARIAN. I'M NOT FEELING PLAYFUL.
DON'T PRETEND TO CARE. YOU DOOMED ME.
I DOOMED YOU *BECAUSE* I CARED.
THIS IS ALL YOU EVER WANTED.
IT'S ALL I EVER WANTED...
...BUT I WANT MORE.

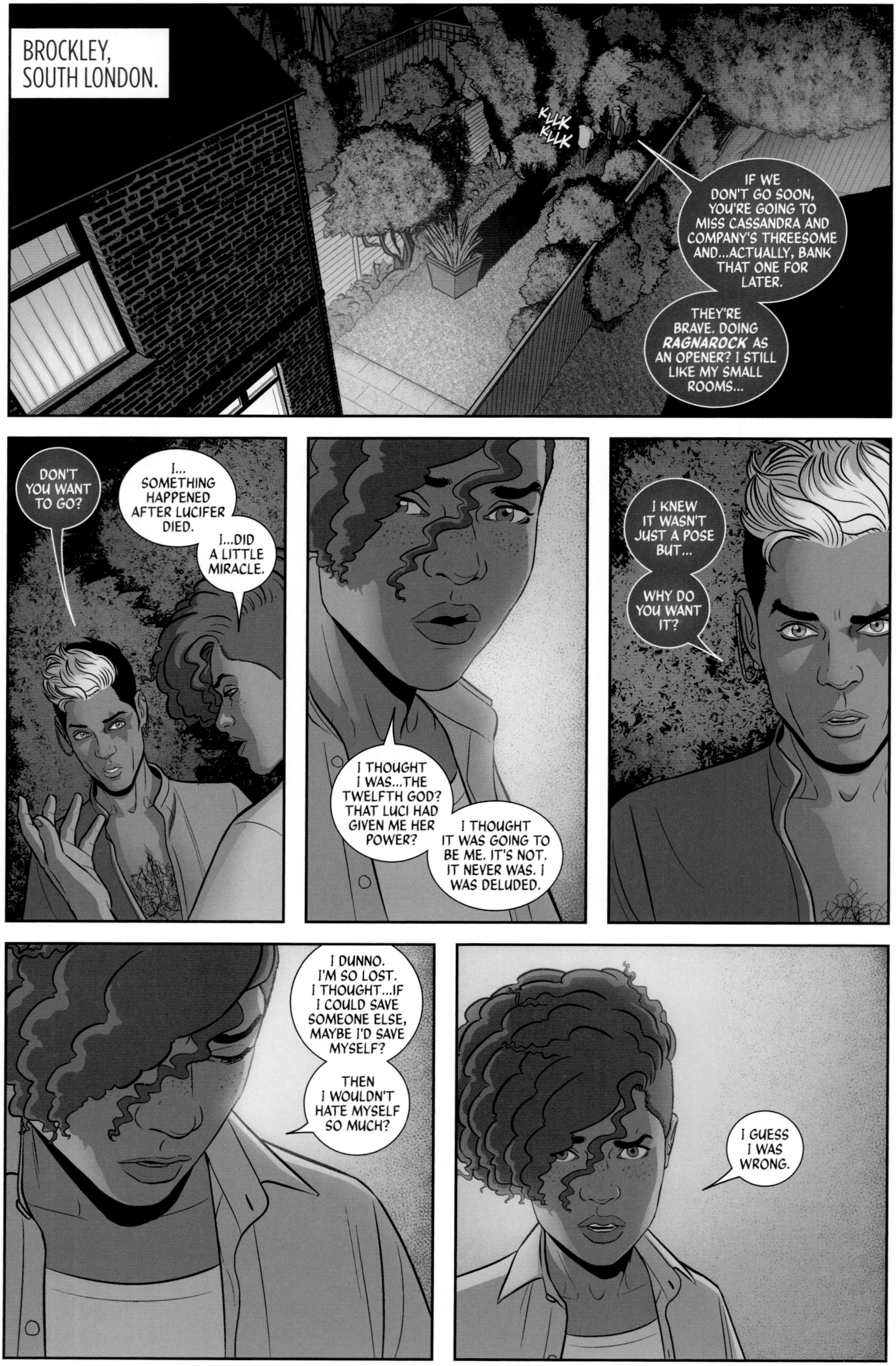
BROCKLEY, SOUTH LONDON.
KLLK KLLK
IF WE DON'T GO SOON, YOU'RE GOING TO MISS CASSANDRA AND COMPANY'S THREESOME AND...ACTUALLY, BANK THAT ONE FOR LATER.
THEY'RE BRAVE. DOING RAGNAROCK AS AN OPENER? I STILL LIKE MY SMALL ROOMS...
DON'T YOU WANT TO GO?
I... SOMETHING HAPPENED AFTER LUCIFER DIED.
I...DID A LITTLE MIRACLE.
I THOUGHT I WAS...THE TWELFTH GOD? THAT LUCI HAD GIVEN ME HER POWER?
I THOUGHT IT WAS GOING TO BE ME. IT'S NOT. IT NEVER WAS. I WAS DELUDED.
I KNEW IT WASN'T JUST A POSE BUT...
WHY DO YOU WANT IT?
I DUNNO. I'M SO LOST. I THOUGHT...IF I COULD SAVE SOMEONE ELSE, MAYBE I'D SAVE MYSELF?
THEN I WOULDN'T HATE MYSELF SO MUCH?
I GUESS I WAS WRONG.

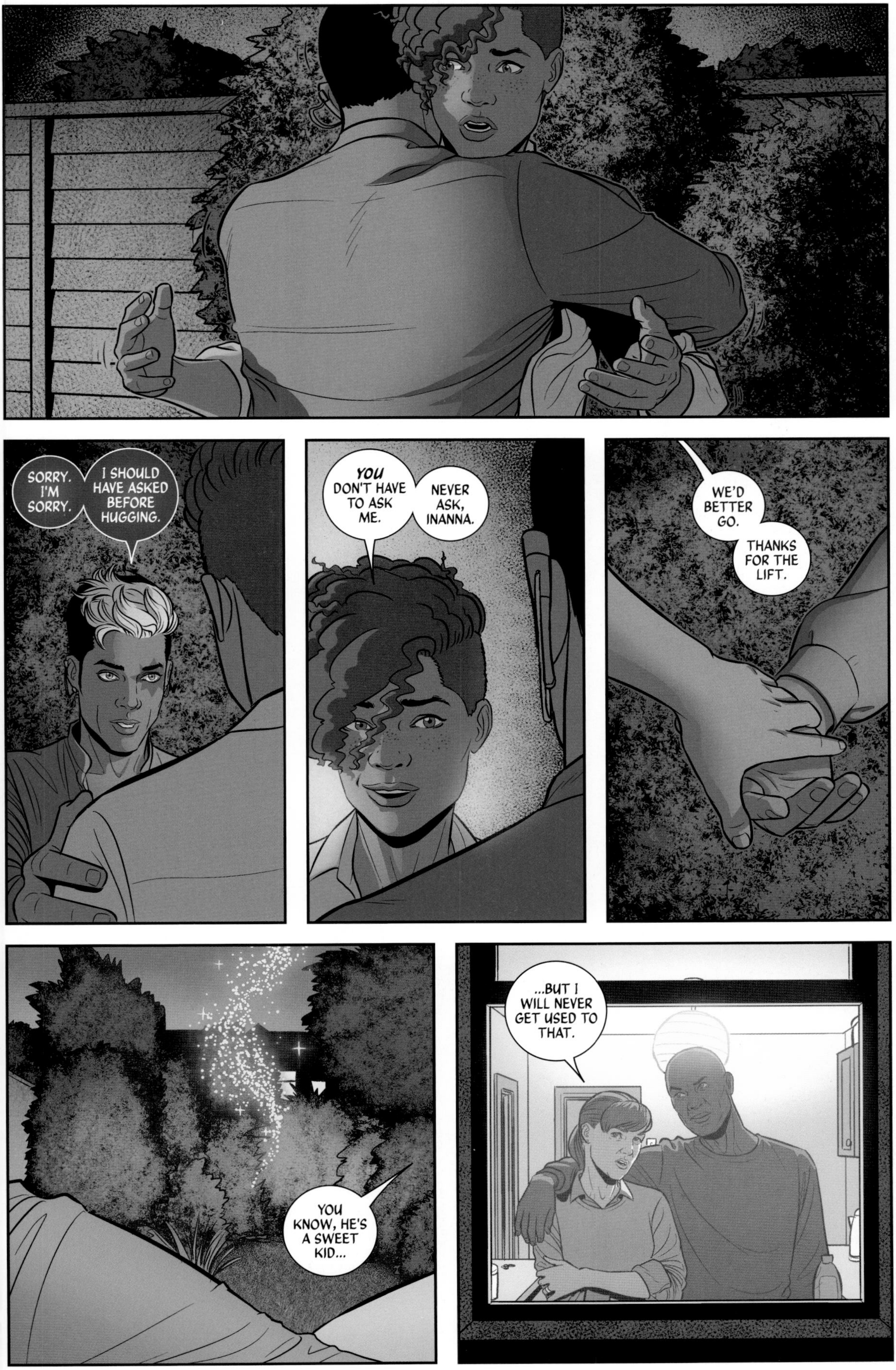
SORRY. I'M SORRY.
I SHOULD HAVE ASKED BEFORE HUGGING.
YOU DON'T HAVE TO ASK ME.
NEVER ASK, INANNA.
WE'D BETTER GO.
THANKS FOR THE LIFT.
YOU KNOW, HE'S A SWEET KID...
...BUT I WILL NEVER GET USED TO THAT.

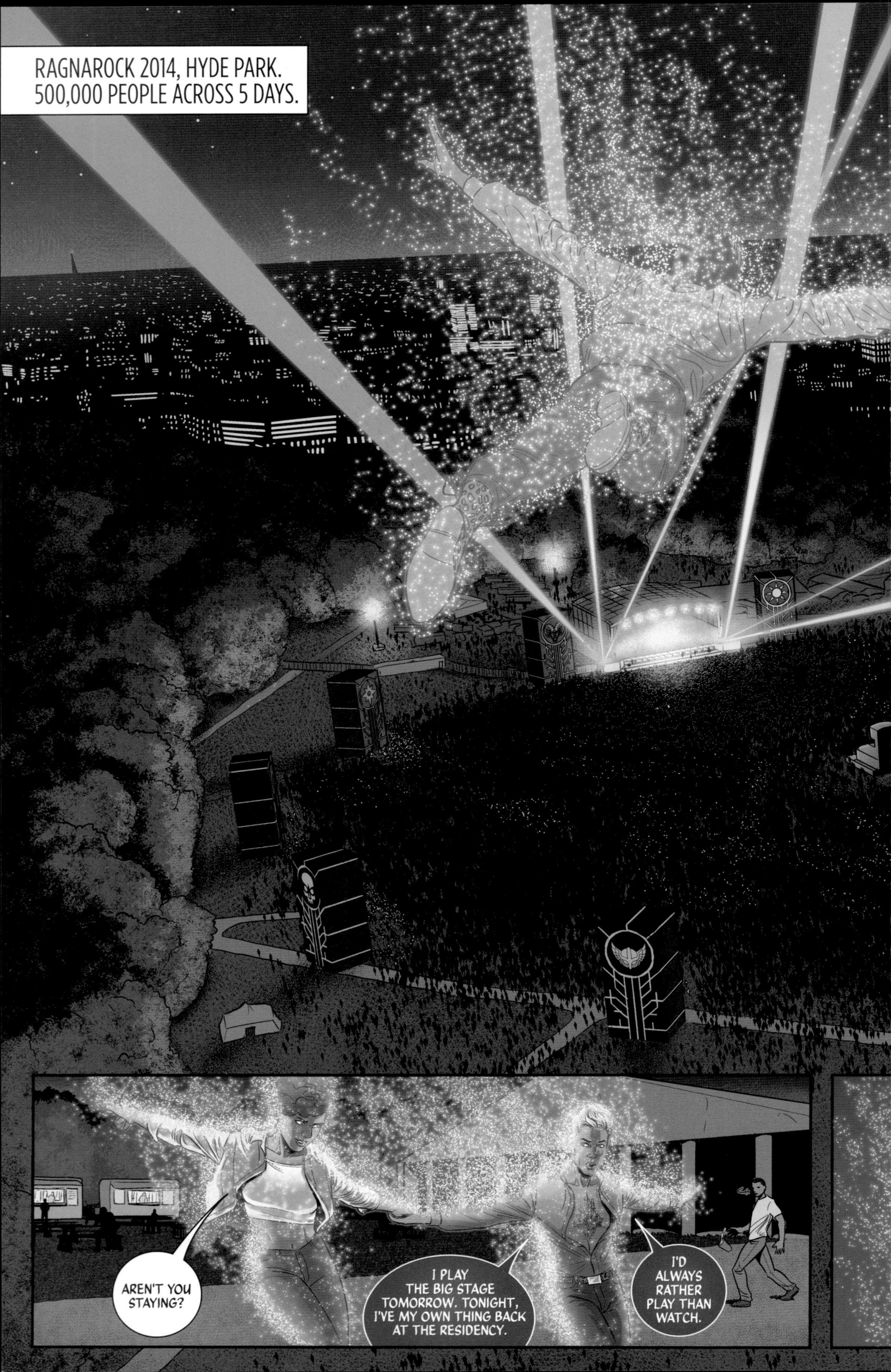
RAGNAROCK 2014, HYDE PARK.
500,000 PEOPLE ACROSS 5 DAYS.
AREN'T YOU STAYING?
I PLAY THE BIG STAGE TOMORROW. TONIGHT, I'VE MY OWN THING BACK AT THE RESIDENCY.
I'D ALWAYS RATHER PLAY THAN WATCH.

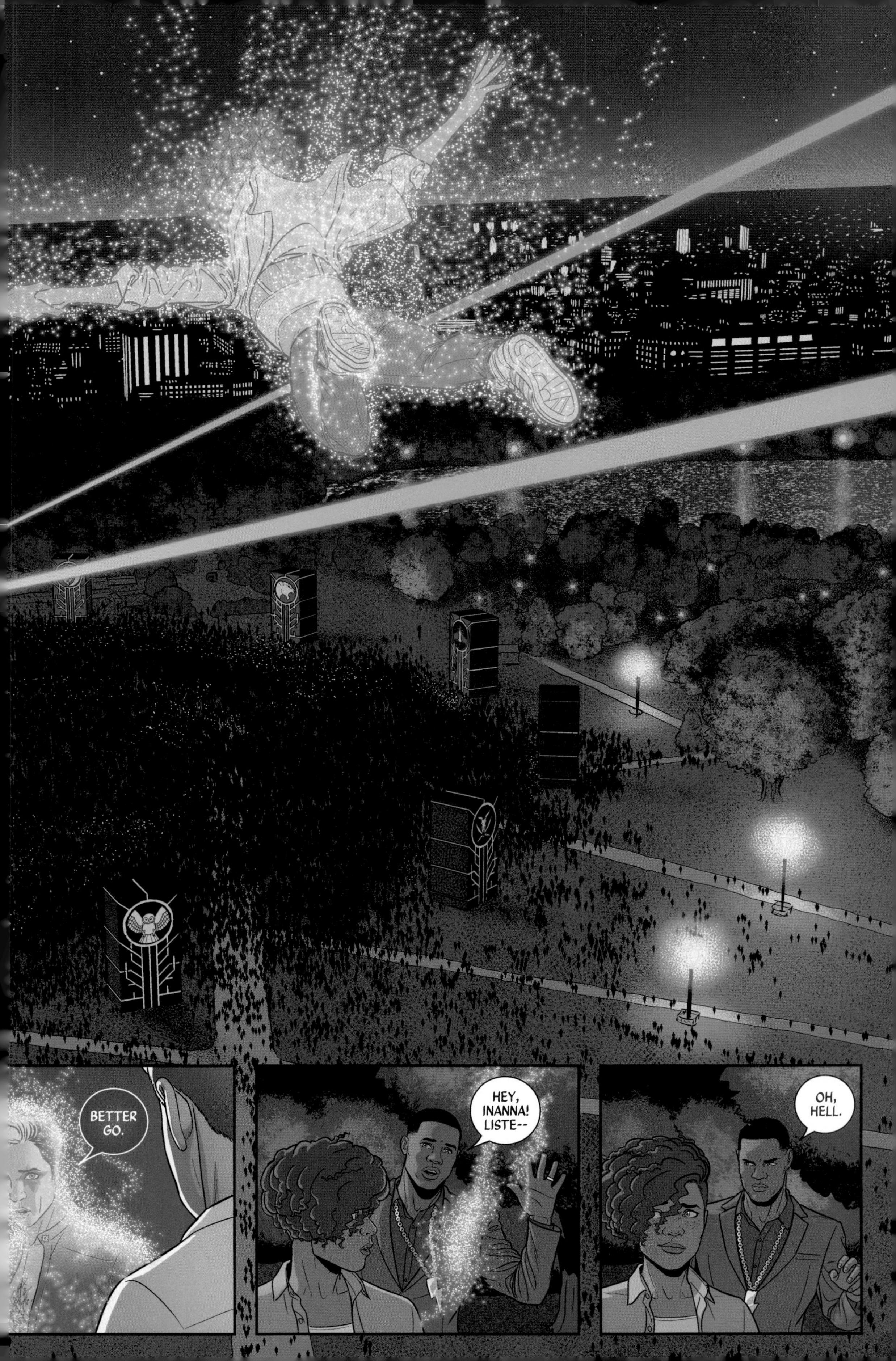
BETTER GO.
HEY, INANNA! LISTE--
OH, HELL.

I HAVEN'T TOLD HIM ANYTHING.

HE WOULDN'T CARE ABOUT THAT. IT'S JUST ME. YOU COULD SAY YOU WERE MARRIED WITH TWELVE LITTLE CHERUB KIDS AND HE WOULDN'T BE THROWN.

I WISH HE WAS.

BUT I DIDN'T WANT TO TALK PERSONAL. IT'S *BUSINESS.*

GODDESS-IN-TRIPLICATE HAS FOUND OUT WHO THE GUYS WITH CROSSES AND CROSS-HAIRS WERE.

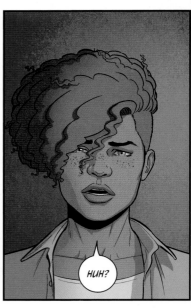

HUH?

ER... CASSANDRA WORKED OUT WHO TRIED TO OFF LUCI.

WHAT?!?

NOT HER STORY

2 AUGUST 2014

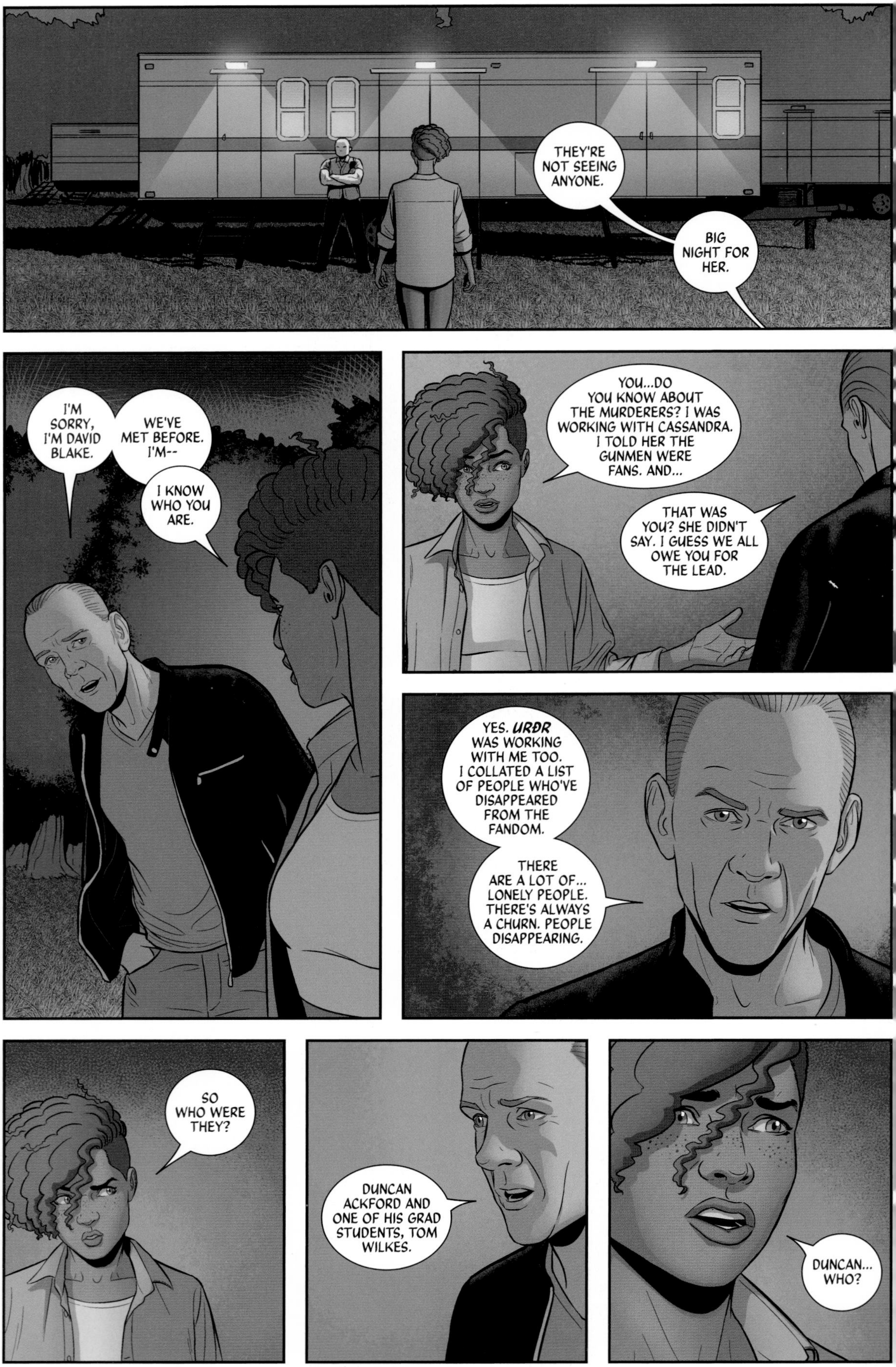
THEY'RE NOT SEEING ANYONE.
BIG NIGHT FOR HER.
I'M SORRY, I'M DAVID BLAKE.
WE'VE MET BEFORE. I'M--
I KNOW WHO YOU ARE.
YOU...DO YOU KNOW ABOUT THE MURDERERS? I WAS WORKING WITH CASSANDRA. I TOLD HER THE GUNMEN WERE FANS. AND...
THAT WAS YOU? SHE DIDN'T SAY. I GUESS WE ALL OWE YOU FOR THE LEAD.
YES. URÐR WAS WORKING WITH ME TOO. I COLLATED A LIST OF PEOPLE WHO'VE DISAPPEARED FROM THE FANDOM.
THERE ARE A LOT OF... LONELY PEOPLE. THERE'S ALWAYS A CHURN. PEOPLE DISAPPEARING.
SO WHO WERE THEY?
DUNCAN ACKFORD AND ONE OF HIS GRAD STUDENTS, TOM WILKES.
DUNCAN... WHO?

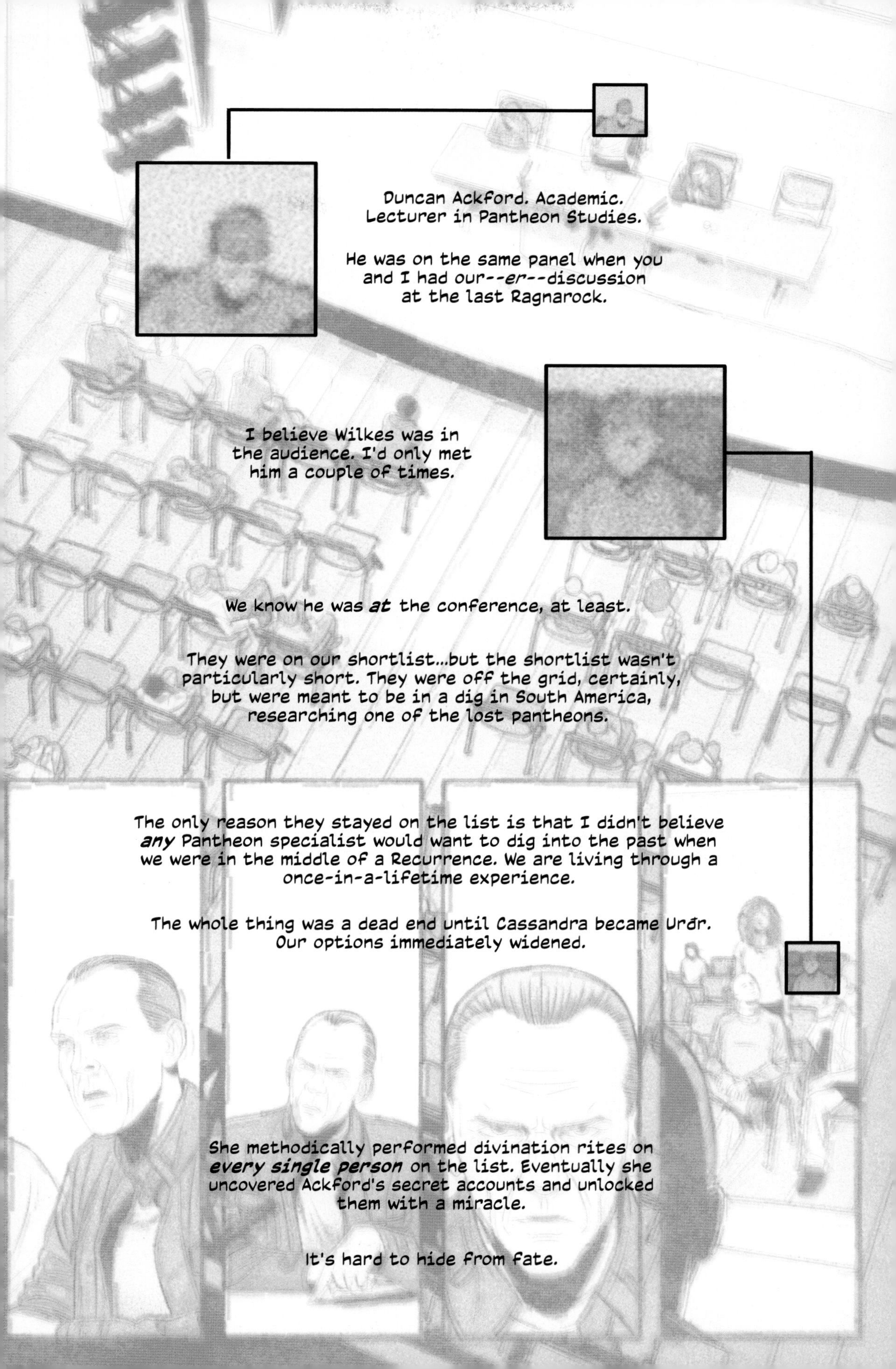
Duncan Ackford. Academic. Lecturer in Pantheon Studies.
He was on the same panel when you and I had our--*er*--discussion at the last Ragnarock.
I believe Wilkes was in the audience. I'd only met him a couple of times.
We know he was ***at*** the conference, at least.
They were on our shortlist...but the shortlist wasn't particularly short. They were off the grid, certainly, but were meant to be in a dig in South America, researching one of the lost pantheons.
The only reason they stayed on the list is that I didn't believe ***any*** Pantheon specialist would want to dig into the past when we were in the middle of a Recurrence. We are living through a once-in-a-lifetime experience.
The whole thing was a dead end until Cassandra became Urðr. Our options immediately widened.
She methodically performed divination rites on ***every single person*** on the list. Eventually she uncovered Ackford's secret accounts and unlocked them with a miracle.
It's hard to hide from fate.

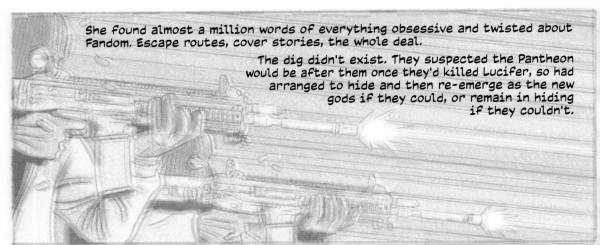

She found almost a million words of everything obsessive and twisted about Fandom. Escape routes, cover stories, the whole deal.

The dig didn't exist. They suspected the Pantheon would be after them once they'd killed Lucifer, so had arranged to hide and then re-emerge as the new gods if they could, or remain in hiding if they couldn't.

Very much the Prometheus Myth cult. Kill a god, get their powers. A ludicrous fantasy.

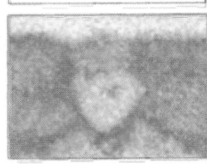

Ackford was lying to Wilkes too, telling him the powers could be shared. He didn't believe that for a second. Ackford had plans to get rid of him if Wilkes caused any problems...

The documents are just disturbing. The researcher part of me knows that intensive study will lead to a lot of interesting work, but when you find your own papers mixed in with theirs, it becomes a little too personal.

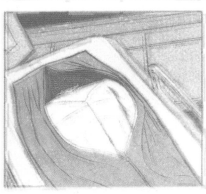

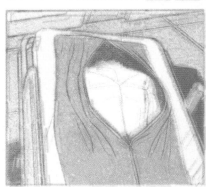

At least we know now. The families can get some peace.

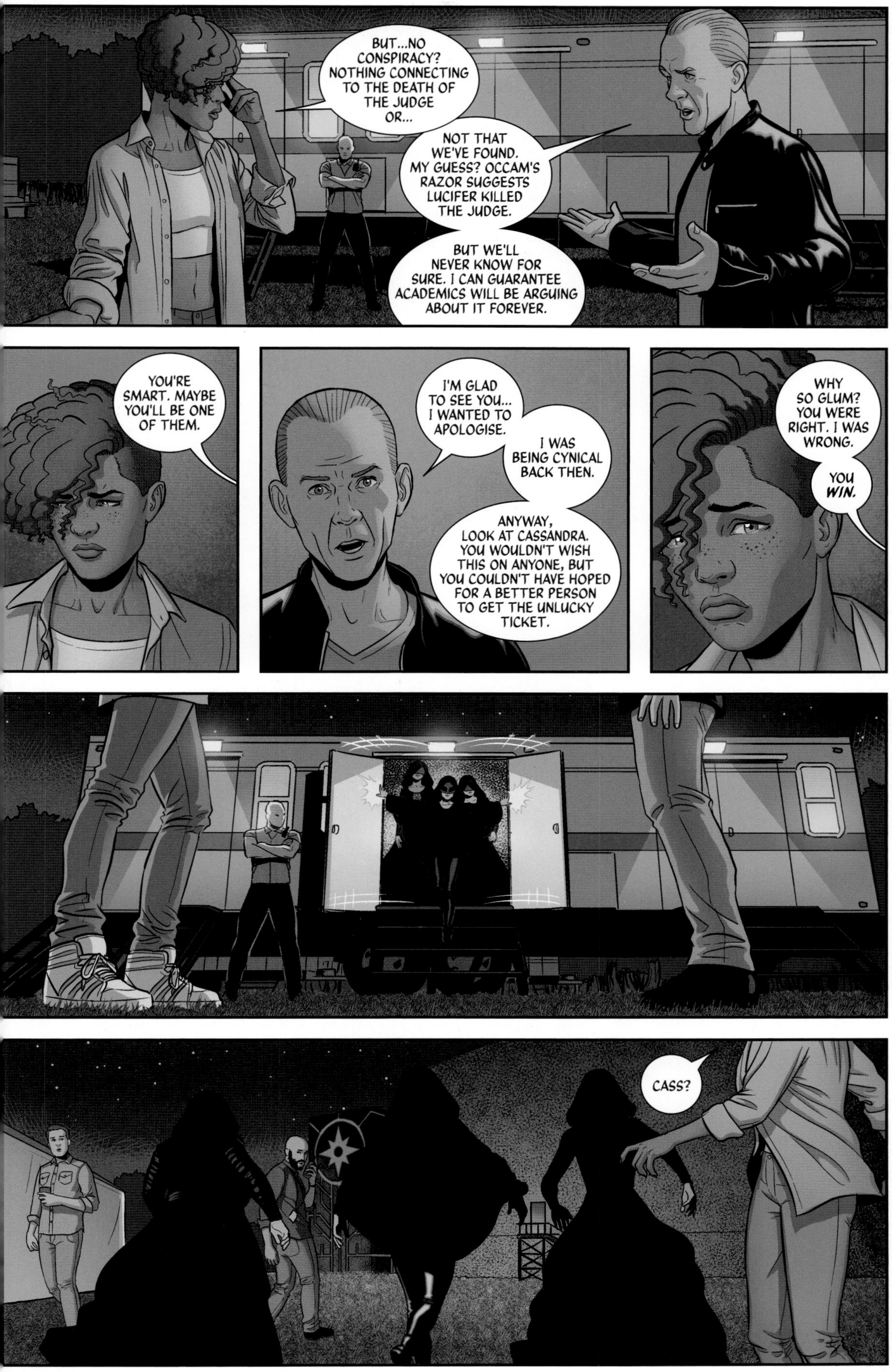
BUT...NO CONSPIRACY? NOTHING CONNECTING TO THE DEATH OF THE JUDGE OR...
NOT THAT WE'VE FOUND. MY GUESS? OCCAM'S RAZOR SUGGESTS LUCIFER KILLED THE JUDGE.
BUT WE'LL NEVER KNOW FOR SURE. I CAN GUARANTEE ACADEMICS WILL BE ARGUING ABOUT IT FOREVER.
YOU'RE SMART. MAYBE YOU'LL BE ONE OF THEM.
I'M GLAD TO SEE YOU... I WANTED TO APOLOGISE.
I WAS BEING CYNICAL BACK THEN.
ANYWAY, LOOK AT CASSANDRA. YOU WOULDN'T WISH THIS ON ANYONE, BUT YOU COULDN'T HAVE HOPED FOR A BETTER PERSON TO GET THE UNLUCKY TICKET.
WHY SO GLUM? YOU WERE RIGHT. I WAS WRONG.
YOU *WIN.*
CASS?

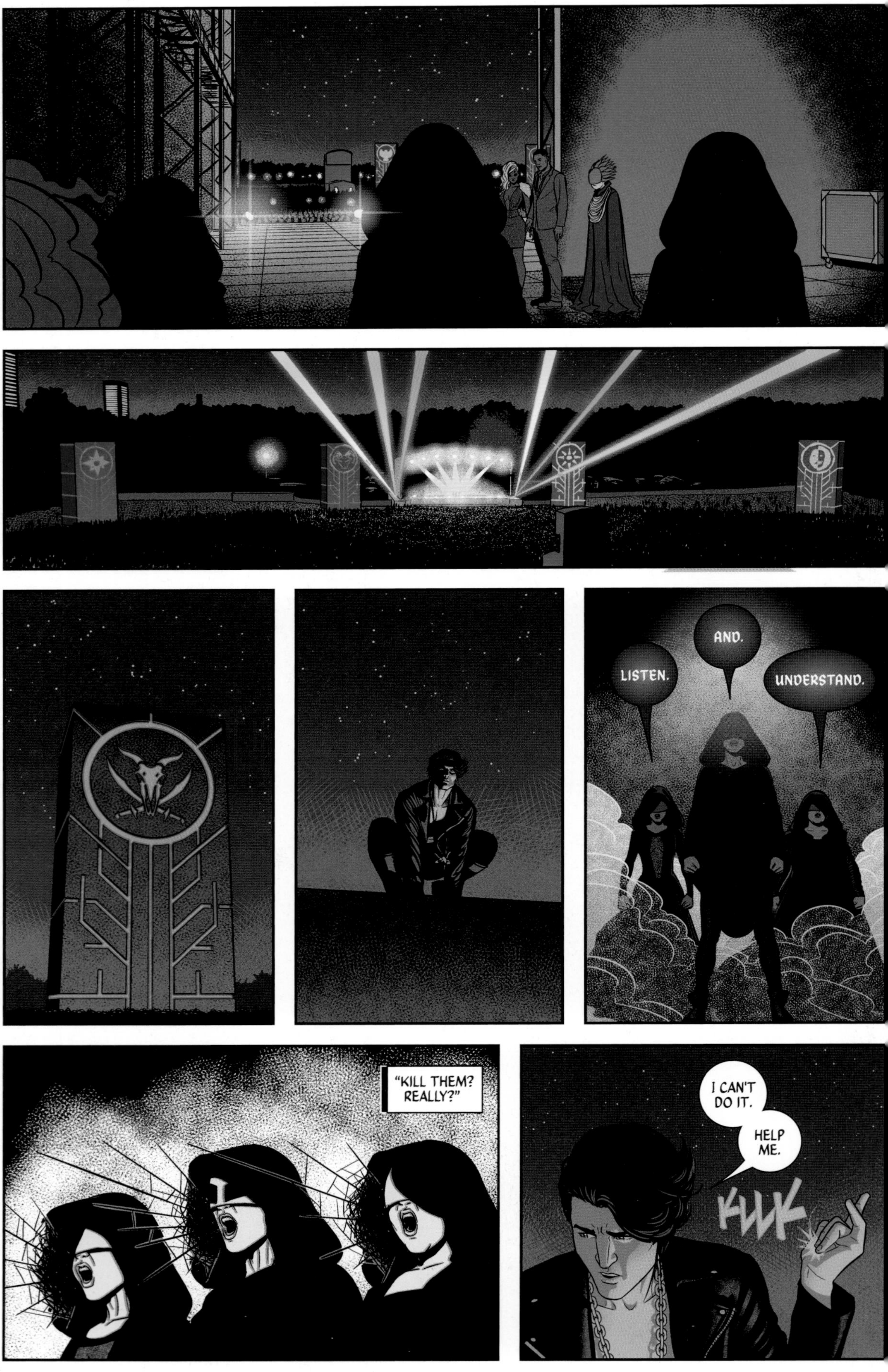
LISTEN.
AND.
UNDERSTAND.
"KILL THEM? REALLY?"
I CAN'T DO IT.
HELP ME.
KLIK

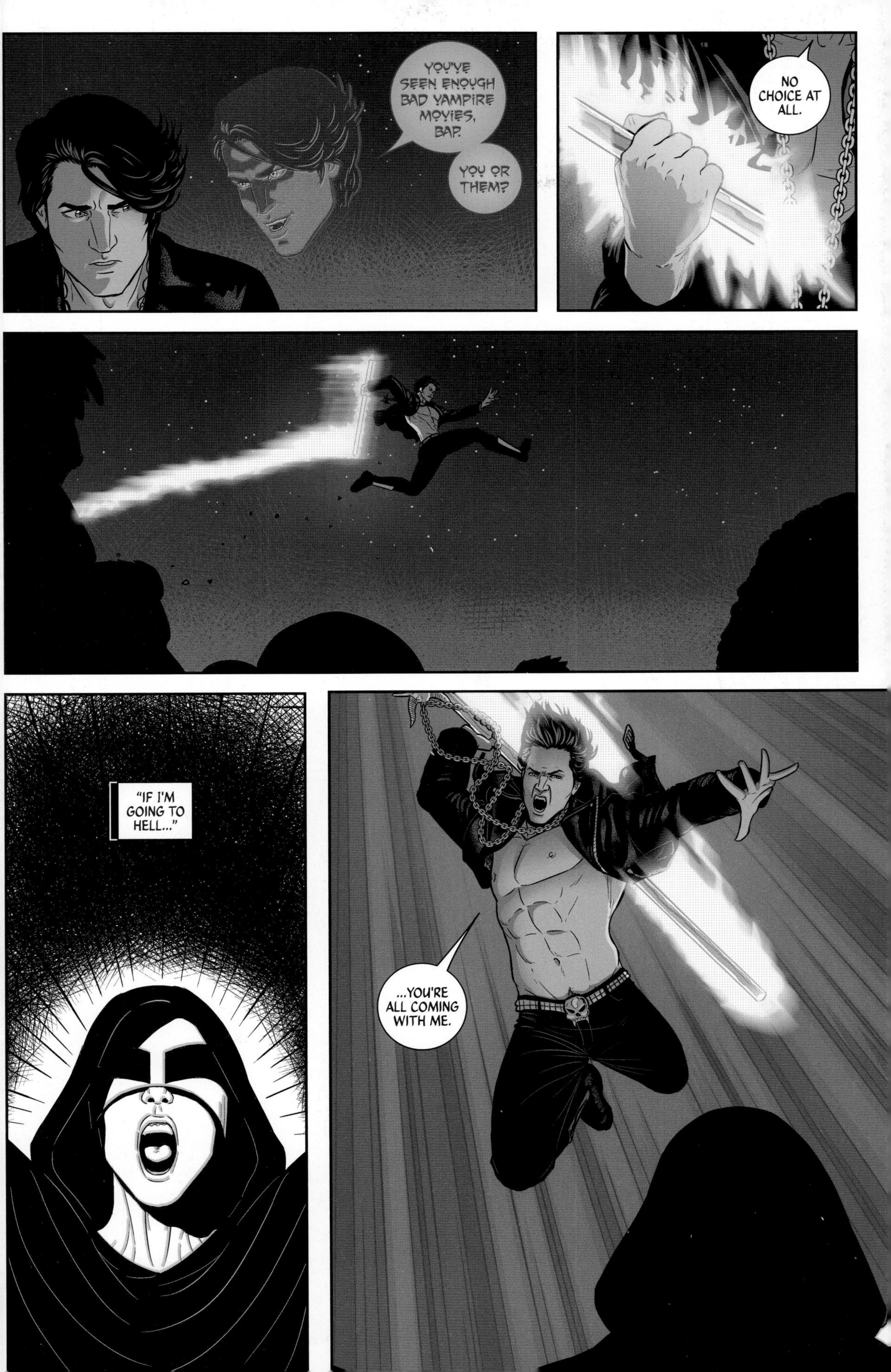
YOU'VE SEEN ENOUGH BAD VAMPIRE MOVIES, BAP.
YOU OR THEM?
NO CHOICE AT ALL.
"IF I'M GOING TO HELL..."
...YOU'RE ALL COMING WITH ME.

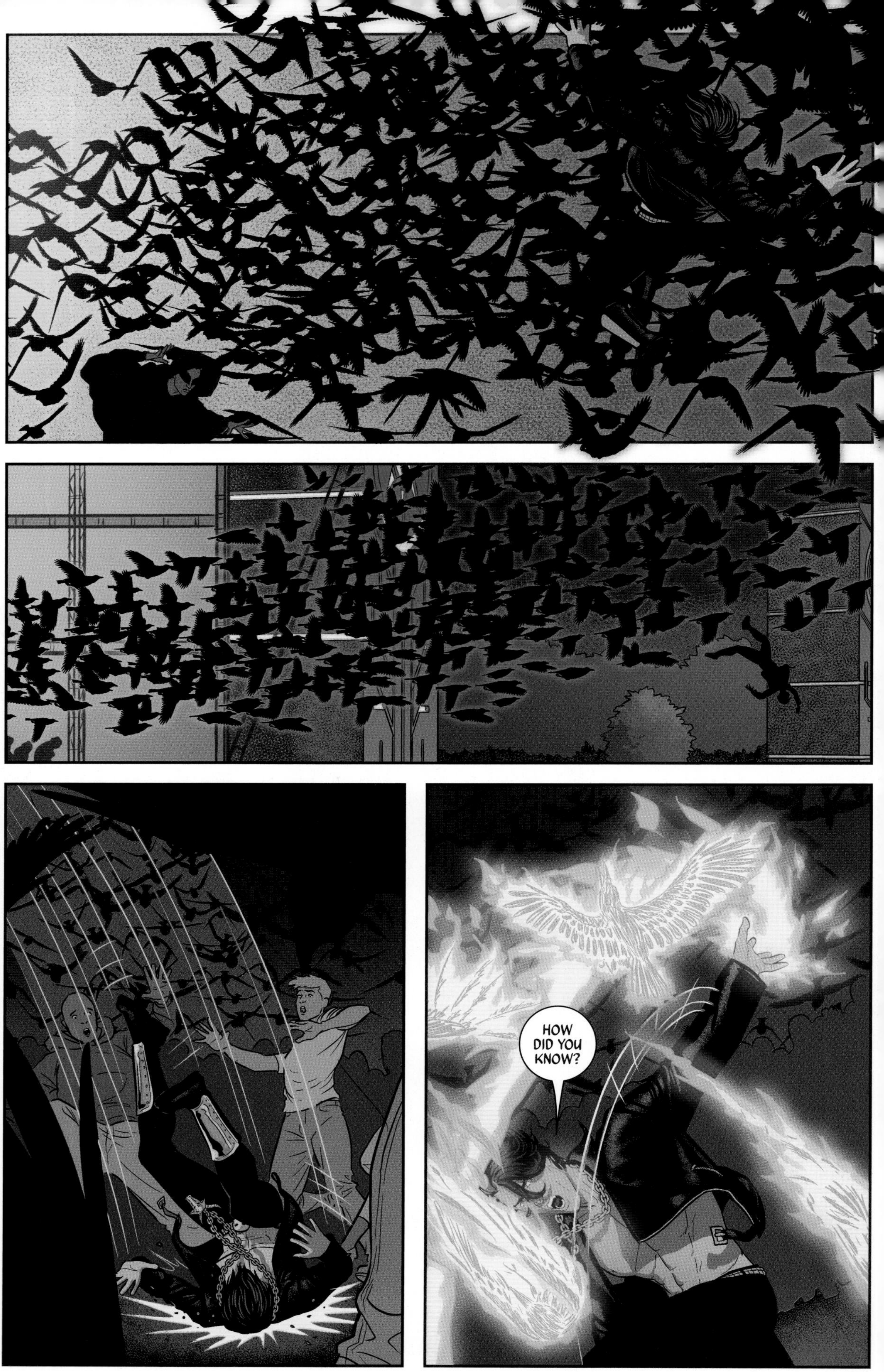
HOW DID YOU KNOW?

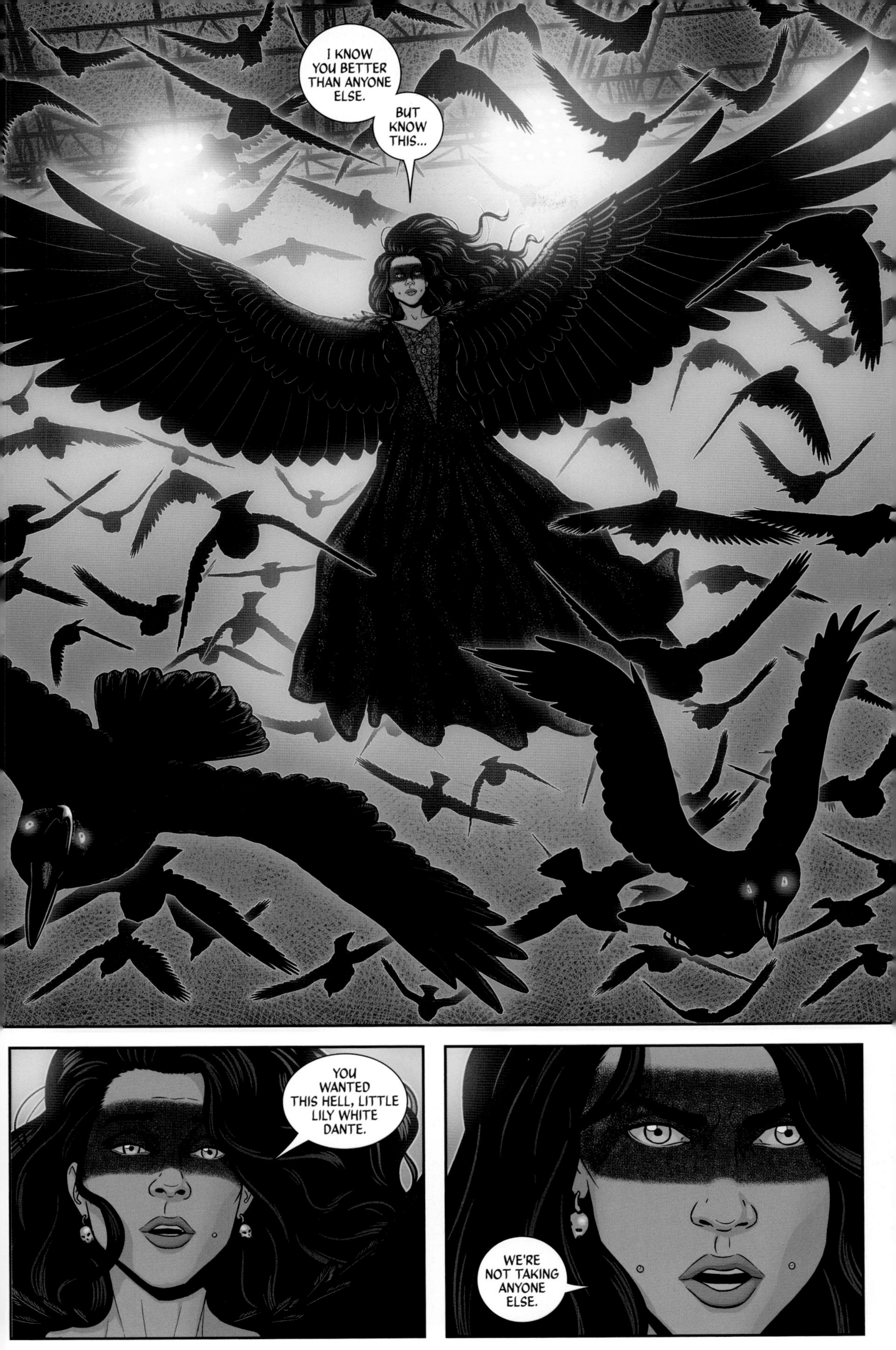
I KNOW YOU BETTER THAN ANYONE ELSE.
BUT KNOW THIS...
YOU WANTED THIS HELL, LITTLE LILY WHITE DANTE.
WE'RE NOT TAKING ANYONE ELSE.

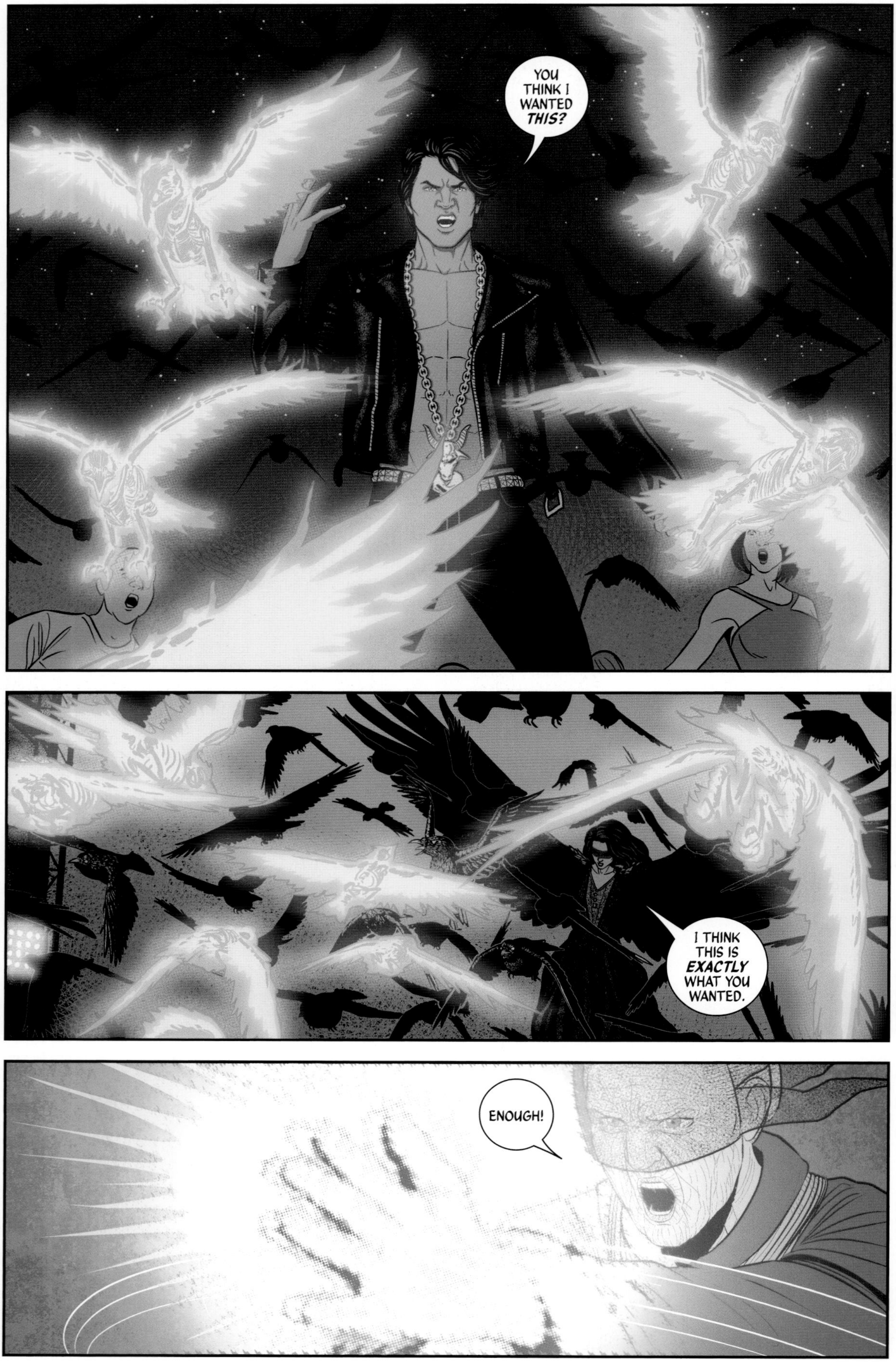

YOU THINK I WANTED *THIS?*
I THINK THIS IS *EXACTLY* WHAT YOU WANTED.
ENOUGH!

YOU HAVE MOVED WITH MURDEROUS INTENT.

YOU KNOW THE COST OF YOUR CRIME. THIS CANNOT BE ALLOWED TO CONTINUE.

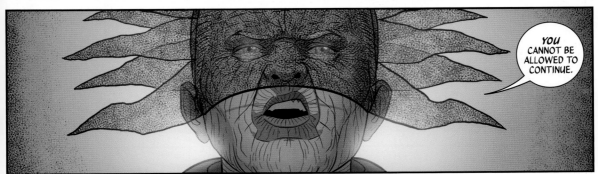

YOU CANNOT BE ALLOWED TO CONTINUE.

I STOPPED HIM. NO BLOOD IS SPILLED. I *GUARD* HIM, ANANKE.

FUCK YOU AND YOUR JUDGMENTAL FUCKING FUCKING FU--

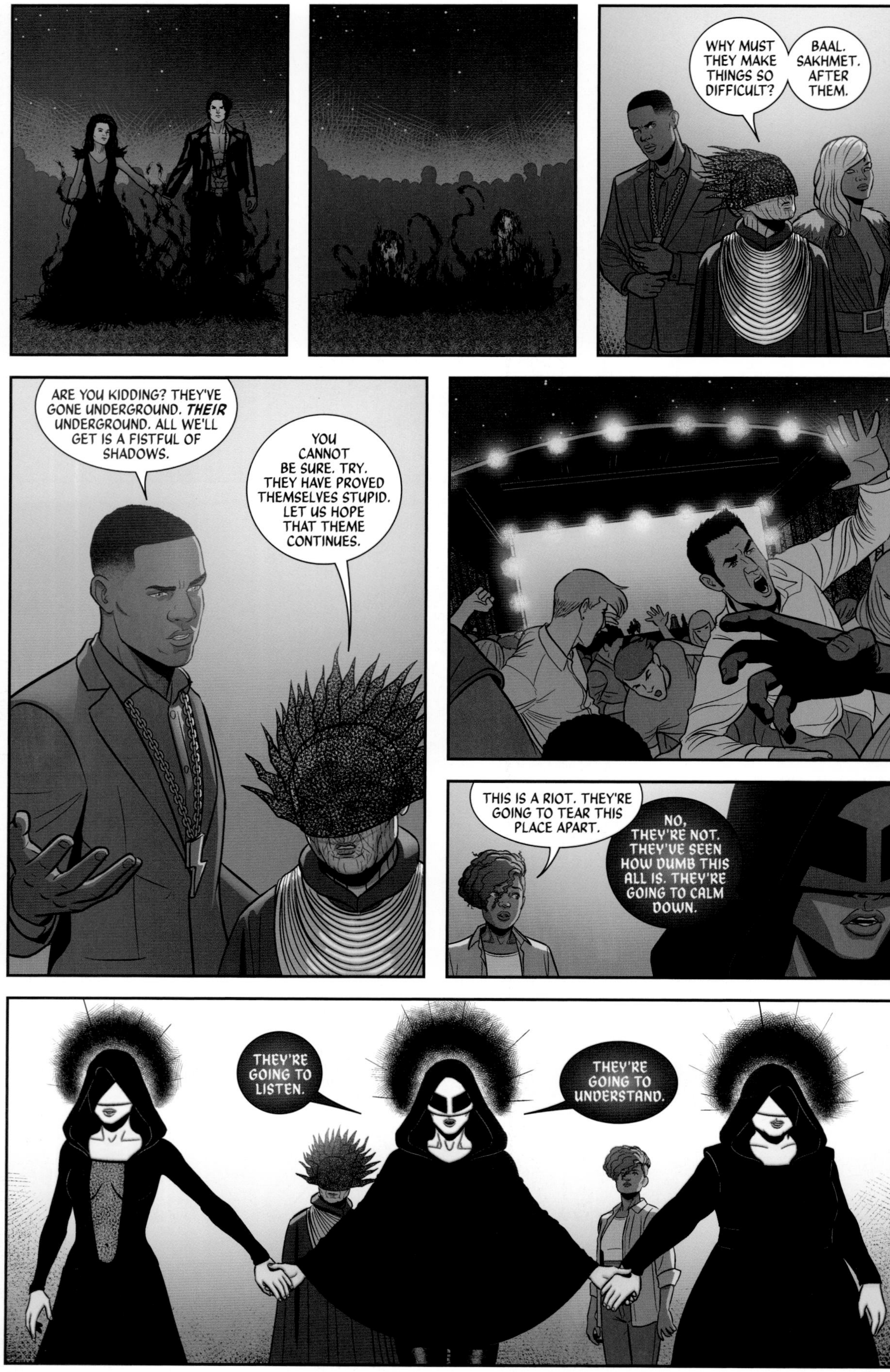
WHY MUST THEY MAKE THINGS SO DIFFICULT?
BAAL. SAKHMET. AFTER THEM.
ARE YOU KIDDING? THEY'VE GONE UNDERGROUND. ***THEIR*** UNDERGROUND. ALL WE'LL GET IS A FISTFUL OF SHADOWS.
YOU CANNOT BE SURE. TRY. THEY HAVE PROVED THEMSELVES STUPID. LET US HOPE THAT THEME CONTINUES.
THIS IS A RIOT. THEY'RE GOING TO TEAR THIS PLACE APART.
NO, THEY'RE NOT. THEY'VE SEEN HOW DUMB THIS ALL IS. THEY'RE GOING TO CALM DOWN.
THEY'RE GOING TO LISTEN.
THEY'RE GOING TO UNDERSTAND.

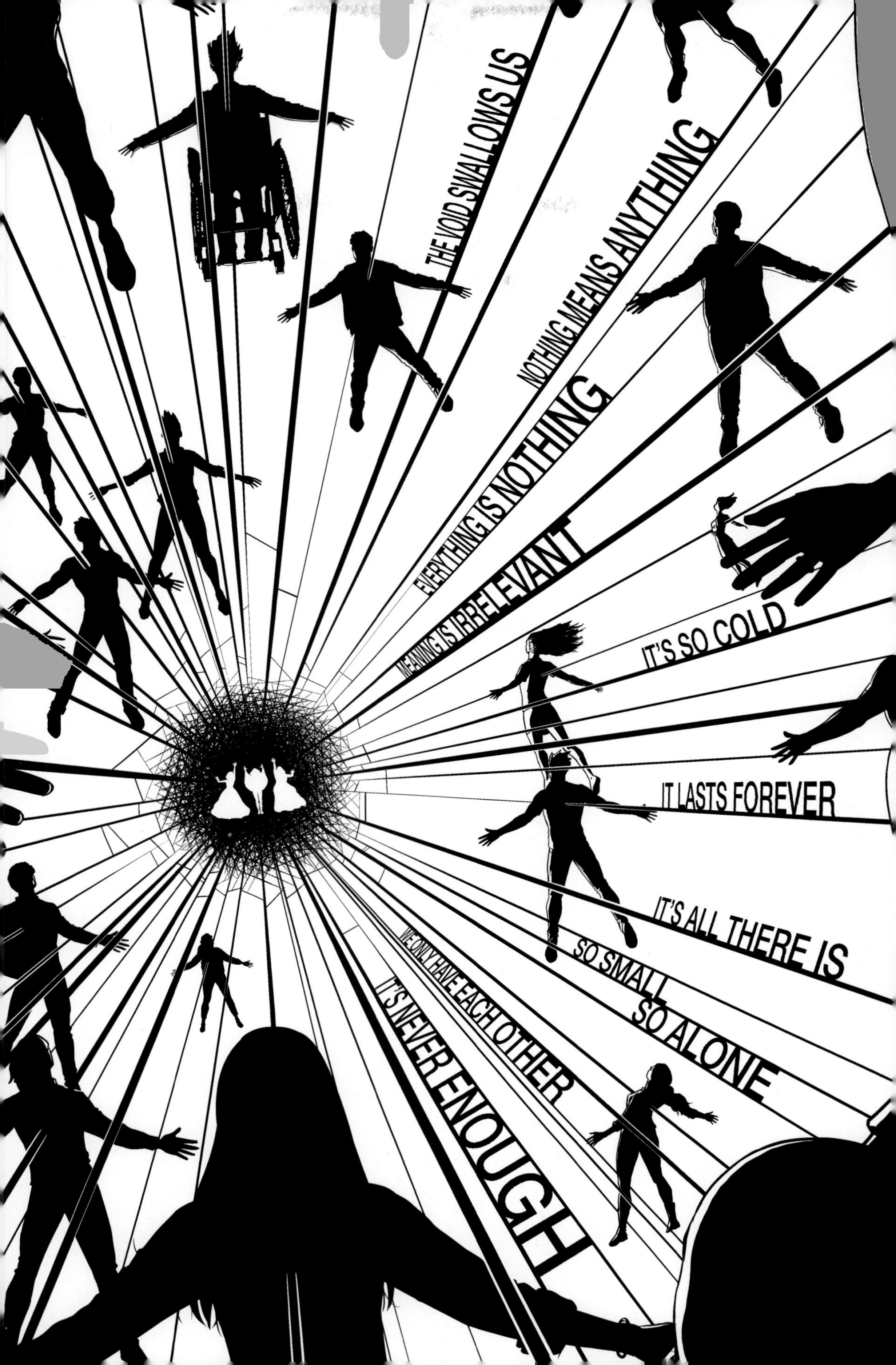
THE VOID SWALLOWS US
NOTHING MEANS ANYTHING
EVERYTHING IS NOTHING
MEANING IS IRRELEVANT
IT'S SO COLD
IT LASTS FOREVER
IT'S ALL THERE IS
SO SMALL
SO ALONE
WE ONLY HAVE EACH OTHER
IT'S NEVER ENOUGH

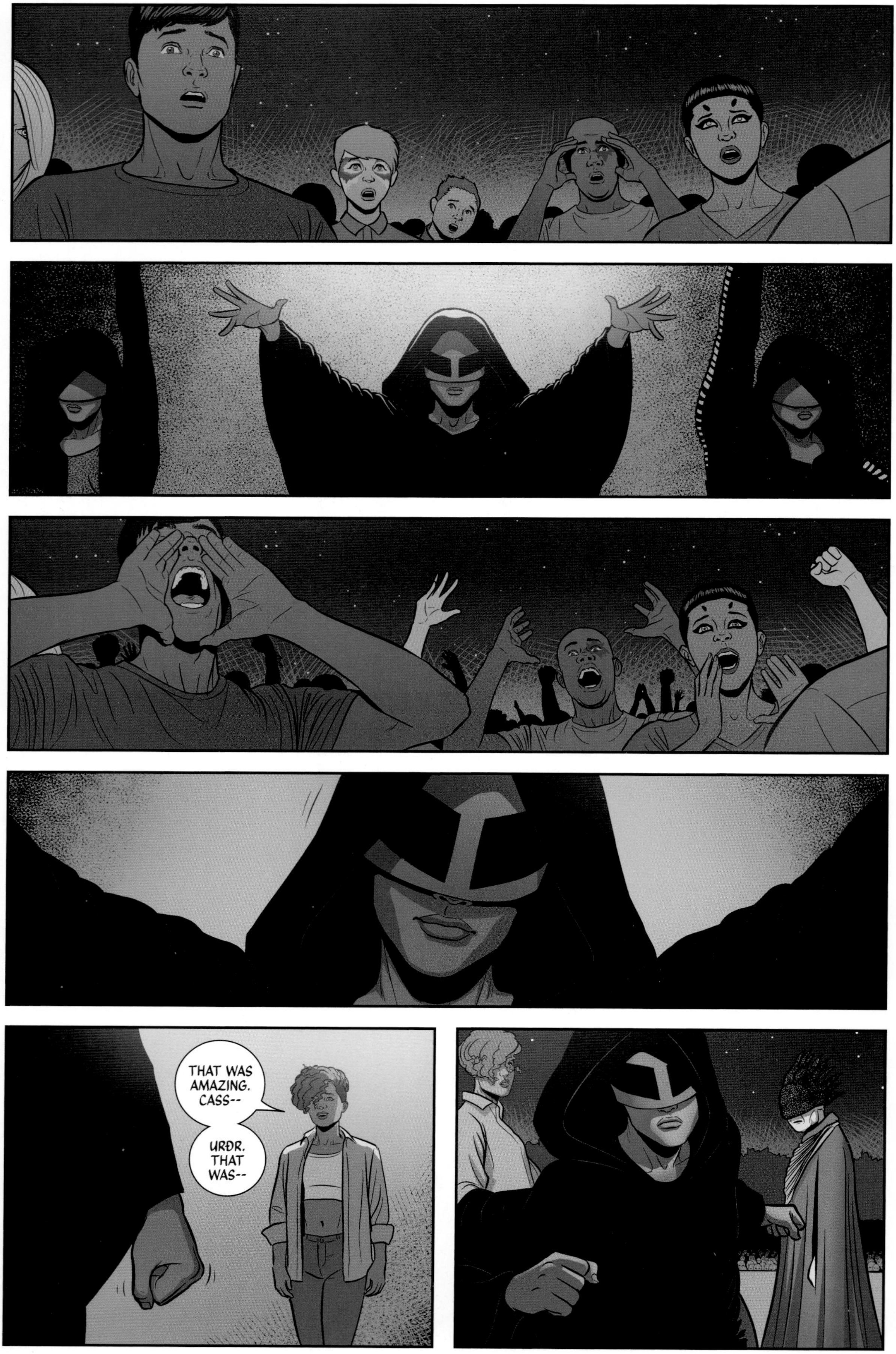
THAT WAS AMAZING. CASS--
URÐR. THAT WAS--

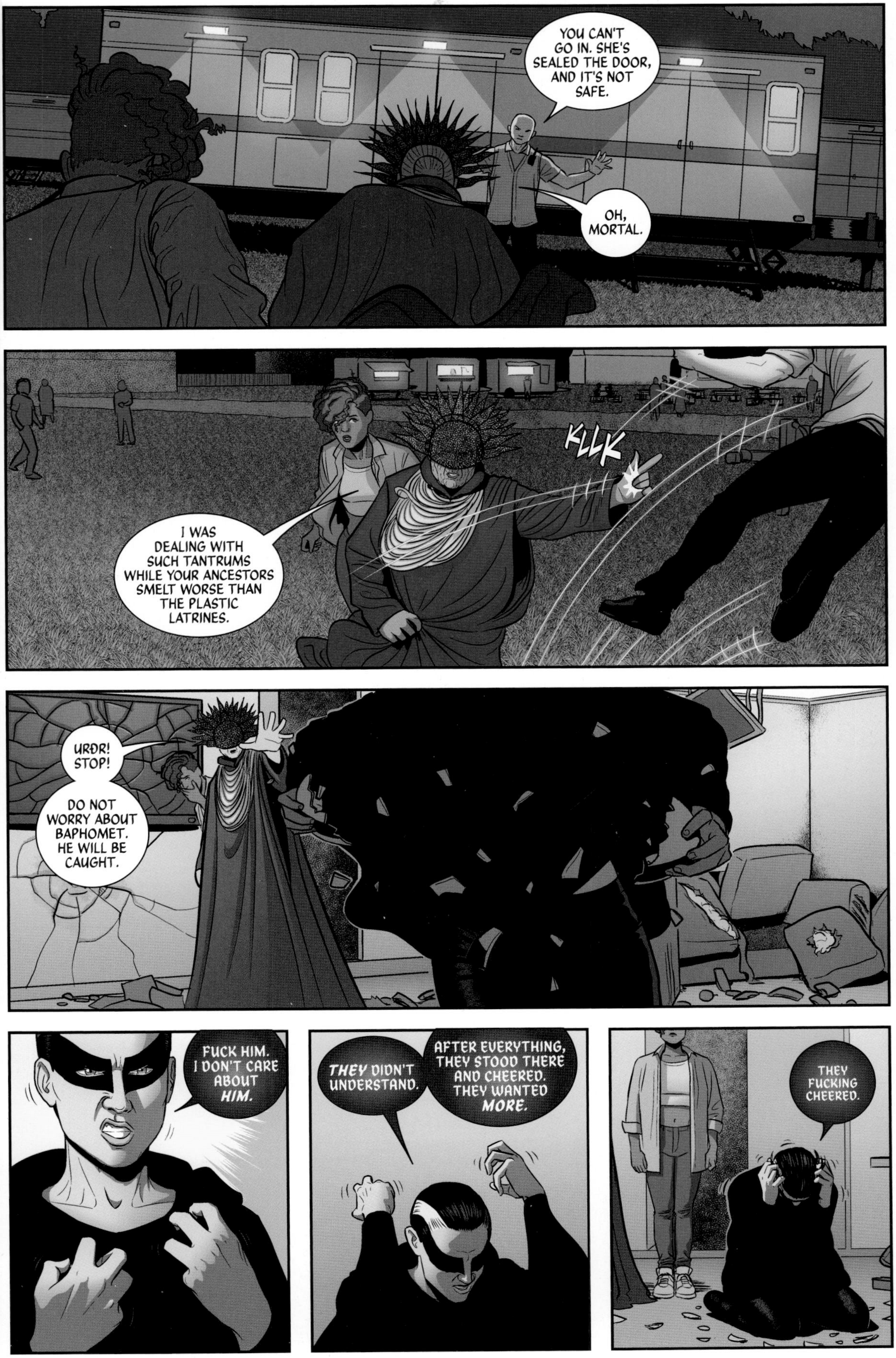
YOU CAN'T GO IN. SHE'S SEALED THE DOOR, AND IT'S NOT SAFE.
OH, MORTAL.
KLLK
I WAS DEALING WITH SUCH TANTRUMS WHILE YOUR ANCESTORS SMELT WORSE THAN THE PLASTIC LATRINES.
URÐR! STOP!
DO NOT WORRY ABOUT BAPHOMET. HE WILL BE CAUGHT.
FUCK HIM. I DON'T CARE ABOUT *HIM.*
THEY DIDN'T UNDERSTAND.
AFTER EVERYTHING, THEY STOOD THERE AND CHEERED. THEY WANTED *MORE.*
THEY FUCKING CHEERED.

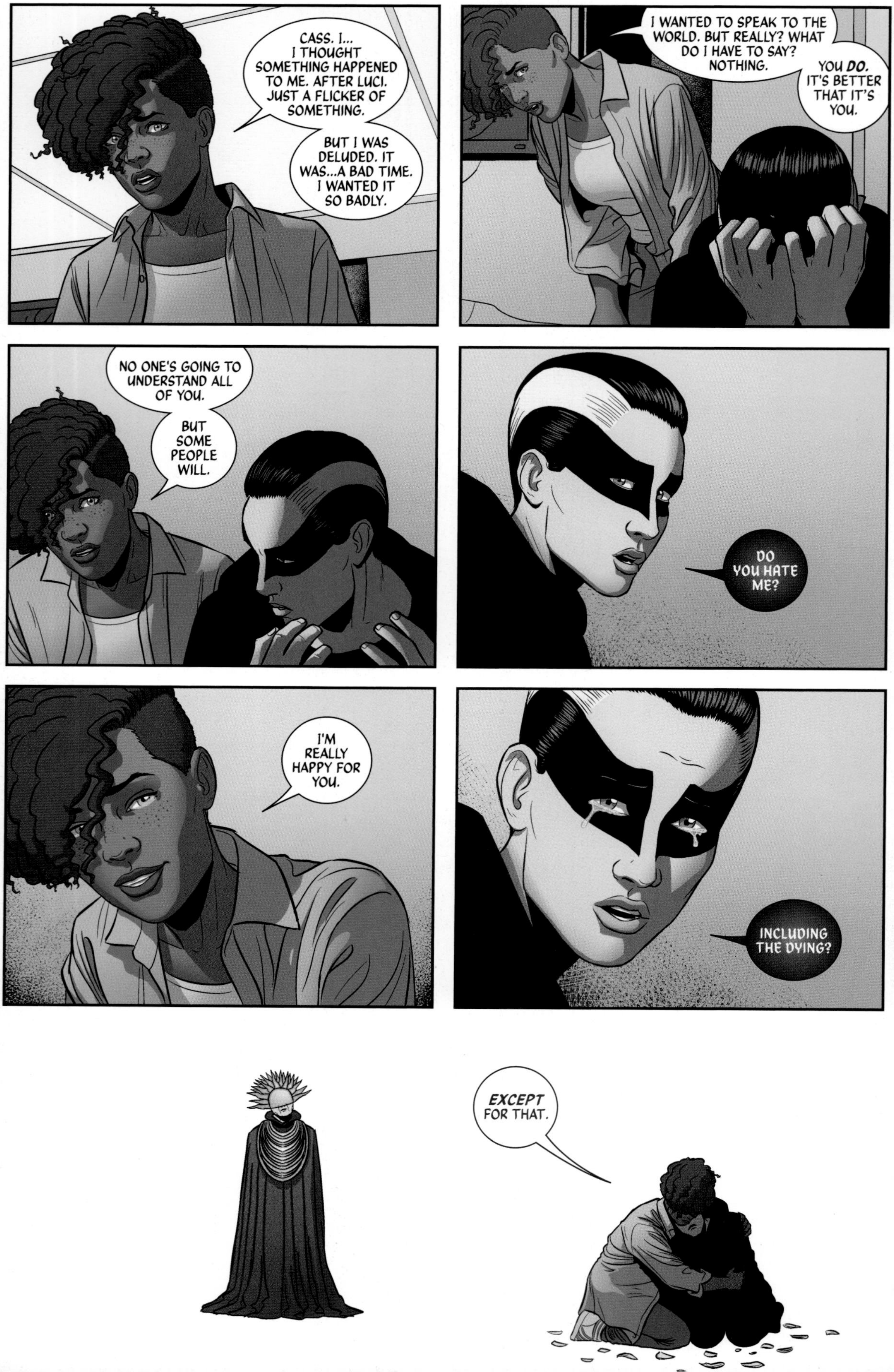
CASS. I... I THOUGHT SOMETHING HAPPENED TO ME. AFTER LUCI. JUST A FLICKER OF SOMETHING.
BUT I WAS DELUDED. IT WAS...A BAD TIME. I WANTED IT SO BADLY.
I WANTED TO SPEAK TO THE WORLD. BUT REALLY? WHAT DO I HAVE TO SAY? NOTHING.
YOU *DO.* IT'S BETTER THAT IT'S YOU.
NO ONE'S GOING TO UNDERSTAND ALL OF YOU.
BUT SOME PEOPLE WILL.
DO YOU HATE ME?
I'M REALLY HAPPY FOR YOU.
INCLUDING THE DYING?
EXCEPT FOR THAT.

WE ONLY HAVE
EACH OTHER

2 AUGUST 2014

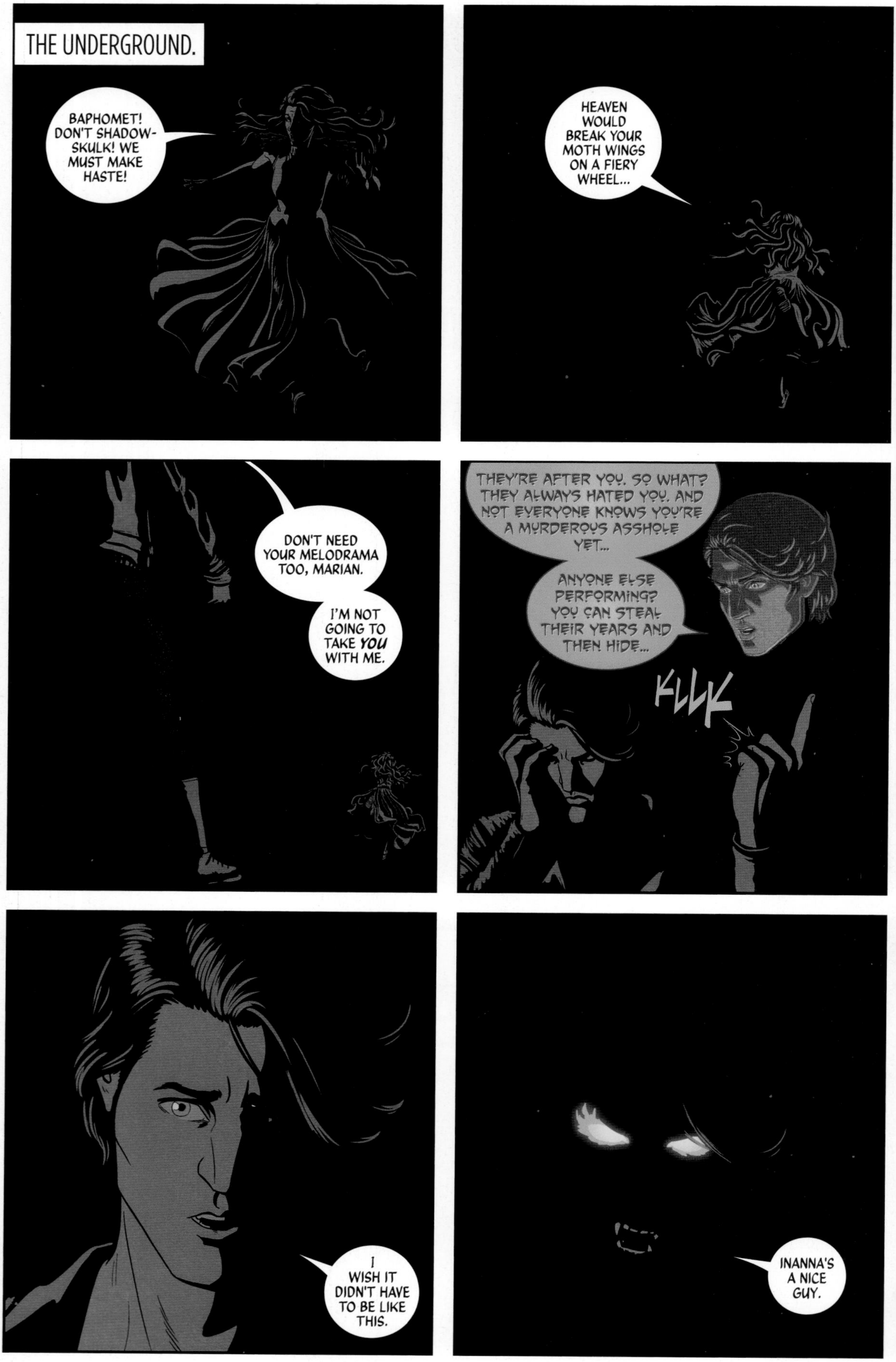
THE UNDERGROUND.
BAPHOMET! DON'T SHADOW-SKULK! WE MUST MAKE HASTE!
HEAVEN WOULD BREAK YOUR MOTH WINGS ON A FIERY WHEEL...
DON'T NEED YOUR MELODRAMA TOO, MARIAN.
I'M NOT GOING TO TAKE YOU WITH ME.
THEY'RE AFTER YOU. SO WHAT? THEY ALWAYS HATED YOU. AND NOT EVERYONE KNOWS YOU'RE A MURDEROUS ASSHOLE YET...
ANYONE ELSE PERFORMING? YOU CAN STEAL THEIR YEARS AND THEN HIDE...
KLLK
I WISH IT DIDN'T HAVE TO BE LIKE THIS.
INANNA'S A NICE GUY.

NEVERMORE

2 AUGUST 2014

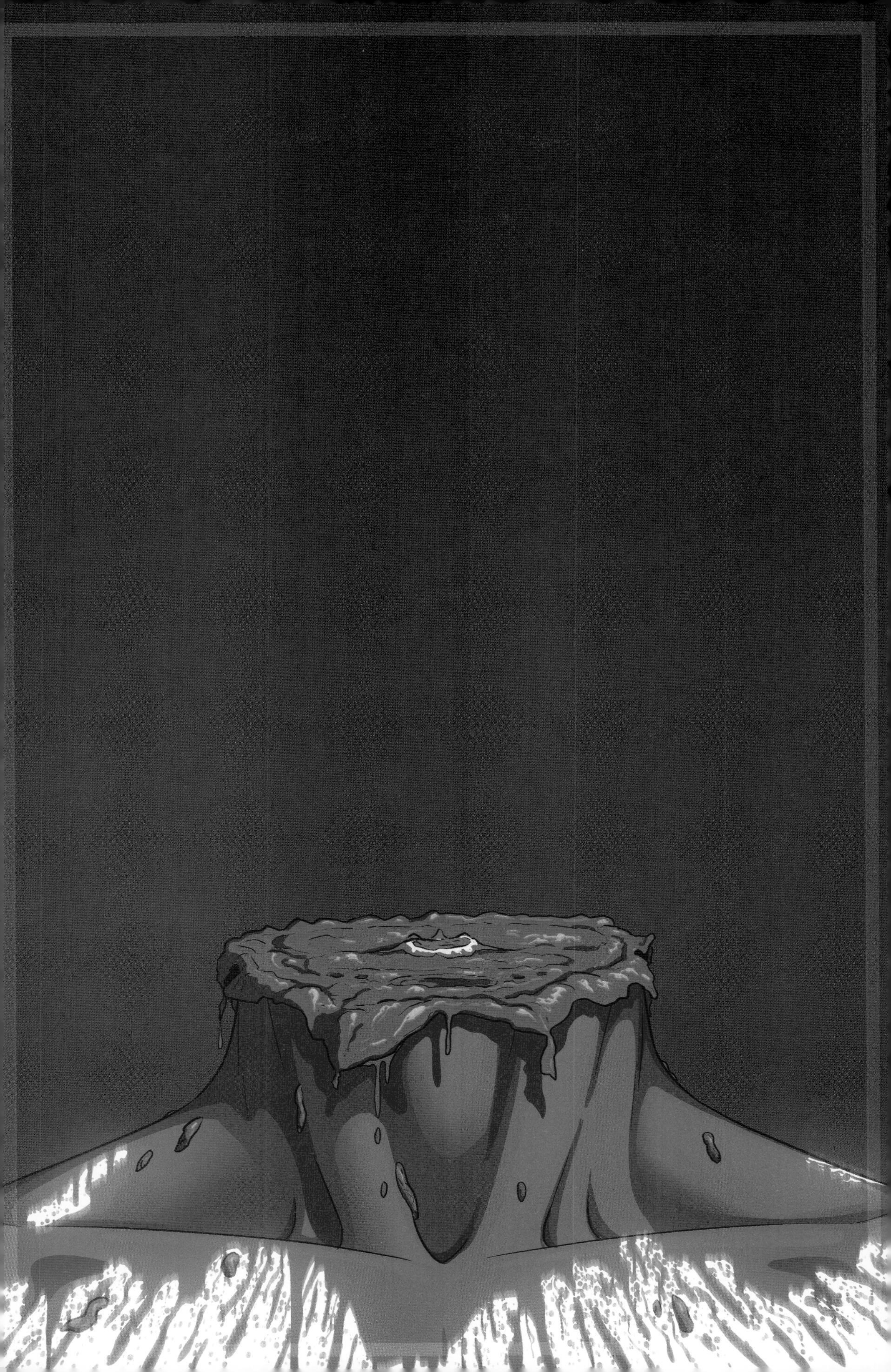

THE
WICKED
+
THE DIVINE

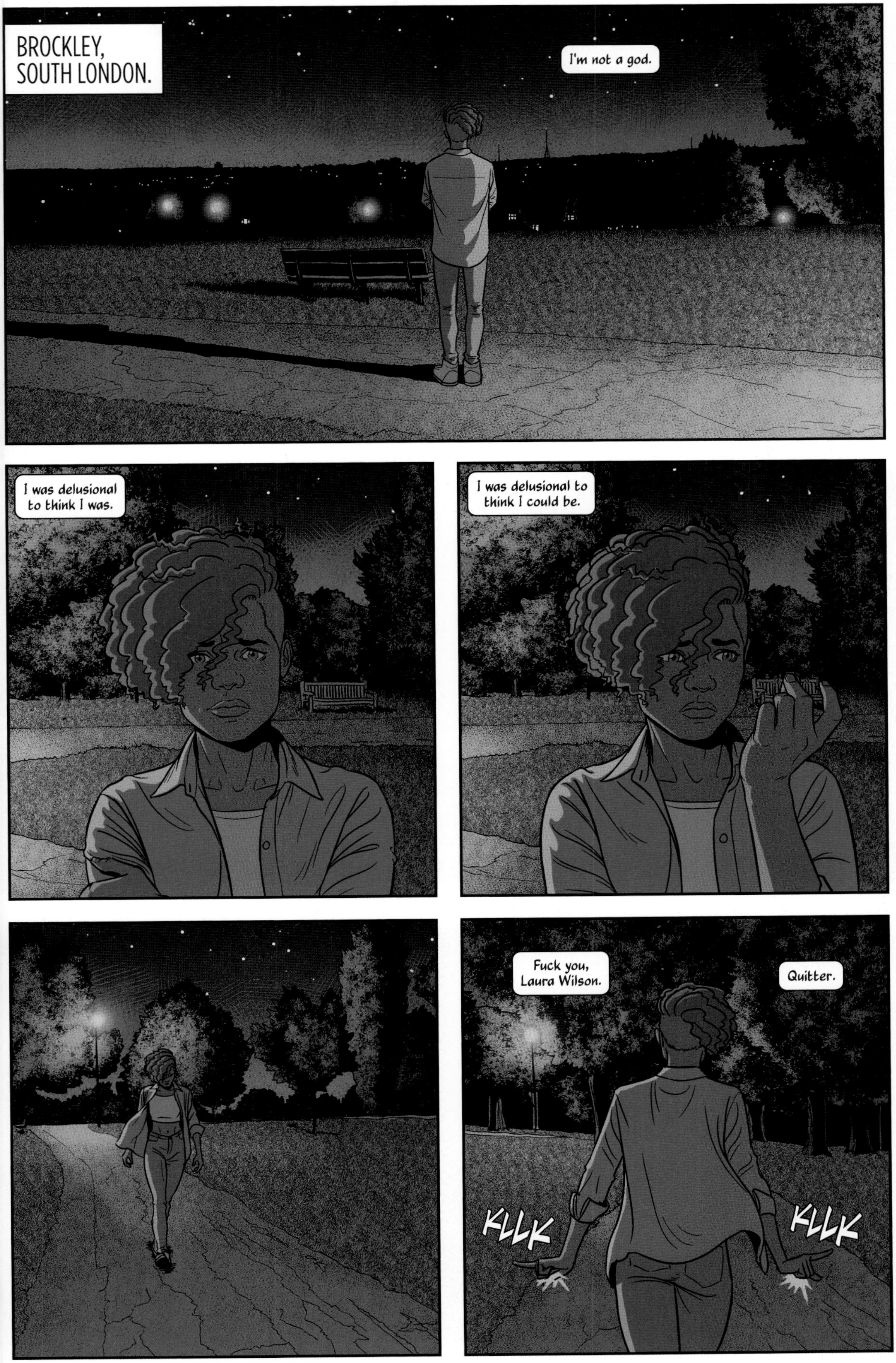

BROCKLEY, SOUTH LONDON.
I'm not a god.
I was delusional to think I was.
I was delusional to think I could be.
Fuck you, Laura Wilson.
Quitter.
KLLK
KLLK

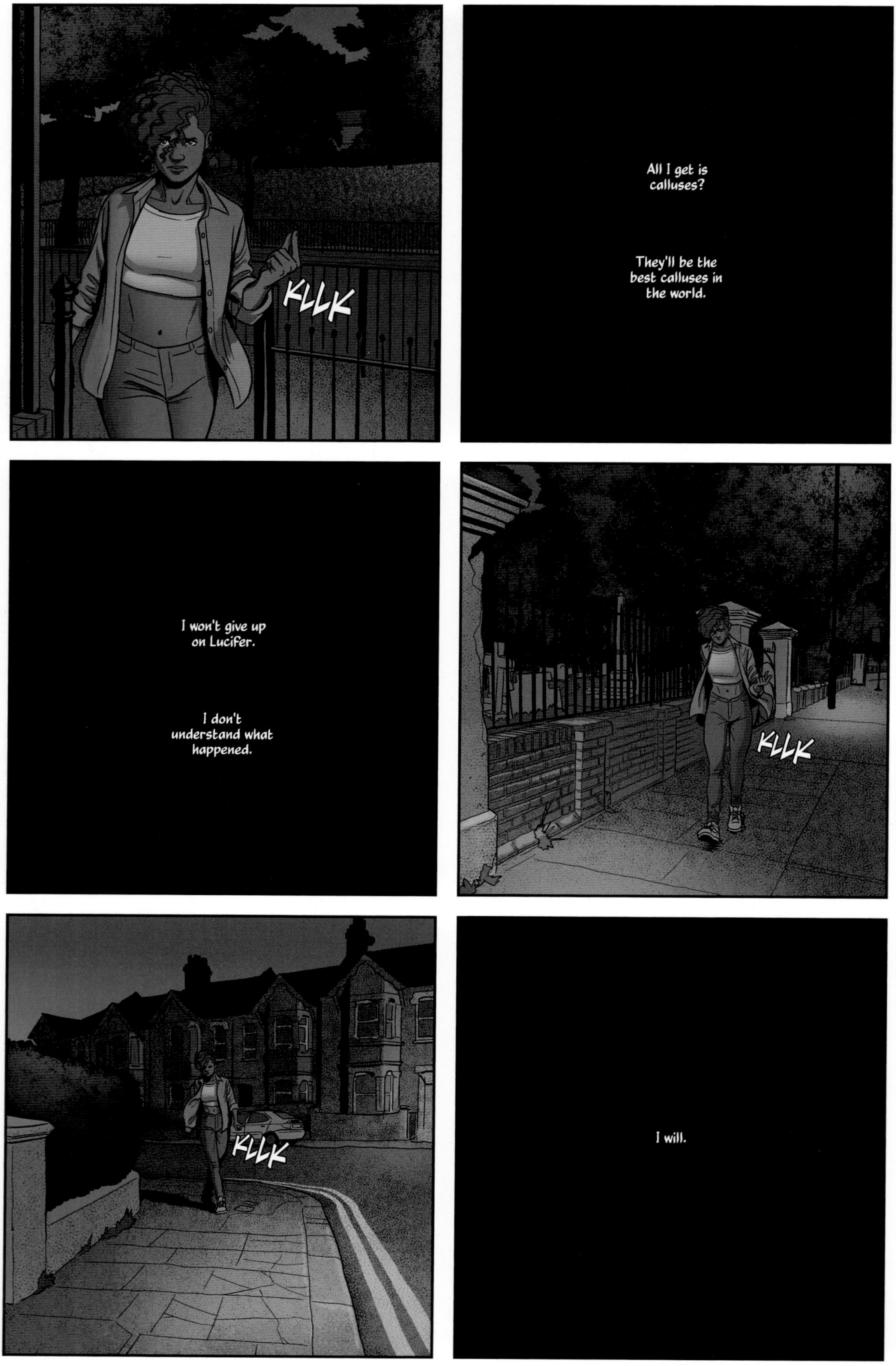
KLLK
All I get is calluses?
They'll be the best calluses in the world.
I won't give up on Lucifer.
I don't understand what happened.
KLLK
KLLK
I will.

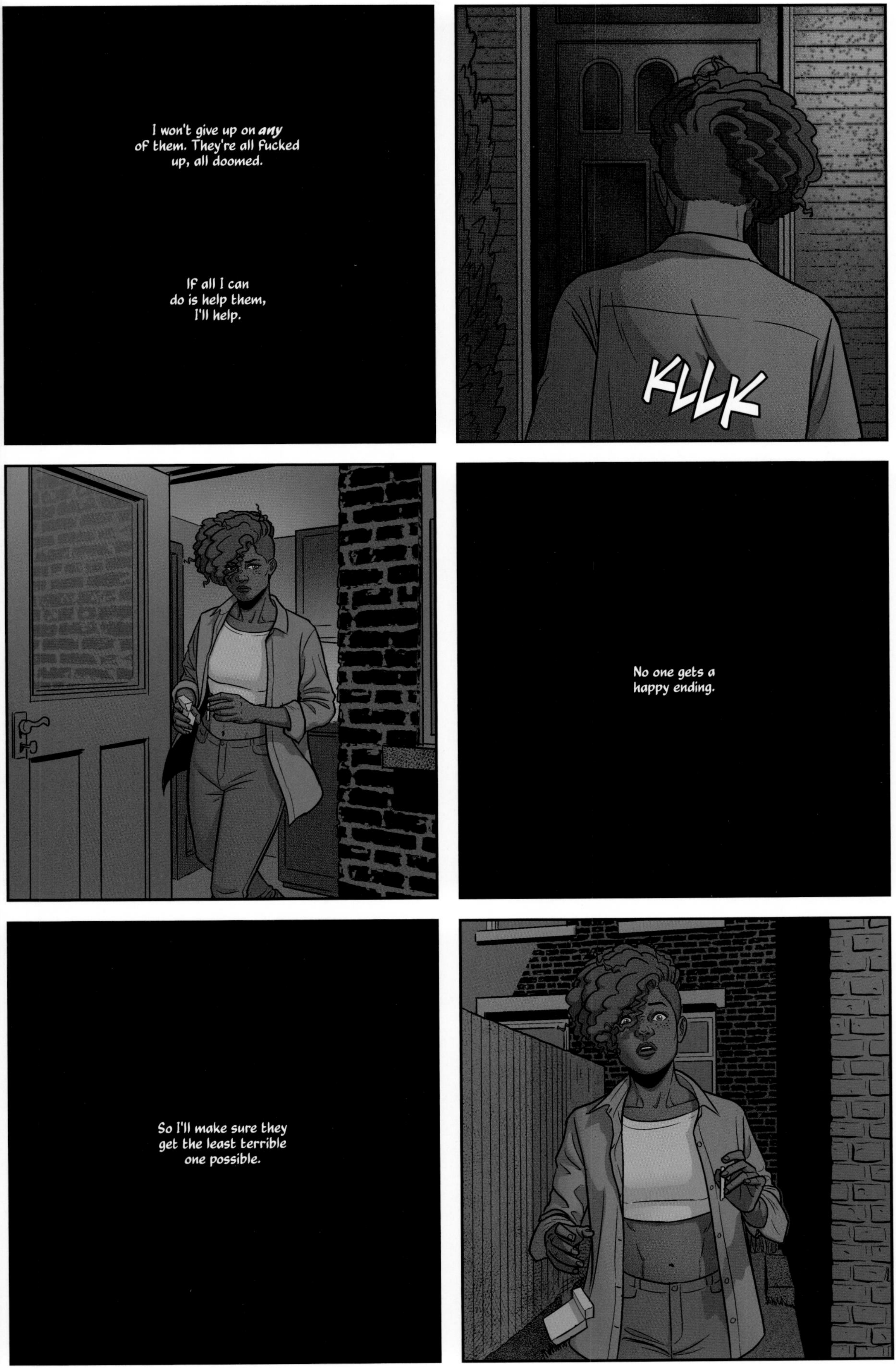
I won't give up on *any* of them. They're all fucked up, all doomed.
If all I can do is help them, I'll help.
KLLK
No one gets a happy ending.
So I'll make sure they get the least terrible one possible.

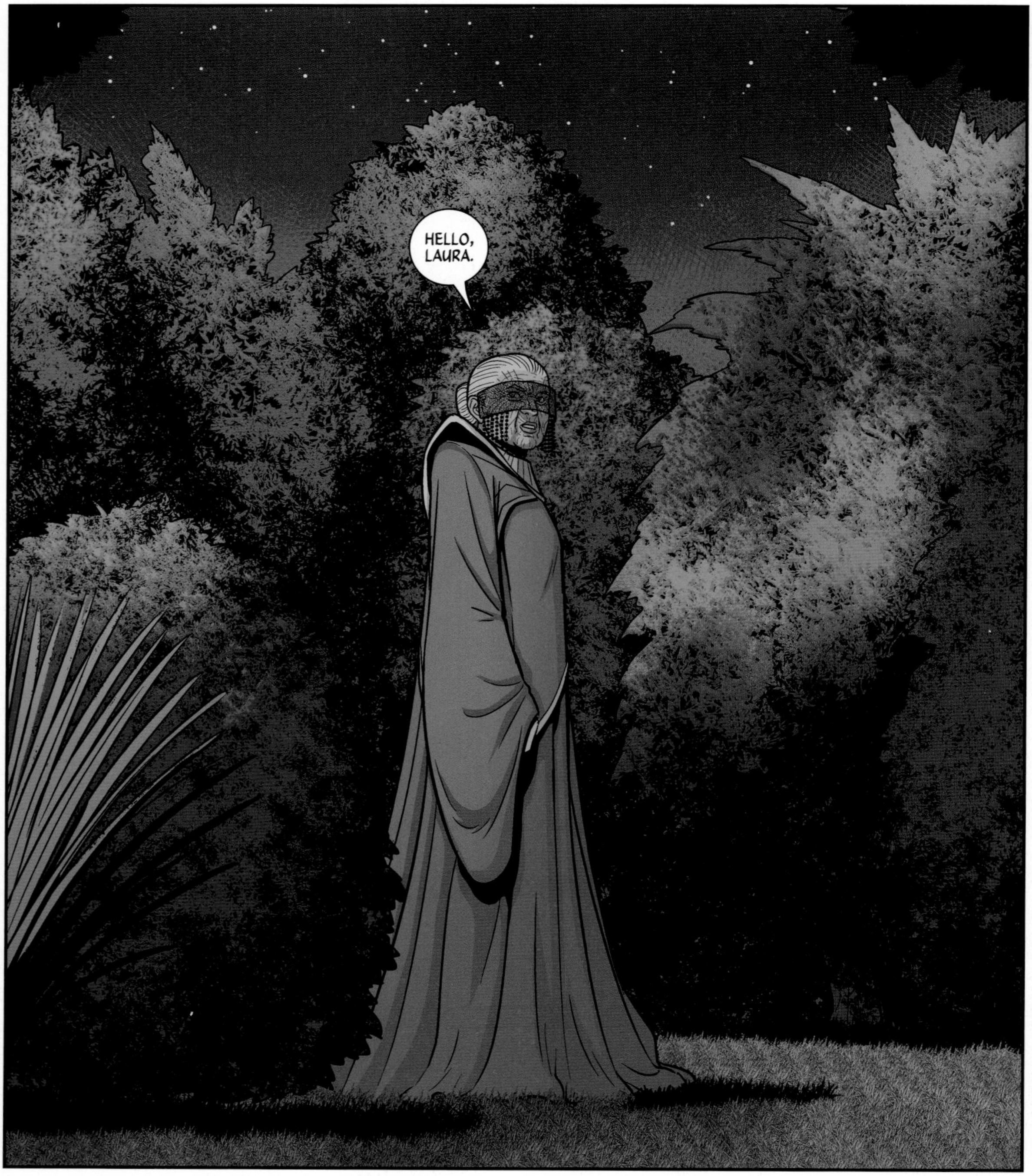
HELLO, LAURA.

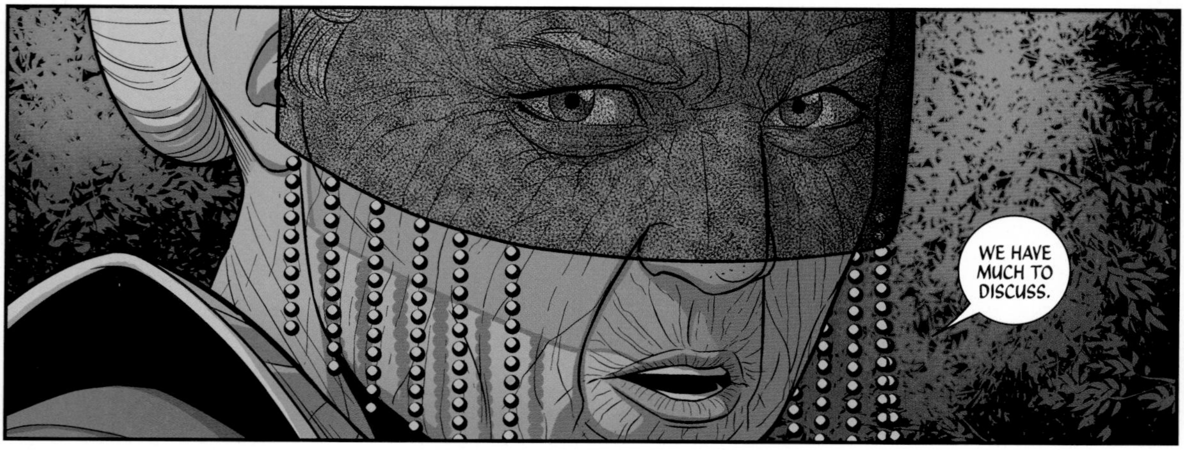
WE HAVE MUCH TO DISCUSS.

IT'S GOING
TO BE OKAY
(SLIGHT RETURN)

3 AUGUST 2014

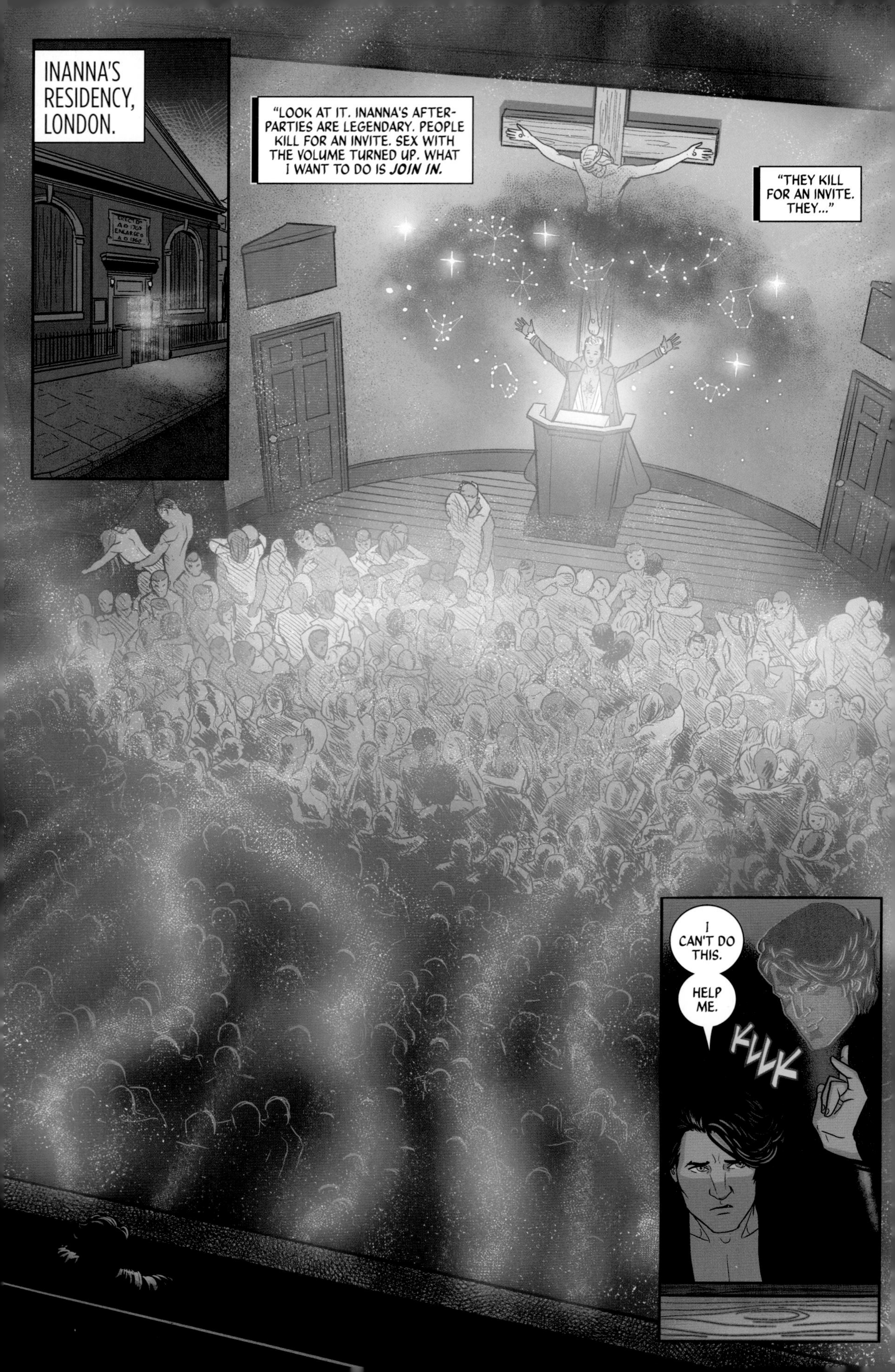
INANNA'S RESIDENCY, LONDON.
"LOOK AT IT. INANNA'S AFTER-PARTIES ARE LEGENDARY. PEOPLE KILL FOR AN INVITE. SEX WITH THE VOLUME TURNED UP. WHAT I WANT TO DO IS ***JOIN IN.***
"THEY KILL FOR AN INVITE. THEY..."
I CAN'T DO THIS.
HELP ME.
KLLK

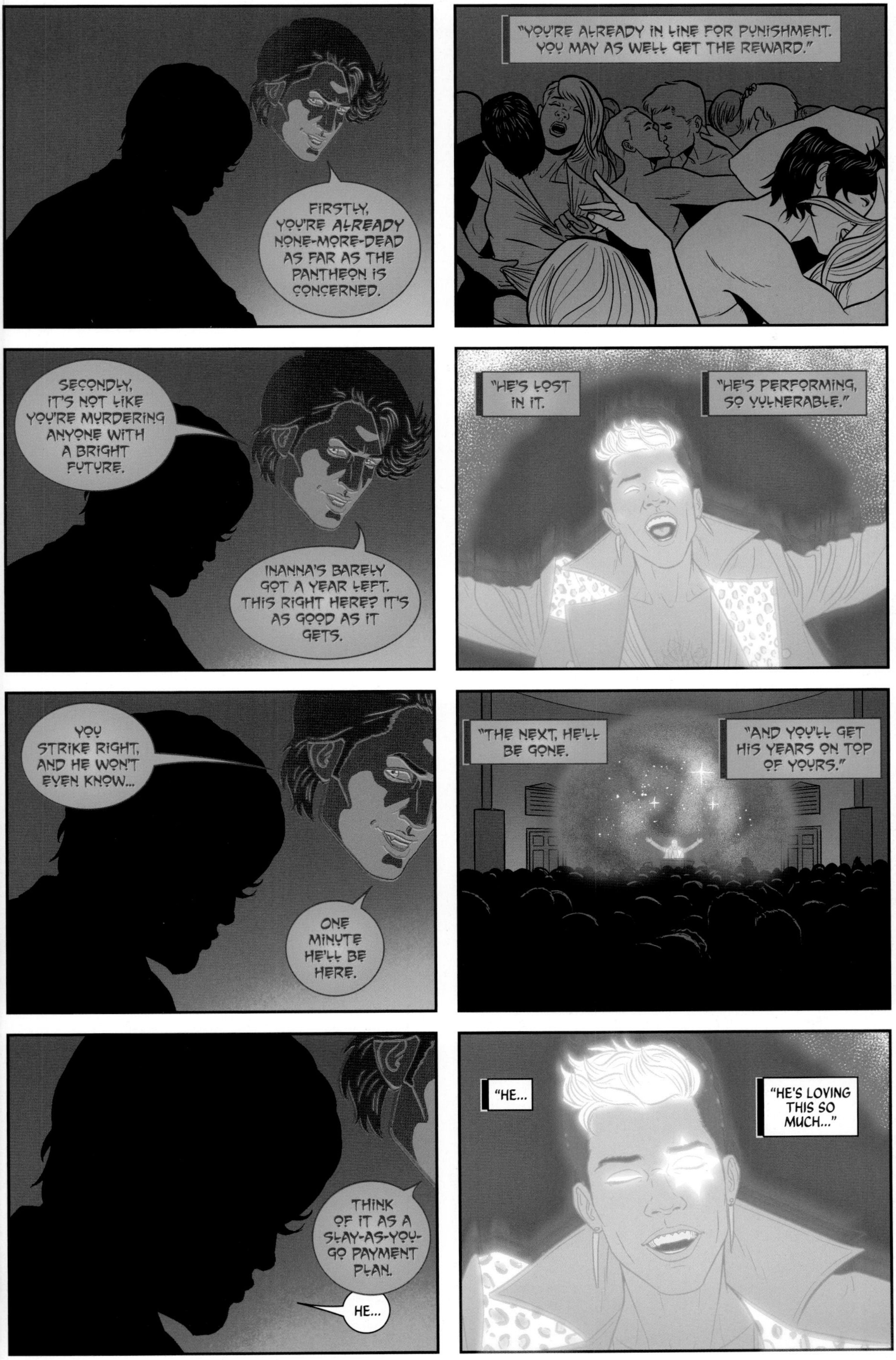

FIRSTLY, YOU'RE ALREADY NONE-MORE-DEAD AS FAR AS THE PANTHEON IS CONCERNED.
"YOU'RE ALREADY IN LINE FOR PUNISHMENT. YOU MAY AS WELL GET THE REWARD."
SECONDLY, IT'S NOT LIKE YOU'RE MURDERING ANYONE WITH A BRIGHT FUTURE.
INANNA'S BARELY GOT A YEAR LEFT. THIS RIGHT HERE? IT'S AS GOOD AS IT GETS.
"HE'S LOST IN IT.
"HE'S PERFORMING, SO VULNERABLE."
YOU STRIKE RIGHT, AND HE WON'T EVEN KNOW...
ONE MINUTE HE'LL BE HERE.
"THE NEXT, HE'LL BE GONE.
"AND YOU'LL GET HIS YEARS ON TOP OF YOURS."
THINK OF IT AS A SLAY-AS-YOU-GO PAYMENT PLAN.
HE...
"HE...
"HE'S LOVING THIS SO MUCH..."

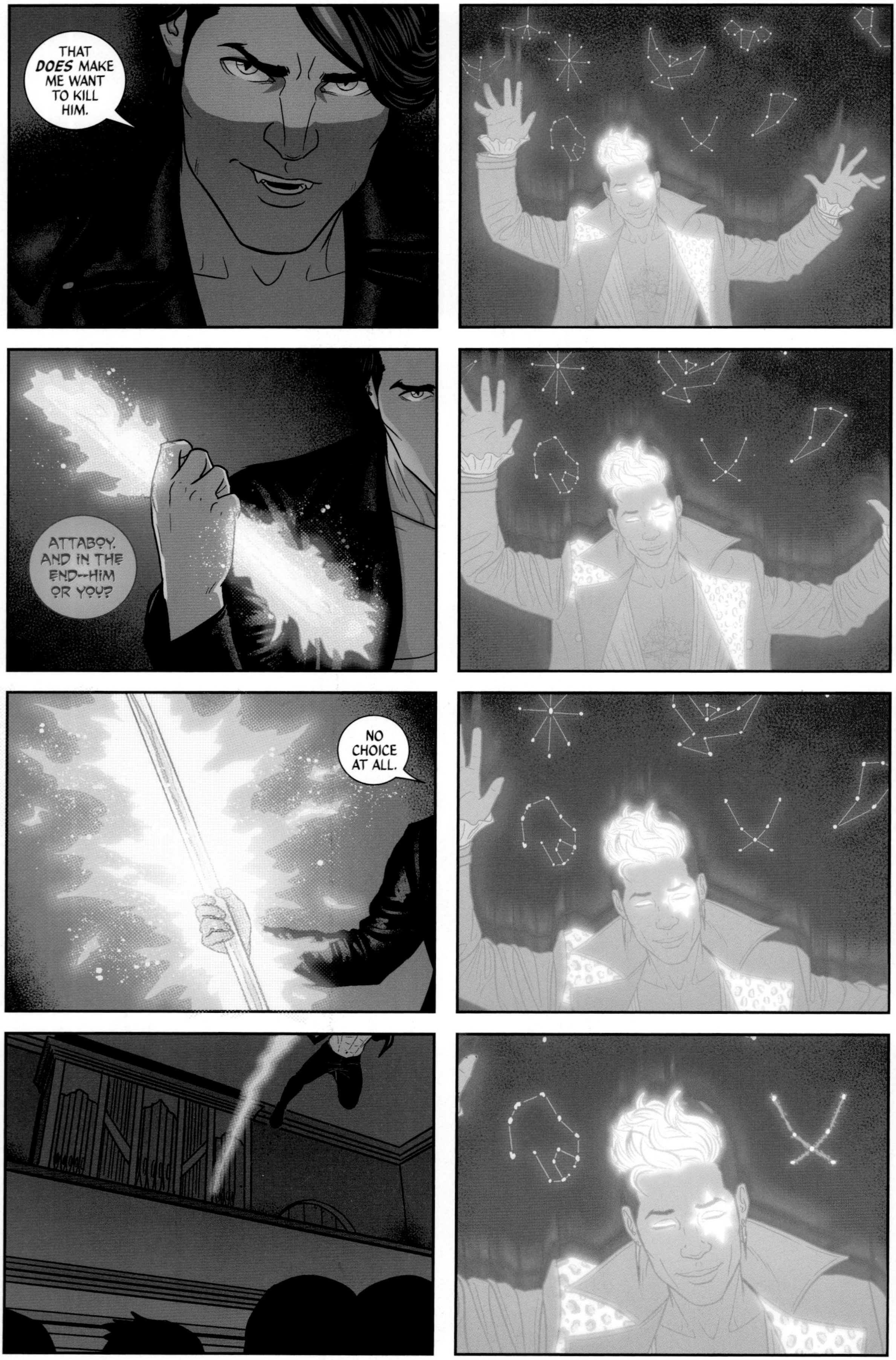
THAT DOES MAKE ME WANT TO KILL HIM.
ATTABOY. AND IN THE END--HIM OR YOU?
NO CHOICE AT ALL.

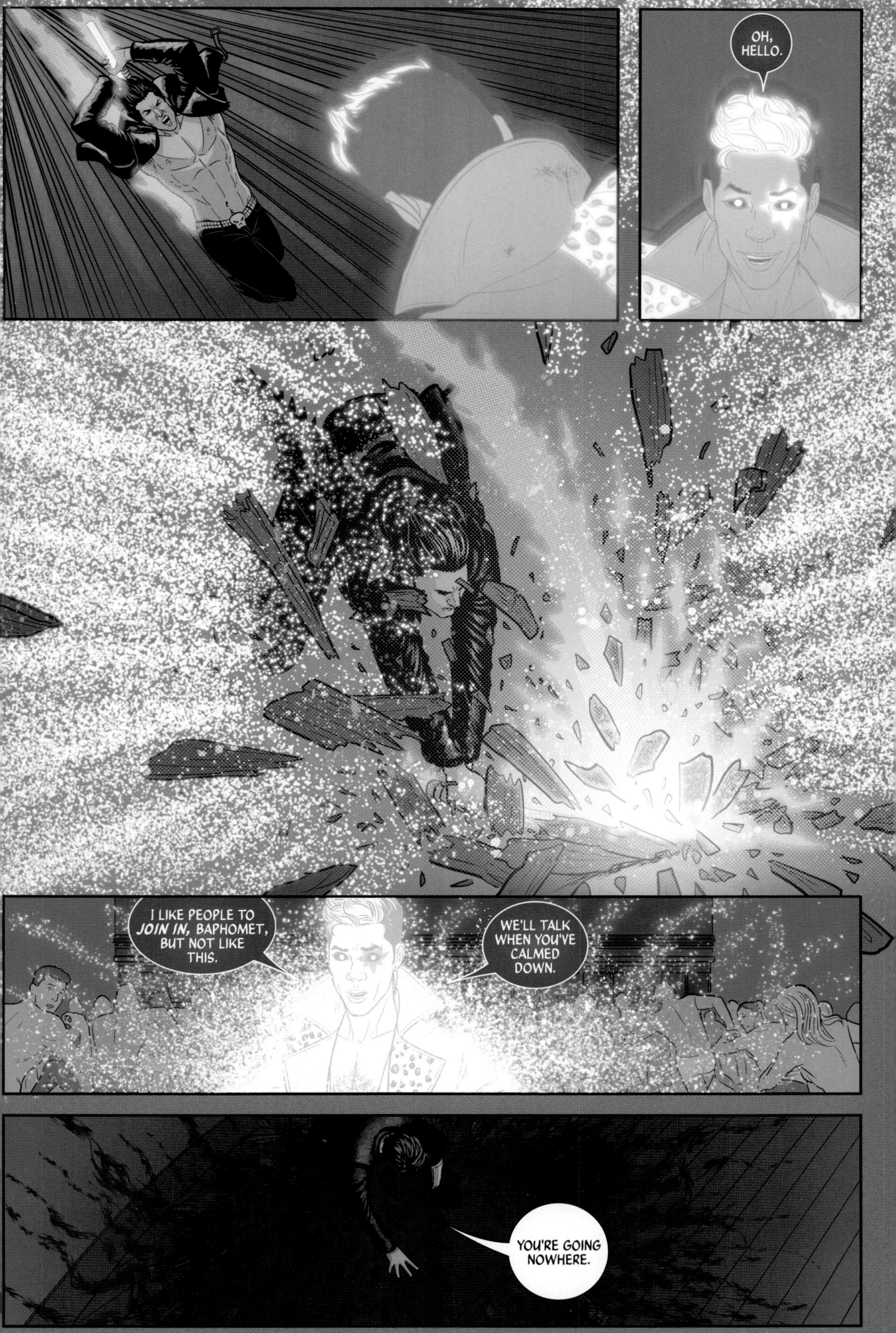
OH, HELLO.
I LIKE PEOPLE TO JOIN IN, BAPHOMET, BUT NOT LIKE THIS.
WE'LL TALK WHEN YOU'VE CALMED DOWN.
YOU'RE GOING NOWHERE.

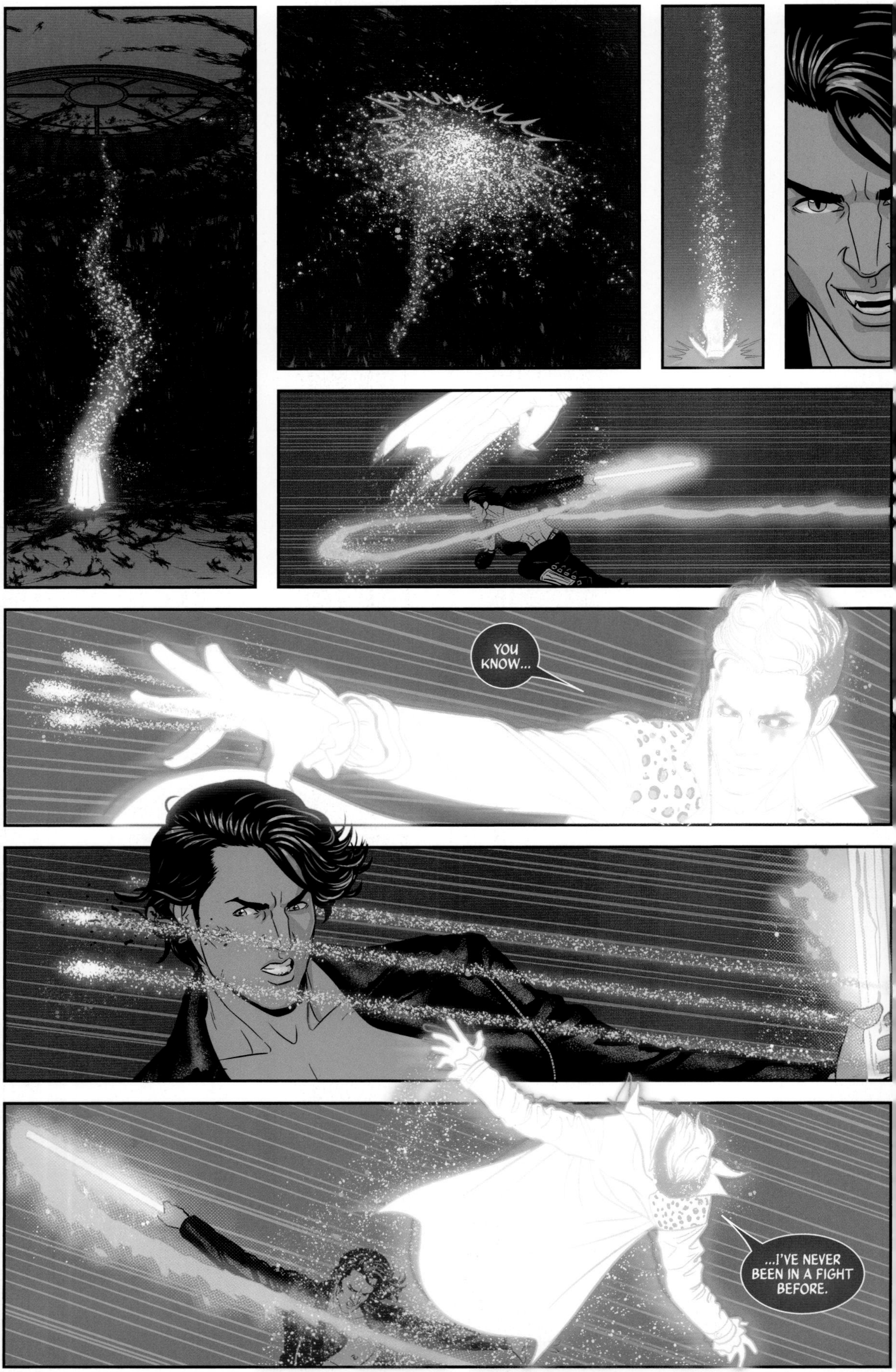
YOU KNOW...
...I'VE NEVER BEEN IN A FIGHT BEFORE.

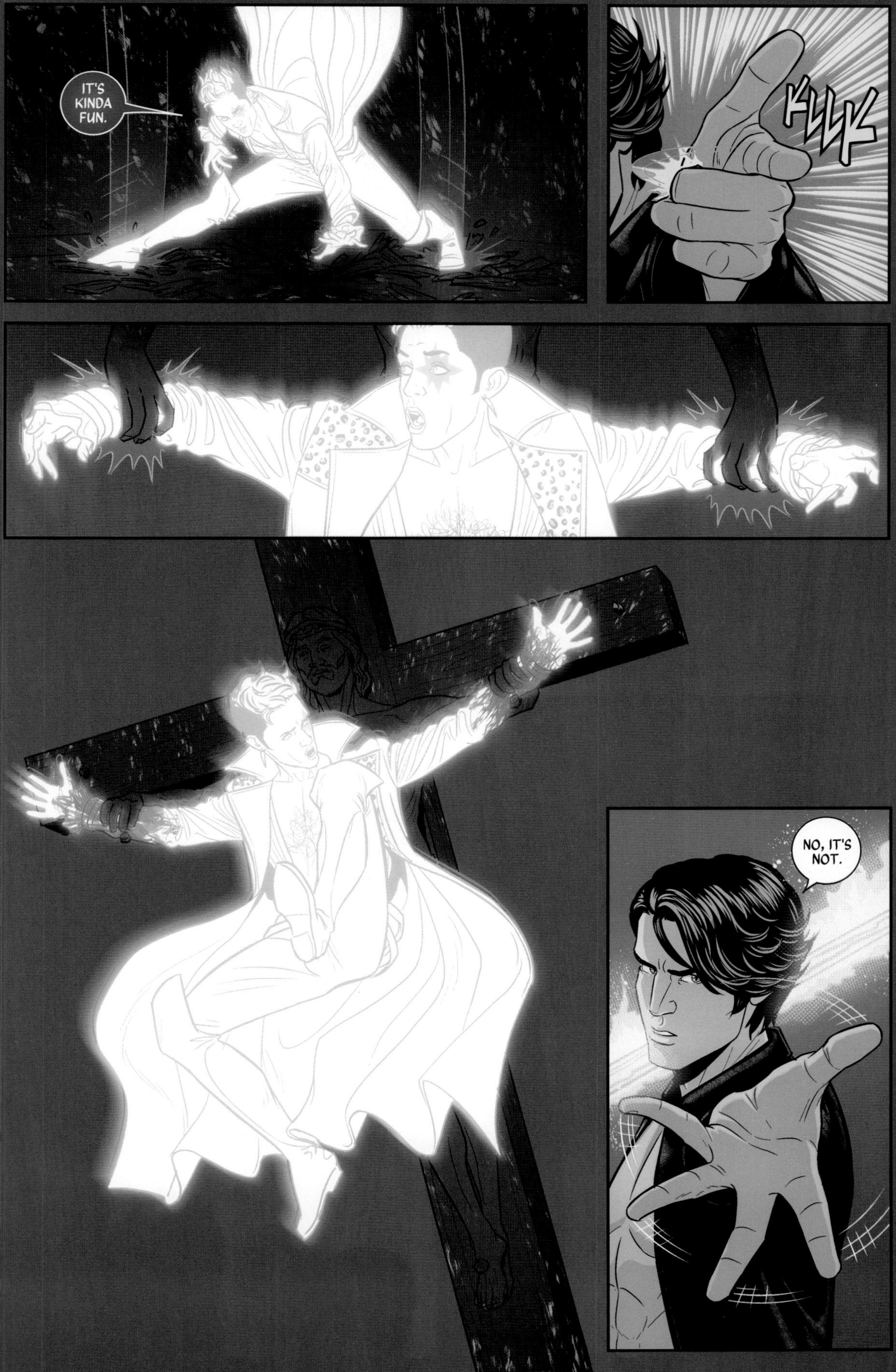
IT'S KINDA FUN.
KLLK
NO, IT'S NOT.

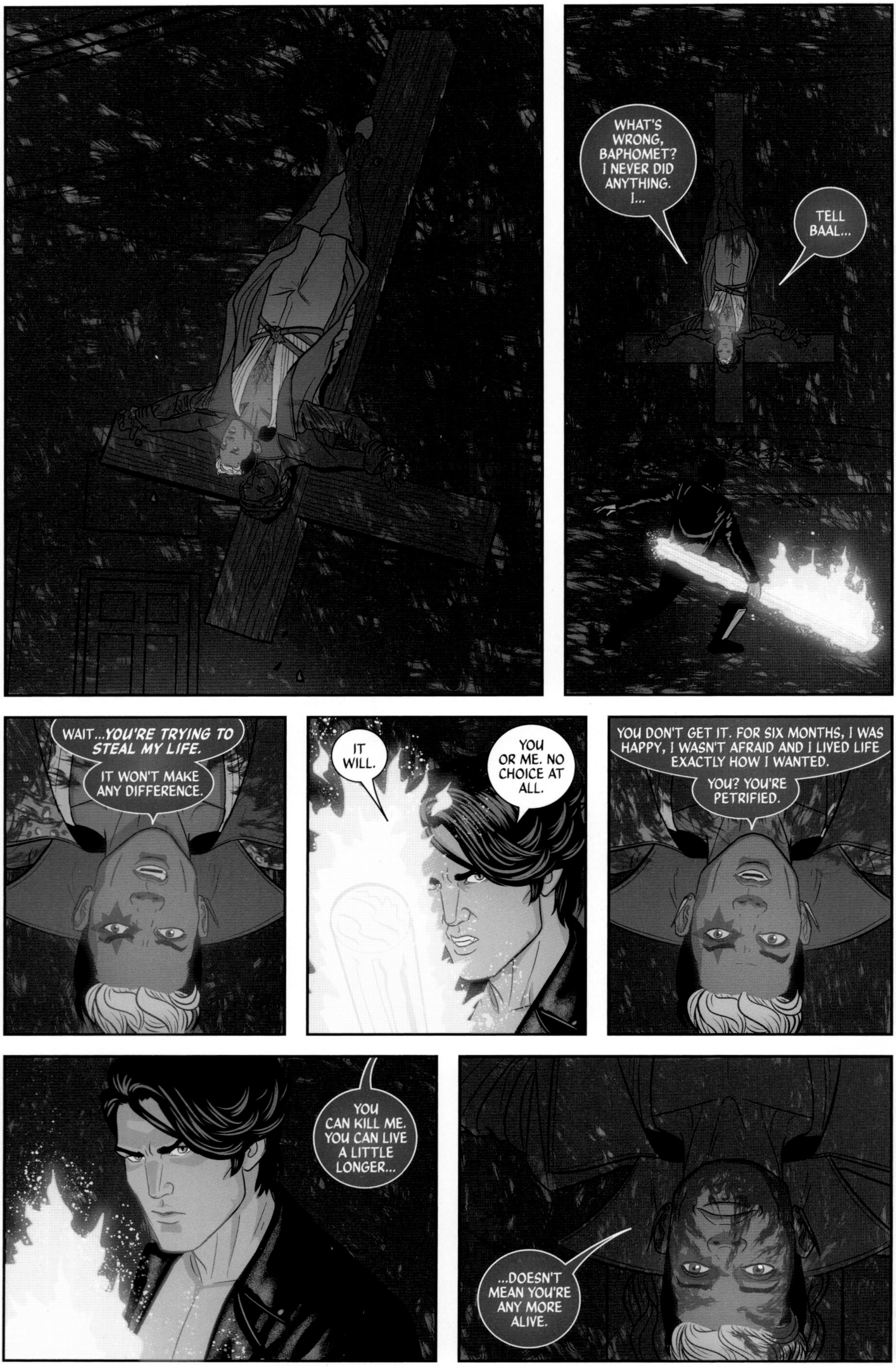
WHAT'S WRONG, BAPHOMET? I NEVER DID ANYTHING. I...
TELL BAAL...
WAIT...*YOU'RE TRYING TO STEAL MY LIFE.*
IT WON'T MAKE ANY DIFFERENCE.
IT WILL.
YOU OR ME. NO CHOICE AT ALL.
YOU DON'T GET IT. FOR SIX MONTHS, I WAS HAPPY, I WASN'T AFRAID AND I LIVED LIFE EXACTLY HOW I WANTED.
YOU? YOU'RE PETRIFIED.
YOU CAN KILL ME. YOU CAN LIVE A LITTLE LONGER...
...DOESN'T MEAN YOU'RE ANY MORE ALIVE.

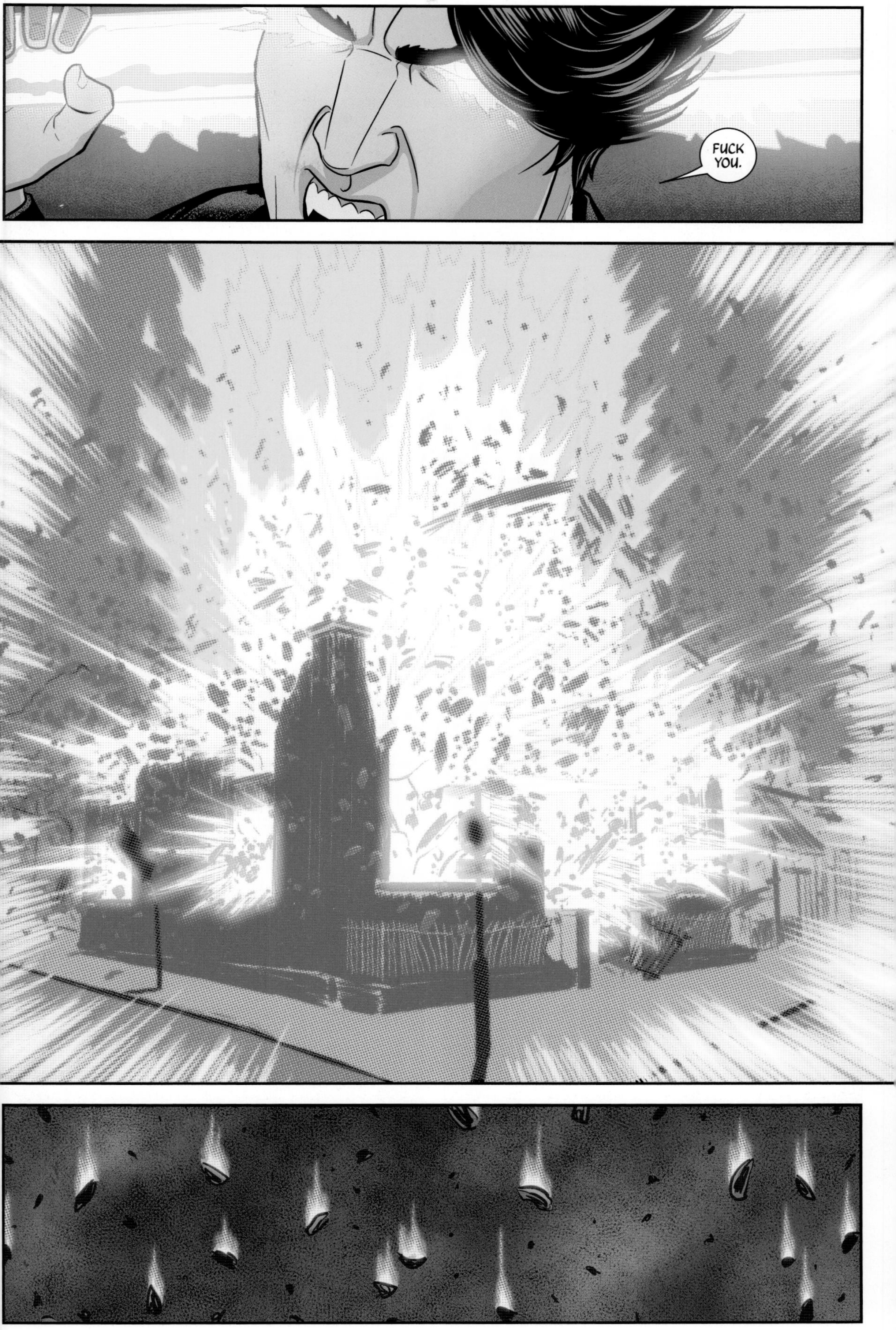
FUCK YOU.

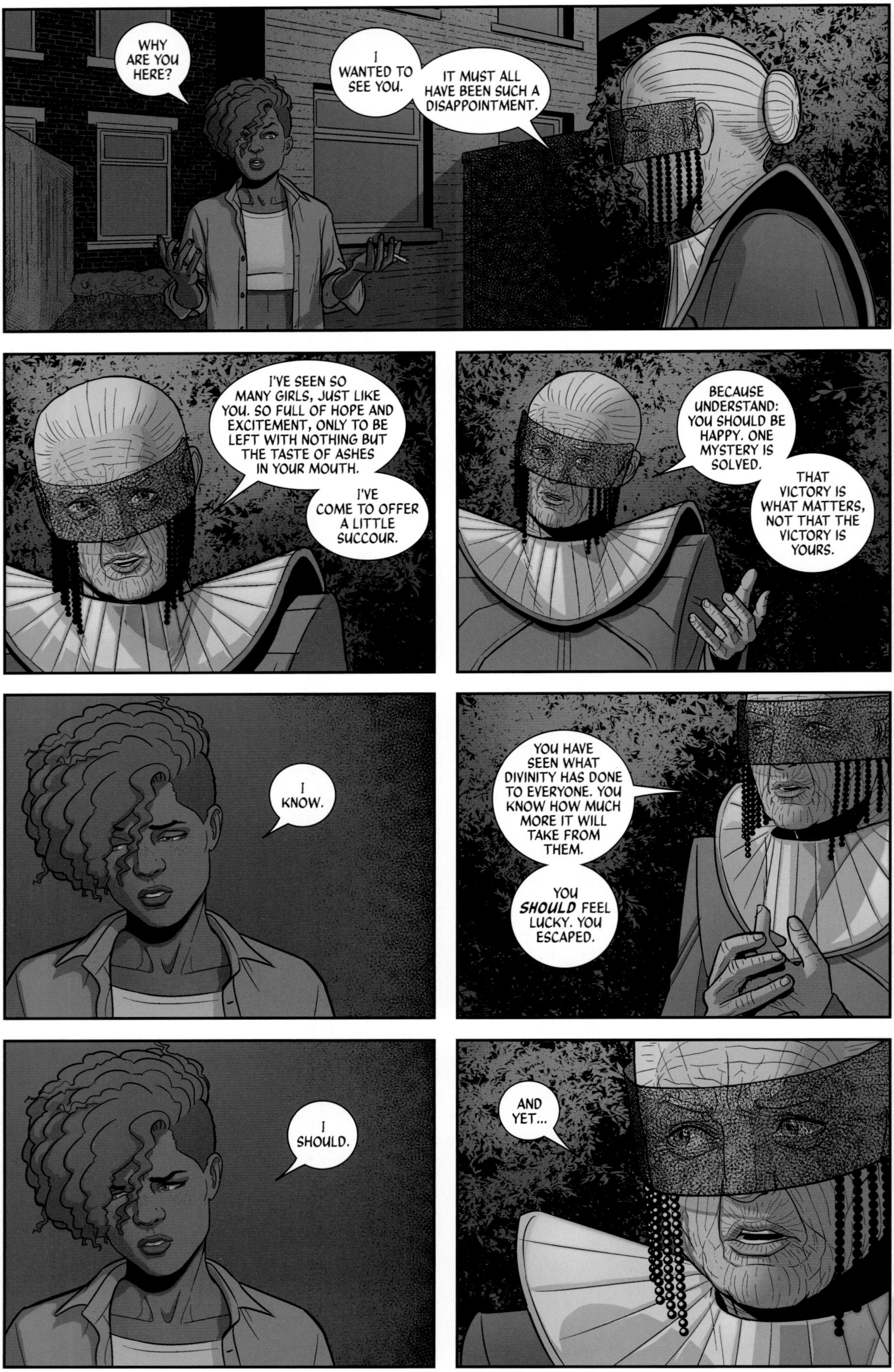

WHY ARE YOU HERE?
I WANTED TO SEE YOU.
IT MUST ALL HAVE BEEN SUCH A DISAPPOINTMENT.
I'VE SEEN SO MANY GIRLS, JUST LIKE YOU. SO FULL OF HOPE AND EXCITEMENT, ONLY TO BE LEFT WITH NOTHING BUT THE TASTE OF ASHES IN YOUR MOUTH.
I'VE COME TO OFFER A LITTLE SUCCOUR.
BECAUSE UNDERSTAND: YOU SHOULD BE HAPPY. ONE MYSTERY IS SOLVED.
THAT VICTORY IS WHAT MATTERS, NOT THAT THE VICTORY IS YOURS.
I KNOW.
YOU HAVE SEEN WHAT DIVINITY HAS DONE TO EVERYONE. YOU KNOW HOW MUCH MORE IT WILL TAKE FROM THEM.
YOU ***SHOULD*** FEEL LUCKY. YOU ESCAPED.
I SHOULD.
AND YET...

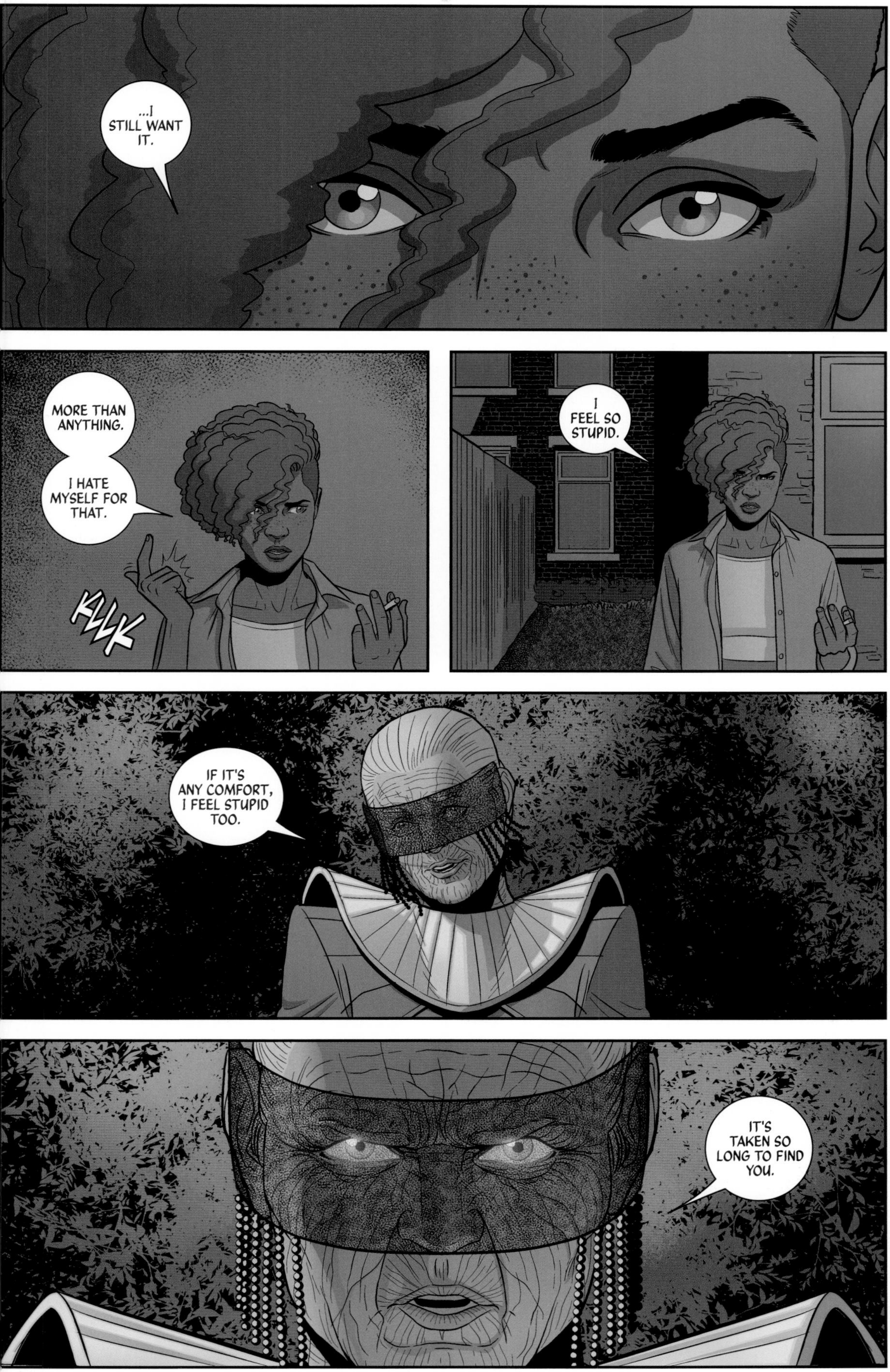
...I STILL WANT IT.
MORE THAN ANYTHING.
I HATE MYSELF FOR THAT.
KLLK
I FEEL SO STUPID.
IF IT'S ANY COMFORT, I FEEL STUPID TOO.
IT'S TAKEN SO LONG TO FIND YOU.

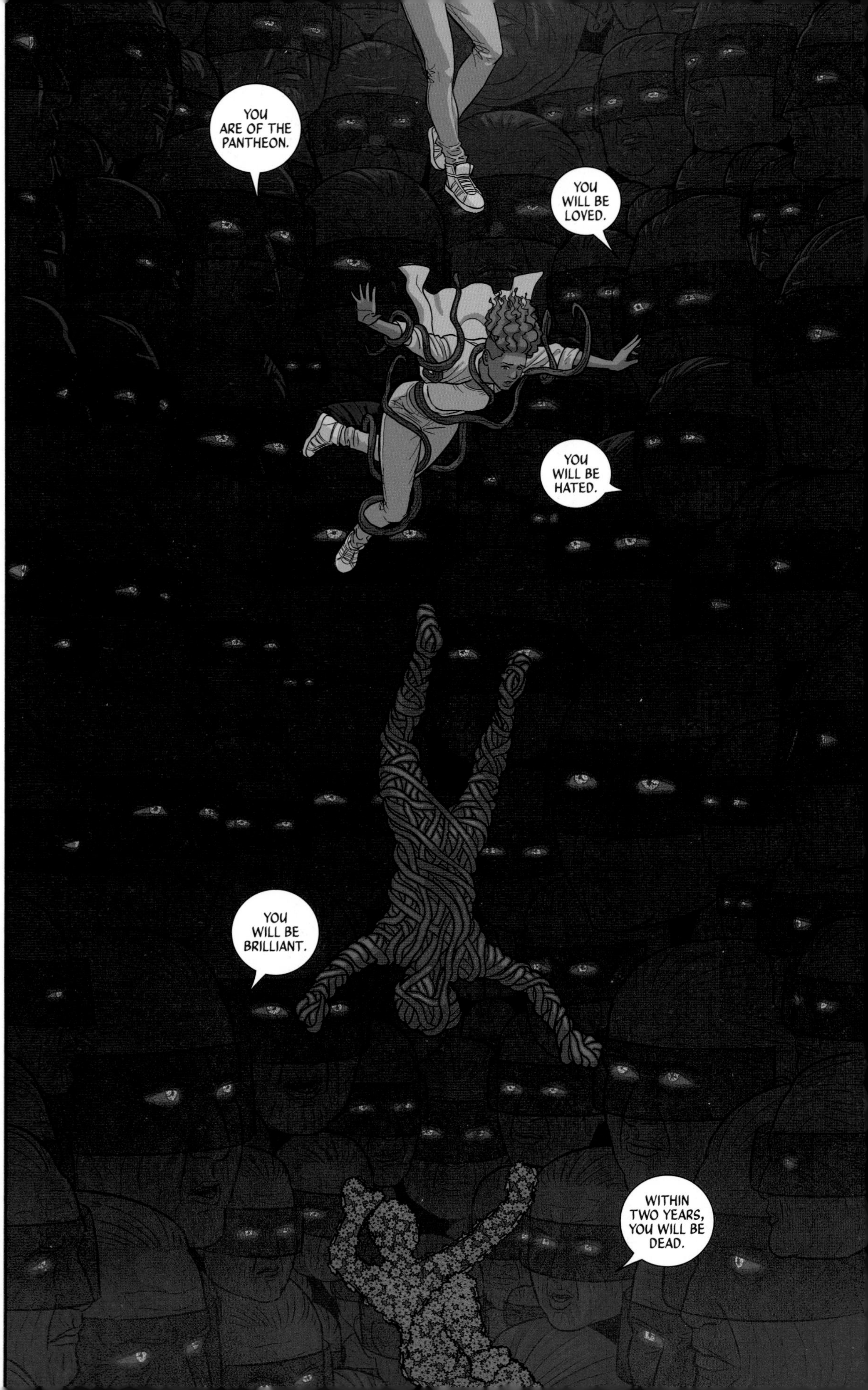
YOU ARE OF THE PANTHEON.
YOU WILL BE LOVED.
YOU WILL BE HATED.
YOU WILL BE BRILLIANT.
WITHIN TWO YEARS, YOU WILL BE DEAD.

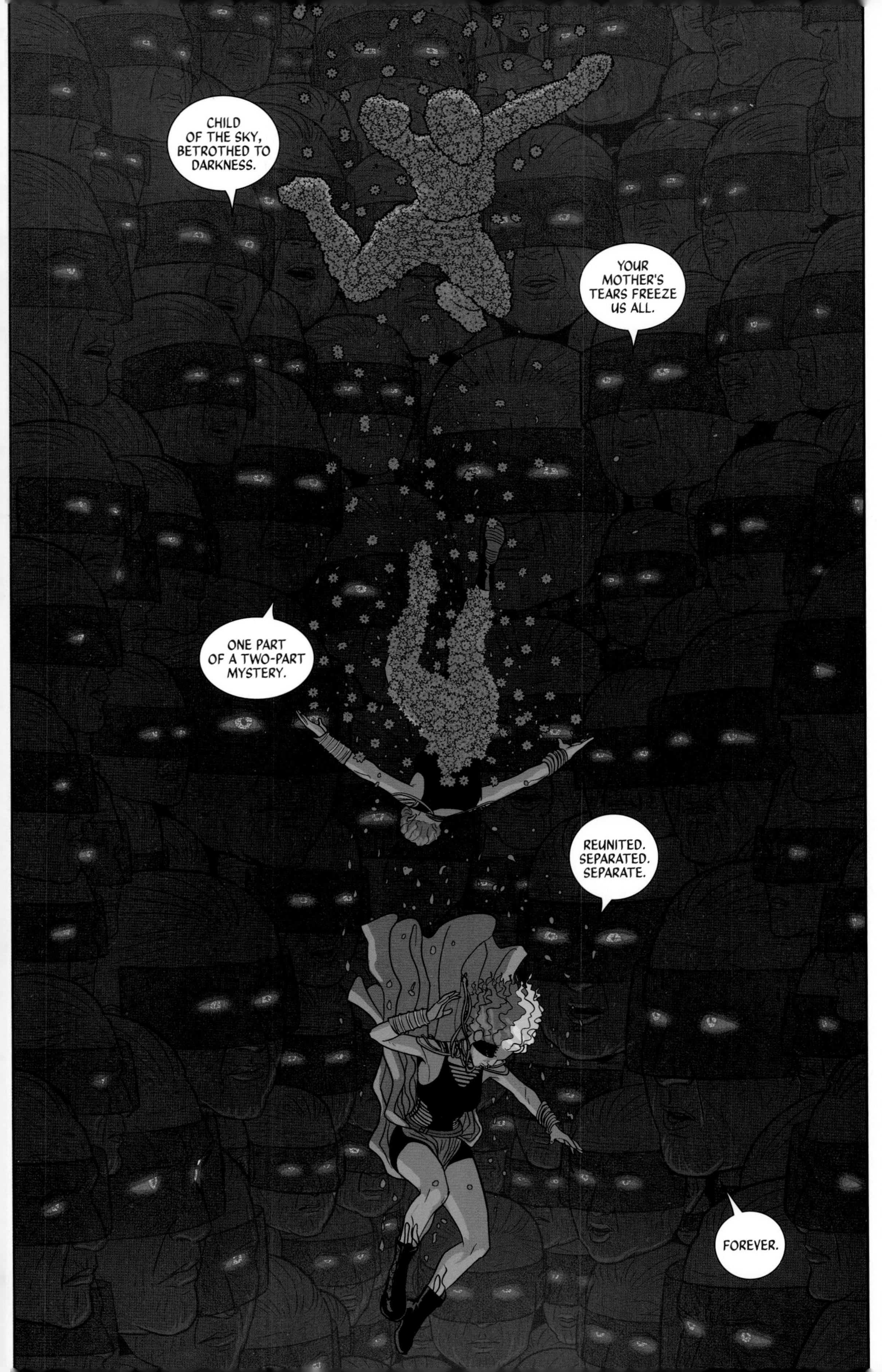
CHILD OF THE SKY, BETROTHED TO DARKNESS.
YOUR MOTHER'S TEARS FREEZE US ALL.
ONE PART OF A TWO-PART MYSTERY.
REUNITED. SEPARATED. SEPARATE.
FOREVER.

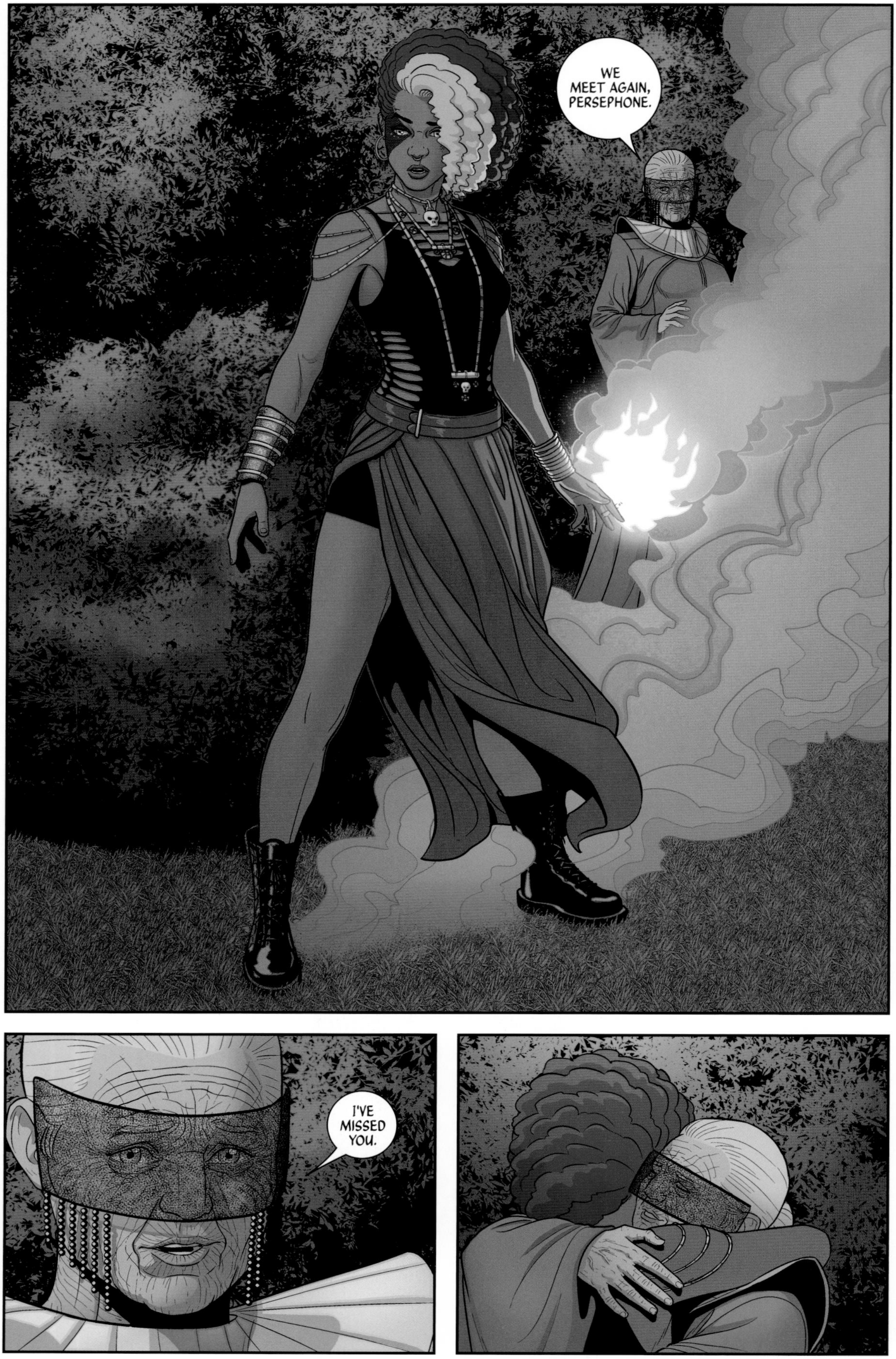
WE MEET AGAIN, PERSEPHONE.
I'VE MISSED YOU.

PERSEPHONE

3 AUGUST 2014

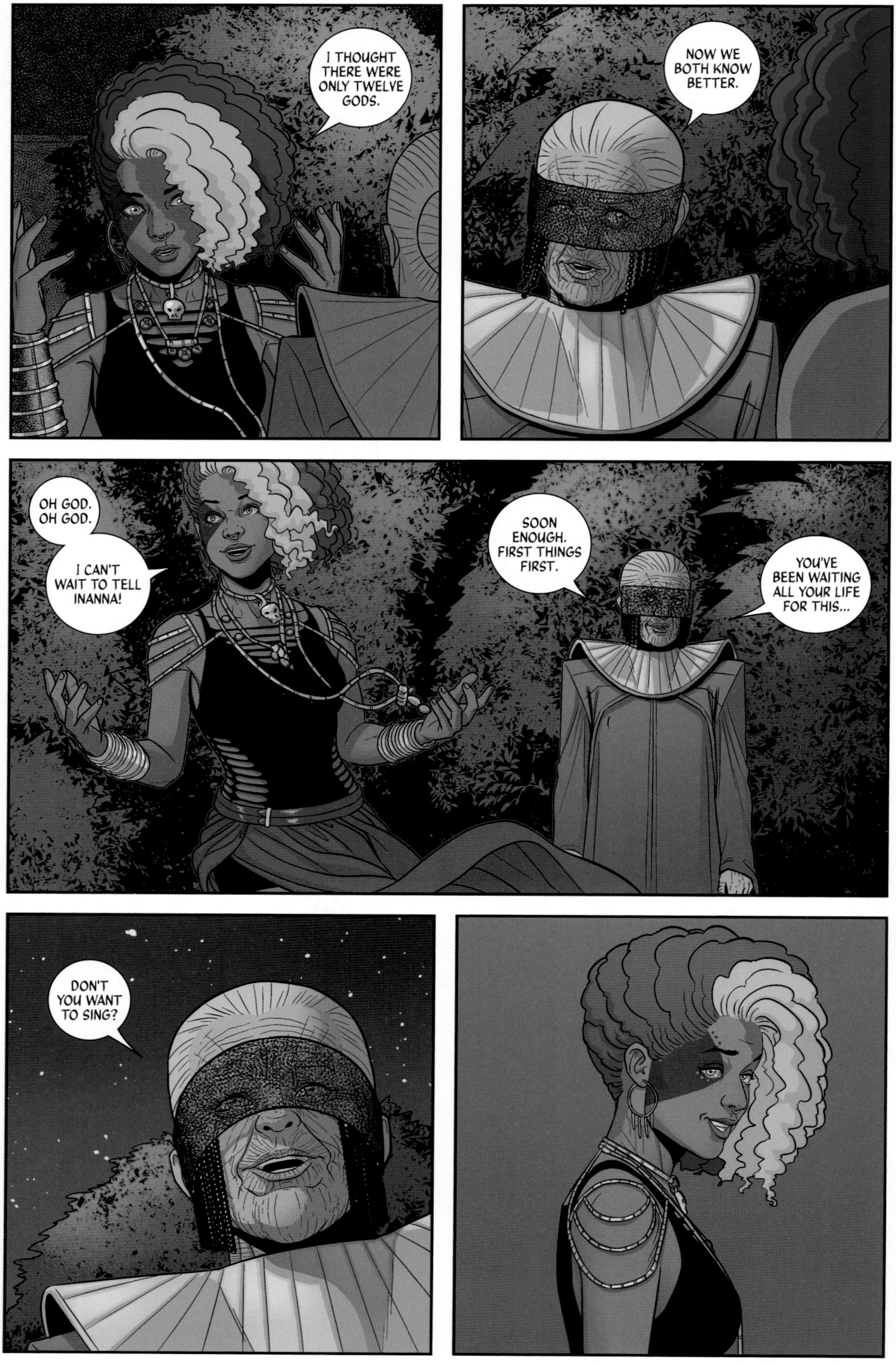
I THOUGHT THERE WERE ONLY TWELVE GODS.
NOW WE BOTH KNOW BETTER.
OH GOD. OH GOD.
I CAN'T WAIT TO TELL INANNA!
SOON ENOUGH. FIRST THINGS FIRST.
YOU'VE BEEN WAITING ALL YOUR LIFE FOR THIS...
DON'T YOU WANT TO SING?

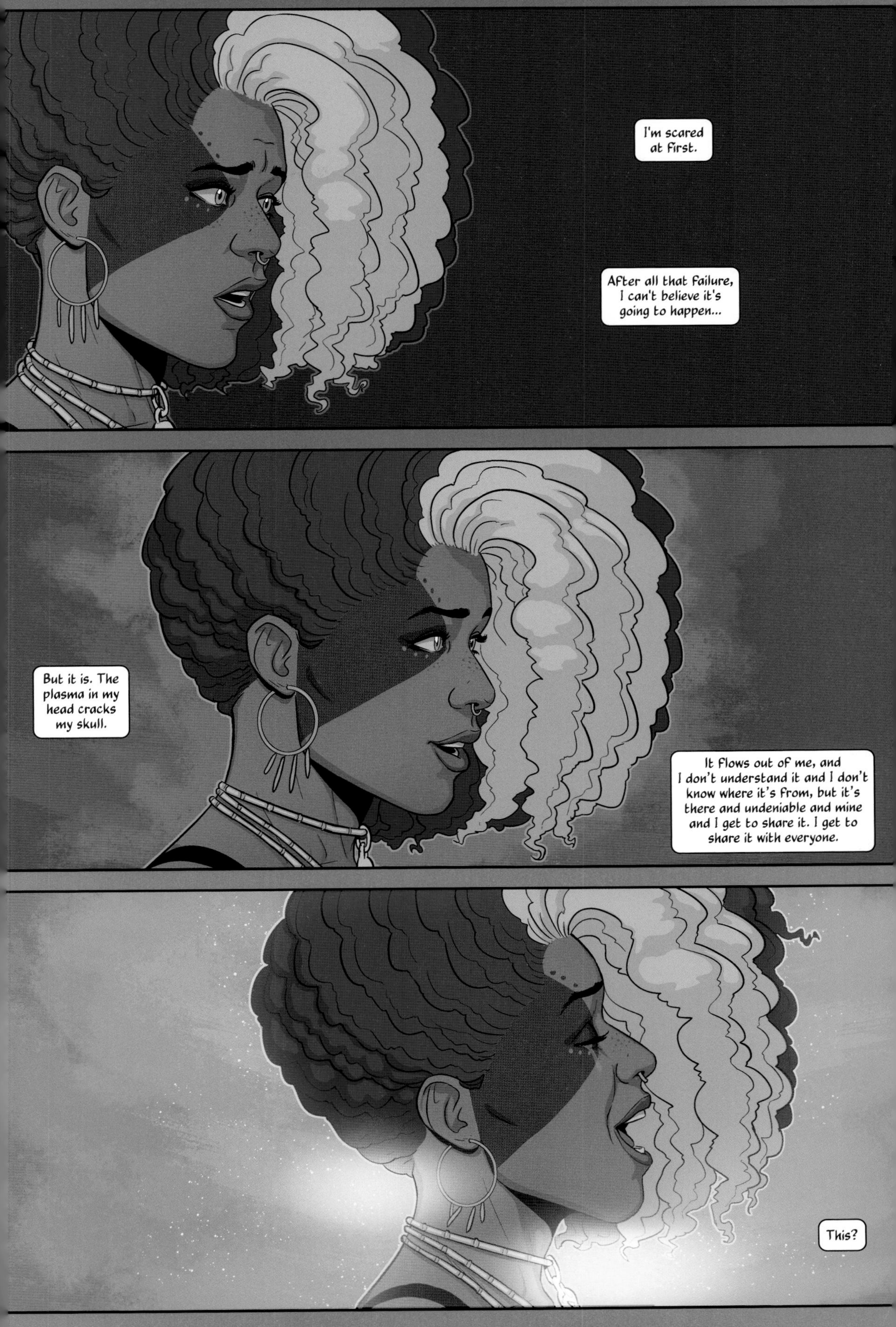
I'm scared at first.
After all that failure, I can't believe it's going to happen...
But it is. The plasma in my head cracks my skull.
It flows out of me, and I don't understand it and I don't know where it's from, but it's there and undeniable and mine and I get to share it. I get to share it with everyone.
This?

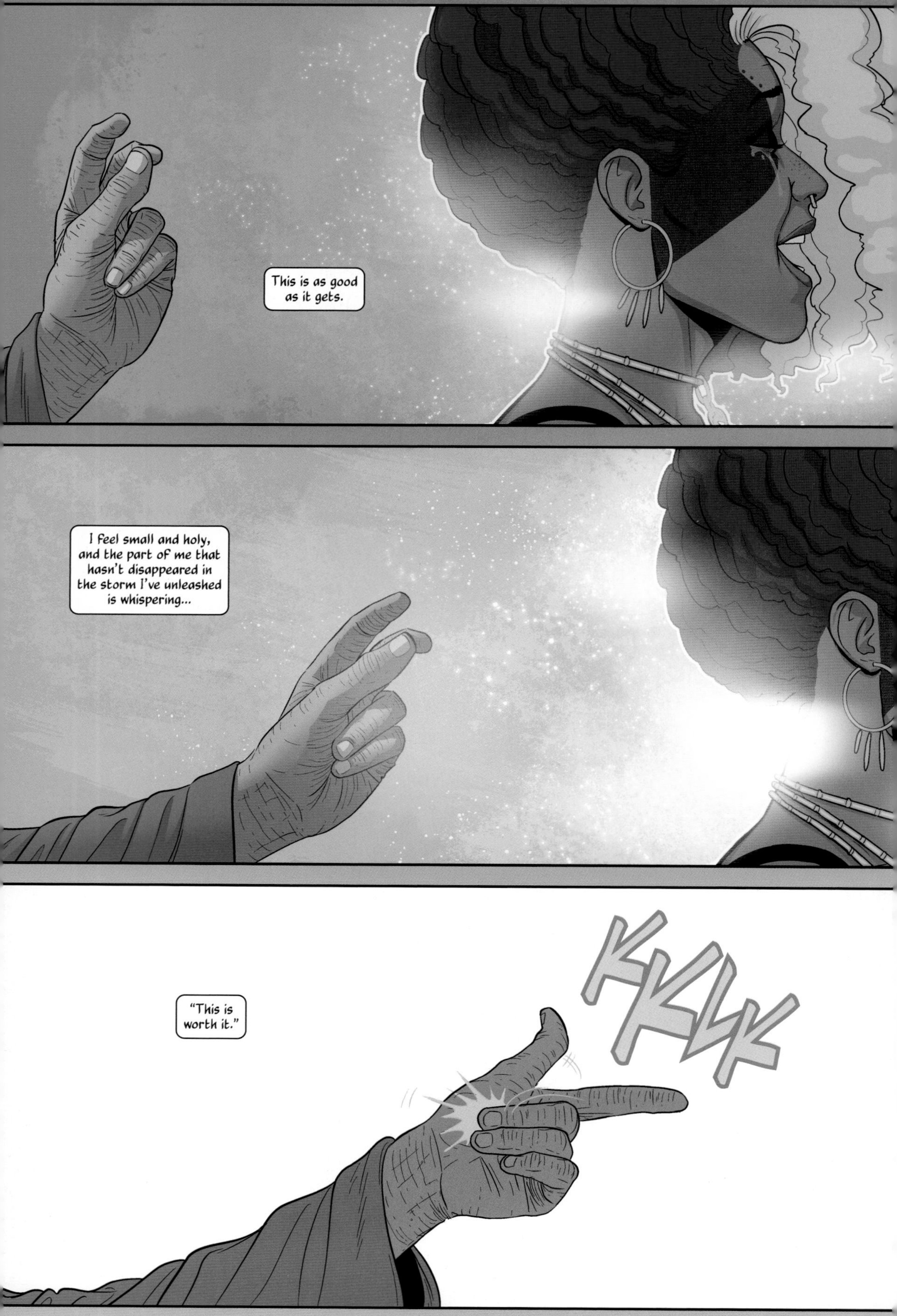
This is as good as it gets.
I feel small and holy, and the part of me that hasn't disappeared in the storm I've unleashed is whispering...
"This is worth it."
KKK

I don't remember
anything after
that.

I guess I'm
grateful.

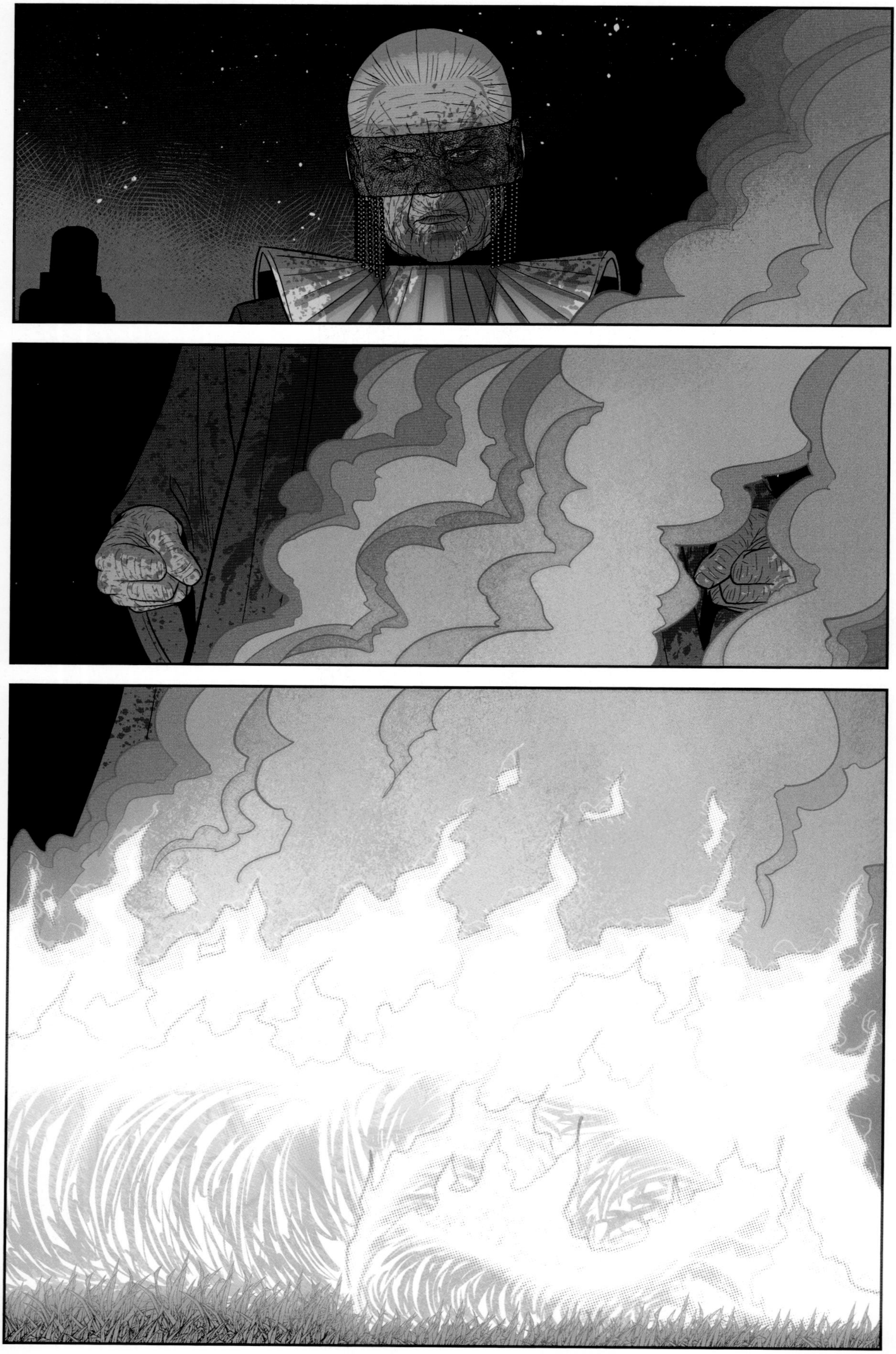

WHAT THE HELL DO YOU THINK YOU'RE DOING?
YOU'RE...
THAT FIRE. THERE'S...
NO.
FORGIVE ME.
I SHOULD HAVE LEFT MORE SWIFTLY.
SOME MURDERS ARE NECESSARY.
OTHERS ARE NOT.
KLLK

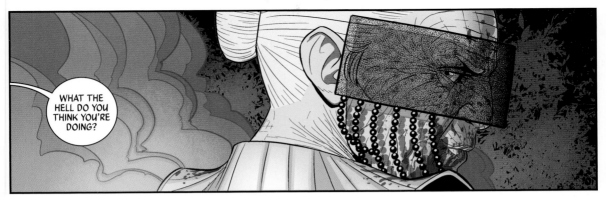

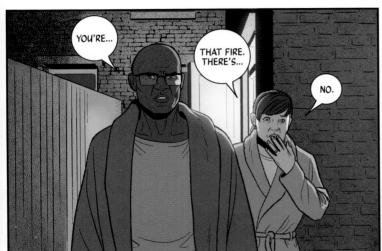

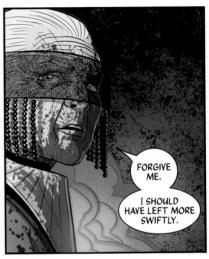

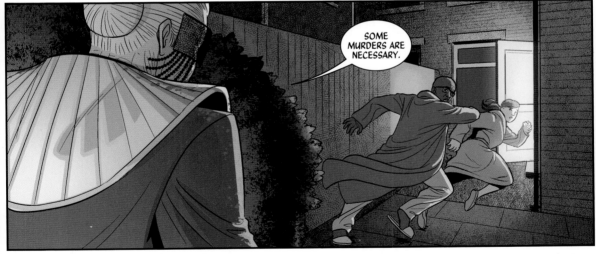

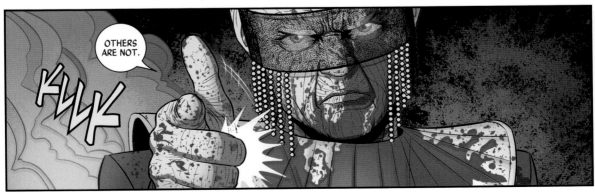

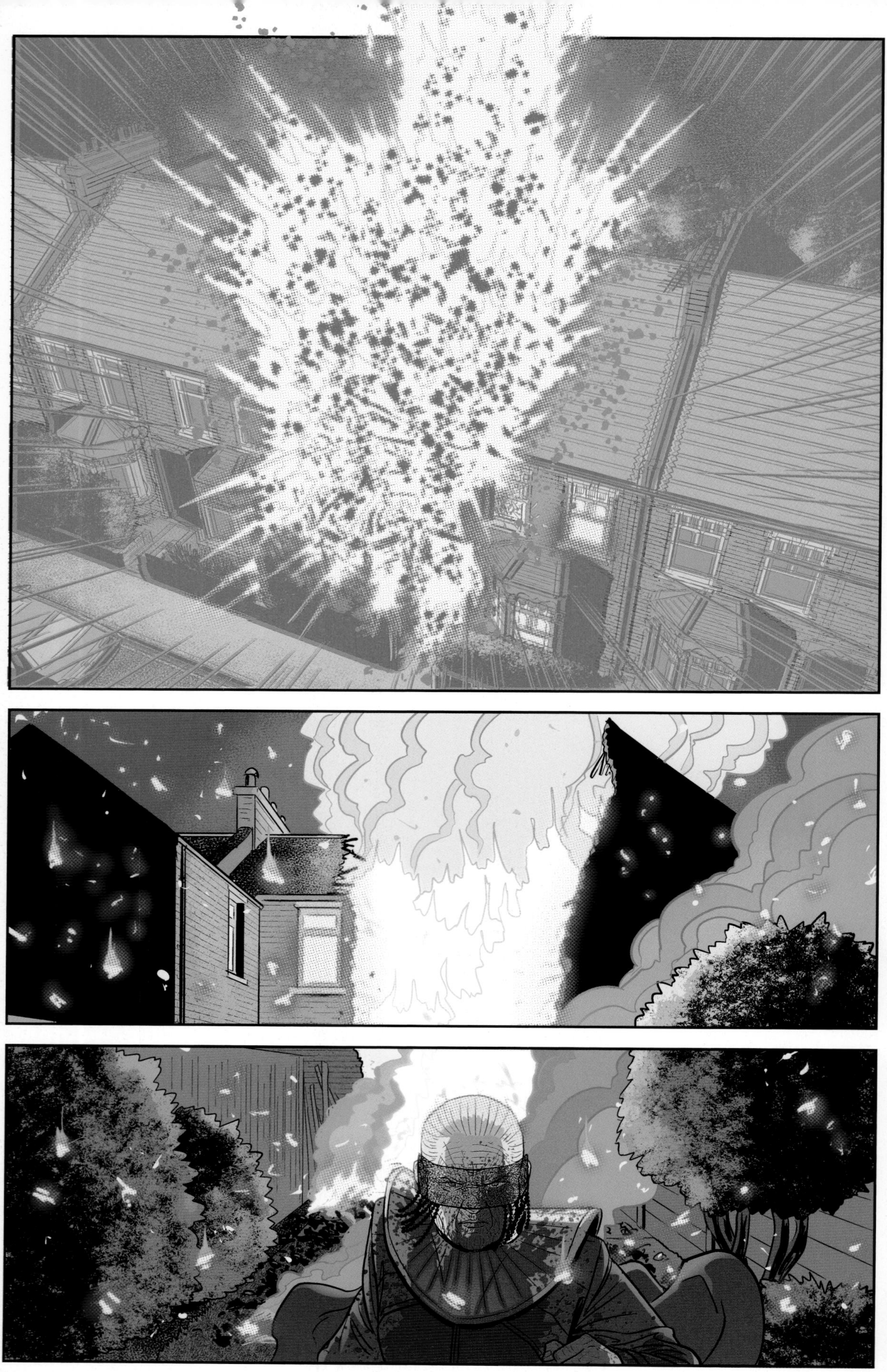

IT WAS NEVER
GOING TO BE OKAY

3 AUGUST 2014

VARIANT ART

How we approach variant covers is something we've grown into. It's not something we were planning originally, but has become a big part of our month-to-month on the book. The variant cover is normally something which is related to what's been revealed in the previous issue, so we only actually show it to the world after that issue hit the stands. For example, when issue 9 was out, we revealed Frazer's Norns. It's oddly enhanced the performative nature of the thing, and people seem to like it. I suspect it'd work a lot less well if we didn't have some of the best artists in the business interpreting our characters. As it's a book about image and iconography, treating the characters like icons worthy of that lavish visual attention seems to underline the theme. You'll find all the variant covers for the issues collected here, plus a special variant we did along the way.

David Lafuente
Issue six cover

Christian Ward
Issue seven cover

Brandon Graham
Issue eight cover

Matthew Wilson, Jamie McKelvie
Issue nine ECCC cover

Marguerite Sauvage
Issue nine cover

Frazer Irving
Issue ten cover

Fiona Staples
Issue eleven cover

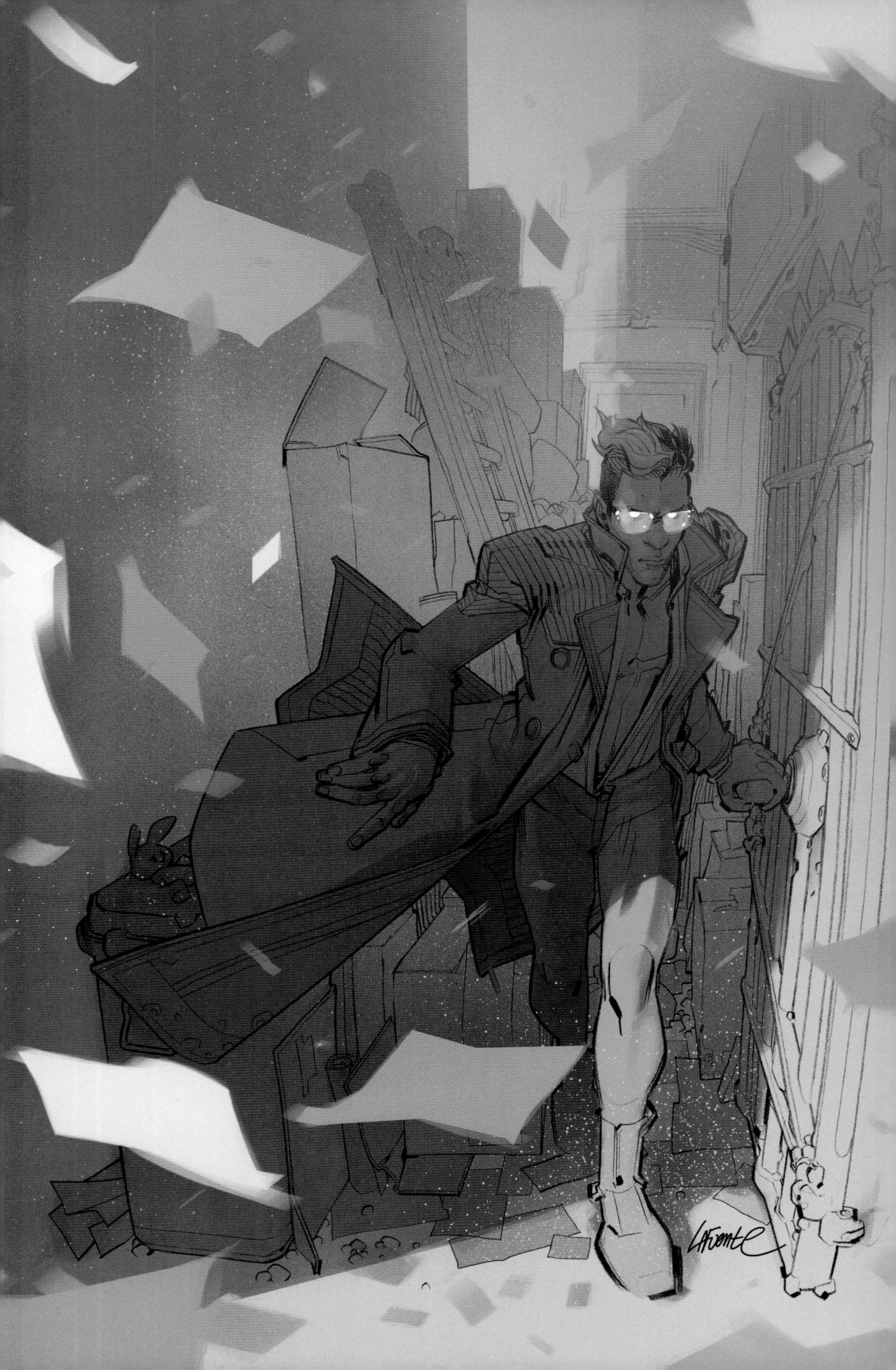
LAFUENTE

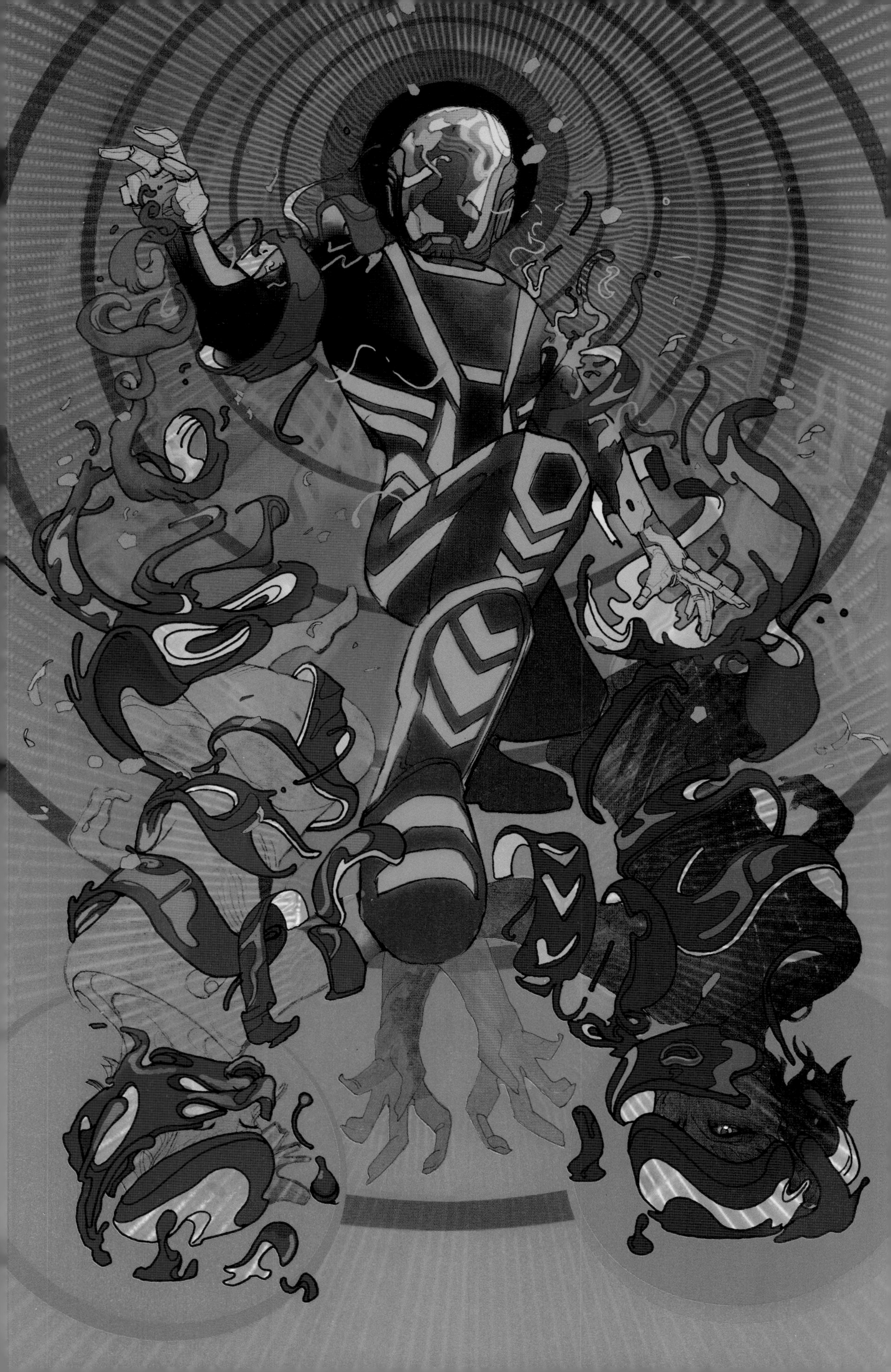

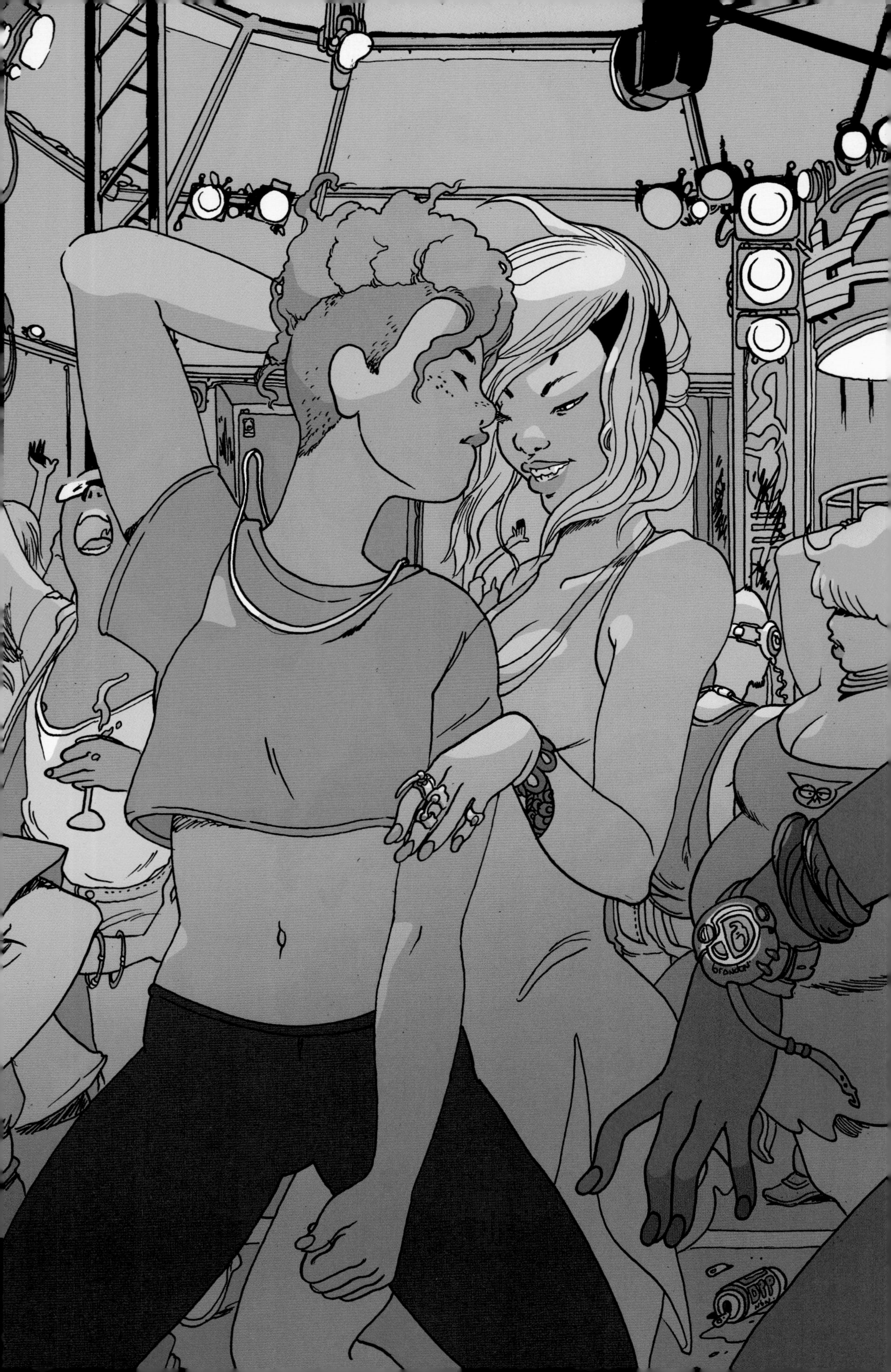
brandon
DRP

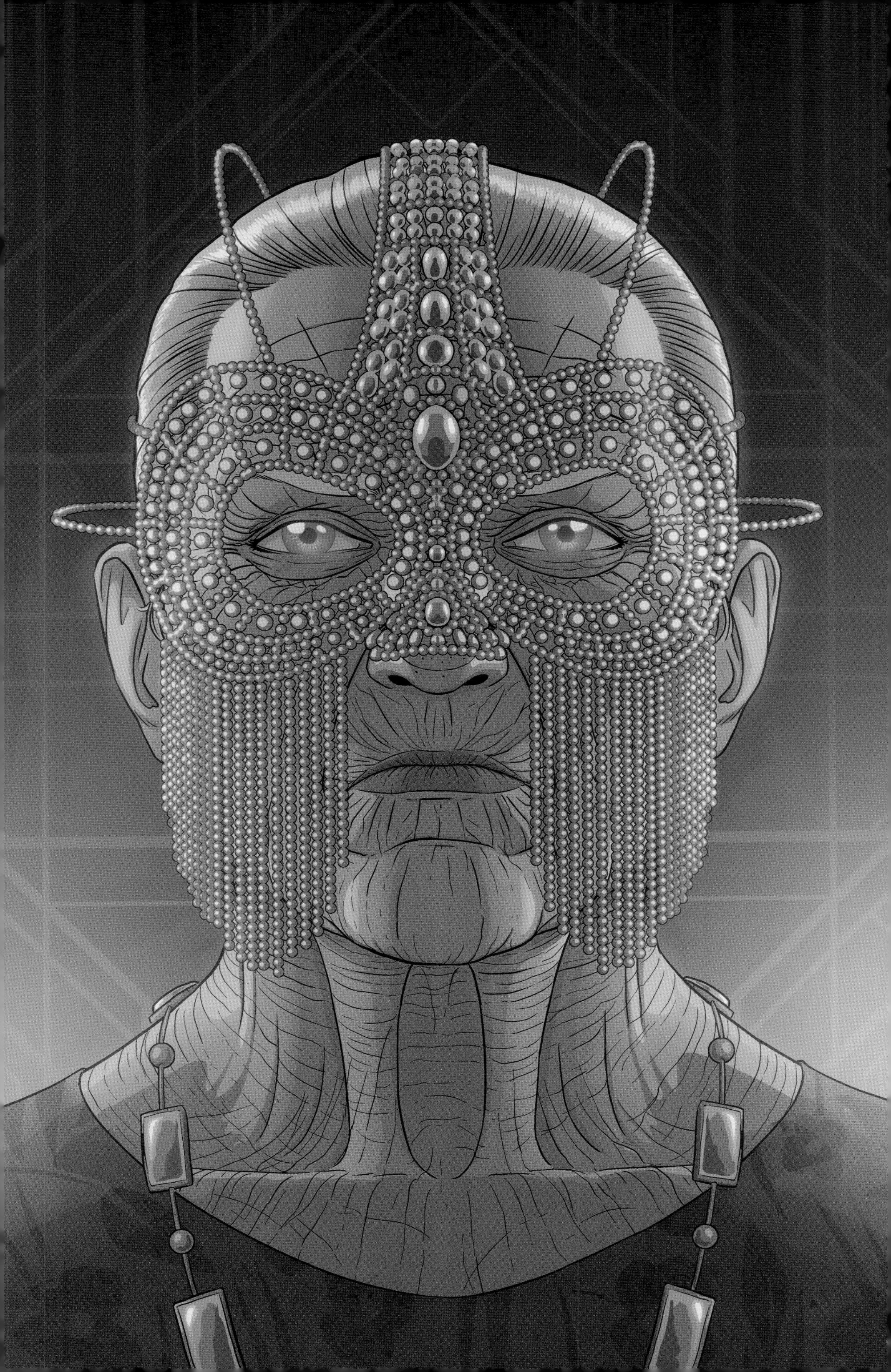

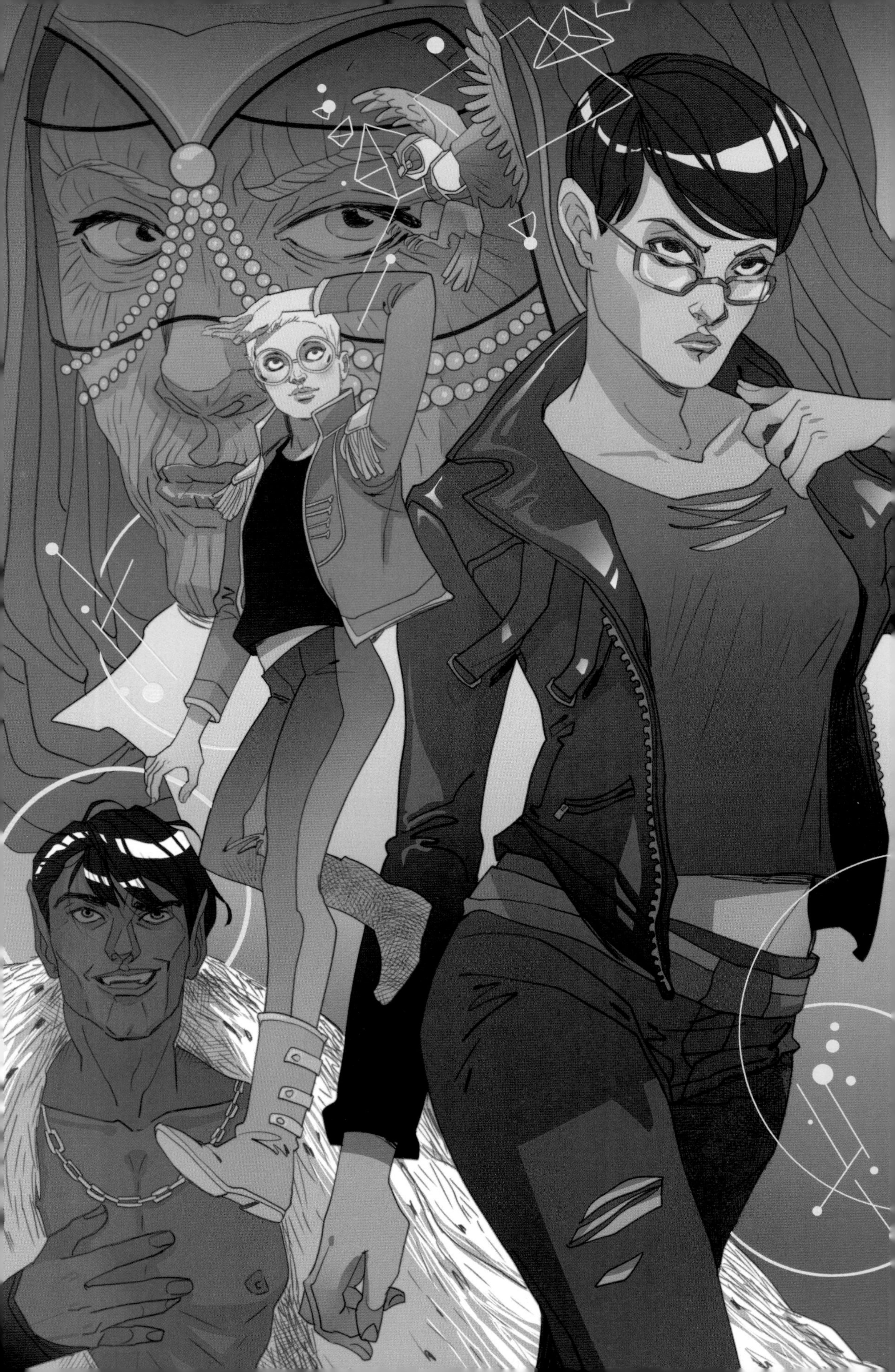

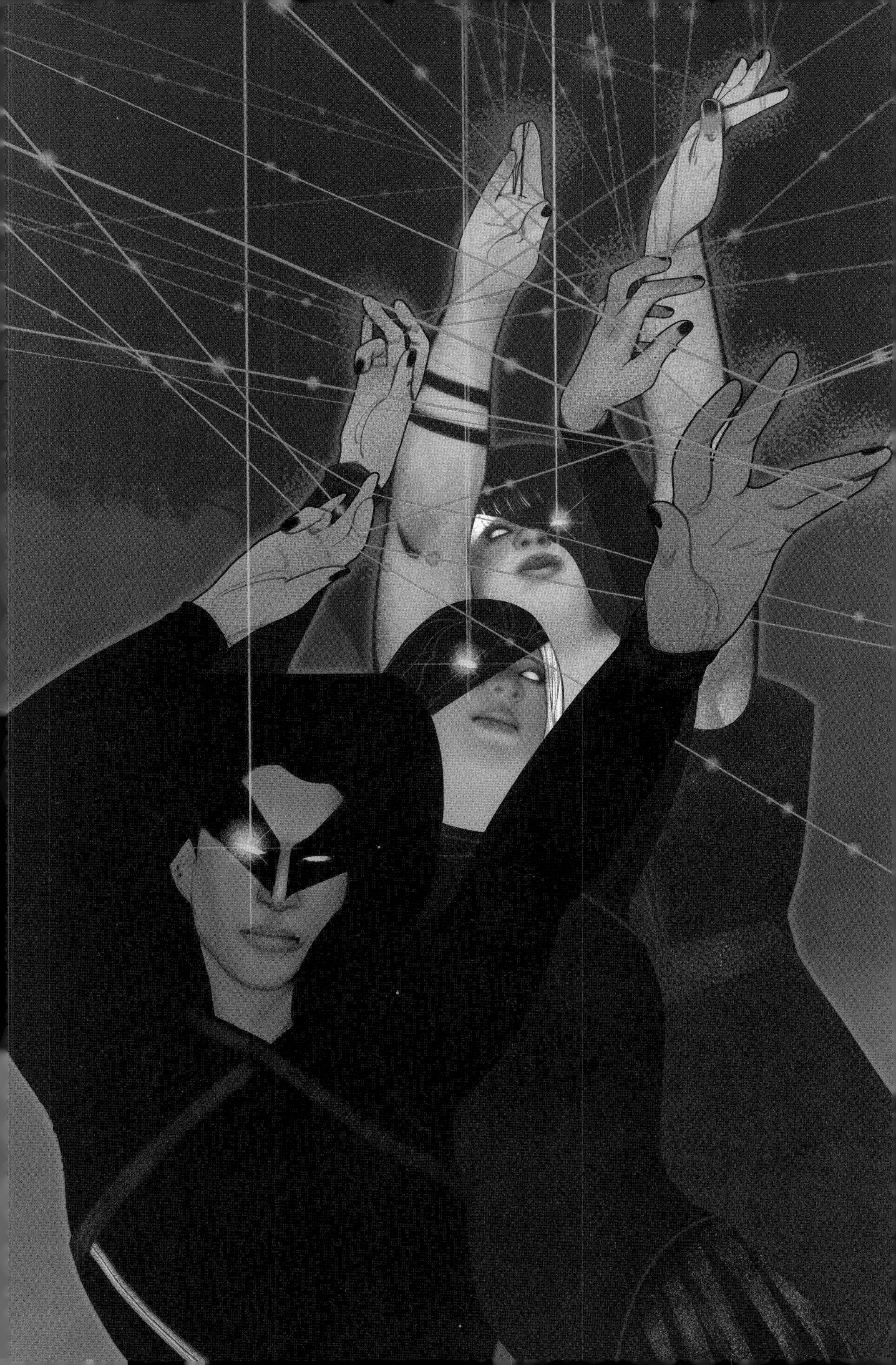

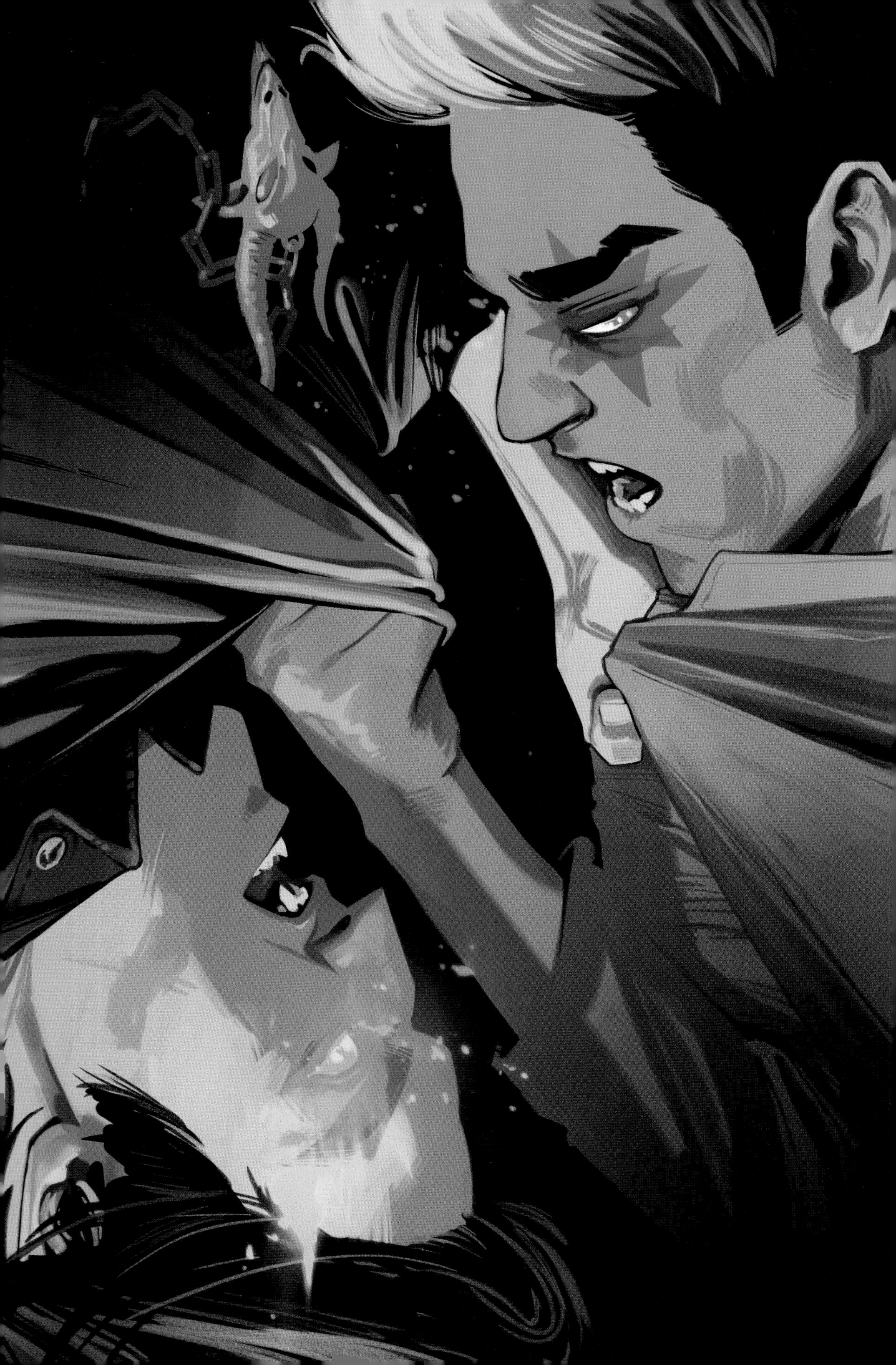

MAKING OF

Creation is basically magic. Dark magic, in our case. When making an issue of *WicDiv*, we have to perform horrific magical rites, sacrificing screaming virgins to the grand demon S'jsafk'arf who gives us lovely pages in return. However, as a cover for our diabolic dealings, we reverse engineer a bunch of steps. First Matt takes the pages, and removes all the colours, and so on. We present all these entirely fake steps on the following pages. It's all S'jsafk'arf's work. He's a surprisingly nice guy, except for all the human sacrifice. You should drop him a line.

FROM SCRIPT TO PAGE

PAGE 18
This is the one real sequence of magic in the issue. It's possible you may want to spread it to more pages if you feel like it... but maybe not. It's a quiet magical thing, as is this issue.

We're in a morgue, at night. It's all still. There is a roof in the ceiling or small high windows. Through it, we can see the night sky. Stars twinkling out there, all distant. Perhaps beams of lights fall across this clinical empty space, from the moonlight...

And then, in the beams of light, we start to get twinkles of purple, like tinkerbell-gone-Purple-Rain.

And then, out of the light itself, Inanna steps out. Not all there yet — just swirling stardust in part.

And then he's there, looking around. He's not entirely at ease. This place is creepy.

CAP: Miracle options.

FROM ISSUE 6 SCRIPT

PENCILS

INKS

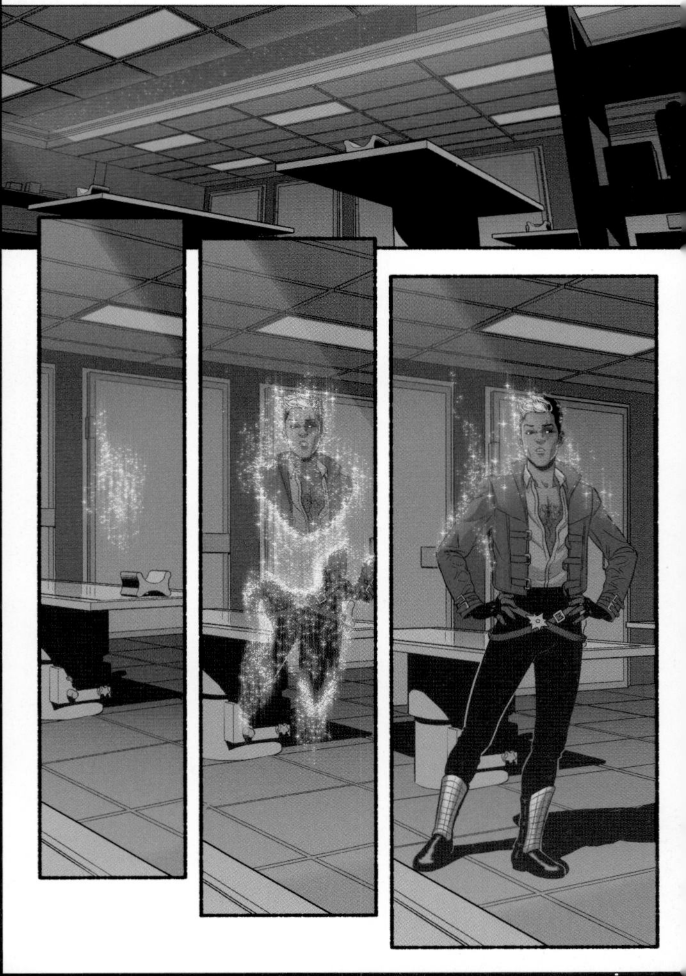

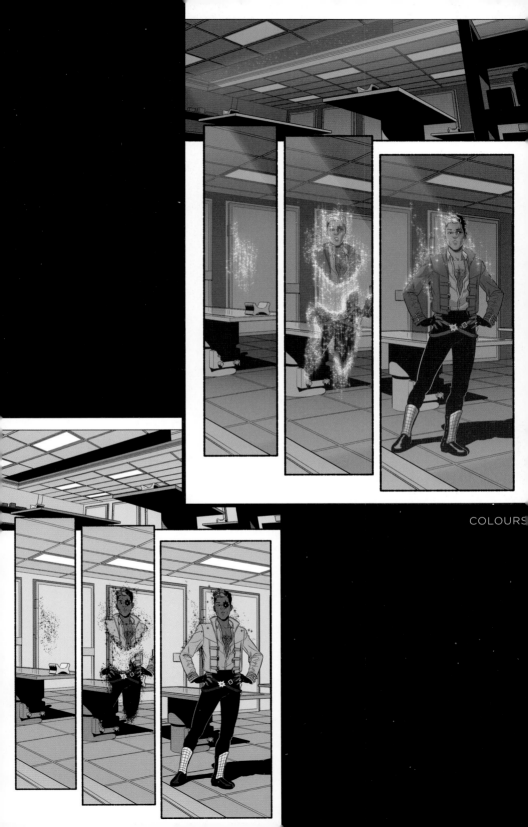

COLOURS

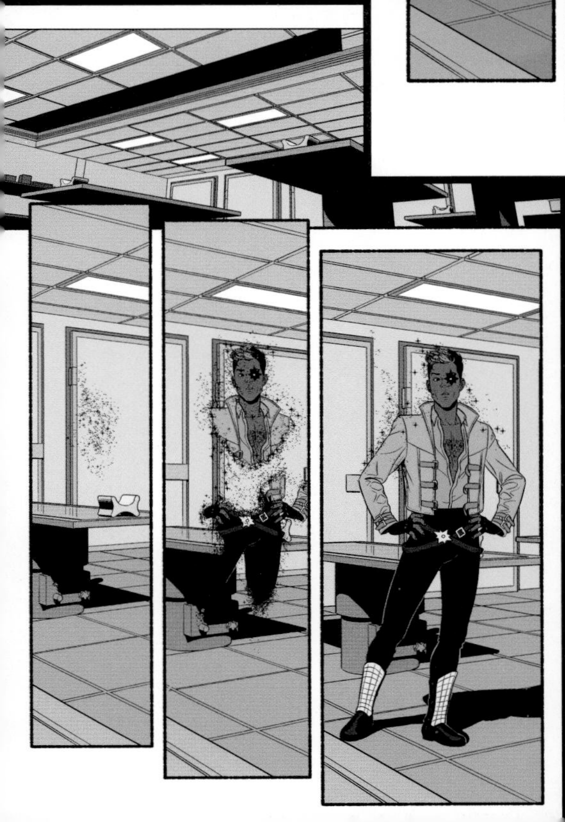

As many of the gods have their own way of speaking, letterer Clayton Cowles spends a lot of time coming up with the best way to represent their unique characters. Here are some of the different options he played around with for Urðr and Dionysus.

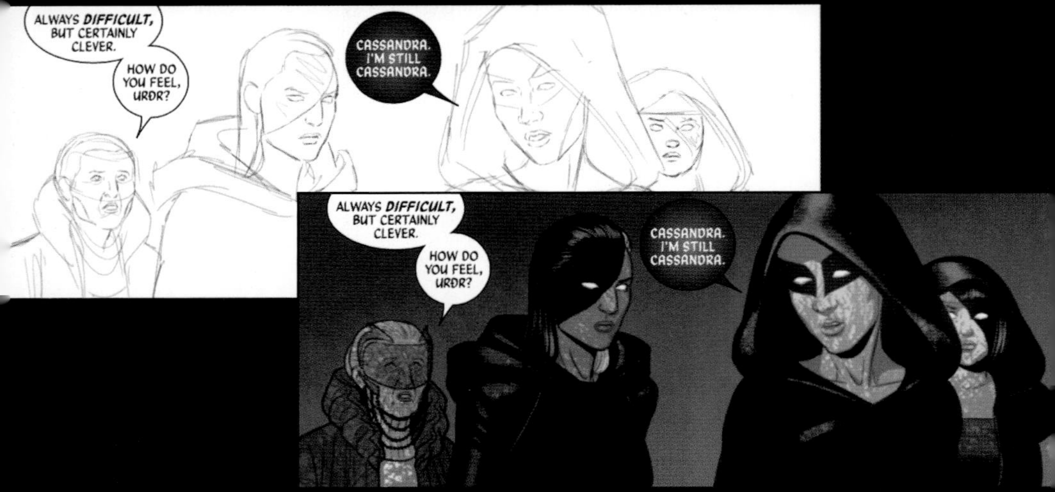

ALWAYS DIFFICULT, BUT CERTAINLY CLEVER.
HOW DO YOU FEEL, URÐR?
CASSANDRA. I'M STILL CASSANDRA.
ALWAYS DIFFICULT, BUT CERTAINLY CLEVER.
HOW DO YOU FEEL, URÐR?
CASSANDRA. I'M STILL CASSANDRA.

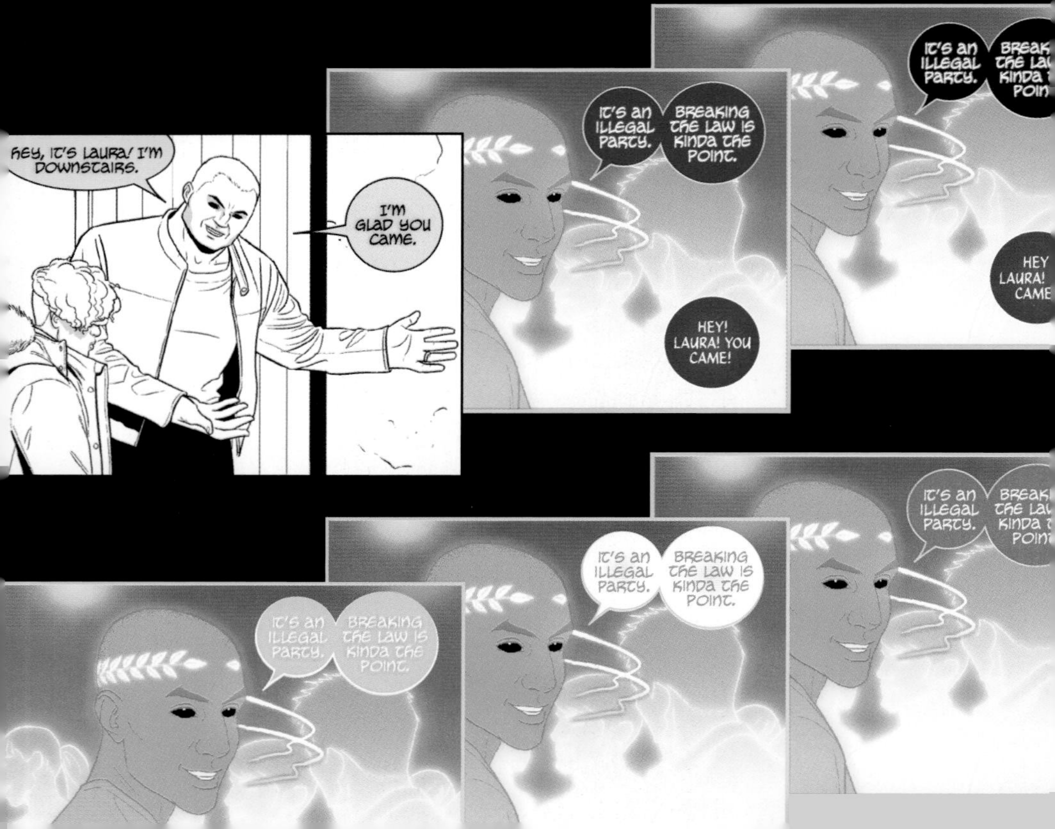

HEY, IT'S LAURA! I'M DOWNSTAIRS.
I'M GLAD YOU CAME.
IT'S AN ILLEGAL PARTY.
BREAKING THE LAW IS KINDA THE POINT.
HEY! LAURA! YOU CAME!
IT'S AN ILLEGAL PARTY.
IT'S AN ILLEGAL PARTY.
BREAKING THE LAW IS KINDA THE POINT.
IT'S AN ILLEGAL PARTY.
BREAKING THE LAW IS KINDA THE POINT.
IT'S AN ILLEGAL PARTY.

FROM SCRIPT TO PAGE

You'll see particular differences here between how the script started out and what was subsequently drawn. Things we haven't shown you, for example, include an extensive email chain between Jamie, Kieron and Chrissy debating festival venues, sites and capacities.

PAGE 4-5

4-5.1

Double Page spread with inserts in bottom right of the spread.

(It could have other insert panels if you wanted to take it that way, but I'm not doing many images in the comic which get the sense of what Ragnarock is... so we may want to lean into the spectacle here. Ideally, it would be a full DPS, but I needed some panels here to lead into the next page.)

We are with Laura and Inanna, high in the air. Like, superman high. They hold hands, falling in star-dust, but with incredible grace – Inanna as Peter Pan to Laura's Wendy. Remember that Miss America panel that opened Young Avengers? That had grace and power. This is very much leaning to grace. We follow them, and before them is...

Well, it's a cross between Glastonbury and a religious festival. Which makes it Glastonbury x Glastonbury.

It's night. Across the countryside below a 100,000 campfires dot the landscape. A moon hangs over the land. The northern star especially glints – Inanna's Star.

The main stage is epochal. Part of me actually wanted to set this at actual Stonehenge, but I don't think that's going to be possible, as Laura needs to make her own way back. Let's set it at whatever Heath is biggest – I'm using Hampstead Heath for now.

While the Stage is at one end, in front of it are several-hundred-feet quasi-stone blocks, arranged in a circle. It's as if Spinal Tap got their Stage Stonehenge, but with the scale flipped the wrong way. They glint in techno-magnificence – presumably made by Woden. There's twelve of them. Each one has a symbol of the gods on it. This would include Lucifer. Perhaps each one could have unearthly fire sparking into the sky. Perhaps except Lucifer's. This looks awesomely ritualistic.

The crowd mills inside the circle, visible through their lighters. The actual people at the gig would be 300,000.

LOC CAP: Ragnarock 2014.

LOC CAP: Hampstead Heath.

4-5.2

And we're at the back stage area. Have you ever been backstage at a festival? Blackstage at Glastonbury, except a fantasy of that – one part Glastonbury and one part Garden of Eden.

We don't have much here, so we can have people milling around. We have Laura and Inanna stepping out of the star-dust, beautiful.

I see this as a long, almost page width panel...

LAURA: Aren't you staying?

INANNA: I play the big stage tomorrow. Tonight, I've my own thing back at the residency.

INANNA: I'd always rather play than watch.

4-5.3

Small panel. On Inanna, turning to light. He's glancing over Laura's shoulder. He's a little trepidatious. He's basically escaping!

INANNA: Better go.

4-5.4

Ball stepping up... and Inanna takes to the air, in stardust. Baal is reaching and caught half greeting.

BAAL: Hey, Inanna you--

BAAL: Oh, hell.

FROM ISSUE 10 SCRIPT

TOP VIEW
STAGE
Pillars (and one more)
CROWD!
CAMPING!
CAMPING
CAMPING
CAMPING
Enormous
GLOW

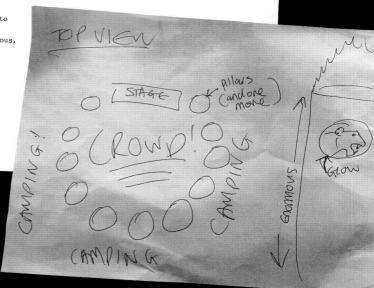

KIERON'S SKETCH

3D MODEL

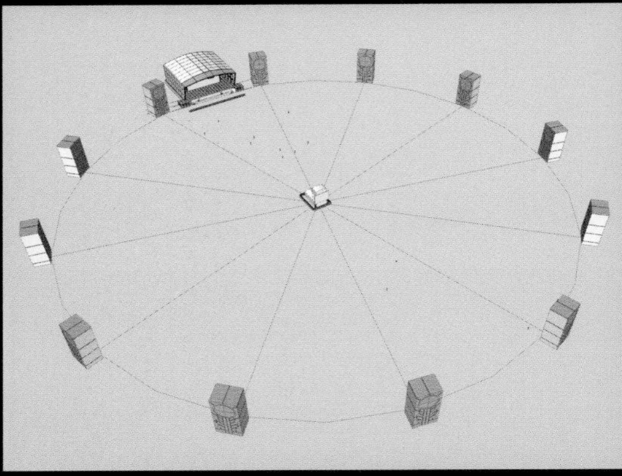

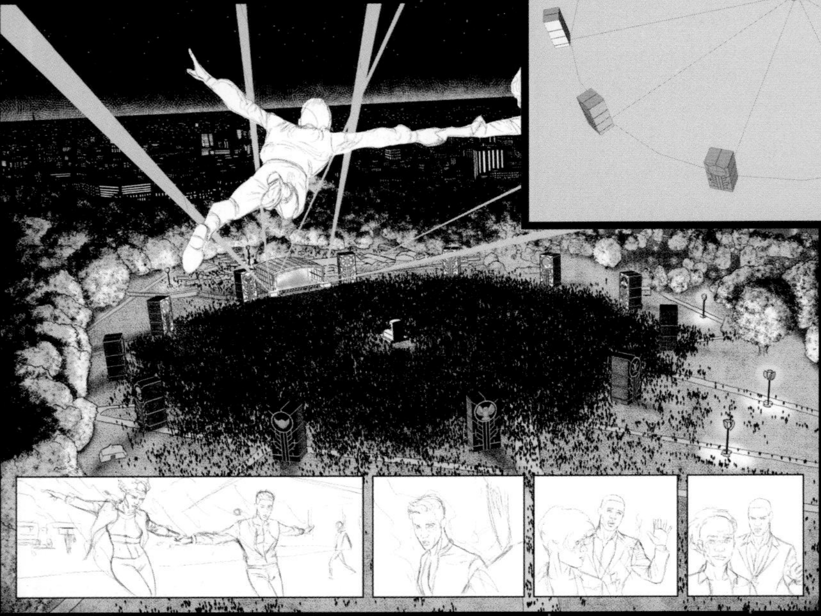

PENCILS

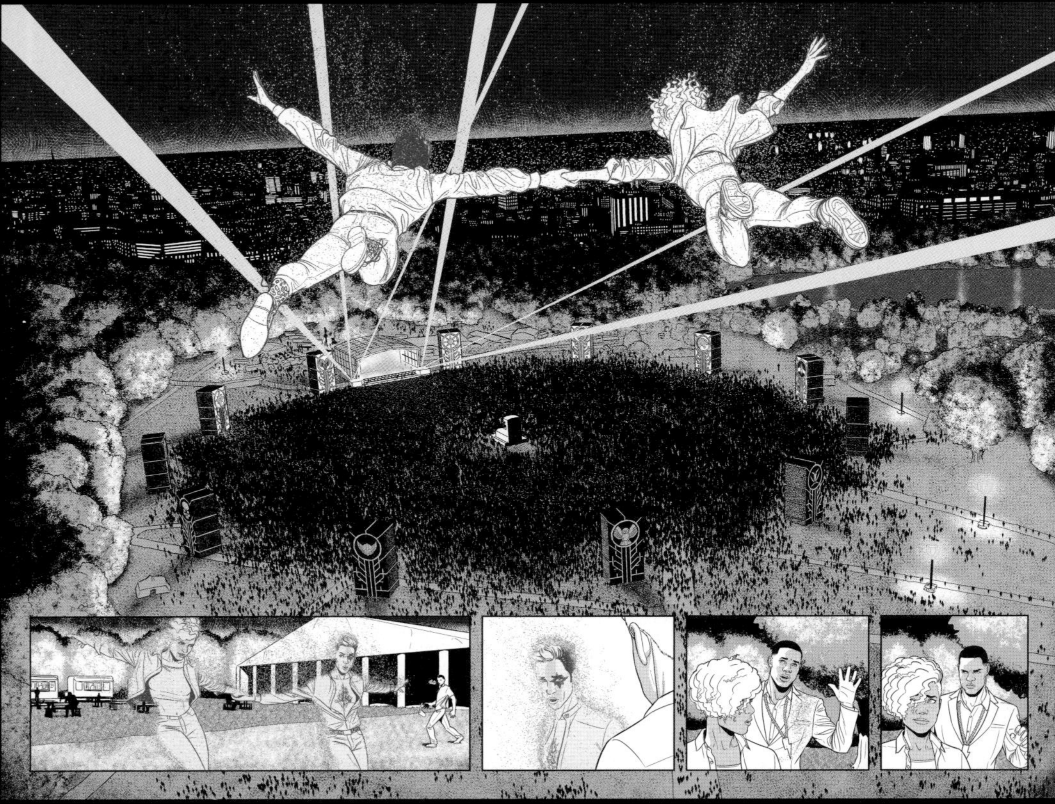

INKS

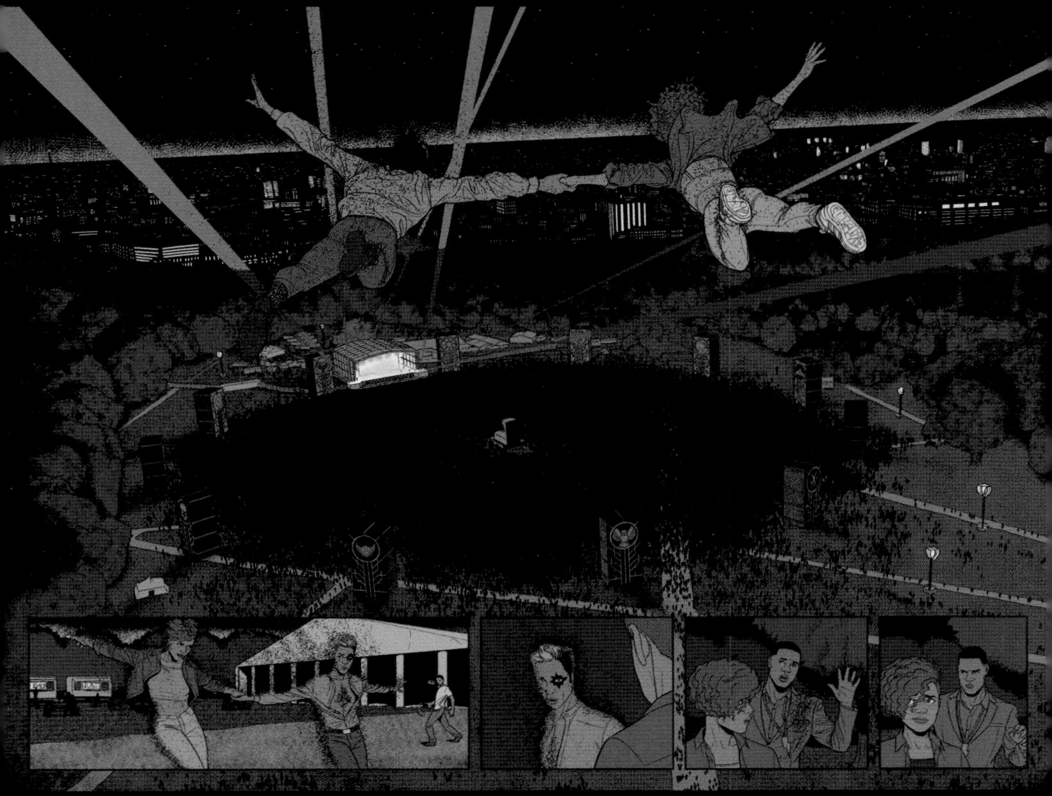

FLATS

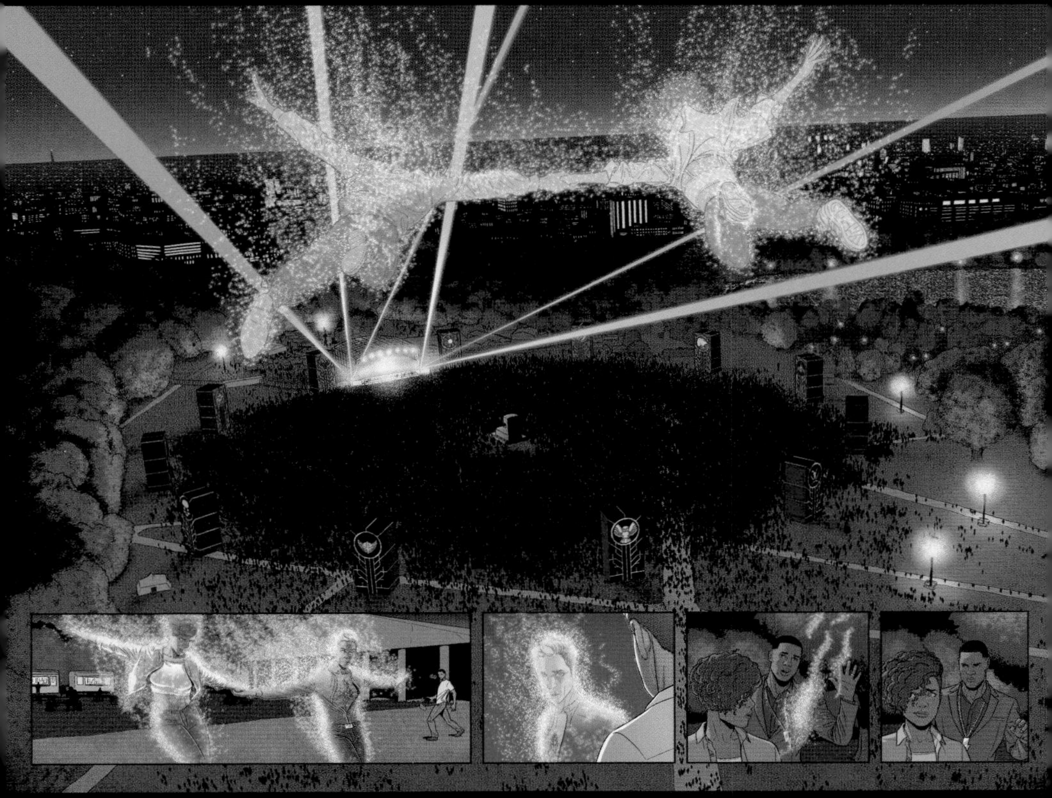

COLOURS

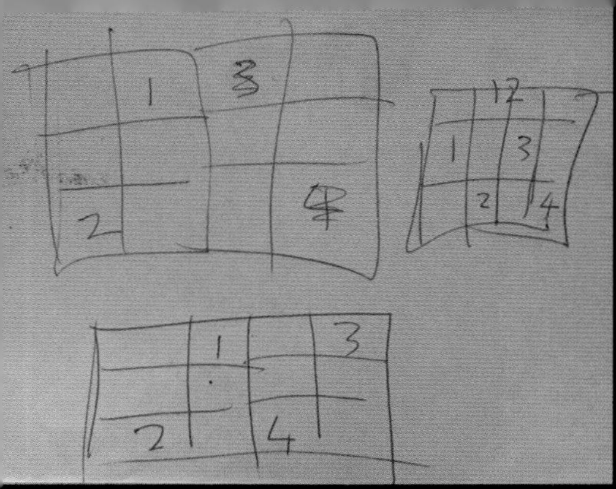

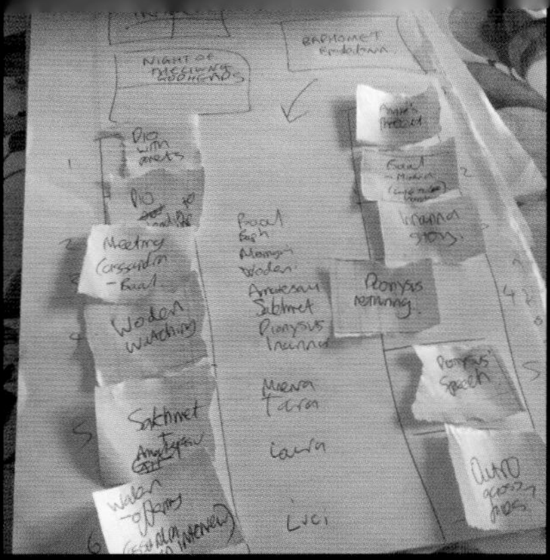

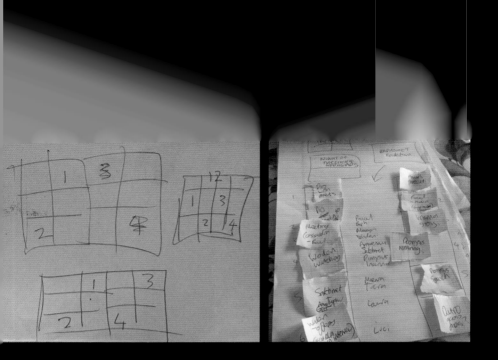

These sketches Kieron did for issue 10 show why we don't let him draw.

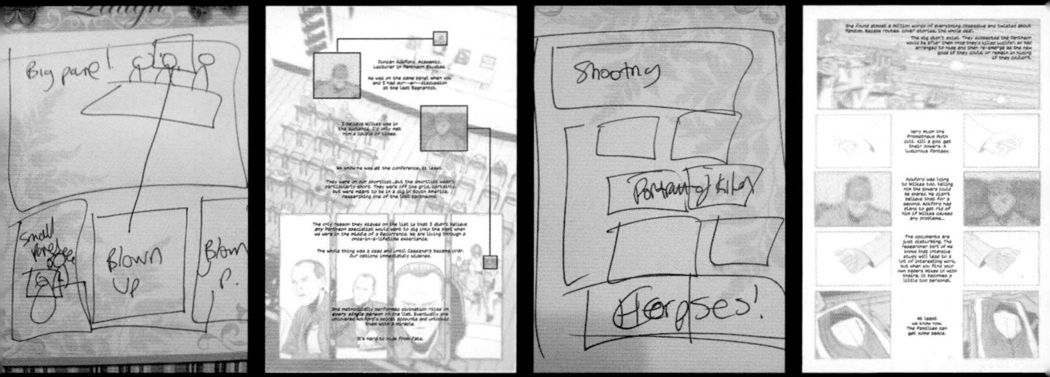

Classic owl correction was required for this panel in issue 7.

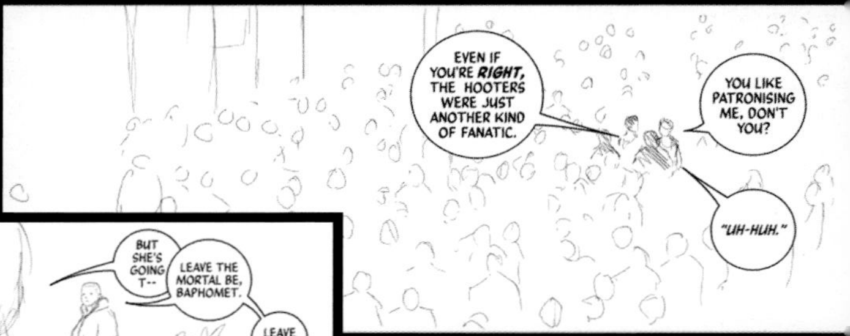
EVEN IF YOU'RE ***RIGHT,*** THE HOOTERS WERE JUST ANOTHER KIND OF FANATIC.
YOU LIKE PATRONISING ME, DON'T YOU?
"UH-HUH."

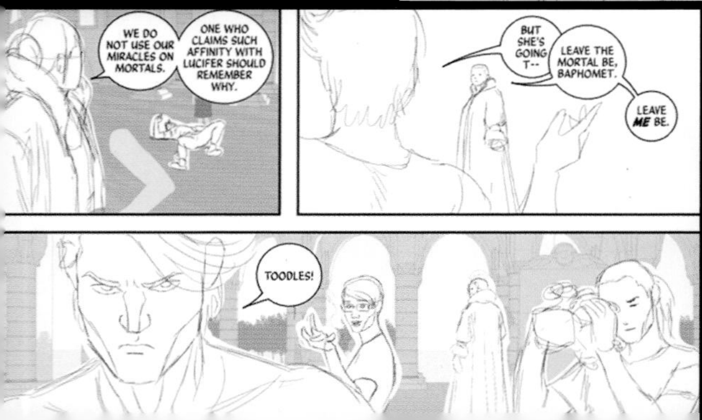
WE DO NOT USE OUR MIRACLES ON MORTALS.
ONE WHO CLAIMS SUCH AFFINITY WITH LUCIFER SHOULD REMEMBER WHY.
BUT SHE'S GOING T--
LEAVE THE MORTAL BE, BAPHOMET.
LEAVE ***ME*** BE.
TOODLES!

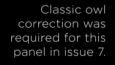

The bottom panel here in issue 10 needed correcting after Cassandra's line was accidentally misattributed to Baphomet. Aww. Grumpy Baphomet was *grumpy*.

THE WICKED + THE DIVINE VOL. 1: THE FAUST ACT

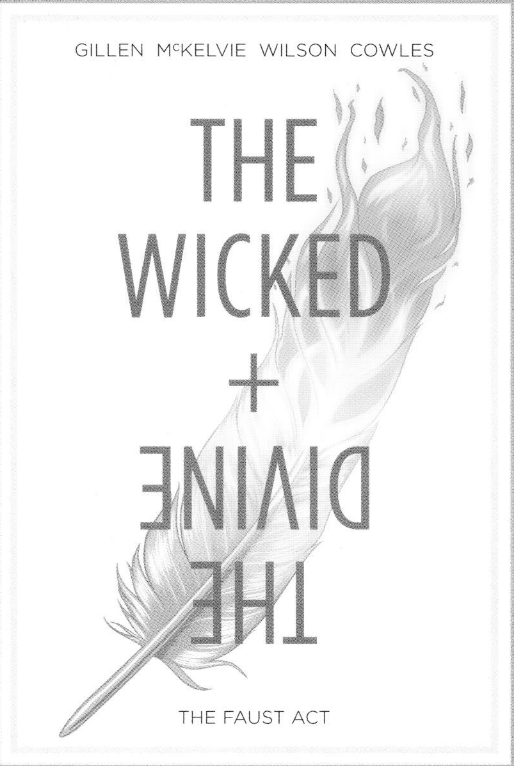

GILLEN McKELVIE WILSON COWLES
THE WICKED + THE DIVINE
THE FAUST ACT

PHONOGRAM: THE IMMATERIAL GIRL ~ AUGUST 2015:

PHONOGRAM
THE IMMATERIAL GIRL

ALSO AVAILABLE:

PHONOGRAM
RUE BRITANNIA
image
Kieron
GILLEN
Jamie
McKELVIE

PHONOGRAM
THE SINGLES CLUB
KIERON GILLEN & JAMIE McKELVIE

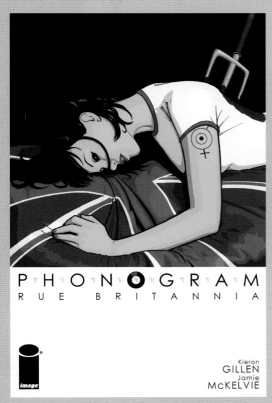

Kieron Gillen writes this.
Jamie McKelvie draws this.
Matt Wilson colours this.
None of them are pictured here,
but they are watching, nearby, amazed.